Scenting Scandal

by

Suzi Love

Dedication

To all the people who kept me going
while I pursued my dream of becoming an
author, I'm truly grateful to all of you.

Special thanks to my family and friends
and all my fellow romance writers,
especially the Unicorns and Sultry Scribes.

Copyright

Table of Contents

Chapter One

St. James Church, Piccadilly, London, 1843

If Lady Laura Jamison had inherited her great-grandmother's ability to portend disaster, she'd have pleaded a megrim, locked herself in her bedchamber, and avoided this morning's humiliation and stomach-churning terror.

To her chagrin, her senses only warned her of more immediate danger. So, when a grubby urchin had slipped a piece of crumpled paper into Laura's gloved hand outside the church, she'd acted on instinct and thrust the note into her pocket. She'd read the message from their informant in private, after her sister's wedding, when she'd have time to consider which, if any, of her family members should be informed.

If the note contained what she thought—a time and place to meet later today—the man must have uncovered something significant about the enemy they were tracking. And if the newly-weds caught even a hint of what was in the wind, their long-delayed honeymoon would be postponed again. No; far better to inform her other siblings at a later time, or perhaps not tell them at all and attend the rendezvous alone.

A brilliant plan except for one large flaw, or rather, one very masculine brick wall, in the form of the bridegroom's cousin, Richard St. Martin, Earl of Winchester. Though Winchester knew better, the obstinate man treated her as a simpering miss who should be sent to a fainting couch with a maid waving smelling salts under her nose, rather than an intelligent woman who was perfectly capable of making her own decisions. Winchester, having promised the duke that he'd guard the Jamison women with his life, was determined to assume the position of battle commander.

During the service joining Becca and Sherwyn as husband and wife, Laura had felt a prickle of awareness across the back of her neck and known that someone, most likely the Earl of Winchester, had been staring at her rather than the minister conducting the church service. And the moment Laura had followed the bride and groom outside to the sun-drenched steps, Winchester had magically appeared at her side and taken her arm, firmly looping it around her elbow.

"The moment we're alone," he'd said, his tone as quietly confident as his manner, "you shall hand over the note in your pocket. I want to know who sent it, and why."

She'd stiffened, thoroughly annoyed that once again the hawk-eyed earl had outsmarted her. No doubt Richard had noticed the sleight of hand between herself and the messenger before the service and, with his eye for detail, had embarrassingly counted the times Laura had needed to reach into her reticule during the ceremony to extract enough handkerchiefs to soak up her river of happy tears.

The final straw had been when he'd adhered himself to her side closer than a layer of boot-maker's glue, ushered her past her bemused family, and swept her down the wide steps to take up positions in a shaded side area, uncaring that the departing wedding guests were recording every titillating fact to spread during afternoon-tea-and-gossip visits.

The steps provided the best vantage point for watching the street below and the bride and groom's departing carriage, but Laura couldn't fathom why Winchester had deliberately moved away from her family. It was a contradictory action from an affirmed bachelor who went to great pains to ensure he was never alone with any one of the dozens of debutantes thrown in his path each season. Despite knowing him so well, Laura felt a tiny tingle of excitement at being singled out by the most fought-over bachelor at her sister's wedding, which was a great pity considering Richard needed mere seconds to burst her bubble of feminine self-delusion.

Winchester patted her fingers and spoke gently in her ear, as if bolstering a wilting older lady, "You may dry your eyes and regain your composure. We are away from onlookers here."

Winchester's unexpected kindness brought another rush of tears to her eyes, though she turned her head away and scolded herself for being a weak-kneed girl, instead of a quick-thinking woman. Having his lean body pressed against hers, scandalously-close, not only jeopardized her freedom later in the day, but the essential maleness of the man distracted her from her objective of finding and removing their main enemy and saving her family.

She scuffed the toe of her silk slipper across the stone step, back and forth, as she tried to recall if her reticule held enough coins to pay a hackney-driver to take her across the city. Tipping back her head, she peered past the wide-brim and lace ruffles of her bonnet; her aunt's choice of hat was as impractical for a lady of action as the expensively-embroidered shoes.

She needed thunderclouds. A solid downpour would scatter the group, deter her attendant and ruin the ugly new accessories. Needless to say, the sky remained a ridiculously bright blue. Her longed-for rainstorm appeared as improbable as the Earl allowing her to sprint down the road and escape.

Laura looked over her shoulder, up the steps, to where her aunt fluttered around Lottie like a bee around a daffodil. Laura's golden-haired sister radiated sunshine in their matching, too-bright yellow wedding-day finery, but, unfortunately, the color drained all vibrancy from Laura's darker complexion and leeched the last vestige of pink from her cheeks. She glanced down at her skirt, groaned, and attempted to smooth the unflattering flares and flounces away with her hand.

Today, of all days, she longed for her peers to regard her as the stylish and poised sister. And she needed the man standing next to her, securing her to his side as if she were a wayward child, to realize she had long since matured into a resourceful and dependable lady.

Despite them being alone, Winchester again spoke very close to her ear, his tone a confusing mix of decisiveness, annoyance and an inexplicable wistfulness. "Ignore those jealous women and their catty remarks." Her head shot up. "The only fruit you resemble is a temptingly juicy one. One which every man present longs to bite into."

Her eyes widened and she stared at him. However, she was no witless Mayfair chit. She'd overheard enough conversations between her brothers and the Duke's cousins, purely by accident of course, to believe the rumors about the Earl were the absolute truth, and that the man only had to flash his dimpled smile for any woman to fall prey to his attractions.

Despite knowing that in her case Winchester wanted her obedience and compliance, not her body, his words sent a rush of goose flesh down her arms. And though any compliment from a known-seducer was dangerous—a lure dangled like an apple before a horse's mouth—more kind words from him shocked her enough to keep her at his side.

Curses on all smooth-tongued men. Because the only way she'd prove her fortitude, financial and personal, and survive three months of the Earl's meddling, would be to keep her wits sharpened to a knife's edge. Richard toyed with her, knowing she wanted nothing more than to kick off her ungainly slippers and flee, and used his most seductive tricks to bind her to him. Oh, yes, the man was indeed dangerous.

But like a child enchanted by the reading of a fairy tale, Laura listened and even smiled at his words, until finally she gave an emphatic shake of her head. "No. Those ladies were entitled perfectly correct with their ridicule of this gown. I resemble an overblown lemon."

He lifted his large shoulder in a shrug and his arm rubbed up and down against hers, and her body again reacted by tingling and burning. A heart could be trained to not race and a woman learned to ignore a rake's sensual comments, but would her traitorous body ever stop reacting to this man's physical presence?

Only last evening, the Earl had implied she was jealous of her elder sister's relationship with Sherwyn, and though there might be a smidgeon of truth to that, she'd been taunted by this man so many times that she'd caught onto his game. Winchester antagonized by hovering and subtly heckling, taunting her to verbally retaliate in a game of advance and retreat.

The Duke of Sherwyn, despite Laura's volatile objections, had requested his cousin's presence in their household in case the madwoman, Lady Hetherington, returned. Sherywn and Becca were about to sail on their honeymoon voyage and Laura's brothers needed to return to their university studies. Yet Winchester, a known stickler for familial duty, had pretended to be coerced into caring for them as vigilantly as he watched over his four younger sisters and his wide-spread investments. Implied he'd been forced by his cousin against his will. Laura had passed several sleepless nights trying to fathom his reasons. Why was he provoking her passions and stirring her anger?

Because every minute of her time was about to be monitored by a man who, though he loved women and adored his siblings, treated them as drawing-room ornaments and shepherded them as closely as a flock of sheep. The girls grumbled, often though good-naturedly, about their brother's smothering. And his use of spies, in every corner of England, employed to ensure each and every one arrived at their own weddings as innocent as lambs and with reputations whiter than fleece.

Laura risked another peek to count how many family members remained on the steps, waiting to wave their final goodbyes to the happy couple. Each face showed their collective worry as they looked at the traffic-clogged street and calculated the odds of the coach reaching the docks before the tide turned.

Her stomach clenched when her new brother-in-law's coachman urged his horses into a gap between top-heavy merchants' carts and expensive conveyances. The street remained as blocked as Mrs. Burn's pollen-swollen nostrils when Laura's strongest herbal brew failed to move it.

She'd assured her family, repeatedly, that any small disasters could be dealt with, swiftly and surely, by her alone. No need for a busy earl to disrupt his life, and no reason her brothers and sisters should fret about her safety because of an unsubstantiated rumor. But to her misfortune, every Jamison shared one disturbing trait: a highly suspicious nature. If they suspected her terror and deathly pallor were due to their old enemy's rumored escape from her asylum, she'd be forbidden to set foot beyond her distillery in their fortress-like garden.

Or if they investigated their footman's extra visit to his actress friend to purchase Laura's concealing face paint, her sister would forgo her honeymoon to hover like a mother hen. The hatchling, Laura, would miss her one chance to be the decision-making sister and the Jamison their jobbers at the Exchange respected for her investment acumen.

Though her two brothers were younger, as males, their ears were deaf to her assurances the assistance of Lady Stevenson, a friend from the Women's Betterment Society, was more than enough. In their minds, only a man of their own ilk, strong and confident, was acceptable to stand in their stead and support their sisters and aunt.

It was hard to decide which was the worst option: Becca spending her honeymoon engrossed in share trading records, or the wedded couple sailing and leaving Laura to cope with Winchester's well-intentioned but frustrating meddling. She tugged on his arm, not wanting a public tussle, and glared at him, a scowl being the first deterrent her brothers had insisted their sisters learn to rebuke forward suitors.

At four-and-twenty years, she'd practiced enough times before a mirror and could now convey extreme displeasure and discouragement to even the most daring gentleman. Winchester, however, always the exception, raised one eyebrow and gave her the look, dubbed by his sisters as Richard's Regal Regard. Fond indulgence overlaid with mild rebuke, a warning to his sisters of dire consequences if they stepped over the bounds of good behavior. Unfortunately, his four sisters had already departed, leaving her as the sole recipient of his reprimands. She wished the ground would open up and swallow her whole.

He bent a good ten inches to whisper in her ear. "Your sister is watching through their carriage window. No doubt worried by your scowl, which I imagine is due to me standing beside you. Unless you convince Sherwyn and his new duchess you're willing to accept my company, they may still refuse to sail."

Her small gasp earned his knowing nod. She was reminded of the times he'd predicted outcomes long before she, highly-sensitive to atmosphere, had sensed any danger. To the Jamison women's unease, Winchester read their thoughts and uncovered emotional frailties, with the same ease as deciphering his sisters' convoluted schemes, as though female's minds were open books with secrets laid out for his scrutiny on a library table.

She sighed. The wretched man was correct, as always. Her sister loathed inactivity. In another ten minutes, the ribbons on Becca's travelling gown would be in knots and her fashionably upswept hairstyle a mass of entangled ringlets. Becca would chew her nails and fret about Laura's share-buying acumen when the railway released its new shares. Her sister would ponder for the hundredth time whether Laura was strong enough to handle the rough-around-the edges jobbers who traded for them at the Exchange. She and Sherwyn might reconsider leaving on their voyage.

"Besides," Winchester said, reading her mind as easily as if she marked every thought with a mountain-high signpost, "the faster those two depart, the quicker you can be rid of my company. For today, at least."

"Then perhaps, my lord, instead of shooting daggers at me, you should try smiling."

"And perhaps, my lady," he repeated, mirroring her exasperation, "you should stop fidgeting." His hold on her hand firmed. "I ask only for your cooperation. For a mere three months. Yet you're acting as if I'm holding a gun to your head. Forcing you to walk a plank."

Laura straightened. Not the plank, no. But he'd forced her to remember this morning's vow to outshine the sun with her disposition. Beginning today, her astute juggling of their finances would outclass the county fair's best performer. Men would admire her for more than a pleasing face and a curvy body. Women would realize she did more than dabble in remedies and medicaments. Despite Winchester's interference, she'd overcome her dislike of mathematics and statistics and be viewed as a success in her share trading. And for her sister's peace of mind, she'd turn her pretend smile into a real one.

She concentrated on restful images. Brooks babbled, birds sang, white fluffy clouds floated. Colorful rainbows arced and.... Nothing, dammit. Her frazzled nerves refused to be soothed. Trying not to alert her aunt, whose over-emotional farewells had already delayed proceedings, Laura tugged on Winchester's arm. His leather-gloved hand held fast. The Devil take the blasted Earl and his oversized anatomy, his overwhelming maleness and his–

She shivered. Everything overpowering about this man, including his unwanted invasion of her senses, ought to be declared illegal. A ticket tied to each limb reading: *Danger. Avoid at all cost.*

His cologne's citrus tang, bergamot with an after-note of lemon, flooded her nose and made her sneeze. Another confirmation that the theory of natural selection being developed by scientists at the Royal Academe was correct. And an extra incentive to elude her keeper, ergot the enigmatic Earl, and pay another visit to her friends, Mr. Charles Darwin and his cousin, both men grandsons of Mr. Erasmus Darwin, famed researcher and theorist.

While she listed to herself the scientific reasons for avoiding the Earl, her herbalist and caring side, or more likely her feminine one, overruled. She reminded herself a few more drops of lemon should be added to the next batch of cologne she blended for Richard. Even as she mentally cursed her siblings for insisting she work closely with Winchester, Laura's traitorous body responded in a physical way to his presence.

Imagining him, an expert financier, being granted full authority over not merely her 'Change transactions, but also her daily household accounts, horrified her. Mortification would nail closed her coffin if he compared her scientific skills with those of her extraordinarily talented four siblings and found her wanting. Or, heaven save her, exposed her failures to the world.

Her nose itched with another oncoming sneeze. Perhaps she could unearth one more handkerchief from the bottom of her tumbled reticule, though considering her recent run of bad luck she'd more likely need to borrow one, from him. With the brief span of time she had to prove her proficiency both in running the household and investing, she'd be drawn and quartered before she'd request a handkerchief or beg assistance from Winchester.

Further along the street the crush had thinned, and a collective gasp rose from the onlookers when Sherwyn's coachman forced his horses into the midst of the tangled traffic and urged them to high-step their way around several halted carriages and down the street. Laura snatched a quick glimpse at the jeweled timepiece pinned to her bodice, and for the first time, her mouth lifted into a small, but real smile. Until she caught the Earl's enquiring glance.

"Half an hour at most until we can end this farce. Then we'll be free to bid each other a far-from-fond farewell."

The Earl snorted, the indelicate sound contrasting with the refined air he presented this morning in his long charcoal frock coat with tailored sleeves displaying decorative gold buttons. A gold-threaded gray vest fitted snugly underneath, while a gold bar sporting an enormous topaz winked from the elaborate folds of his thrice-about neckcloth.

Laura twisted her neck a little more and looked lower. Immaculate trousers – with the newer style front fastening instead of a buttoned-over flap – covered an acre of legs and finished at blindingly-polished walking boots.

Living up to her family title of Miss Inquisitive, she moved her gaze higher again and back to his thigh's evident musculature, honed from time spent on horseback. The mechanics, and easy access, of one row of buttons down the simplified closing on his trousers fascinated her, purely from a scientific point of view.

Botheration. The air had warmed all of a sudden. She lifted her ivory and lace fan. Even waving the fragile creation rapidly back and forth didn't dispel her flush. Not blush, as she'd never admit to such a state. Dealing with the Earl might be a hardship, but she and her sisters had never found it taxing to peruse the Earl's decidedly-masculine physique. She risked one more peek. No, not difficult at all. When her appraisal reached his face, she saw a wide smile and a display of even white teeth, and she smiled in return.

"Uh, uh," he said, wagging a finger. "You misunderstand the reasons for my happier expression. Unlike you, I'm looking forward to the next three months and the chance to study your fiscal strategies. I'd like to compare my investing skills to those of your astute sister's."

His mouth widened into a roguish grin. "I'm also flattered by your scrutiny of my anatomy and amused by your blush, especially after your studies into animal reproduction."

Her free hand flew to her cheek and her heavy reticule knocked her arm. "I never blush." To have him observe her ogle him was embarrassing and gave her another reason to be irritated by his company, petty though her reasons might be. She tugged, but her hand was imprisoned under his. With her nose raised a fraction, she said, "For the sake of propriety, I was ensuring your garments were intact. You've a reputation for disappearing into dark corners and re-emerging with your clothing askew. As though hasty hands ripped your garments from your body."

"Tut, tut, my pet. Has jealousy driven you to spying?"

"Jealousy? Over the class of females you consort with? I was reassuring myself your clothing was intact for the sake of my elderly aunt. The entire congregation watched that woman, the Countess, beckon you to the back of the church. Heaven knows what you were doing while the bride and groom were signing the register."

Winchester chuckled, long and low. "I doubt even my sullied reputation could support the story that I dragged the Countess into a shadowy niche for a quick tumble. At least, not with my sisters watching me like hawks." He dipped his head closer. "I may excel at dispensing pleasure, but I like more than a few minutes to enjoy a rendezvous."

She forced herself to stand motionless, to not react to his latest coarse taunt. "I've no interest," she said, between calming breaths, "in knowing any details of how you entertain—"

Louder noises erupted from the street.

"Oh, dear. Their carriage is slowing again," her Aunt Aggie announced from her loftier position. "Becca's quite likely to have drawn up another list of instructions for you, Laura."

Laura moaned. "I hope not. She's already left enough lists to paper my bedroom walls."

Lottie, the optimist, said, "Perhaps they simply forgot something vital in their packing."

Sherwyn's younger brother jogged past. "I'll see what's delaying them."

As they watched Brian lope down the road, Laura took advantage of Winchester's distraction to tug her arm free. "It's your fault they've stopped."

He growled and threw up his hands. "How can the coach stopping be my fault?"

"You were supposed to use your notorious powers of persuasion for something besides seduction." She poked his chest. "To convince Becca you held uttermost confidence in my ability to manage in her absence."

"As of an hour ago, we became related by marriage. And despite what you think of me or how I live my life, I take familial duties seriously. If we do discover a new stock syndicate is being formed by Lady Hetherington, I'm far better qualified to deal with her than you are."

"And as I've informed my siblings, I'm quite capable of organizing our affairs. Without the meddling of a condescending—"

"Laura," Aunt Aggie said. "Remember your surroundings." Her hissed reprimand echoed down the steps. "Refrain from such disrespect. The Earl's offer is extremely kind. Apologize, and accept his assistance. With grace."

Winchester smirked and made a great show of bending closer, to better hear her apology.

"I'd rather be boiled in oil than—" Gloved fingers pressed against her lips.

From the steps above, Laura heard Aunt Aggie clucking, her favorite way of expressing her disappointment in the behavior of her great nieces.

"I wouldn't continue, if I were you." The Earl leaned in and spoke in a whisper. "Brian is arguing with the honeymoon couple. Most likely convincing them all is well. Urging them to continue their journey. And your sister, who's as stubborn as you—"

She nipped the closest finger to her teeth.

He yanked back his hand, and with his head bowed muttered, "Bloody hell." Then the dreadful man met her gaze and gave a slow grin. "Sorry." He held out his finger. "Russian leather. No blood. Better luck next time."

Clamping her mouth shut, Laura faced the road, raised her hand and waved. "The coachman is rousing the horses again. Everyone," she said, forcing another smile into her stiff cheeks, "keep waving." Even to her own ears, her voice sounded strident and strained. Over her shoulder, she spoke to Winchester in her most commanding tone. "There'll not be a next time for us. As soon as they're out of our sight, you'll remove yourself from my presence."

His sigh whispered across the nape of her neck, lifted the fine hairs there, and sent a small shiver across her shoulders. For an idle moment, she savored the warm brush of air and imagined the same heat caressing other areas of bared flesh.

"... in the short term, my promise stands. Until Sherwyn returns, the smooth running of the Jamison household is my responsibility."

She shook her head and reeled in her wayward thoughts.

"No need," she said, unclenching her jaw and showing her teeth in a false but placating smile. "I'd be most distressed, kind sir, if you put yourself out on my account. Becca left me a list of instructions as long as my arm on which shares to buy and sell, and how to deliver my orders to our Stock Exchange agents. To excel at my duties, I need only follow each and every step. Rather like climbing a ladder."

"People have been known to tumble from ladders. Land in the wrong place."

She narrowed her gaze at him. "Very true. But for all I know, aligning myself with you may land me in deep water. How do I know you're trustworthy? You could be copying those scoundrels Becca had imprisoned. Snaking into our household to steal our secrets."

She'd tried to appear apprehensive, but when his jaw went slack with shock, she couldn't stop help but chuckled.

He waggled a finger. "You, pixie, are provoking me. Deliberately."

"Do, please, stop calling me such a childish name. If you haven't noticed, I became a woman several years ago."

His gaze flicked over her body, scorched where it touched and left her tingling in its wake.

"Trust me, Laura, I'd noticed."

Chapter Two

The Earl of Winchester had paid attention, rapt attention, to all three Jamison sisters when they'd glided down the aisle. Every man present had been enthralled by their graceful beauty, but Richard, having already known them as the prettiest girls in the village, considered their transformation into the most self-assured ladies in the city doubly stunning.

Becca's new-found wealth had allowed these butterflies to emerge from their country cocoon to climb and circle above their elegantly-coiffed but empty-headed peers. The difficult climb from near-destitution to modest affluence would have worn any other girls to exhaustion, yet until Michael and Jonathon were educated and full-grown, these three invincible ladies carried the burden for their continuing prosperity.

Richard understood only too well the consequence of the trio practicing non-traditional female roles, rather than gossip-and-stitch. Knew he could never marry a woman of their ilk, intelligent and confident. His future countess would be their complete opposite.

He silently scoffed at himself. If his obsessive interest in the trio was due entirely to the novelty of their unusually shrewd minds, why had his stimulated blood immediately chilled when he'd observed the gaze of every man under eighty fix on one place?

Correction, two yellow-clad places. The softly swaying rear ends of Laura and Lottie, as they'd swished and swirled in an attempt to stay two paces behind the bride, Lady Rebecca Jamison. Swathed in creamy lace and with a smile as radiant as the sun outside, Becca had rushed with indecent haste towards the altar and an equally impatient Sherywn, the love-match between the duke and his now-duchess a rarity amidst the calculated unions of the *ton*.

From the rear at least, Laura and Lottie had appeared as similar as twins. Lottie, admired for her classic beauty and sweet nature, had already refused several offers of marriage; though considered by some to be headed down the path to spinsterhood, the young lady believed herself far too young for marriage at twenty. By year's end, she'd be consoling more desolate suitors, while following her sisters' examples and delaying marriage until she'd mastered her currently preferred science.

Privately, Richard considered phrenology ludicrous. Despite enjoying, three or four times, Lottie's experiments where she'd run her fingers through his hair and traced his head bumps, supposedly to reveal his soul's deepest secrets. And despite his friends, their brothers, issuing repeated warnings to the girls to never be alone with a man when they tested their scientific theories.

Richard agreed whole-heartedly. Sisters were precious. His own weren't allowed within ten feet of most of his friends who were, to an elder brother's view, all rogues, rakes, or scoundrels. The type of men who attended balls as guardians but strolled the perimeters with an eye to securing their next mistress. Men like him.

So why had such honorable convictions not stopped his dishonorable thoughts when Laura had floated past his pew, gown billowing like a hot-air balloon? Every man with a heartbeat had prayed a nor'easter would whirl down the aisle and lift Laura's skirts. And he'd prayed hardest. Convictions had warred with sheer unadulterated lust, and he'd wrapped his hands around the Order of Service, squeezing the engraved parchment to within an inch of its life as an alternative to throttling every man who lecherously leaned into the aisle to follow every movement of Laura's lemon-frothy hips.

If he could bring himself to renounce his vow to his sisters, sworn during the first wretched week after their parents' death, those long legs of Laura's and the hundred fantasies they stirred could be his. All his. He'd begin at her toes, nibble, lick, and work his way upwards, not stopping until he'd tasted forbidden fruit and...

He groaned. Heaven save him for lust had addled his wits. Contrarily, if he'd read similar thoughts on the face of any drooling young pup, he'd have leapt across the pews and planted him a facer. Embarrassed himself, and Laura, with his possessiveness. The gossips would squeal with delight to see him break his own rules and behave like an obsessed suitor.

Far better onlookers saw the relationship between him and Laura as sparring siblings because, in private, his indifference was becoming harder and harder to maintain. More so, when Laura studied him surreptitiously, or so she thought, and compared him to other men. When she recorded his suitability as her mate as part of her quest to ensure the survival of the human species. Blast the woman and her speculating eyes, because no matter how sexually innocent her assessments of his anatomy might be, his body leapt to readiness faster than any seasoned street walker lifted her skirts.

And damn his randy thoughts for creating so many pictures of them cavorting in his bed. In that arena, if nowhere else, he was certain their passionate natures would prove a perfect match. He clenched his fist at the thought of giving up something else. The intelligent and strong children their couplings would produce. Because if he had Laura's body under him once, he'd be old and wizened before he tired of her.

Across dinner tables over the last few weeks, he'd displayed nothing more than mischievous teasing when he'd questioned Laura about her evolutionary beliefs. He'd lifted his nose in an exaggerated scoff over her year-long trials as she waited to catch whiff of her perfect olfactory match dancing past her in a ballroom.

Fool that he was, he'd stood by, still as a block of marble, while the woman who could be his soul-mate sucked in long pulls of scent. Or rather, she'd inhaled and analyzed the odor of a man's sweaty body after he had romped after up and down a ballroom in a quadrille. And though he might tease, he'd neither interfered nor objected to her unfounded beliefs. Not even when she'd waxed lyrical upon being uncovered from cataloguing some unsuitable fop's sweat-dotted skin.

Twelve more weeks would strain his honor, his good intentions, and his self-control to the limit. After every ball, he'd see the women home in his carriage, and Laura would fill his ears with her latest findings, or the latest swain on whom she'd pin her hopes for future happiness. Night after night, Richard would smother his irritation at Laura's eagerness to wave him goodbye, knowing she would rush to her garden workroom and, while in the throes of euphoria, enter her reactions to her would-be-lover in her log books. Several more encounters with the same gentleman would be arranged and Laura would happily record her comparisons of the man's scent under different conditions.

Meanwhile, he'd console himself by adding a name or two to his own suitable-spouse list: a catalogue of his friends, daughters and nieces, sweet girls ready to make their come-out in two or three years, charming chits who'd fit into his schedule and his mold. Yes, keeping a dozen or so society misses under his scrutiny would take his mind off Laura's husband list.

He shuddered. Suddenly, the idea of stretching his rules and taking a wife earlier than planned seemed like an extraordinarily good idea. He glanced at Laura. The main spoke in his carefully-planned wheel stood with him, mouth open as normal, about to either amuse him or abuse him. Either way, he looked forward to it. So how the hell would he survive future years in the company of Laura and her perfect-match of a husband?

He copied her and kicked at the step in frustration. Good God, he was a master of self-assurance. He'd ignore the inquisitive and assessing looks she gave him when she thought he wouldn't notice. He sighed. To his misfortune, he noticed everything she did or said.

But he'd school himself to play the role of mentor with such brilliance, her brothers and sisters would applaud his aptitude for match-making. He'd find Laura's perfect husband as quickly as possible. And at those long and interminable dinners, he'd prove his own unsuitability by arguing until their fellow diners rolled their eyes and closed their ears to another of their battles of wit.

When their companions' eyes glazed over and they turned to more interesting conversation, he'd be free to let his eyes roam and his senses feast on Laura as she raved about the wonders of evolutionary science.

It was more likely that he'd need to dig his fingers into the elegant carvings on his chair to stop himself leaping across the table like a lunatic and shocking everyone at the sixty-seat table. He'd been in control of himself and his minor kingdom since he'd turned eighteen. So, for pity's sake, why did being within thirty yards of Laura turn him into a wet-behind-the ears randy youth?

After her olfactory tests had proved he wasn't her ideal mate, he should feel relieved, not affronted. And rather than reveling in a bachelor's escape from the clutches of another would-be countess, Laura's rejection had prompted him to childishly extol his own virtues. For an earl who also held minor titles and controlled several estates, being categorized as 'Examined and Disregarded' was as abnormal as it was lowering.

"Laura," he said, dodging lace frills. "Picture my brutalized face if Michael and Jonathon caught me, the one man able to resist your charms and ignore your demands, composing appalling odes to the length of your lashes like your other fawning fops."

"Is that why Sherwyn needed to coerce you into acting as my keeper?"

Ah yes, trust Laura to demand to know the reason he complied with his cousin's wishes.

"I was the only able-bodied male available for the time required." He shrugged, feigning ignorance. "Perhaps Sherwyn realizes I'm not as gullible as those pitiable sods you flirt with simply to lean close enough to sniff their cologne. And catalogue the ingredients."

"You're insulting those gentlemen. They're all very sweet. I cannot stop them composing poetry to me. Besides, not all odes are appalling. Monsieur Lamarck's odes to evolution were –"

"Stop, please." He held up a hand. "No evolutionary theories this morning."

He looked down at Laura's bizarre bonnet, recognizing her great aunt's outlandish taste and comprehending why, as a devoted niece, she'd wear such an unsuitable hat.

She laughed at herself and her heightened senses, made jests about following her nose to uncover people's deepest secrets. In truth, her heightened sense of smell was a startling gift which allowed her insights into people's wants and needs. Yet once she'd sensed a person's greatest joys or worst fears, her compassionate nature stopped her using the knowledge in a hurtful way. He hoped his face never displayed his true feelings. Prayed his many and varied licentious imaginings of Laura, partly clothed or entirely naked, were hidden from her family.

He'd tried, often without success, to conceal the exaggerated stories about strings of courtesans or wild romps with bored ladies of title from innocent ears—including Laura's—as being regarded as a cad, or having well-bred ladies avoid his company, grated on his innately honorable nature. How the gossip columnists imagined he found the time or energy, he'd no idea. Managing estates, escorting sisters and accounting for a sheaf of investment portfolios kept him running from one dawn till the next.

According to his plan, he had another three years before he needed to choose a bride, when his youngest sister would whirl her way through London ballrooms for her first season and, he prayed, the others would be married. Until all four were comfortably situated, they remained his primary consideration. After which he'd select a bride, a quiet and biddable chit, who was the opposite in every way to his passionate mother and his exhausting sisters.

A sensible young lady, who wouldn't turn his hair grey or disrupt any facet of his life, business or personal. He intended passing his days with a woman of sedate charm and his nights with a placid bedfellow. Not a passionate woman who'd embrace the pleasures of sex and demand to be taken, night after night, in every place and position she desired.

Enthusiastic games would be reserved for the bedchamber of his mistress. He'd sworn to never watch another well-bred lady, one as exciting and intelligent as his mother, miscarry babe after babe because she stirred her husband's baser instincts. Because her husband was so enraptured with his wife that he had no control over his rutting nature.

Laura stared at him, no doubt trying to read his thoughts. Her famed perception stood tall between them, the main reason he would never weaken, succumb, or beg this remarkable young lady to become his countess.

If he invited this termagant into his household, she'd unravel the secret he'd taken pains to hide since his first day at boarding school. Pity might become the only chain keeping Laura with him, and though during some lonely nights he thought he could suffer anything if only Laura lay beside him, a marriage based on nothing more than sympathy and compassion would kill him.

"Your male relations understand my stance on marriage. I abhor marriages based on notions of romantic ideology, and I believe love matches create more unhappiness than joy. My convictions exclude me as a suitable suitor for you and make me the safest choice of escort, especially compared to the fortune hunters and rakes I've seen sniffing around your skirts recently." Under her intense scrutiny, he shifted his feet. "For a woman as passionate and exciting as you, I'd prove very poor husband material."

He realized how his words might be interpreted when she said, "Are you complementing me for my passion? Or lamenting that I'm not the milk-pudding-miss you profess to require as your bride?"

He stiffened. "My countess will not be as bland as you imagine. She'll be admired by everyone, including me of course, for her competency in running several large households."

"Of course." She rolled her eyes. "Because sewing and pianoforte and menu-planning and…reciting the bible…. are vital for any woman's sanity. Mind you, your countess will need some distraction during the long boring months waiting to deliver your heir. And, of course, a possible spare or two. Stitching handkerchiefs may be the most excitement she experiences if her marriage to you is as boring as it sounds. I don't believe you're stupid enough to settle for a young girl who completely lacks wit." Her gaze met his, confronting and demanding. "A chit with whom you've nothing in common, malleable enough to bend to your will and willing to be held at an emotional distance."

He stared straight ahead, unable to meet her eyes. Laura, and this damnable conversation, would strip his long-held convictions regarding marriage from his bones.

"It's the way of our world, Laura. Men of rank list their requirements and choose the wife who best meets their needs. My countess needs to have enough spine to act as my hostess, yet be biddable and undemonstrative."

"Poor, poor girl. Selected like a horse from Tattersall's to carry on your breeding program, and then ignored for the remainder of her marriage. No doubt you'll desert her in favor of your latest mistress."

"You've no right to scoff at my rationale. Not after you've terrified every bachelor in London by scribbling notes about them in your little books. Only giving the poor sods a tick of approval if they have a pleasing aroma. You're selecting your husband the same way I intend finding my wife. By examining their credentials. Your scientific theorizing degrades their worth as men far more than my plans for my countess. At least I'm choosing her for her ... ah...gentler traits."

When she scowled, he clasped a hand to his chest in a dramatic fashion and gave her a wide-eyed look. "Consider your lack of traditional female skills arts as providential. Instead of wasting your time testing me as a potential husband, you can treat me as an older and wiser financial advisor, as well as a loyal sentinel."

She frowned. "Once again, I can't decide if I should be insulted or relieved."

He searched for a non-committal response, but couldn't reassure her without revealing his thoughts. A fast change of subject would be better.

"You realize that if you were a man, I'd call you out for insinuating I might steal from you."

"Then treat me as if I'm a man."

He looked down, his gaze lingering at the dip in her fashionably-cut neckline. "Hard to think of you as a man when you dress like that. Perhaps knowing I'm a better shot than London's weak-kneed dandies frightens you." To make her want to check she was covered, drifted up again. "Curses to Sherywn for teaching you girls how to shoot. He bolstered your self-confidence at far too early an age."

"We needed to protect ourselves. Our father is…" She shrugged. "Well, if an archaeological dig opens, he disappears for most of the year. The boys are studying."

"Still, young girls shouldn't have been left to run wild."

"Stop acting high-and-mighty. You loved our tomboyish company."

"It was different as children. But once girls leave the schoolroom, things change."

"Hypocrite. Chastising me for reveling in my bit of freedom. Choosing a simpering miss when it's time to set up your nursery." She narrowed her gaze. "Yet I've seen the women, or rather, the wanton females you take to bed."

"Are you going to remind me, every time we meet, of the countess holding a conversation with me at Featherstone's ball?"

"That woman did not converse with you. She devoured you, gobbled you up. I feared there'd be only the heels of your shoes protruding from her bosom. I was ready to summon footmen to grasp your legs and retrieve you. If her efforts to entice you back to her bed had become any more heated, you'd have burst into flames."

As he turned back to watch the street, he heard her reciting botanical names and, despite summer warmth and a melting-sun dress, he felt her shiver.

"This morning," he said, giving her hand a pat, "I rose before dawn to organize the arrival, on time and suitably dressed, of four capricious ladies. Being the target of your ill-tempered barbs is a stroll in the park by comparison. I believe your washed-out appearance and uncharacteristic churlishness are due to your worry about Lady Hetherington. Imagining that lunatic gathering more men gives us all nightmares. So I sympathize, I really do. But–"

When she started to interrupt, he held up a finger. "Be warned. If you're about to weep all over my new coat, in front of the worst gossips in London, I shall turn tail and run."

She looked down, kicked the step. "I-I never weep."

"Liar. Your eyes were red when you left the church."

He meant no offense, knowing her behavior was out of character, but she stiffened her spine, lifted her face and glared. The swift return of Laura's fighting spirit pleased him, though he covered his mouth to hide his satisfied grin. Then he covered her hand with his, securing it on his sleeve with what he hoped was a light and reassuring touch. What he'd prefer to do was bundle her in his carriage and drive her out of London to somewhere safer. With Lottie and their aunt, of course.

"There's no shame in accepting assistance." He dipped to see her face beneath the brim. Damn! Her eyes were moist, with those tears she'd denied shedding. "From a….a… friend."

"Friend?" She swiped at her face with a gloved fist. "Everyone believes us to be sworn enemies."

He shrugged. "Let others think what they like. Despite our bickering—" He gave her a small smile. "Which I'm certain you do to irritate me—"

Her own lips twitched. "And to stop your head from swelling any larger. Saving you from having to purchase new hats."

He chuckled. "But on a more serious note, I expect you to be sensible. To yield some ground. Let me deal with your finances."

"No, blast your arrogant hide." She tried to tug her arm free. "This is my chance to prove to you—" She sucked in a sharp breath. "To *everyone that* I'm more than the middle Jamison sister. More than the uncivilized one who tinkers with medicines and perfumes and such."

Richard's ears pricked at an odd sound. Comprehension struck like a fist to his gut.

He wrapped his arms around Laura, who was shouting, "Gun! Gun."

Michael yelled from behind them, "Run. Take cover. Someone's shooting."

Chapter Three

Laura had turned to run, when an intractable force grasped her bodily and threw her off her feet, hurling them both sideways. Winchester, or to be precise, his muscled arms, had circled her body, heavy, protective, and immovable. Women screamed on the street below. Footsteps pounded across the stone steps.

Laura and Richard hit the ground a few feet from where they'd been standing and he rolled, his arms wrapped around her. The cocoon of his body stopped her from slamming onto the harsh stone, and he kept her lifted free of the blistering gravel on the pavement. After a series of rolls and tumbles, they pulled up in a tangled heap, a foot short of the tree-lined fence that separated church land from a row of buildings.

Not out of danger but, thank God, no longer sitting ducks. A large palm spread across the back of her head and gripped, as the Earl thrust her head into the concave shell of his chest. Her rib cage hurt as she struggled to open her lungs. She sucked in noisy streams of air, bobbed her head skyward and fought for normal breaths. His hand brushed her hair.

"Shush. Just breathe. Slowly."

His mouth nuzzled, soothed, and hot breath lifted her curls. Under his guidance, she managed to slow her breathing to ease the ache in her chest and calm herself. She turned her head to listen, before peering out from under his arm. Sweat dripped off her brow and splashed onto the gravel below her chin, while drops fell from Winchester's face onto her.

From beyond the high-piled vegetable cart, which provided a little protection, came chaotic noises—the terrified whinny of horses and high-pitched shrieks from humans. By the mix of lower-class voices calling to each other along the pavement, the crowd was confused about what had happened. Though not Laura.

She'd been stunned for a few seconds, but hadn't needed any announcements to know a bullet had been fired. Not after several other incidents in recent months. They'd been physically threatened, and Becca had witnessed the murder of their friend who did the book-keeping at the Women's Betterment Society.

For well-bred ladies to participate in share trading was scandalous enough, but the Jamison women had a reputation for uncovering crimes. Laura had been nearby when their enemy, Lady Hetherington, had sent a marksman after Becca. Little wonder that several friends had been ordered by their parents to avoid her company. And the Jamisons were about to become the talk of the *ton* once again.

"Laura!" Aunt Aggie's voice sounded distant and panicked. "Where are you, Laura?"

"Laura's with me," Winchester called back. "Safe. Behind the carts."

"Is anyone hurt?" Laura couldn't keep the panic out of her own voice. Her jaw stayed clenched shut until Michael called out, "All fine here. Auntie and Lottie are behind the church. We're around the side. Watching."

She and Winchester drew in ragged breaths. Their tangled bodies rose and fell in a shaky rhythm.

"When I release you," he said, between more sucking breaths, "rise up half-way. Run to the fence. We'll follow the hedge up to those trees. Stay beside me."

"But you'll be exposed—"

"No arguments. Go."

She rose into a half crouch, his spread palm on her neck an unvoiced reminder to stay bent over. His assumption of command would normally gall her but, right now, she was grateful to place their well-being into his hands.

Terror had held her family in its grip once before. Now, with Becca and her brothers leaving, responsibility for her aunt and sister fell on her shoulders. Loathe as Laura might be to depend on Winchester, his size and experience gave him an advantage.

Stories abounded of his efficient yet ruthless dealings with crooks. And she'd had a ringside view when he'd helped Scotland Yard toss Lady Hetherington's first band of criminals into goal earlier this year. If the Earl's well-honed survival skills helped sniff out a new threat and eliminate it, she'd swallow her pride and obey his heavy-handed orders.

Time was suspended as she picked up her hems and scuttled towards the hedge, hampered by layers of petticoats and skirts. He matched her, pace for pace, as they followed the fence line up towards a gnarled elm tree. Yanking her behind the wide trunk, he sagged back against the bark and enfolded her in his arms. His chest heaved, more than her own.

"You're safe." His voice sounded gruff and fraught.

Surely his anxiety wasn't solely for her welfare? Still, firm hands remained clasped around her waist as she dragged in welcome breaths. She burrowed into his chest and surrendered to the fatigue that had been racking her mind and body for the past two weeks. Something about his soap-scented linen shirt nagged at her senses, a tiny incongruence she'd ponder later in her distillery.

From the moment the Duke had asked his cousin to step back into their lives, the Earl's presence had disturbed her equilibrium. His habitual nosiness and his interference in her daily routine upset her carefully laid plans. Plans that included her and select candidates for her future marriage. Plans that couldn't include him.

When she'd begun using her highly-developed sense of smell to test gentlemen's aromas, and therefore their suitability as a marriage partner, she'd never dreamed Winchester would be eliminated first. Never dreamed his skin's natural oil combined with a cologne, one she normally loved and mixed especially for him, would disturb her own senses so much she'd want to sneeze.

Her experiment tested and meticulously recorded the high and low aromatic notes emanating from a man's skin. She matched them with her own aromatic pitch in identical situations—happy, stressed, or excited—using her perfume-making procedures.

According to the theory of sexual selection, any sensually-compatible man should be tested further. She'd read the earlier treatises of scientists such as Thomas Malthus and Erasmus Darwin, and believed wholeheartedly she could aid human survival by choosing her most compatible mate. The perfect man would give her strong and healthy children who wouldn't desert her, unlike her father who'd abandoned his children in favor of excavating Roman ruins. So far, the only man who challenged her intellect and ignited her passion had distressed her olfactory senses and made her sneeze.

She wriggled in his grasp. "Please let me go. I must get to my aunt."

Winchester listed the reasons she couldn't leave their shelter. Told her why it was too soon to expose themselves. Gave assurances her family were in a safe place. Still her gut clenched. "If anything happens to Aunt Aggie, it'll be my fault. I promised Becca I'd take care of her. And Lottie."

"Laura, listen to me. Your brothers are with your aunt and your sister. Some idiot shooting bullets on a crowded street isn't your fault. It's no wonder you're exhausted. You carry too much weight on your shoulders."

Only the sight of her brothers standing to the right of the church, presumably shielding her aunt and sister, let her relax a little. She twisted her finger in a hanging gold thread of Winchester's loosened vest button and willed away a rush of tears.

She'd rejected the Earl's guardianship because he reminded her of a prowling lion whose dark eyes dared you to come closer; a golden predator ready to devour her in one quick bite. Her core was as female as all the others. If the king of the jungle roared, his pride would fall in behind him, and unless she stood strong against Winchester, she'd never stand on her own two feet and earn the respect of her father.

Booming laughter sounded from across the street, and a rough voice called, "Cowards. 'Twas only a barrel. Somethin' fallin' on stones be'ind yonder church."

Others joined the uproar, satisfied the first man's guess was correct while, several feet away, her family called out to remain behind shelter. Laura waited and fretted. Her fingers worried at the Earl's button as seconds dragged into minutes, and they listened, tensed for a repeat gunshot. Movement in the street resumed, while muffled conversations changed into a more boisterous buzz, with bouts of loud laughter, as the footpaths filled with people.

Brian arrived at a run from down the street to lean a hand on the tree beside them. He bent forward, gasping. "We can't find any sign of a weapon. Or a shooter. Whoever it was seems to have disappeared."

Michael, donning his cloak of elder-brother-in-charge, called orders to those concealed behind one of the protruding niches along the outside wall of the aged-darkened church.

"Jonathon, keep watch at the corner while we move the ladies to a safer place." He pointed up the adjoining street and called to Laura, "You and Lottie wait up there in the park with Aunt Aggie. I'll bring our carriage."

Michael, already jogging down the steps, called to Winchester, "Can you leave the ladies in your care while I fetch our coachman?"

The Earl stilled and his hands clenched. Laura saw a pronounced tick in his cheek and empathized, having often battled similar conflicts: accept an honorable but meeker role, or rebel against society's rules and rush into danger.

The Earl of Winchester, with his rigid ideas on the role of a gentleman, would disagree with Laura's thinking and the beliefs of the women she associated with. But women could, and should, deal with tribulations as well as any man. And she owed it to her brother-in-law to ensure his cousin didn't suffer through his over-zealous sense of duty.

This was one arena where Laura disagreed with her friend, Mr. Charles Darwin, and his notion that man's eminence over woman was the natural outcome of sexual selection. Because her family's well-being was her responsibility, not Winchester's, and her ability to find their attacker and uncover Lady Hetherington's hiding place had nothing to do with her gender.

Chapter Four

"Sorry, Michael," the Earl of Winchester said, as he pointed across the street. "But if I'm to catch our shooter..." He looked at Laura. Her expression, or lack of it, forced him to forget his plan to track the gunman down the alley.

Terror had pressed her generous mouth into a straight line. Fear had leached her cheeks of every remnant of color and her face resembled a wash-day sheet, blanched white. Tremors rippled across her shoulders.

Only by clenching his fists did he stop himself reaching for her. Only determinedly widening his stance stopped his feet taking flight and charging off in a rage, after the walking-dead-man who'd dared shoot at them. At Laura.

He damped down his urge for revenge until later. Until Laura's argumentative nature resurfaced and she berated him over a multitude of offenses, minor or major. And she didn't look exhausted and defeated.

He nodded to Michael. "I'll stay with Laura," he said, not shifting his gaze from her face. "And the other ladies. Go. Fetch your coach."

It took little time for Winchester to shepherd the ladies to the park, seat them on a shaded bench, and answer numerous distraught questions from Aunt Agatha. He kept his eyes on Laura, knowing the instant her aunt was settled the stubborn woman would be unable to contain her curiosity and would rush away to inspect the shooting area with her brothers. He cursed every member of the Jamison family, especially Laura, for their recklessly inquisitive natures.

When she started to rush away, he caught up to her and planted himself squarely in her path. "No. I forbid you."

As soon as he'd spoken, he closed his eyes and cursed his own reckless mistake. Laura was conditioned to rebel against any demanding man, thanks to her father. He watched, resigned, as her brows shot skywards.

"F–forbid? You. Forbid. Me. Absurd. Stand aside."

He shook his head. "Your imperious tone doesn't work with me, pixie."

Meeting his gaze, she pleaded. "I need to reassure myself

Becca's coach was around the bend before the shot came. I must know if they're safely away to their ship."

Heavens, how could he refuse when she looked at him like that? Eyes wide with regret and fear and shining through it all, her determination to make her sister proud. He groaned. He'd do anything to smooth away the worry lines from her forehead. He thrust his free hand into his trouser pocket, stopping its disobedient path towards her face, towards the lock of dark hair dipping into one eye. No touching. Not now, not ever. Not if he wanted to keep their relationship as sparring-friends. Not if he intended marrying a milk-and-water miss.

Winchester's ideal wife would accept his bidding with a smile, but without questioning his every thought and action. While Laura's ideal husband would match her fervor and idealistic passion, as she rushed into the seedier parts of the city in her attempts to improve the lot of the underdog. Laura's fiery temperament meant a lifetime of fights and reconciliations, while her non-conformist behavior would provide gossip fodder for three generations of society's matrons and would tarnish the reputations of his marriage-minded sisters.

He pushed aside regret in favor of action. "Then at least wait here, until I assess the situation."

She twisted her soiled gloves in a relentless loop through her fingers, leaving them as wrung out and limp as a floor-washers wet rag.

"No, "she said. "I'm not some namby-pamby miss you can order to sit in the corner."

Her unrelenting urge for action matched his so he knew these moments of submissiveness would aggravate like an abscessed tooth. ,

His first instinct was to rope her to the park bench beside her aunt, but he hid his worry and took both her hands. "Your stubbornness will be the death of me. I'm terrified you'll rush out there by yourself. Please, pixie. For once in your life, let someone help you."

"I do. My family. And stop calling me pixie."

He shrugged. "Can't help it. The name suits you. Now, let me, as a gentleman, do as I promised. Let me help you."

She stared at him, silent, brooding and gnawing her bottom lip with her teeth.

He shook his head and chuckled. "I've never waited this long for a woman to accept an offer from me."

She arched a brow. "Any offer you make to a woman is bound to carry barbs and require close inspection."

He grinned. "And our conversations are always prickly. I'm never sure if I'll survive." He pointed a finger at her nose but stopped before he touched her sprinkle of freckles, tiny brown dots he wanted to touch with his tongue. "We shall assess the situation together. Because if I leave you here, you're bound to do something reckless."

He cleared his throat and tried to sound imperious, not besotted. If his friends discovered that, in the midst of danger, he'd fantasized about licking a woman's facial spots, they'd lock him away in Bedlam.

He held out a hand, clasped hers, and started towards the street. "You'll stay behind me at all times. Understood?"

Thankfully, she gave a brief nod. "Yes."

As they walked towards their male relations, Winchester watched Laura out of the corner of his eye. She straightened and looked him in the eye. Meeting his gaze, he read her dammed stubborn determination and sighed, frustrated yet resigned. She moved away from the shelter of the hedge, her crumpled skirt flapping around her ankles as she strode across the ten yards separating them. Lord save him. Between his compulsion to keep Laura safe and her stubborn determination to prove herself, she'd be the death of him.

For the second time, Winchester heard the firing of a bullet. Louder, closer. Much too close, and somewhere near Laura.

He yelled, ran and threw himself on top of her. "Are you hit? Are you hurt?"

"No, no, I'm fine."

But color had drained from her flushed cheeks, and spots of blood dotted her bottom lip where her teeth had broken the skin.

"You–you may remove yourself."

"No. Not until I know you're safe this time. That was far too close. Let your brothers do a more thorough search first."

"They searched before and found no one. I doubt they will this time either."

He growled, the sound jangling in the small space between them like the loose gravel rattling on the macadam road near their heads.

"I damn near lost ten years off my life when I heard that bullet go past you."

He felt the shudder rippling along her spine. His body lifted and fell in time to her inhalations, his larger physique melding itself to hers and fitting her curves in perfect symmetry.

He dropped his head beside hers, muttering words he hoped she either couldn't hear, or wouldn't recall. Only when the road trembled with the noise of booted footsteps pounding towards them did Richard grasp the urgency of moving, as he couldn't allow her to be caught in this compromising position by her brothers. Certainly not with the man she purported to loathe; one whom she declared, at every opportunity, to be arrogant and irritating.

"Let me up." She gave a little push. "People are coming."

Though reluctant to give up the comfort of her hot breath blowing against his neck, he stood and reached down to help her do the same. It was ridiculous for a man of his experience to long to keep hold of the most inappropriate would-be-countess in London, and despite her curves being covered by layers of bulky clothing. Not when he'd only to beckon for any number of wanton women to come running.

Turning aside, he scanned the street and tried to shrug off this peculiar and unwanted effect she always had on him. Perversely, when she twisted free of his hold, turned to her brothers and threw herself into their combined embrace, his teeth clenched and his scowl returned and deepened.

Why accept their comfort and not his?

"Idiotic," he muttered, kicking at the ground.

Laura had been watching her brothers walk away, but now she turned to him with a puzzled frown and asked, "What's idiotic?"

He shrugged. What could he answer? That he'd fooled himself into thinking a few moments of intimacy during a dangerous situation, twice repeated, might mean she'd change her opinion of him? Hoped she'd give up her nonsensical ideas of selecting a perfect husband by his perfect scent? Of living a perfect life? Because he knew her imagined perfection didn't exist? Or, on the rare occasions a perfect union did happen, like with his parents, fate decreed a tragedy would snuff out their idyllic lives far too early?

He shook off his morbid thoughts, bent to retrieve her shawl, turned away and shook it several times to dislodge the collected debris.

"Bloody hell." Shocked disbelief made him forget he was a gentleman who should temper his language in front of a lady. He felt the wrap tugged out of his hands, and watched as Laura lift the fabric up to her face.

"It's only a small tear. It can be mended."

"That, you stubborn woman, is the hole from a bullet. One that almost killed you."

***

Laura ignored Winchester's outrage, and lifted her shawl higher and closer to her face so she could examine the shredded threads. "I'm not an imbecile, Winchester. I do realize what caused this hole." She peered at the spot. "Botheration."

She reached inside her reticule and fumbled around, all the while muttering at her seething companion. "In contrast to a heedless man, who I shall not bother naming," she glared back at him, "I was trying *not* to draw more attention to us. If my aunt realizes how closely the bullet passed by my head, she'll be pacing the corridors and checking windows every night."

Laura glanced around to ensure no one was near enough to notice, before she furtively withdrew a pair of spectacles from her bag and placed the gold rims on her nose.

He shook his head. "Why you bother hiding those blasted things, I'll never understand."

"Spectacles distract and detract from a woman's countenance."

"Nonsense." He reached out and straightened the frame over her nose. "It'd take far more than a gold chain and two pieces of glass to detract from the beauty of your face."

She frowned. "I never know whether you're teasing, or being sincere."

She studied his profile, but he'd blanked his expression, leaving her curious, puzzled and frustrated--a familiar jumble of emotions around this confounding man of late.

"Plus," he said, turning those all-seeing St. Martin eyes back to her, "some men find the thought of a woman with intellect, one capable of reading a book, an appealing proposition."

"Not the men I've met. Spectacles indicate a bluestocking. Nothing more."

Thrusting the glasses onto the tip of her nose, she lifted the fabric and studied it, doing her best to ignore his looming presence. "It's a pistol shot." She spun in a slow circle, scanning the street and the people crowded around. "So our shooter hid reasonably close to where we now stand."

Two constables arrived and were besieged by the milling crowd, but Winchester stared only at her. 'There is no need for you to speak to the constables. I can answer all their questions. I'm putting you, and the other two ladies, in your carriage and ordering your coachman to take you home and bolt the doors."

"Winchester, you're being ridiculous. Speaking to policemen isn't going to send me into an attack of the vapors. We're all familiar with police procedures. In fact, we all visited Scotland Yard after we assisted in sending Lord Hetherington to goal. It was our descriptions of her acts of lunacy that helped commit Lady Hetherington." She pointed down the street. "They will be finished with those other witnesses soon. I'm not leaving until I hear what they've learned."

She turned away and started counting paces across the street. To her irritation, Winchester matched his stride to hers and accompanied her, their shoulders barely six inches apart. Laura strode into the midst of a group of men standing under a tree. They, and Michael, had their heads bent and were searching the ground, using walking sticks and bare hands.

"Twenty is here," Laura called to her younger brother.

Jonathon nodded, and she watched him with her usual awe. With lightning speed, her youngest sibling could reconstruct the physics of any situation within his engineering brain. His gaze swiveled from side to side as rapidly as one of the mechanical arms in their factories and he muttered calculations under his breath.

"Jonathon, can you describe the trajectory? Pinpoint an exact target?"

"We already know the target, you contrary woman," Winchester snarled, interrupting their conversation. His eyes were ablaze, sparkling with anger, and he gave her arm a light shake. "You were the target. You were the one they meant to murder. Both those shots were aimed at your blasted obstinate head and your smug hide."

"Nonsense." She released his fingers, one by one, from their tight grip on her sleeve. "From that distance, it's impossible to say for certain which of us he was aiming at. Michael, you had the best view from the back. Who was standing near the steps? Behind us, or beside us?"

"No, Laura. Much as I'm loathe to think it, Winchester's guess is probably correct. The gunman was either aiming at you in the front, or me, standing directly behind you."

Jonathon rejoined them, counting out his paces as Laura had done. His face was drawn, his mouth pinched, an indication he was trying to calculate the whys and wherefores of a particularly difficult problem. Jonathon tackled problems methodically, scientifically, rationally, the same way in which Becca tackled mathematics. Unfortunately, Laura had to admit that her own approach was often the opposite to theirs, being more intuitive, and often similar to Lottie's studying people's actions and reactions through phrenology.

"They're correct, Laura. By my calculations, the gunman stood here." Jonathon turned towards the church, lifted his arm in mock firing position and pulled an imaginary trigger. "Firing directly across the street, the first in his line of vision were Laura and Winchester, with Michael and Aunt Aggie directly behind."

"Aiming for the back rows would have been too risky unless he was a crack shot," Brian said. "So we must assume it was either you, Winchester, or Laura."

She turned to Winchester and looked him squarely in the eye. "So, shall we draw up a list, starting with me, of all the people who wish to put a bullet between your eyes?"

"My eyes?" The Earl widened his stance and settled his feet at an angle, his customary battle position and one she'd faced many, many times before. "The hole from the bullet is in your shawl. You were waving it."

"Stuff and nonsense!" She stabbed a finger towards his midriff. "It's far more likely to be an irate husband. One you've cuckolded."

She heard his hiss of indrawn breath and saw his fists clench at his sides. The angry lion was roused. He leaned closer so her brothers wouldn't hear.

"Not that it's any business of a well-bred lady, such as your aunt believes you to be, but I never dally with married women. Ever."

He shrugged, the negligent lift of one shoulder not enough to dislodge the perfection of the line of his fitted coat. "Besides, why spend my nights worried about an out-of-town husband arriving home unexpectedly? Not when there are willing widows, an entire city of them, throwing themselves at my feet."

She opened her mouth. Widely. In vain. No retort emitted. At this worst possible time, her quick wittedness had deserted her.

He raised his rakish brows, gave his best roguish look, and

waited. When she didn't respond he continued to taunt her. "Ah, I see, my pet. Jealous again. Wishing you were either not so well born, or that you were a widow. You'd then be free to join the queue of women awaiting my attentions."

She'd rather die rather than acknowledge it, but his words had struck a chord with her. But she was certain that if she laid bare even a smattering of her feelings, the man's head would grow so large with conceit that he'd become wedged between the door posts. No doubt he'd blame that consequence on her, as well.

His grin, and his mesmerist's eyes widened. "What? No sharp retorts? None of Lady Laura Jamison's infamous barbed jabs aimed at the most tender parts of my anatomy."

Her teeth ached from clenching. Her forehead would need several heated irons to smooth the furrows between her brows.

But Winchester blithely carried on, despite knowing how dangerous it was to goad her further. "Perhaps we should summon a doctor after all. Shall I call back your brothers? I fear the bump on your head may have caused you to lose your senses."

Drat the man! A curse on everything about him. If she must be thrown into his company for her sister's sake, suffer his verbal sparring for her brother-in-law's sake, why couldn't the Earl be ugly? Two feet shorter, rotund, and with a wart on the end of a bulbous nose.

Still, she was generally considered a commonsensical person, apart from those few regrettable occasions when she'd acted a little rashly, after which her family had persisted in labeling her Leap-before-you-look-Laura.

Therefore, she reasoned, by accepting Winchester's assistance, no matter much it irked her, her poor aunt could be driven home all the sooner. And after that, with her aunt snugly resting under her mound of quilts, Laura could sneak out and go the shipping office to check that the ship carrying Becca and Sherwyn had sailed on time.

"I've decided you're quite correct. It's too terrifying to contemplate, but both those bullets may have been meant to kill me. My staying here will only put all your lives in danger, and I couldn't bear it if anything happened to you. Aunty, Lottie, and I shall return home and lock ourselves inside."

Winchester shot her a disbelieving look. "Why the sudden change from brash adventurer to cowering debutante?"

"I'm a logical person. I've considered all sides of this argument and have conceded to your superior knowledge?"

Not that she would tell him, but her last reason for following Winchester's instructions and returning home like an obedient child was so she could dispatch a couple of their roughest and toughest footmen to aid her brothers. She prayed that by sending extra eyes and ear to help Michael and Jonathon search the area around St. James, it would take far less time. She wanted them to spend as little time as possible roaming the streets on foot, leaving themselves open to another attack.

She wouldn't rest easy until every one of them retuned home for luncheon. Winchester suspected something else had changed her mind but, thankfully, he didn't waste more time arguing with her, but turned and walked off in the direction of the alley.

Devil take the man! When he reached the narrow opening between two high-walled buildings, he stopped and turned back to look at her. He lifted his arm in a wave, grinned and began to whistle. He disappeared into the alley's dark depths as if he hadn't a care in the world, as if a madman hadn't tried to plough two bullets into their heads. Leaving her with only the sound of his tuneless whistling echoing through her head.

Winchester assumed that being born male made him indestructible and impervious to harm, and his skin harder to pierce than the hide of an African rhinoceros. Perhaps his belief in male superiority came from keeping company with clinging females, who were dim-sighted enough to regard his imprudent actions as heroic. The insipid ones that Laura loathed, and who swooned on the footpath in maidenly distress if their hems became soiled crossing the street. It wasn't in her nature to expect a gallant knight to scoop her up and carry her across a muddy road. She'd rather grab whatever was on hand and build her own bridge across.

In this, she and the high-and-mighty Earl of Winchester differed. She might be female, but she was stoically bred and had learned to rely on her own resources, rather than beg for help. She needed no conquering hero to feel obliged to, and if she wanted to play the frail romantic heroine from Penny Dreadful novels, she'd suitors lining up before her at every ball and vowing to do anything she required.

No, no, no. These three months were her chance to prove to her family she could cope in any situation. If she'd slipped momentarily and let emotions get the better of her, it was only to be expected. She had been shot at, twice, and she could be excused a small level of feminine distress. Winchester's shoulder had been nice to lean on and his hard body had provided wonderful comfort when she'd nestle into his body for those few seconds. But she couldn't afford to make a habit of depending on him.

She acquiesced to his masculine ability to scour the rougher alleys around the church and have a better result than she could, as a woman. Although she failed to fathom it herself, one steely glare from Winchester shot fear into the hearts of the lowest criminal. In those grubby and crowded back streets, onlookers were more likely to provide information, albeit with a little coercion, if he was alone.

Still, she had many other avenues to pursue. And if their assumptions were correct, and mad and bad Lady Hetherington was roaming loose on the streets again, it would take their combined forces to defeat her for a second time. She stiffened her spine. After all, she was a Jamison.

She herded Aunt Aggie and Lottie into the carriage, with their coachman carrying his shotgun across his lap, ready and willing if they were attacked. As per normal, the family had made plans to gather here, at Grosvenor Square, for luncheon and to share any new gossip.

Laura managed to accomplish her secret tasks. She sighed with relief at the shipping office when she was assured that, yes, the ship had sailed on the tide. And once alone in the carriage, she had a chance to read the note in her pocket and reflect on the news from their investigator without Winchester reading over her shoulder.

At home, she tried to hide her distress from her aunt, pretending that she'd been upstairs resting. And though Lottie doubted her explanation, she wasn't prepared for her sister to know how worried she was about their brothers. Nor that she was especially anxious to set eyes on Winchester.

Though she did admit to herself that, on this one occasion, she'd be desperately relieved to see the irritating man swagger through the door. This one time, she might even forget propriety and do something most unladylike and most unlike herself.

Like kiss the Earl's cheek; the dimpled one.

Chapter Five

Two hours later, Jamison House, Grosvenor Square

Richard, Earl of Winchester, stood at the bottom of the flight of worn stone steps and gazed upwards, studying stately Jamison House and its five levels of red brickwork.

The house testified to the foresight of previous generations, who had built in an area of the West End that represented solid family values and financial security. Though any financial stability currently enjoyed by this family was due to Becca's mathematical genius and her determination to elevate her siblings from country poverty to city surplus. He metaphorically dipped his hat in admiration of a fellow investor.

This residence radiated a magnetic pull Richard couldn't resist. He wasn't drawn here to discuss railway shares with Becca, or to indulge sweet Lottie's fascination with his skull as a phrenology specimen, nor to tinker with Jonathon's latest mechanism. And though he enjoyed sharpening his wits by parrying quips with quick-minded Michael, his compelling reason for returning, time after time, was to reassure himself of the well-being of the fifth Jamison.

Laura's knowledge of curative plants and herbs astounded and fascinated Richard, and her siblings and servants were grateful for her remedies. Yet her father continued to ignore her unique gifts. Her disparaging pater reserved his sparse praise for Michael as heir, or Becca as financier.

Richard's hackles had risen a month ago when the Earl had paid an unannounced visit to his children, only leaving his latest Roman site because funding for the dig had run out. The bastard had harangued Laura, before family and guests, over her inadequate contribution to the family's coffers. Richard had been halfway across the drawing room before he'd realized his fist was raised and his sights set on the old hypocrite.

Michael, being closer, had stepped in front of his father, allowing Laura a moment's grace to steady herself. Only the presence of ladies had stopped Richard from reprimanding the older gentleman, physically and verbally, for not respecting his daughter.

In his wilder days, Richard had scuffled with the best of them in a few tavern brawls, but never had he felt so driven to plant his fist in a man's face.

He'd ridden to Jamison House early the next morning, telling himself the whole way his presence wasn't necessary. Laura's two brothers wouldn't return to university and leave their sisters to battle with their demanding father. Even knowing that, Richard couldn't concentrate on the letters and accounts his man of business piled on his desk each morning, until he'd seen for himself that Laura's self-worth wasn't again being shredded by the old earl and his self-interested attitude. He wouldn't rest easy until the old man had gained what he'd come for—more funding—and had left again

Laura fearlessly argued with every other man, including him, yet she accepted her father's criticisms with such silent stoicism that Richard wanted to scoop her up and carry her far away from the soul-destroying comments the Earl heaped on her. A bizarre compulsion that would no doubt anger Laura and make an enemy of her father.

Being both financier and brother, Richard understood the value of Laura's herbal remedies, soaps and scented products for their large household. He wanted to stand on the Earl's rooftop and broadcast Laura's accomplishments far and wide. And though it wasn't his place to do so, he wanted everyone to hear about Laura's work at the Women's Betterment Society, where she helped financially-strapped women support themselves in ways other than on the streets, or on their backs. Laura allowed the women to replicate her potions and sell them to the hundreds of middle class gentry, who were desperate to imitate every aspect of their beloved Queen Victoria's life and use the potions to cure their ills the way her doctors did.

Richard saw the heavy brocade curtain in the bow window of their drawing room twitch and, even from this distance, knew it was Laura watching him. He lifted a hand, waved, and reassured her with his everything-is-fine grin. When the hand clutching the drapery released and the fabric dropped back into place, his smile widened. The splinter of light between the curtains' side partings told him Laura still peered out at him, and the knowledge that she cared enough to wait for his safe return swelled his chest and filled him with a sudden urge to hum, sing, or whistle.

Displaying his happiness was undoubtedly a stupid idea,

especially following Sherwyn's lectures—his last duty before his wedding—when he'd issued a few stern words of warning to his brothers and cousin. The Duke had stunned all of them when he'd given a long list of advisements on how to survive in his absence. He'd spoken with the authority of one now related to the Jamison women, of their contrary attitudes and fiery temperaments. He'd left them his list of three solid rules for males dealing with them.

Never betray your feelings — like their many over-eager suitors.

Never let them acquire the upper hand.

Above all — never, ever let them know you want to worship at their prettily-shod feet.

The sisters, though all ridiculously beautiful, showed an unusual indifference to their looks and placed much more value on how a woman proved her worth in the world. Even impervious and controlled Sherwyn had tripped over his tongue when reintroduced to Becca, Laura and Lottie after his four-year absence. The Duke's nonplussed attitude when confronted with a room full of dazzlers, instead of the young girls he'd known, had become the day's jest for the entire Jamison family. Until Becca had stomped on his toes and captured his attention, as well as capturing his heart.

Following his cousin's path would be a fatal mistake. Richard sucked in a deep and calming breath. He'd been very careful to avoid being alone with these ladies, especially Laura, as he'd no intention of becoming entangled, physically or emotionally, with any well-bred lady. Not yet anyway, not until he'd seen his sisters down the aisle.

Nor would he love a woman as desperately as his father had loved his mother. Loving relationships invariably led to heartache and grief for one or other of those involved. Not a path he intended treading, no matter how much Laura tempted him.

The two Jamison brothers compared their sisters to the Royal Flag. Becca's redheaded attributes and fiery temperament defied disagreement. Lottie's pale hair, light as mythical strands of spun gold and offset by the bluest of bird's shell eyes, inspired poetry.

Flanked by the flag's red and white stripes waved Laura, the most unpredictable of the three sisters, whose locks gleamed with the blue-black sheen of a raven's wing. Their vibrant and varied hair colors, red, blue-black and white-blond, resembled the navy's ensign and, to many, the girls were as dangerous as the Admiral's fleet.

To his own mind, Laura's midnight coloring reflected the

concealed depths of her psyche: intelligence that intrigued him, honest humor that made him roar with laughter and her never-ending quest for knowledge that equaled his own.

He sighed, surrendered to momentary regret over his desire for the unattainable, before he primed his cannons for the next round of battle. Luscious Laura, as he'd dubbed her in a loose-mouthed moment one drunken night, remained as distant from his ideal countess as the moon. Strange that he was eminently suitable as the man with whom she played their games of friend and foe and advance and retreat, yet she considered him totally unsuitable to be the perfect husband she was determined to seek and marry.

For his own sanity after she married, he'd shock the world by delaying his sisters' marriages and setting sail to the Continent. Or India. Or the Americas. Or whatever point on the globe that was most distant from Laura's devotion to her carefully-chosen match. Worse still, would be watching the vitality seep from her body and doubts override every future decision if she chose wrongly, and her days with her spouse were miserable rather than exhilarating.

In the past, his friends had teased him over his deliberate avoidance of Laura, yet it wasn't because of an often-chased bachelor's normal dodge from being alone with an unmarried woman. Though he cursed his titles and wealth as a blasted nuisance when they made him a target for marriage-minded chits. In his heart of hearts, he believed Laura deserved far, far, better than him.

Better than a man who publicly decried her notions of sexual selection to preserve the strength of their species. More than a rogue who preferred light dalliances with a list of willing widows, rather than risk involving his heart in deeper relationships. More than a man who'd concealed his inability to read an entire page aloud, without stumbling over every third or fourth word during most of his four and thirty years.

He didn't honestly know if he was more ashamed of his childhood reading troubles, or of having been too cowardly to ever disclose his struggle. But if Laura learned of his hard school years, the ridicule and bullying, he'd be unable to look her directly in the eye. Overcoming his handicap had been far less humiliating than asking for help.

He'd merely had to spend hours, days, and weeks alone while he repeated words and phrases until he'd locked them in his mind and could recite passages by rote. Yet his terror of disclosure persisted in nightmares, featuring boys from his old school who thronged through London's busy financial center to broadcast news of his illiterate childhood. Over and over, his tormentors pronounced his secret shame until his business cohorts mistrusted his financial acumen.

Richard shook himself. There was no time for such mawkish thoughts when Laura remained in danger. Striding up to the door, he rapped the brass knocker, hard and loud. Experience had taught him the Jamisons' servants were a ramshackle lot, a group of lame or stray curs the sisters had collected from the streets. The butler, using the term in a loose fashion, acted more as a protective guard than a dispenser of visitors, cards and tea.

No one responded, as normal. Cursing under his breath, he raised his arm to create a louder racket on the paneled oak door. All of a sudden, it flew open and the subject of his many erotic dreams popped up under his sleeve.

Richard leaned over her to place his open palm on the door frame and stared down at her, his shoulders sagging a little upon seeing Laura ensconced within her own walls and her cheeks flushed with a little color. As he'd searched the labyrinth of narrow streets around St James's church, he'd not been able to clear from his mind the look of fear etched across her face. Oh, fearless Laura might be ready for any adventure and as expert at hiding uncertainty as he was at concealing his craving, but he knew every one of her moods and terror was something she rarely showed.

He rested his forehead on his sleeve and battled to subdue his tumultuous emotions. Laura, with her determination to prove her competency in caring for her aunt and sister, would subject him to a tongue-lashing if she saw how anxious he'd been over their journey home. He didn't want her to compare him to her father, with his constant pecking holes in her self-esteem, yet he could barely restrain himself from grabbing her and running his hands over her body and assuring himself she was hale and hearty.

If Laura noticed the strength of his angst she'd be furious. But if she glimpsed the depth of his desire she'd be blinded. Wanting Lady Laura Jamison and having her were two entirely different things. The wanting he'd accustomed himself to. The taking would be an unforgivable sin against his cousin and bride.

When he looked into her eyes again Richard caught a hint of his own feelings reflected back. He half smiled, contrarily pleased that

Laura had fretted over his safety. Surely though she wasn't as frightened for his safety as he'd been for hers? He'd learned self-preservation as a stripling lad whereas Laura, despite her declarations to the contrary, was of the fairer sex and therefore needed shielding.

Before he could blink, the confounding minx lifted her hand to his eye level and casually fluttered her fingers, before turning and disappearing down the hall. He watched her retreat, all swaying hips and a flurry of lavender skirts, with nothing left but the lingering of her enticing aroma. The scent was one of her preferred mixes and the one he loved best: violets, determined to grow and thrive, strong in color and fragrance, and yet fragile beneath their wildness. Exactly like Laura.

Stiffening his spine and strengthening his resolve, Richard stepped inside and closed the door. No sign of the butler, although the footman who considered himself a cohort in the Jamison's undercover affairs poked his head around the kitchen door.

"Your lordship," the burly sod said with unusual deference, startling Richard into imagining his manners had finally improved. "Oh, dearie me. 'Tis not good," the footman said, as he frowned and caused plough-deep furrows across his enormous brow.

"Ah, what isn't good?" Richard's head was already spinning, and he hadn't yet confronted Laura, or her family.

"Well, I can see that milady left you high and dry. Again. Don't show ye any sorta respect, does she?"

The man's grin wiped out Richard's momentary hope that the servant might have developed a respectful attitude. He bit back his reprimand, despite the galling realization that the man was correct, and followed the noise towards the gathered family. All eyes turned to him as he strode into the morning room, mainly displaying their interest, yet Laura's managed to burn straight through to his soul, blast her. He needed to resolve the situation with the shooter and retreat again.

Michael stood near the mantle, recounting his movements for the last three hours for the benefit of his sisters and aunt. "I coerced Jonathon into returning to university. But only by promising, on your behalf, that you will not put yourselves in danger again. Even if it means refusing all invitations for a time."

Michael pointed at Laura. "Do not roll your eyes at me. I'm as worried as Jonathon about leaving you. Neither of us would go if we didn't believe Winchester," he waved towards him, "and his friend, the firearms expert, will keep after the shooter." He shuddered. "So, if you wish to leave this house, you'll need to ask Winchester to escort you. He promised Sherwyn he'd escort you and keep you safe."

Winchester walked across to shake hands with Michael. "I swear I'll protect them with my life." He looked at Laura. "And discover who tried to kill your sister this morning."

Unsurprisingly, she jumped to her feet, her face tight with anger. "Untrue. You've no proof I was the target." She strode across to him and, unheeding of her enthralled family, stabbed her finger on his vest button. "You, my lord, have far more enemies than I."

He caught her finger and held it still. "Perhaps you should take a seat while we discuss the shooting."

"Why?" She gave an exaggerated eye roll. "Do you believe I'm the type to swoon?" He might have believed her bravado if he'd not glimpsed that same fear in her eyes. "Besides, this morning's events may still prove incidental to the wedding."

Richard shook his head. "Stop pretending. Every person in this room believes Lady Hetherington paid someone to shoot at us. Mainly at you." He walked to Laura's empty chair and picked up her shawl, waving it aloft. "Exhibit A." He scowled at her. "That bullet almost went straight through your obstinate noggin."

With a swirl of muslin, Laura turned and went to stand beside her aunt's chair. "Aunt Aggie refuses to cower in her bed, and so do I."

Ignoring Laura, he turned to Michael. "I believe all the ladies, but most especially Laura, must retire to the country. If not your estate, then one of mine. Whichever provides the best protection."

Laura stalked across to stand before him, hands on her hips, and her glare alive with defiance. "Leaving is out of the question. Now, more than ever, I need to visit the banking district. Unhampered by glowering men. Becca regularly meets her informants at the coffee-houses on Threadneedle Street, and I'm going to continue her routine.

"Now that, my reckless friend, is out of the question." Winchester bent closer to her. "All sort of reprobates loiter about those areas, waiting for plump pigeons to pluck."

"Don't be daft. As if I cannot avoid pickpockets and thieves." She waved a hand towards Lottie and her aunt, who followed their conversation in mesmerized silence. "How do you think we've survived all these years?"

"I shudder to think."

"Despite your worries, my lord, I shall speak to our jobbers at the Stock Exchange. They will know which men are spending the most money at the auctions."

Even Richard couldn't do his own bidding on the Exchange and had to employ jobbers, because many of his peers still considered it low trade for an earl. Ridiculous, when everyone knew estates needed more than a wad of capital sitting in a bank to support families and titles these days.

"I must also assist at the Women's Society," Laura said. "It's not that long since Peggy was murdered and the women feel vulnerable. When they hear that Lady Hetherington may have returned, they'll be terrified. They can't afford any more threats to their financial security."

"Face the facts. It's more than likely that madwoman has already organized another consortium to bleed those women dry." He pushed the shawl closer to her face. "Isn't this enough proof that these people will do anything for money."

Laura scowled. "It would've been better if that bullet had hit your head instead of my beautiful shawl." Ignoring her aunt's shocked gasp and her brother's loud objections, she added, "Because your skull is too thick for a bullet to penetrate."

"Oh, my goodness, Laura," Aggie said, waving her fan before her flushed face. "You're embarrassing us all. Winchester, please accept my apologies. My niece is overwrought after such a harrowing morning. We shall retire for luncheon and leave you two alone for a few minutes. During which time, Laura, I expect you to reach a compromise with the earl." She pointed a finger at her niece, who had the grace to at least look slightly uncomfortable. "There will be peace in this household while Baca and Sherwin are away. Do I make myself clear?"

Laura nodded. "Yes, Auntie, I shall speak to Winchester."

"No, young lady, you will apologize for disbelieving him. The next few months will run much smoother if you accept that in these matters—our personal safety and railway investments—the earl's experience and knowledge is far superior to ours."

Aunt Aggie spun turned towards the door, her ample form rushing in the direction of more sustenance.

Winchester halted their departure long enough to say, "If Laura insists on venturing out, I shall accompany her wherever she wishes to go. So, Michael, feel free to leave as soon as you need to."

"As soon as we've eaten," Lottie said, "Auntie and I shall go to Bond Street." She smiled at her brother. "Don't fret. We shall have two footmen accompanying us. If Lady Hetherington is in the City and gathering her old servants and cohorts, we'll know as soon as we speak to the owners of the shops she used to frequent."

"Quite right," Aggie said. "No matter how much a Lady wishes to remain hidden, one thing remains certain. She will always revisit her favorite dressmakers. And buy her gloves from the shop that stocks her preferred colors and sizes. We shall find her."

"Good Lord." Michael raised a brow and looked at Winchester. "Did you realize women were such creatures of habit with their shopping?"

"I can see the truth in that, having been dragged from shop to shop by ladies —"

"*Ladies*?" Laura flashed him a wide-eyed look. "We've all seen you prowling Bond Street. Apart from your sisters, the females who cling to your arm are not ladies. They're pro—"

"Laura!" Michael held up a hand, palm outwards. "Do not utter that word in front of our aunt. Or your sister."

"But you've no idea what I was going to label Winchester's..." she smiled with exaggerated sweetness, "friends."

"No," Michael muttered, "but I can well imagine."

She smiled again. "Pretty women?"

Michael groaned aloud. "Winchester, good luck. You'll need it with Laura." He was still shaking his head when he escorted his aunt and sister from the room.

   ***

Winchester had plenty of time to reflect on Michael's parting comments later that same afternoon while he sat in his carriage outside the Women's Society. He was waiting, with growing impatience, for Laura to reappear. As he twiddled his thumbs, he recalled, word for word, how his cousin, Sherwyn, had described Becca's early treatment of him. As if Sherwyn, the Duke, was her lackey; a boot scrubber in Becca's own personal army.

Richard's fists clenched. His teeth ached from grinding them. Damn all the irritating Jamison woman to hell and back. He was the Earl of Winchester. His afternoon hours entailed more than trailing behind the skirts of a commanding chit who had, as per usual, had refused to apologize to him that morning. Instead, she'd given him a sketchy itinerary for her afternoon's outings and lectured him about being ready to leave when she was, and had completely ignored his persistent questioning over the contents of the note she'd received at the church.

He'd made a new resolution. Now, if only he could follow through on this one and not let Laura either argue or coerce him out of it. He roused his footman from the game of cards he was playing with the coachman, and waved the man towards the pathway leading to the front door of the old house. Richard refused to lower himself to the indignity of knocking this second time, so he prod the footman ahead of him up the path. He'd only taken a few steps between the neat rows of colorful flowers lining the walkway when the door swung open.

The Lady he'd been waiting for emerged in a rush and that same startling flurry of purple skirts. She waved a gloved hand in a goodbye gesture to the group of women watching from the doorway as she sped past him on the path. He instinctively stepped backwards and almost toppled into one of the low gardens, only recovering his balance when the footman grabbed his elbow in support.

"Hurry along, Winchester," Laura called over her shoulder. "We've much to accomplish. And I've news you will wish to hear."

Only that carrot, cunningly dangled before his nose, forced him to cut short his non-complimentary retort. He merely muttered a couple of words, before hauling in a calming breath and following her to the carriage. *His* carriage. He watched her instruct the driver and ascend with the assistance of the footman. *His* driver and *his* footman. Once they were both seated and the coachman — *his* coachman — rocked them into motion, she tugged off her bonnet and tossed it onto the seat.

He followed the flight of the hat, a winsome straw arrangement with sprigs of violets and numerous dangling lavender ribbons well-suited to her capriciousness, and watched it slide, unheeded, into the corner. Though he winced, he suppressed his urge to rescue the neglected item. Best to avoid irritating Laura by mentioning such a trifling matter, for they argued enough over his nit-picking on her household accounting. Not to mention their all-out wars over taking more care with her personal safety.

Although Laura placed fashion-following lower on her list of interests than the distillation of herbs, he took a far greater interest in her accoutrements, especially adoring the sight of her ballroom-gowned as Lady Laura Jamison in her preferred colors of amethyst, ruby, and burgundy. Darker colors highlighted the glimmer of banked fire in her eyes and complemented the loose curls dropping over her slim neck and down to her—

Heaven help him!

No, his mind mustn't be allowed to wander there. For them, unmarried and unchaperoned, to even be out and about in a carriage was unseemly. Though with her sister and aunt fully occupied, and Laura's missions of an urgent nature, they'd been compelled to take the risk.

Dammit, he regretted this outing already. Regretted his compulsion to guard her whenever she mingled publicly. Under his breath, he counted backwards from fifty, a practice he'd adopted when dealing with four impetuous younger sisters. The same rigid self-control he called on often when trying to deal with Laura, a female who considered herself well outside his reach and yet was within his extended family.

"We agreed," he said, trying to appear amicable despite his clenched jaw, "you would not walk out the door of the Society alone. You would wait until I'd first secured the area. Yet... yet you hurtled out--" His control slipped, and he stopped. "You tore down that path as though hell's fires burned your tail. And if you recall, only this very morning you cheated death by a hair's breadth. And not once, but twice." He nodded several times. "My constitution cannot withstand any more shocks today."

"Fiddlesticks." She flicked a gloved hand through the air between them. "Your constitution's sound as an ox. Nothing disturbs your complacency."

He glared at her. "You'd be surprised how shattered my nerves have become in recent weeks."

She waved another imperious hand, again dismissing his troubled nerves as a matter of insignificance. Ha! If only she knew.

His latest stresses, all to do with the Jamison family, had stopped him from following his normal regime and prevented him from doing anything but worry about her. Including seeking out or seducing any new conquests. His cousins would tease him, as they had Sherwyn, over his forced state of celibacy. Though for him, to be truthful, it wasn't forced, as much as self-inflicted.

If taken in small doses, he enjoyed the high-class social whirl. He escorted his sisters to balls and soirees, checked the credentials of every man they danced with, and took advantage of those stuffier occasions to keep his hand in by flirting with a refined lady or two. He didn't even mind, not too much anyway, dancing with a succession of pink-cheeked debutants or grateful wallflowers. Though for reasons he'd yet to fathom, none of the women had tempted him in the least, and that included the handful of brazen widows who'd flung themselves in his path.

Lately, he'd found all females as boringly similar as the leaves on an oak tree. Their conversations were distressingly repetitious, and the ladies so vain they copied each other's turnouts to the last ribbon. They'd over-practiced their ballroom demeanor before mirrors until, in the midst of a conversation about weather, he'd cough to smother his yawns and silently beg his partner of the moment to stop pontificating before he slid down the wall and snored. They should have berated him for his lack of interest, rather than smile so hopefully up at him. At least speaking to Laura always kept him awake and on his mettle. Though he had just missed what she'd said.

"—and we're being talked about again for mixing with women who are idealists. Many of our friends are speaking publicly against the Queen and the strict rules she encourages for governing women in their own homes."

"Oh, please," he muttered, although he couldn't help his grin. Laura's conversations never bored him. "Spare my ringing ears. Not another of your lectures on why women should have the same rights as men. None of that is possible until all men have equal rights. You know that."

She sighed, her wonderful breasts rising and falling like the daily arc of the sun across the sky. To his mind, the movement of her breasts was far more fascinating than any of nature's other wonders.

"Yes. I do know that. Laugh at me if you wish, but one day, there'll be radical changes. And I, for one, want to be a part of it."

He reached across and took her gloved hand in his. So small, her bones so fragile. Yet, underneath the strength of steel.

"I don't laugh, pet. I wouldn't dare to, not when my sisters preach the same ideas to me. Day and night. And if it's any consolation, I hope that I'm standing up with you the day women earn the right to represent themselves in the 'Change. The idea that you must hide behind initials, scribble illegible names on your stock certificates--it's a blight on the name of progress. If Prince Albert wants to see England become the greatest financial power in the next ten years, he must see that low-class men, and women, are included in his plans."

Looking across, he noticed Laura laughing.

"Now who sprouts radical teachings?"

He grinned, shrugged. "What does that make us? Two of a kind."

For a long moment, the air charged again with those same turbulent currents, and once again, he felt the arc, the sparks, leap and dance between them. If he touched it, he'd burn as it glowed with fierce heat.

She looked down at her lap, twisting the tips of her gloves into knots as she did when nervous. "Heaven forbid we admit to being alike in any way."

He swallowed, hard. "And heaven also forbid we admit to liking how the other thinks. Or the sort of person the other is."

"Yes." She drew a long breath, another nervous habit. He knew her well. "Far too late to change our opinions of each other now. So, let's concentrate on finding Lady Hetherington and her motives for returning to London. Find out if she's forming another syndicate. And, if I'm to keep to Becca's investment schedule, we need to mix with our peers. Hear if anyone has given permission to lay railway tracks across their estates."

"I'll speak to my man of affairs and send him to the stock auctions." When she went to speak, he held up a hand, palm out. "No, hear me out. "He's used to acquiring that sort information for me, and I swear I'll pass on everything he learns. There's no need to put yourself out in view. Far too risky." He raised his brows. "And, if you promise to not leave my sight, you may accompany my sisters to Bentwood's ball this evening."

Her eyes widened. "You intend playing out the role of protector in front of a room full of people? Pretend you're Michael?"

"I'll be glued to you as closely as the soles on your pretty little dancing slippers throughout the entire evening. As I was at the church this morning."

She huffed, the sound dripping with sarcasm. "Oh, yes, look how that turned out. I was shot at. Twice. Though now that I think about it, it's a wonder you even noticed."

"What do you mean? Of course I noticed. I was with you."

"Not all morning. You appeared from the back row only after you'd managed to escape the clutches of your countess."

He groaned and threw back his head. "Not that again. When are you going to forget that man-eater, as I have?"

"Perhaps when she stops gobbling you up with her eyes. Not that I care what happens between you in private. It's only in public, I feel embarrassed. On your behalf, of course."

"Of course. You're thinking of my welfare. Always." He sneered. "Will this evening be easier to bear if I promise to not look at the countess? Not even once."

"Possibly, but can I believe you?" The little demon—or did one call her

a demoness?—tapped a finger to her mouth and fluttered her eyelashes in a falsely provocative manner. "Should I believe things spoken between lips touted in gossip columns as the most kissed in all three hundred upper echelon British families?"

"Bloody hell! Enough. There's only one way to stop your irritating taunts."

She raised an imperious eyebrow. "Oh, and what's that?"

He reached across the seats and grasped her waist. He lifted, spun her about and laid her across his lap. His mouth came down to cover hers, to silence, dominate, but above all pleasure her. When he drew back to suck in a shaky breath, her eyes were wide, her mouth open, and her heart raced under his palm spread across her back. He'd discovered a way to silence Lady Laura Jamison, at last. Excellent.

So he grasped the opportunity she presented with her widely inviting mouth to descend, again and again, and cover her soft, enticing lips. After several long minutes of pleasure, he pulled back. Chest heaving, lids drooping, he was unable to form a coherent thought.

He was unable to speak. But she wasn't.

"Delicious!"

After a stunned second, he threw back his head and laughed. Laughed aloud. Laughed with true joy, for the first time in many months. Trust Laura to have the last word.

Never mind. He only needed to see her dazed expression to know he'd won the last round of this battle. If only he could win every battle with luscious Laura so easily.

"I do regret eliminating you from my list of suitable candidates to be my husband." She sighed. "Because I certainly enjoyed our kiss."

Winchester's moment of euphoria dissipated as quickly as soap bubbles in a tub of dirty laundry, when he realized he'd also enjoyed their kiss.

Far too much for a man who'd sworn to never dally with any woman he liked and to avoid any relationship that might cause him future pain.

Chapter Six

Laura dragged her feet that evening, as she trailed her sister and aunt along the hall to the balcony above the polished staircase. Her heart had wedged itself firmly in her mouth, and no amount of panicked swallowing could dislodge it.

Aunt Aggie assured her the mixed hues of her gown complimented her dark coloring. Yet, until she saw that same appreciation reflected in those other eyes, she'd hover in the no man's land of doubt that assailed her whenever she attended these large social gatherings.

Beside her, Lottie whispered, "Be truthful. It's Winchester's approval you seek."

"Stuff and nonsense. Why should I care what such an aggravating man thinks?"

"We both know why. And your flushed cheeks when you returned this afternoon advertised the fact clearly."

Laura swallowed hard. "Any color in my cheeks was from rushing hither and thither seeking information on Lady Hetherington's whereabouts. Nothing more."

Her sister looped their arms together, leaned closer, and smirked. "I'm positive," Lottie said in a loud aside, "Winchester will be offended if you refer to today's solicitous behavior towards you as nothing." She arched a brow. "And when bullets were fired in our direction this morning, your exasperating earl," she nodded in his direction, "had no regard for his own safety. His sole concern was assuring that one person was removed from the firing line. That person being Lady Laura Jamison."

Lottie was well known for sensing people's deepest feelings and being able to predict where their emotions and actions might lead them. But having her sister apply her intuitiveness to the relationship between her and Winchester disconcerted Laura. Their push-pull confrontations left her flummoxed and she felt no compulsion to imagine what their future held. Truly she didn't.

Besides which, she already understood what must happen.

As soon as Becca and Sherwyn returned from their honeymoon and resumed their duties, Laura would no longer be thrust into

Winchester's company. Avoiding each other would suit both of them admirably. Until then, she'd keep at least a long arm's distance between them. Preferably two. Out of kissing distance. That way, no harm could come to her person. Or to her feelings.

The three Jamison girls had retreated into a low key but acceptable form of social life for several years before Becca enlisted Sherwyn's assistance, and he in turn insisted Becca and her sisters accompany him to the top houses in society to search for papers. Financial constraints had pushed the cash-poor Jamisons to the fringes of society, living in the country and unable to mix with the town's high fliers. At least until Becca's railway investments had begun to return staggering profits, and before the days they'd called a wealthy duke part of their family.

For better or for worse, the Jamisons had been thrust back into the whirl of social engagements. Although, after several months of being under scrutiny, Laura still hadn't reconciled herself to the never-ending list of rules and obligations associated with wealth and position. It galled her to be watched by matrons eager to find fault, and to know she'd provide gossip fodder for the next day's visits and tea.

Despite being labeled the outrageous one by her family, she preferred to carry on her daily life unnoticed. She enjoyed slipping like a ghost between groups of people at balls, absorbing the mixture of sounds and scents, taking notes and experimenting with new blends and fragrances in peace and privacy later. She glanced up, caught Winchester's gaze upon her, and stumbled.

Lottie's grip on her forearm tightened and she looked at her in puzzlement. Aunt Aggie walked ahead, speaking non-stop over her shoulder as she stepped onto each tread, one hand on the curved top rail, the other lifting her skirt the allowed three inches from the floor. A light hand on the rail remained Auntie's only concession to her age, as not once did she need to look at where she placed her slippered foot.

"How does she do that?" Laura asked her sister.

Lottie returned Laura's bemused look, as they held tightly to each other to prevent any accidents in their own descent with the sweeping skirts of their elegant ball gowns. To their amusement, or aggravation, their aunt stepped with head-held-high dignity to unerringly descend the long staircase. As she walked, she carried on one of her one-sided conversations, laden with the heavily-punctuated words she favored in the presence of others.

Laura shook her head. How a lady who displayed the outward dignity of a duchess, yet who held the inward fortitude of a washerwoman from Cheapside, managed to so easily blend her many character traits remained a mystery. She snuck another sideways glance at Winchester. He'd covered his mouth with his hand but, from Laura's higher position, she saw his amusement over her portly aunt's light-footed glide down the stairs. She smiled. Though they argued over many trivial things, they were a perfect match in their sense of amusement.

"Lady Laura," Aunt Aggie announced in her duchess-going-visiting voice, the one she used when she wanted everyone within ten feet to overhear. Inwardly, Laura groaned. Her shrewd aunt always had a reason for adopting her fawning social voice.

"Auntie," Laura said, pointing at the standing clock. "It's time—"

"My dear, you look most becoming in that gown." Her aunt ignored her growled warning, but her distress earned her a concerned look from Winchester. "And I'm soooo glad we chose the ruby net over the gold underlay. My lord, doesn't our darling girl resemble a fairy princess?"

Laura walked towards the entrance, praying the distraction of accepting cloaks from the footman would stop her aunt's comments about her gown. But to her dismay, Winchester halted. When he shook his head, she froze in her tracks and could barely breathe as she waited to hear why he'd disagreed with her aunt. Despite knowing she'd acted like a shrew earlier in the day, if Winchester broke habit and made a single derogatory remark about her, she'd turn tail, scurry to her bedchamber and pull the covers over her head.

"No, not a princess, Lady Jamison." His eyes were sinful-black rather than sweet-brown tonight as his all-encompassing gaze ran over her gown —up, down and up again— until she felt as hot as if it were his hands roaming free over her body. "In those rich colors, Lady Laura resembles–"

"No!" Laura leapt towards him. "Remember, we're supposed to act like friends this evening. Jamisons united with St. Martins."

To Laura's shock, the Earl simply smiled, displaying those ridiculous baby-chubby dimples. Every other man outgrew such child-like things, but not Winchester. Oh, no.

A more suspicious woman might believe the wretched man

contrived to appear so adorable for the sole purpose of unsettling her, though she knew the appeal of his facial features had tempted hordes of women in the past. And quite probably would continue to do so far into the future. Ah yes, his tactics worked. A man as handsome as him would never lack for female attention, an hypothesis she would do well to remember. Perhaps she should write in her notes like a mantra: *A woman should never surrender her heart to a man with the face of a cherub. Because though he might look like the Archangel Gabriel, his soul may be blacker than Lucifer's.*

"I simply meant to comment," he said in a silky tone, while his eyes flashed devilment, "that a princess is normally depicted in story books as golden haired and blue-eyed and even tempered–"

"Ha!" Laura's hands went to her hips. "In other words, my lord, all the things I am not!"

He laughed. "No, it's true nobody could mistake you for any of those, at least not today when you appear to be…out of sorts. Yet, in your wine-colored gown, you remind me not of a princess, but of a magnificent rose. One who stands strong and blossoms, even after the weather turns foul and others around you have long since wilted."

Aunt Aggie made a loud *oohing* sound and covered her heart with her hands. Lottie gave an over-loud sigh. Even the footman were murmuring.

"I may swoon," Aunt Aggie said, "over your poetic and perceptive sentiments. So aptly said of our dearest Laura, my lord. I am certain your kindness will lift the poor girl's spirits."

Despite Laura's growled warning, Winchester ignored her and faced their aunt directly. "Is Lady Laura worried about attending Lord Brentwood's ball this evening?"

Aunt Aggie, obviously coerced by the cherub's winning smile and his confiding attitude, placed her gloved hand on the sleeve of Winchester's immaculate black evening coat and leaned closer.

"Oh, yes, poor dear. She fusses over the outcome of every ball we attend. She begins the evening supremely confident that this will be the one when she detects her perfect partner for a happy marriage." Aunt Aggie sighed dramatically, and stretched even closer to Winchester's ear, forcing Laura to do a quick and undignified forward shuffle in order to hear. "But so far, the medley of men our dear Laura has approached have proved dreadfully disappointing. Not a single one of them holds the right…appeal… for someone as sensitive to aromas as my niece."

"Auntie, please." Laura pushed between the two confidents, certain her face now resembled an overripe persimmon, and her mortification was being noticed by every servant within ten feet. Not to mention the man standing before her. "We must go or we shall be late, and Lottie and I are already promised to partners for the first dance."

She kept her head dipped as she accepted her cloak from the waiting footman and swept out the door towards the waiting coach, taking the seat furthest from the door in an attempt to distance herself from the Earl. When Lottie stepped inside the coach, Laura tugged her hand and pulled her off balance, forcing her sister to land beside her in a puff of billowing skirts. When Lottie's eyes went wide with amazement, Laura squeezed her hand—a signal for her sister to allow Laura's panicked action to pass without notice, something generally unachievable when Winchester hovered with eyes as sharp as a circling hawk.

She flinched when she heard his chuckle, and peered across Lottie and out to him, letting him know she was aware of his motives as well. He'd seated their aunt by the nearside door, ostensibly for easier access for the older lady. Yet Laura knew in her bones it was another of Winchester's calculated moves, as it left the seat across from her vacant.

Did the man have no shame? She rolled her eyes and watched his smug smile widen. With a casual air, he strolled around to her side, leapt inside with enviable agility, and made a huge show of seating himself. His long legs stretched across the dip between them and discomforted Laura. A feeling, akin to fingers tickling across bare skin, made her squirm in her seat and long to tug off her gloves and scratch.

Her fingers clutched together and twisted the tips of her soft suede gloves into knots, and sweat broke out inside her palms. After forcing herself to unclench her hands, she reached down and smoothed out imaginary catches in the skirt's netting, twitching one caught fold. When the gown held fast, she frowned, before noticing he'd shifted his right knee so it pressed down towards the seat and beside her bottom.

She glanced up and saw that the edges of his mouth were turned up into a half-smile, noticeable only by her at this angle. From their positions, the other two wouldn't know his leg was on the edge of the satin underlay of her gown, or that, no matter how much she surreptitiously tugged, it was caught under him. She dipped her brows and flattened her own mouth, wanting him to see her displeasure.

Winchester reached down with one gloved finger and, in a slow and deliberate movement, hopped it along the netting. His finger lingered over every fourth or fifth hole and pressed into the satin. She sucked in a quick breath.

"Heavens above, Laura," her aunt said. "You're jumpier than a rabbit this evening."

Laura forced herself to sit still. She needed to focus on something apart from the six foot or more of muscled form sitting far too near to her. She shifted her thoughts to the inane, concentrating on the mist visible through her window, rather than recalling the earlier earth-shattering announcement made by the mountainous man opposite her.

Patting the folds of her skirt for the twentieth time, she thought about her choice of cut and color. Unmarried girls were, as a rule, urged towards lighter colors that reflected the optimism and expectancy of a rainbow after the rain.

Not steered to the deeper and more dramatic contrasts Laura preferred. She was thankful her aunt allowed her three independent nieces to choose clothing suited to their strong characters. Apart from this morning's wedding-lemon fiasco, of course. Their Aunt Aggie encouraged her nieces to join the women's movements springing up around the city, often lamenting that forward-thinking had been frowned upon for women during her own youth.

Secretly, the girls shuddered at the thought of their already radically-minded aunt being exposed any younger to revolutionary ideas. They could picture her marching the streets with a laden picnic basket under one arm and a raised clapboard in the other.

But nothing was a big enough distraction to shift Laura's thoughts from the warm limb she could feel through her skirts. She gave herself a severe talking-to: *do not look him in the eye, and do not betray your feelings*.

"Sherwyn told me a little," the Earl said, leaning back in his seat and casually directing his conversation to Aunt Aggie, "about Laura's friends and their theories about evolution. And her own search for a scientifically-selected mate."

Laura bit her lip and stayed silent.

"I'm certain Laura will soon find a suitable husband because…" He waved a casual hand. "Well, because she is one of the most courageous and selfless ladies I've ever had the privilege of meeting."

Her aunt gave him a beaming smile, taking the Earl's second compliment of her niece in under half an hour as a direct reflection of how well she'd raised her girls. She leaned across to pat Laura's hand. "There, you see, my love. His Lordship believes a wonderful gentleman will soon present himself to you. Besides which, you told me you weren't in any hurry to find a husband."

"I'm afraid any change of heart on Laura's part is my fault," Lottie said, making her presence known for the first time. "Now that Becca is wed, Laura feels pressured to marry next and, therefore, free the way for me."

Aunt Aggie waved a dismissive hand. "Nonsense. Such silly rules are no longer important. Though, in my younger days—" The girls moaned, but their aunt ignored them and spoke directly to Winchester.

"Each girl had to marry in correct turn, with no variations. It was terrible if the eldest was a stick-in-the mud, or had some other failing and no man wanted her." Laura rolled her eyes. "But, my darling girl, we live in more enlightened times. No woman is expected to wait until her elder sister is married, or even betrothed. If you truly believe your aromatic senses will allow you to select the best husband for you, then hold strong to your convictions." Her aunt waved her hand in an encompassing motion. "We shall all support your beliefs, however long it takes."

"Sherwyn told me," Winchester said, directing his conversation to Aunt Aggie, "that Laura has been keeping records of her reactions to different aromas. A scientific search to find the best husband man?"

Laura heard the question in his comment but refused to be drawn into another discussion or argument with him.

"And you, Lady Charlotte, are you following in the footsteps of your sisters and using scientific methods to select your husband?" No one spoke. "Or do you believe in the more tried and tested methods? Alliances of titles and estates?"

Lottie chuckled. "Oh, no. Neither of those methods would suit me."

"Ah, but your beauty is more than enough to attract a thousand husbands."

Lottie's hissed breath sounded over-loud in the cramped space, and Laura felt her sister go rigid beside her.

Winchester frowned, not understanding her sister's reaction to words that would thrill most debutantes. But since they were young girls, Lottie's golden-haired beauty had attracted attention and, to Lottie's mind, far too many people admired her visible attractions and never bothered to look further. To some degree, Becca and Laura had suffered the same problem, but they had learned to turn it to their advantage, especially when Becca needed their peers to view them as impressionable chits who would be impressed to hear of their latest investment acumen.

"At last," Aunt Aggie announced, breaking the tense silence. "It's our turn to descend."

Laura sighed with relief to be spared from having to explain her sister's feeling to the Earl. Thankfully, their aunt was happy to do the talking for all of them.

"The carriage queues for balls these days extend from one square to the next."

Laura smiled. "Yes, Auntie. Soon it will be more convenient to walk from our home."

"Walk?"

The shock on their aunt's face sent both Laura and Lottie into peals of laughter. Winchester's lips twitched, but he refrained for laughing aloud.

"We could never walk to Lady Brentwood's ball," their aunt said, a hand to her heart. "She'd imagine us very ill mannered."

The girls wisely refrained from any more teasing when a footman opened the door and assisted their aunt to descend.

When they joined her, the older Lady Jamison lifted her nose another half inch and murmured, "Remember, my dears, we are Jamisons. Never let anyone intimidate you."

Laura sighed, before giving her well-meaning aunt a quick kiss on her wrinkled cheek. She gathered her skirts, and her courage, as they ascended the front staircase to begin the long tedious process of greeting their host and hostess. She only needed to endure a half hour of social formalities, or as she called them tiresome trivialities, before she would be free to join her friends.

Winchester's cologne wafted from behind her, teasing her

nostrils and relaxing her with his strong presence at her back. Glittering ballrooms were more his world than hers so, in these settings, she accepted his assistance as willingly as he received the lotions and colognes she mixed for him, deferring to his expertise without argument. Why, then, did she find it so hard to reconcile herself to him in other parts of their entwined lives?

Working with so many distressed and battered women had clouded her judgment of all men and their motives, until the only men she trusted were her brothers, her new brother-in-law, and ….

She forgot to concentrate and tottered on the lip of next step, but was saved from toppling by the warm spread of Winchester's hand across her back, his reassurance stirring her emotions and body through layers of clothing. Supporting, comforting, and dare she even think it—exciting. She stilled and savored the moment. Allowed her spine to relax into his supporting hand, and imagined her life if Winchester had proved to be the one; the perfect mate whose aroma compelled her to his side.

She half turned on her higher step, for once able to meet him eye to eye. For a fleeting second, she glimpsed his unguarded expression. Open, before he closed it off to the impersonal one he generally assumed around people. A look of kindness, concern and, yes, perhaps in that moment, a tiny glimpse of the deeper emotions she knew him capable of. The kind of devotion she'd observed him showing to his four sisters on numerous occasions.

She swallowed down the lump clogging her throat. "Thank you," she said. "It's nice to know you're behind me tonight."

His eyes widened. He stared at her for a moment, before rubbing his palm in a small unseen motion over her back. "You really do worry about events such as these, don't you? I thought your aunt exaggerated the situation, as I've never known you to be afraid of anything."

"I'm not afraid. More disheartened. In the last few months, we've attended so many similar events. Stood in so many queues. Been introduced to countless gentlemen. And yet, I've not found a single man who comes close to meeting the requirements on my list."

His mouth turned up in a slight sneer. "Huh! Has is occurred to you, my sweet, that you chase the impossible? There's no such thing as a perfect man. Especially amongst the ton."

"Tut-tut, Winchester. How cynical you sound. But does that

assessment include you?"

"As you've pointed out on numerous occasions, minx, I'm far from perfect."

He touched a finger to her nose. "The fact that you're not perfect isn't the problem, as I'm sure you realize."

"Ah, so you're agreeable to accepting a husband who isn't perfect?"

"Yes, I mean...no." She moaned. "Bother you, Winchester. You're tying me in knots again."

He peered up the stairs. "Tying you in knots is the most fun I'm likely to have all evening, if this line doesn't start moving soon."

"Don't fret, my lord," she said, with a sweet smile. "We'll be through the greeting process shortly, and then you can resume your normal activities." She leaned closer to his ear. "Prowling the ballrooms for your latest conquest."

He waggled his brows. "I'm gratified you take such a keen interest in my love life." His words, spoken so close to her own ear, lifted the ringlet her dresser had artfully arranged and sent a shiver rippling down her neck. "Most young ladies of your station would never dare mention the word *conquest*. And few would understand the implications."

"I understand the implications perfectly. How could I not after the Countess's last display at the music recital yesterday. What I cannot fathom is how that woman knows exactly where you will be at any given moment."

"If you're implying I send the information to her ahead of time, you couldn't be more wrong. I do my best to avoid contact with her."

She raised a brow and tilted her head to the side. "Perhaps she has a spy amongst your servants. A footman who is the jealous suitor of one of your maids. One who is smitten with your good looks."

His lips twitched but he didn't smile. "Once again, I'm gratified you've taken the time to notice my appearance, and to remark upon it in a favorable manner." She rolled her eyes. "But I never dally with my maids. Bad form, don't you know? Although, on the other hand, I have noticed the blue-eyed Irish one you keep on your staff at Grosvenor House. Do you think the rules of gentlemanly behavior governing dallying with servants applies to one's own exclusively, or to those working in the establishments of one's friends as well?"

"Humph." She glared at the man's complacent attitude. "I know you're teasing me. You may do many things that stretch the bounds of society's approval, Winchester, but your gentlemanly instincts are too deeply entrenched for you to do anything to completely embarrass your sisters. And dallying with my servants would not only earn you their wrath, it would earn you my bullet between your eyes. Then your pretty face would no longer be able to attract any female."

He clasped his hand to his chest in a theatrical manner and leaned closer. "Harsh words, lovely Laura, coming from one who uses her own beauty and winning wiles to twist men around her little finger. Including your own footmen."

She scowled at him. "What do you know of my dealings with my footmen?"

"Only that when I tried to bribe one of them to send me information on your daily movements–"

"You what?"

He grinned at her, totally unrepentant. "For your own safety, my sweet. I knew you'd never agree voluntarily to sending me a list each day of your gadding, so I wanted to ensure that I knew where you were at all times. Unfortunately, your staff are ridiculously loyal to you."

She patted his hand, and gave him a smug smile. "As are yours, my lord."

When he froze between taking one step and the next, and his mouth dropped open in shock, Laura couldn't help but let out a peal of laughter. Oh, yes, she did so enjoy getting the better of him whenever possible.

"You mean…you mean you've bribed my staff?"

"Tried to bribe one of them, actually, but alas with little success. Like ours, yours are loyal to their master. Or at least to the one who pays their wages. But our cook's second cousin is married to your second footman, so we felt he should also owe some loyalty to the Jamison household."

"Because my footman has a distant relationship with someone from your household, you assumed that he should spy on me? His master?"

"You assumed you could spy someone to spy on me, so I see little difference. Except that you're wealthier than I, therefore your first thought is to use coin to pave your way to anything you need."

"Good grief. I always knew you were devious and cunning, but I had no idea that you'd also resort to using underhanded tricks to defeat me in our ongoing battle of wits."

She shrugged. "Why not? You do, and you cannot deny it."

"I'm allowed to use every means possible to protect the women under my guardianship."

"If you say that you're allowed be heavy-handed in your dealings, and I'm not, simply because I'm female and you're male–"

She sucked in a deep breath, praying for the fortitude to not punch the aristocratic nose that was unfortunately wavering far too close to her clenched fist. Luckily for Winchester's much admired facial features, at that moment, they were required to greet their hosts in an amicable manner. As soon as they had cleared the greeting queue, Aunt Aggie rushed off to greet her cronies and settle in for a good gossip.

Soon, both she and Lottie were surrounded by a large group of avid admirers. Laura was cynical enough to understand that part of their new popularity had to do with their newfound wealth, which, despite their best efforts to keep the news quiet, had become a topic of gossip. Everyone had discussed the arrest of the Consortium members three months earlier, and the part the Jamison family had played in their capture.

Cayle had tried his hardest to damp down rumors of their enormous profits from Becca's railway investments, and he and Michael had thrown out enough threats to would-be fortune hunters that men trod warily around the Jamison women. Knowing the girls had the backing of not just their brothers, but the Duke of Sherwyn and the Earl of Winchester, two renowned men of power around town, forced many men to retreat.

And Laura thanked the Lord for it every day. As it was, the respectable gentlemen who crowded to be included in her inner circle of friends exhausted her some days.

"May I request this dance, my lady," Winchester asked from in front of her.

She opened her weary eyes and rubbed a hand across her brow. "I am afraid I am already promised for this dance, my lord."

"Perhaps the next then."

She shook her head. "No, I am promised for the next several dances."

Winchester bowed acknowledgement and backed away, but not before she'd caught a look of disappointment on his face. He always danced one or two dances with her, yet she'd assumed he did it as a mark of respect to his cousin. Part of his duties as stand-in guardian.

Perhaps she wronged him, and he really did enjoy twirling the room with her as much as she enjoyed her time spent in his arms. Winchester danced the same way he did everything: expertly, with grace and ease.

Finally escaping the dance floor and the clamor of more eager would-be partners, Laura crept behind the branches of a large palm in a corner of the room. From here, she had a clear view of her aunt, now twirling down the center of the floor in a reel, partnered by another of her ardent admirers. It seemed Aunt Aggie was the only one of them who truly enjoyed the dancing for entertainment's sake.

Lottie danced with men only to examine their minds, to dig deeper into their innermost thoughts and uncover their secrets. And to try to see the bumps on the heads. That was her main objective: to enhance her knowledge of the science of phrenology.

The younger Jamison sister vowed Laura must wed before she had any intention of even considering marrying. A delaying tactic on Lottie's part, as she knew of Laura's vow to wed only the right man; the perfect man.

And for herself, partnering a gentleman in a giddy whirl of turns, dips and bows, was a way of catching hints of the man's scent close up. As he swung past her nose she'd inhale deeply, sucking into her senses the essence of the man for closer examination and evaluation. Tonight however, she felt only despondency that after weeks, even months, of such sniffing, her nose was as weary as her feet in her new slippers.

"Hiding again?" Lottie's whisper sounded loud in her ear.

"Yes. Retiring for a breather away from tedious conversations about the weather. And even more boring ones about their latest hound's hunting achievements."

"Isn't it ridiculous that these gentlemen, ones who have reportedly attended university, cannot converse about anything more than how over-heated the ballroom is tonight, or their latest prowess in a horse race."

"I never felt under pressure before, but now that Becca is married, I feel pushed to find a husband so that you too may start thinking about marrying. We're not getting any younger, as the tabbies delight in reminding us at every opportunity."

"There is absolutely no need to rush on my account, Laura. If the gentlemen I meet at these dreary social functions are typical examples of a good husband, I'm in no hurry to secure one as a husband. Can you imagine trying to hold a conversation over the dinner table each night?"

"What did you do today, my lord?" Laura said, imitating what could only be Lord Hutton's dreadful nasal drawl. "Terribly exciting day, what, as I looked at another horse, what, at Tattersall's, and read the paper, what, at my club."

The Earl of Winchester, in his concealed position several feet away, covered his mouth with his hand in a quick effort to smother his chortle of laughter. Laura's imitation of that pompous and boring gentleman had been exact. It worried him that Lord Hutton's age was exactly the same as his own, as they had been at Eton together.

Laura had also considered him pompous when he'd lectured her about her safety, which had become the topic of high concern in recent days. Still, better that she remained safe from harm and thought him an arrogant stuffed-shirt, than he allowed any one to hurt her. Over that, he'd never forgive himself.

He leaned forward to catch her next words to Lottie, knowing he should feel guilty at listening, but prepared to do anything—even underhanded tricks as she called them—to protect her.

"My plan to sniff out a husband didn't seem so difficult when I devised it, Lottie, but now I'm beginning to despair that the perfect man will ever present himself to me. I must revise my experiment somehow. Perhaps I am being too fussy in my criteria. Perhaps I need to bring forward the next step."

"Laura, think carefully before you do anything so rash. If you are found out, your reputation will be ruined. Then you'll never make a good match."

"I don't want a *good match* as society knows it. I simply want a man who will know me as I am. And respect me that way. Not continually seek to change me. I'd go mad married to a man who lectured me on the rights and wrongs of life every single day, from breakfast to dinner, like many men feel entitled to do with their wives. I need some freedom."

"I admit, the way we were brought up made it difficult for any of us to settle for an arranged marriage, a comfortable fit. We're all searching for that elusive rainbow."

"Settling for second best is not what either of us want." She grasped her sister's hands. "Lottie, I need your help. If you combine your skills with mine and find me a husband, first, then we can both concentrate on finding you a husband later. By using the same combination of scientific methods. I'll record all our findings. Test all the men, and then write it down so we can compare their characteristics. That way, we can sort out which ones are a perfect match for both of us."

"You're forgetting, Becca didn't need either of our skills in the end. She didn't get a chance to test her theories on lovemaking with any gentlemen. Sherwyn forbade her the instant he heard of her intentions."

"Yes." Laura gave a little giggle. "The look on his face was worth framing. While he acted the gentleman and refused to assist her bedroom experiments, Becca flaunted her list of men who would happily help. She walked out and left the Duke with his mouth open, catching flies."

"Ah! But it did push Sherwyn into revealing his own feelings. He couldn't stand the thought of another man touching Becca. And as he'd once given Becca her first kiss, he wanted to be the one to also teach her about lovemaking. "

In his hiding place, Richard couldn't contain his shock. As Sherwyn's closest confident, he'd known that his cousin and Becca had anticipated their wedding night. The grinning glee on the Duke's face in the weeks prior to their marriage had told the story, though Richard hadn't known of Becca's ultimatum. No wonder his cousin had almost turned gray overnight.

For a duke and a gentleman who'd vowed to avoid all close relationships with women while he'd repaired the family fortunes, Sherwyn's position had been untenable. He'd bedded Becca long before deciding to marry her, or he would have risked the stubborn woman calling his bluff and asking some other rake to deflower her.

Good Lord! Sherwyn hadn't stood a chance against one of the strong Jamison women. And what would he do if Laura confronted him with the same situation? He prayed he'd never need to choose, because he already knew how his body would react and he had no idea if his mind would be strong enough to turn her down. Watching other idiots make fools of themselves by clamoring for Laura's attention had turned his stomach until, several times, he'd almost marched onto the dance floor to remove some letch's hand.

Those rogues made themselves far too familiar with her perfectly-rounded posterior for him to stay detached. If Laura copied her older sister's example and wanted to take one of them to her bed, to experiment with sex, he'd be quicker than her brothers to challenge the recipient to a duel. Despite knowing he was the last person she'd want interfering in her life, and knowing he'd never be the one to take Laura's virginity.

Through his own choosing, he backed away every time any mention from the family's hovered around the topic of a union between them. Deep down, he recognized that he wasn't good enough for someone like Laura, someone whose presence on this earth made every day better.

Yet, he'd need to be dragged away screaming and kicking before he willingly conceded the right to any other man. Unless he helped by finding her perfect man for her. Ensuring her future happiness. Only then could he rest easy.

Lottie announced, "I'm off to test my particular skills on Henry Mortimer."

"You won't need to, Lottie. Henry's so smitten with you already, he'd even reveal the name of his latest lady-love, if you asked him. My search is going to be harder. I need a tutor in the sensual arts, but one who knows the meaning of the word discretion. An unknown trait amongst the majority of these men."

Richard frowned, wondering yet again what skill Lottie possessed that could be added to Laura's scientific experiments, her testing of men. He swallowed again, trying to ignore the lump in his throat. It galled him to know that Laura contemplated any sort of sensual play with any man except him. He banged his head against the wall behind him, cursing himself for his predicament.

If he declared himself to her, his own feelings, his hidden yearnings where she was concerned, she would construe it as some sort of a promise. A vow she had a right to assume he made to her, the sort of thing any respectable lady expects from a respectable man. Though such promises were not ones he should make to her, hiding secrets from her as he did. He was damned if he did, and damned if he didn't.

Lottie moved away from her sister and went to greet her latest dance partner, leaving Laura cowering behind her leafy coverage. He stiffened his spine, and his resolve. Leaving her open to harm and hurt was unthinkable. Somehow, he must make her see the foolishness of the plans she and Lottie were concocting out of desperation.

"Good Lord! What are you two thinking?"

He spoke so close to her ear that she startled, jumped, spun around to face him. Her eyes, as dark as the night outside the balustrade doors, widened in shock and surprise. Sparks flashed in them, like the stars that twinkled outside in the inky sky.

Those flashes, those bright sparks, made Laura unique. They encompassed her character. She held secret dark depths that were few were privileged enough to glimpse, yet she possessed a temperament fiery enough to ignite sparks, flash fury and defy the Gods when aroused or cornered.

Christ, he wanted her! Who was he fooling with ideas of finding her another man? He wanted her. He alone. Wanted to capture some of that zest for life, that passion, and hold it against himself. Let some of it fill the empty spaces in his own being. They'd fit together like the soft leather of her gloves molding to her capable fingers.

Why, then, did he still resist? Because he couldn't bear to imagine the day in the future when she discovered what he'd successfully kept hidden for so many years. To have her uncover his weakness, have her reveal his ineptitude, even to gain her pity, would destroy him. No, better to stay away.

When she took several quick swallows, he watched, fascinated, and followed the tinge of red creeping up her face. Laura embarrassed?

Amazing. Interesting. Worrying.

"You were eavesdropping," she said, stabbing a finger into his chest. He took hold of the accusatory finger and held it still, assessing her expression, trying to read those deep thoughts and concerns. Wishing he could do more to ease the burdens he knew she uncomplainingly shouldered for her family.

"Perhaps you could explain to me the exact nature of this secret skill Lady Charlotte wields so easily amongst men. The one everyone hints about but leaves me guessing."

Laura shrugged, a gesture he recognized well, as she'd used it on him countless times when wanting to deflect the topic of conversation to something more amenable to herself.

"Men are inclined to tell Lottie…"An idle flick of a few fingers. "… things." The minx excelled at off-putting gestures.

"Things?"

Another shrug, upwards and sideways, a gesture she'd practiced to distract the fops who fawned over her. The edge of her gown loosened, so that the neckline slipped another tantalizing inch. Being as crassly male as the rest of her leering flowers, the tiny glimpse of the side of her curved breast caused his mouth to dry and his pulse to speed. It would not, however, deflect his line of questioning.

With a nonchalance he was far from feeling, he reached over, tugged the small puffed sleeve of her gown higher, and lifted the neckline with it.

"Is that another of the gestures you practice in front of the mirror?"

Horror flitted across her face, before she recovered her equilibrium. "My gown slipped."

"I noticed," he said with dry irony. "Every male with a pulse notices when you perform that same act for him. That is precisely what I need to speak to you about."

"Oh, please, someone come to my rescue. I sense another of the Earnest Earl's lectures about to commence."

"The Earnest Earl?" He couldn't hold back a startled chuckle at this unheard title.

"One of many names we Jamisons have labeled you on occasion." Her honey-sweet smile belied the sarcasm with which she delivered the words.

"Have I become so staid and calculated in executing my duties as stand-in guardian for Sherwyn, that I'm now being accused of becoming overly earnest?

"Ironic. Every other woman of my acquaintance accuses me of being overly frivolous, lacking in attention, and the normal accusation is of my insincerity."

There was another sickly-sweet smile, this time with a small glimpse of her barred teeth, as she asked, "How is your dear, dear friend, the Countess, this evening?"

"Tut-tut." He waggled a finger under her nose. "That green-eyed monster reappears. But to set your inquisitive little mind to rest, I've managed to avoid the Countess. You should be commending me on my finesse as a sneak-thief, rather than condemning me on my acquaintances."

"Unfortunately, we both know the Countess has been far, far more than that to you. And if her presence at every event we've attended for the past week is a guide, she urgently seeks another acquaintance with your bed posts."

He laughed. "Laura, Laura. Your evil mouth will be your

undoing. What if someone should overhear you? They'd think you a brazen hussy."

"Do you think I really care about these shallow creatures?" She waved a hand towards the chattering crowds in the room beyond them.

"Yes, I heard the disparaging comments you and your sister made about many of these fine upstanding members of our peerage. Which brings me back to my main concern."

He sighed, knowing no matter how he addressed the predicament she would revile his advice. "Sweetheart, you're far, far too lovely a lady to be drawn into any scandalous arrangements with gentlemen. You cannot draw these men into experimenting with you, as many of them—No. The majority of these men, most especially the ones who'll forget their principles and agree to introduce a young lady of good birth to the sensual arts, are rakes, rogues and scoundrels. They'll assume you're far more experienced than we both know you are."

"You've no idea of the level of my experience." Her nose rose in that haughty manner he'd come to watch for. *Hauteur* in Laura meant strength of character to spar with him. What he loathed was the times her head and shoulders drooped, like a kicked dog with its tail between its legs. "Not that it any of your business, but I may have already commenced on my research. Filled countless note books with descriptions of the sensual liaisons I've had with innumerable men."

"Liar."

"I beg your pardon?"

"If, little innocent, you'd had countless encounters with men— men of experience, not wet-behind-the-ears boy who snatch a kiss on the balcony between sets—your breath wouldn't catch in your chest every time I step near you."

He deliberately pressed the length of his body closer to hers. "Like that. And your midnight eyes wouldn't grow extra stars when I bend my head to nuzzle your neck and nibble your ear."

He matched actions to his words, and her breath caught so hard that he feared she'd stopped breathing completely. He lifted his head and stared into her eyes, frozen as wide as saucers.

"Breathe, sweetheart, breathe for me."

Her eyes closed and she gasped for air.

"Those are the reactions of an innocent. Pure, sweet, breathless anticipation. That's how I know no man, at least no experienced man, has touched you. Yet. But be warned, little tempter: if you allow any one of those idiots over there to lay a hand on you, you shall be responsible for the messy consequences when I catch up with him."

Her hand went to her hips and she assumed her usual position of defiance as she challenged him. "How dare you!" A finger to his chest again. "You. Are. Not. One of my brothers."

He scowled at her, his own temper rising to match hers. "If I was your brother, and having these sort of thoughts about you, my lovely, the authorities would lock me away. Wherever they put people of depraved natures."

"Ooh! You're not my keeper. And I'm not some young chit like them." She flicked a hand towards the young timid girls sitting in demure fashion with chaperones. "I'm quite old enough to take care of myself."

A tell-tale tear leaked from the side of one of her eyelids, a demonstration that Laura's bravado of late resembled the thin ice covering the pond at the beginning of winter. One hard push and it would crack wide open. His anger deflated like the air leaking out of the hot air balloon they'd viewed yesterday.

"Sweetheart, it's not cowardice to allow others to assist you. You take so much weight on your own shoulders that I hate to see you bent over with the heavy burden. Please, I beg of you, at least until the honeymoon couple return, accept my offers of help and don't fight me every step of the way. No one will think less of you."

"You will." As if fearing the words slipping out of her mouth, she put a hand to it and silenced it.

With a gentle tug, he pulled her hand away. "What I think is, that lovely and lively Laura is one of the most courageous and selfless ladies I've ever had the privilege of meeting."

She studied him, head tilted to one side, appearing stunned by his revelation.

"Really?"

He nodded. "Truly. As to the other matter you were discussing with Lottie, those tests, like the ones Becca did–" He shuffled his feet, unable to finish. Ridiculous. Now he suffered from embarrassment.

"Yes?"

"If–if you're determined to test the waters. To find out why people indulge in affairs. If you have such a strong desire to experience passion first hand, let me make it clear that I will not stand by and let you attempt these–these studies—with anyone untrustworthy."

"Fine. If that is what it takes to put your mind at rest and your scowling face out of my sight, I'll seek out men of whom you shall approve."

"Damnation! Can you not understand my problem here? There are no blasted men out there of whom I can approve. Not a single one of them." He lowered his head to mutter, "Not when I think of you as mine."

She bent closer, frowned. "What did you say?"

He closed his eyes and prayed for deliverance from a conversation he should never have started, and now longed to finish. His stomach tied itself into tight knots. Through half clenched teeth, he ground out, "I said, the next dance is mine. Your aunt will be searching for you by now, anyhow, so we must go."

He placed Laura's hand on his sleeve, and when another cluster of couples strolled past, merged with them to lead her back through the crowd. With a quick maneuver, he placed them in the center of the floor. He lifted her gloved hand in his, held it high, and awaited the commencement of the music. As the strain of the waltz began, he led her off into the steps, letting years of training take over as his mind drifted to other questions.

"Oh, it's a waltz," she said in a surprised voice, as he swung her through a turn at the corner.

He smiled, relieved. She'd obviously been as distracted as he was, though possibly not for the same reason. His preoccupation occurred from his mind obsessively returning to thoughts of Laura coming to his bedchamber; Laura begging him to teach her all he knew about seduction and pleasure.

Her dark hair would flow like a river across his pillow as he laid her naked on his bed. Starting at her toes, he'd happily spend hours demonstrating all the places on a woman's body that she could find exquisite pleasure, until she screamed her release like a wild animal calling her mate. Calling him to finish what he'd begun.

And, oh, how he wanted to finish it, though he also knew that once he started on that path with Laura, there would be no ending. His wanting her was bound to increase threefold when he'd tasted her once.

Without thinking, he pressed her closer and swung her into another turn, his leg extended between her thighs, his half arousal pressing against her skirts. Damnation! His arousal. He'd been so lost in the feel of her in his arms, and his fantasies of her in his bed, that he'd forgotten they also twirled between dozens of other couples and in front of hundreds of onlookers.

Her eyes widened, an incredible look he adored; a look of dawning understanding, of purely feminine recognition of a male who wanted her in a physical manner. To his consternation, it had occurred more and more frequently of late. She sucked her bottom lip into her mouth, drawing his eyes to the action like a child counting cakes on a tea plate.

Hungrily. Greedily.

He shifted positions for the next twirl and swung her out a little, then tightened his hold and pulled her close again, while they executed another perfect movement of the waltz. Their bodies fitted together as if welded like metal joints in one of the factories they invested in.

He nudged her legs apart as he thrust further forward with his knee, pushing his groin against hers, just enough to help push himself over the edge of insanity. Her breath hissed in and out, hard inhales and exhales that matched his own, as well as his rising level of excitement.

"Of course we're waltzing," she said, with a quick shake of her head and more deep breathing through the turns. "What must... you think of me. Making such... inane comments."

"I think ... little one...you're as unfocused... as haunted... by the idea of us. Together. In bed. Or any other place. As I am."

He swirled her around another corner, marveling at how perfectly they blended together, like butter melting on his morning toast.

"It's a ludicrous idea. You don't love me. You don't even like me."

He threw back his head and laughed, as he slowed their steps and dodged other couples dancing past. "Loving is very seldom the reason people in this City of Sin bed each other, little innocent. And the nuisance is, lovely Laura, that I like you far, far too much for my own health. Or yours."

"Then–then why... why do we always argue?"

He grunted. "Have you never heard the saying...

... *opposites attract*? We fight because we continue to deny the attraction between us; the sensual pull that tugs us together, no matter how much we pretend to dislike spending even an hour in each other's presence."

Keeping his eyes fixed on hers, he shook his head. "In all probability, sweetheart, the time has arrived to relinquish all our presence. To give in to the inevitable."

They'd almost come to a stop as the band played the last notes of the tune and the twirling couples around them slowed and halted.

"What is the inevitable?"

He smiled softly, stilled, but didn't release her. "The inevitable is that your charms become too strong for me to resist. You and I ... are destined to become lovers."

He took the hand she held suspended in the air, placed it again on his sleeve, and made his way towards where he could see her aunt peering with an anxious expression into the crowds.

"*There* you are, Laura, darling. I wondered where you were. If I had known *Winchester* was with you, I need *not* have worried. It's so comforting to have a capable man like him to attend to us tonight. Don't you agree?"

Laura opened her mouth to state her thoughts, most likely to disagree, but he gave her no chance.

"If we are to avoid causing a scandal, it may be better to not allow Laura to voice her strong opinions on having me as an escort tonight, though I fear she would not agree with your assessment, dear lady."

He dipped a little bow to Lady Jamison, and that delightful lady tittered. Predictably, Laura continued scowling at him. Funny, he wouldn't have it any other way. Igniting strong passions in her, even if directed against him, proved the most entertainment he'd ever had in long monotonous years around similar functions.

"Richard, my darling man, where have you been hiding? I've been searching everywhere for you."

Hell! He didn't have to glance down at the woman now clutching his arm, with claws like a jungle cat's, to recognize who'd stalked him once more, cornered him again. At the worst possible time. No. He only needed a glance at Laura's scowling expression. With difficulty, he unlatched her claws from his coat fabric and removed her hand, taking a small sideways step, determined to put himself out of her reach.

"Countess." His required bow was executed without directly facing the lady, though nothing deterred this hunting countess once she'd decided on her path. Or, in this instance, her prey.

"Richard, sweetie, come dance with me. I long to have your arms around me again."

In unison, the Jamison women audibly groaned. They'd delight in tearing verbal strips off his hide later. Never mind. A little ridicule could be endured. However, the clinging Countess's continual hints to everyone within hearing regarding them resuming their past association would not be tolerated.

"I regret, Countess, we are about to depart."

The Countess of Newbery ran her eyes over the older Lady Jamison, and then turned towards Charlotte. She ran through the formalities of greetings before her intense scrutiny fixed upon Laura. Warning bells clanged in his ears. This woman was an infamous cat, vicious and gossipy when she was thwarted, and by the sinister look in her eyes, her intention might be to unleash her wrath upon Laura.

"And you, Lady Laura; the room is abuzz tonight with your strange exploits." She giggled, a deliberately ridiculing noise.

He stiffened, ready to spring to her defense.

"Several gentlemen have spoken of a lady, a blue-stocking spinster so engrossed in her extreme scientific studies she has sunk so low as to take the scandalous step of—"

The Countess hesitated in a theatrical fashion, paused, waited till she'd gained the attention of every avid listener in their vicinity.

"Sniffing! Inhaling men's–" Another dramatic pause. "Oh, one can hardly dare express the word in this exalted company. Yet, apparently, and do correct me if it is untrue, Lady Laura, but one shocked gentleman had the ridiculous idea you actually meant to inhale his... his bodily moisture. "She made a tut-tutting sound of utter disapproval, waited again until her audience were captured, absorbing every word she dropped into the conversation. "His perspiration." She lifted the back of one gloved hand to her brow in an expression of her utter shock and horror, and gave a loud groan.

Around them several other ladies made the same tittering sounds, and snorts and moans of disapproval were expressed. Words describing physical functions of any sort, no matter how minor, were never, ever, ever mentioned in a ballroom. True ladies were expected to swoon at such a thing. Expected to give a public demonstration of their sensibilities being overset.

The Countess directed a smug smile in Laura's direction. "So, please, do reassure me this horrifying rumor is untrue."

Satisfied with the drama she'd created, the Countess turned to Richard, smiled, expected him to agree with her. He stood speechless with anger. Thankfully. If he spoke, he'd make matters much, much worse, because the language he'd use would also be scandalous for a ballroom. His fist clenched at his sides and his jaw tightened.

Three sets of Jamison eyes sparked with anger. The Countess pretended to not notice the growing tension in the air. Conversation in the groups around them ceased. Nearby couples strained to hear what was being said.

"No, I assure you, Countess Newbery, that everything you heard is true. I am fast becoming a scenting scandal. Not only do I mix perfumes and colognes for my family and friends, what some would see as engaging in trade--oh, tut-tut, shock and horror, how dreadful I am--but I've also been studying the perspiration--"

From nearby, Lady Tilton could be heard give a loud gasp and supposedly swooned, as her husband said out loud, "Oh, good grief, Matilda. Not again. Where is your vinaigrette?"

Richard felt the time had come to end this little scene, before the group of gossiper around them increased and rumors started circulating the ballroom of an open dispute between two ladies.

"Ladies," he announced loudly. "We are leaving."

He took Laura's arm before she could protest, and prodded her in the direction of the door. Lottie took up her aunt's arm and followed closely behind them.

As they walked away, the Countess, not content with the amount of scandal she had already attempted to stir, called after him, "Richard, darling, I shall speak with you later."

It took the next thirty minutes and all of his considerable maneuvering tactics to escort them through the crowded room, collect their wraps and assist them to his coach. A long half hour in which none of the Jamison ladies spoke.

Finally, after the coach had rumbled into motion, he broke the taut silence.

"Lady Laura, I know that you have acute smelling senses."

Silence.

"I know all about your distillery, your perfumes and colognes and soaps, the medicaments you mix--"

The three women sat as still as statues, even the older Lady Jamison who normally chattered incessantly. The idea of her niece causing a scandal with her sniffing had distressed her visibly.

He tried again to start a conversation and lighten the dismal mood. "But Sherwyn also hinted at some sort of experiment that Becca helped you conduct. Although, every time Brian, Tony and I asked, my cousin would fix us with his superior and smug look and merely announce that we needed to find out firsthand."

He glanced at the faces of the three women, all knowing the secret that Laura still hid from him. But all three faces were carefully blanked of all expression. There were no tell-tale hints, not even from Aunt Aggie.

"The only thing Sherywn would say, with repeated emphasis, was that it almost turned his hair gray when he discovered what Becca intended doing. And with whom. Therefore, Sherwyn thought it fair punishment that every other man should discover what it entailed by investigation. Rather than by him informing us."

Silence from the three ladies.

"He said it would spoil the surprise for us. And then he'd laugh, in a ridiculously smug manner that always set my teeth on edge. Now, I find myself puzzled by what he meant. And yet, fearful of finding out. Does it have something to do with your ideas of sniffing every man in existence, Laura?"

He sighed. "Well, let me start off on another foot and apologize for any embarrassment the Countess caused to you this evening. I am extremely sorry that I ever introduced her to any of you. She is not a lady to have brought up a subject that was intended to cause distress to you, Lady Laura."

Aunt Aggie finally spoke. "Winchester, we do not hold you to blame for any words that spewed from the mouth of that spiteful woman. It has become obvious at every event we have attended for the past sennight that the lady has her sights set upon becoming your wife. She will go to any lengths to embarrass anyone she fears may be in competition for your favors."

Hell! He had no idea how to handle this.

"What an awkward situation that places me in, my lady. The Countess is, of course, only as human as every other woman. I cannot deny my charms are so great, so notorious, that women fight over me in ballrooms now. Though, if women find me irresistible, can it be deemed my fault?" He dramatically clasped his hands to his chest, a tired-and-true pose of Shakespeare's Romeo.

Aunt Aggie and Lottie both laughed at his attempt at a jest, but Laura refused to give in and laugh, or to even glance at him. Silence descended for another ten minutes before Laura suddenly asked, "Did you discover anything from the gentlemen in the billiard room?"

He heaved a sigh of relief, glad she had steered her mind away from tonight's fiasco and back to their more pressing problem. The danger lurking around them from the shooter.

His next twenty minutes were spent revealing every snippet of gossip he'd picked up from his peers from around the card room, or on the sidelines of the dances.

"I've confirmed that a new investment consortium has been trying to whip up interest amongst the social elite. Members of the new Syndicate have been cornering men, and women, at every opportunity. Wherever there has been a gathering in the last two weeks, a representative of one of the lower order syndicates has made himself known. They're trying to entice a large number of new investors. And each time, the name of the syndicate is different. Whoever is controlling the smaller groups has covered their tracks extremely well. One syndicate has no idea who leads the others."

He had their absolute attention now. Excitement over their current mystery was better, far, far better, than the tense silence he'd endured for the first part of the carriage ride to Jamison House. The sight of Laura's pale strained face was like a knife to his gut. She sat straight as a plank of wood, fists clenched and ruining her beautiful new skirt, her eyes close to spilling tears.

Never in his life before had he experienced such a fierce need to soothe the hurts of another person, despite adoring his four sisters and always being on hand if they suffered any illness or injury.

He sighed again, before forcing himself to continue in as normal a voice as possible. "It's become obvious that the Consortium is making secret investments again, but whether or not this new one is being led Lord Hetherington's estranged wife, that I have been unable to discover. It's what worries me most."

"Yes," Lottie said. "That is our most pressing question. Is this being masterminded by the same demented lady who tried to kill our sister? The same one who organized so many of Lord Hetherington's sordid blackmail schemes the first time."

"We do know that the ghastly Lady escaped before she could be locked away in Bedlam with all those other mad people," Aunt Aggie said, "but so far Thompkins and our footman have uncovered little news of her. Other than the idea that they think she may be the unnamed woman buying several high class bordellos." She sent a sharp look towards her nieces. "Not that I like the idea of you girls conspiring with Madame Faberge and the other owners of establishments of entertainment–" She broke off and glared at him, when a small laugh escaped his lips.

"Laugh if you will, Winchester, but my girls associate with the notorious Madame Faberge. I assume you know her."

He smothered another grin. Conversations with this family were never ordinary, dull, or boring. "I do know *of* Madame and her establishment, yes."

Across from him, Laura rolled her eyes.

"Well, it is rather *hard* to stop the girls from associating with these *sort* of females, when they are so *desperately* in need of assistance with their finances. And *my* girls are *so* wonderful at that sort of thing. And then of course by knowing them, Thompkins, our butler–"

He nodded, wondering where this was headed.

"Thompkins could then send out his boys, street urchins that we employ for a few coins and some food, to provide us with information from around the streets, you understand."

He nodded again, as it seemed to be all that was required of him.

"Thompkins and our footmen are a godsend at spying around some of the houses of ill-repute, and they are reporting to us who owns which ones, and which ones are the most profitable...that sort of thing, you understand."

This time he burst out laughing. "Forgive me, my lady, but it is somewhat unusual for a lady of your station to be discussing the owners of...ah... houses."

"Well, I fear for the lives of our family, you understand, so we must all help find the culprits quickly. I will not sleep easy until they are all behind bars."

He nodded, understanding her fear for her nieces, intrepid as they tended to be. He feared for them himself.

"I've my own sources at all the normal places trying to discover if the lady has been able to round up her old servants. Ones who were loyal to her, not to the husband she tried to murder. So far, no one has tracked her down to where she is living. I've spoken to many men tonight, and no one who has been approached for money has been told who is the main organizer. Only that a group is being formed and if they want to be included, they must first agree to accept all the terms without argument. Only then will they be allowed to join a small group. Each syndicate joins the honeycomb of interlocking groups. There is very little information available, because they've been promised absolute discretion after they register their interest."

"Not like last time, then," Laura said, "when their names were made known after we shattered the upper rungs of the organization. When blame fell, it fell on them. Their reputations were blackened inexorably."

"To stop that happening again," he said, "they've been promised that, this time, there will be no shady underhand deals. No blackmail. No coercion. Though so far as I know, no gentleman has been daring enough to risk trying it. And already there are rumors of some instances where men have said no and are now being pressured into joining."

He looked at the women, unsure how to deliver this news. "In fact, the talk at the ball was that Joseph Longman, a green young man not long ago launched onto the Town scene, and known by many to have a ready supply of cash, had refused twice before to listen to anything about the Consortium. He'd publicly ridiculed the men just last week who discussed investing, as he said his father and his cronies are certain it will end just as the last one did. In tragedy. With a loss of money to investors. And in a loss of face to those silly enough to get caught in the web of the unscrupulous organizers."

He sighed. "Apparently Longman made his feelings known far and wide, and now, tonight, he's not made an appearance. When two friends went to collect him earlier, the young man couldn't be found. They assumed he'd changed his mind and had made his own way to the ball. They searched for him for two hours before realizing he hadn't ever arrived."

Lottie became visibly upset. "Dreadful news. I know Mr. Longman quite well. He's the most sensible of all the men I've met recently. Keeps his rather large feet firmly planted on this earth. Doesn't have his head in the clouds as so many of these idiotic fops do."

"I agree," Laura said. "I've danced with Mr. Longman several times. He's a sensible sort. Not the type to disappear up some actress's skirts."

"Really, Laura," her aunt said, shaking her head. "But knowing the steadiness of that dear young gentleman, it does seem suspicious. I shall feel dreadful if harm has come to Mr. Longman because we didn't send that lunatic lady to goal, rather than the asylum."

The three women turned in unison to look at Richard.

He groaned, but knew he had no choice. "Fine. No sleep for me tonight. I shall endeavor to discover Longman's whereabouts. If no one has seen him this evening, I'll assist his friends in locating him. Would that satisfy the three of you?"

Three pairs of Jamison eyes gleamed in triumph. Three Jamison smiles told him he'd done the right thing.

But it was Laura he watched the closest. She met his eyes without her usual frown of disproval, and her half smile displayed a glimmer of admiration, perhaps even a hint of liking. No wonder so many of the younger bachelors in the upper ten thousand were known to compete for one of those approving smiles from Luscious Laura. And it was quite obvious why many not-so-single men gave Laura a second or third going over with lustful eyes.

Men would walk over hot coals to have a woman smile at them like that, though not him of course. His future countess's charms wouldn't include any facial expressions that could make other men fall at her feet.

Laura smiled again, a tiny turning up of the corners of her mouth, while her aunt continued to express her gratitude. And like a fish being reeled directly into a frying pan, Richard heard himself agree to not only locate the missing man, but to afterwards report his findings to them.

Good grief. He was doomed.

Chapter Seven

The Earl of Winchester stepped inside the foyer of the first club on his list for seeking information, and was immediately drawn to the commotion. He joined a large group of his peers, one of many groups crowded into the generally subdued common room, and listened to their discussions on the current status of Mr. Joseph Longman.

As Richard mingled with the crowd surging in and out of the adjoining rooms, he overheard enough to be certain that the two main topics were the young man's adventure and the chances of Longman recovering from his attack. Longman was well-liked amongst all levels of his peers, so the club was agog with news of his abduction.

"....dragged from his rooms while he dressed for the evening."

"Heard the poor lad was bound and gagged and driven to the outskirts of the city. He was kicked and beaten by several men."

"Dreadful situation. The lower classes are too full of themselves, if they have taken to attacking harmless young lads."

Richard moved between the rooms and picked up snippets of conversation as he went.

"Lost consciousness…Lucky for Longman that a clergyman passed by…He'd been offering comfort to a dying man at a manor house…Spotted Longman's body beside the road."

"Bloody hell. Will he survive?"

"We can only hope. The clergyman found enough in the lad's pockets to piece together the pertinent facts: Longman's name and where he lived. Clever man, that clergyman. He deposited Longman with the closest doctor, and then sent off quick messages to the most likely addresses."

"Pity it took so long."

"But at least his family is now on their way to collect him."

"Dreadful news. Any clue as to why he was abducted? Was it robbery?"

"Bit of a puzzle, apparently. Money missing, yet he his signet ring was left. Nor did the ruffians steal the diamond stick pin from his cravat."

"Either the abductors were sloppy thieves, or they wanted Longman for something else."

"Yes, but what? There was no demand for money."

Richard agreed with these men. Abducting Longman and then releasing him made no sense unless the robbers had been interrupted and, from what he'd pieced together, the clergyman hadn't found Longman until he was almost frozen to death.

Another man said, "We can only hope Longman recovers his senses. Throws some light on the matter."

"Meanwhile," another voice added, "policemen from the district Magistrate's office have been assigned the case. They've taken the clergyman back to the spot where he found Longman. They're trying to retrace the route the carriage took out of London. Hoping someone noticed it pass."

"Let's hope they uncover the truth, and quickly," Richard said to one group of acquaintances. "We all know how rumors spread. Stories become exaggerated out of all proportion."

The men around him nodded their agreement. "That's likely to cause even more unrest," one said. "There's been more than enough disturbance amongst our ranks recently." He looked directly at Richard and asked, "Have you heard anything about this new investment syndicate?"

Richard shook his head. "Have you?"

The man, a pompous old baron known more for his gossipy nature than for any shrewd investing, said, "Only that it's a closed club." He sniffed. "By invitation only."

The baron obviously hadn't been asked; yet several others nodded to say they had received invitations to a meeting, though details were to be sent later to all those who'd answered 'Aye'.

When he'd garnered all the news he was likely to hear that night, Richard left the club and ordered his driver to go slowly through Grosvenor Square. Apart from his obligation to see if any lights remained lit in Jamison House, he was drawn to the dwelling and its occupants; compelled like a bee scenting honeysuckle.

His coachman, following orders, halted a few houses further along the square, and a footman opened the door. Richard leaned back against the richly upholstered interior and debated whether he should, or should not, disturb the household.

The first argument for descending was the glow of a lamp in an upper window. The light glowed strongly, so someone was awake and waiting to hear his news. And though he'd not admit this to another living soul, he already knew that was Laura's bedchamber.

A true gentleman would never acknowledge knowing where a lady slept. It was one of those ridiculous rules of proper behavior where even males and females from the same family were, whenever feasible, housed in separate wings. The sexes were always to be distanced from each other by as many corridors and solid walls as possible.

Heaven forbid that any well-bred young lady should encounter a man without his coat and cravat. Or if a highly-strung girl should glimpse her father or brothers without a shirt, her sensibilities were supposed to be so badly affected that she'd suffer a severe paroxysm from which she'd need days to recover.

So a known womanizer shouldn't know that Laura dressed in that chamber each morning, and laid her pillows on the bed there each night. He'd absorbed these facts through osmosis, and of course because he paid close attention to every word she uttered. If she knew he remembered every quirky thing she said and did, she'd no doubt berate him about it, and compare him to the sycophants who followed her movements like adoring lap dogs.

He banged his head back against the padding, repeated the action, and hoped to knock some sense into his thick skull. If Laura's neighbors around the square noticed him mooning like a love sick fool under her window, he'd be the laughing stock of the City by morning. On the other hand, knocking on her front door would awaken half the household. Either way, the Earl of Winchester was destined to make a spectacle of himself over a lady, who always seems to entangle him in her dramas in one way or another.

He slid back the roof, ready to order his coachman to drive on to his own home. He stopped and listened. A voice, assuredly feminine, called out. Despite the pitch being lower than usual, he instantly recognized the voice and its not-to-be-denied command.

He screwed his eyes shut and prayed that when he again looked at that window, the third from the corner on the second floor, there'd be no sign of her. Then he'd feel free to move on with a clear conscience, knowing he'd kept his word and come to deliver any news.

"Winchester." The hissing of his name in the relative quiet of this time of night sounded like a loud and piercing scream. Certainly not a whisper, as Laura had probably intended.

From above him on the driver's box came the unmistakable sound of Peter's laughter. Even his staff understood that every interaction with Laura diverged from normal. And that his own actions, and reactions, when near her, were completely out of character.

Muttering a resigned curse, he opened the carriage door and stepped down to the pavement. Pretending he couldn't hear his footman's unrestrained amusement, he braced himself and looked up at Laura's window. And immediately wished to God he hadn't.

Laura's upper torso looked to be suspended in mid-air as she leaned out, far past the window ledge, and waved her robe-covered arms in complete disregard for either propriety or her own safety. Her robe was pulled open across the stretch of her chest and, though he couldn't see through her night rail, he could easily imagine those two unrestrained breasts, full-grown and luscious, squashed down onto the timber ledge.

His heart skipped a beat and words stuck in his throat, partly from the image she presented, and partly from fear of her tumbling if he yelled. He glared at his open-mouthed footman, who stood shoulder to shoulder with him in front of the fence, silently ordering him to drop his gaze from the spectacle. But Peter, his coachman, had joined them and paid no heed to his master's annoyance. The ex-boxer looked skywards, enthralled by the sight of Lady Jamison, well-regarded by all his servants due to the free curatives she dispensed to them or their families, hanging from an upper story like a Vauxhall acrobat.

Why, oh why, did Laura never think before she acted? Not only was Peter enjoying the sight of her dishevelment, she was hanging, like meat in a butcher shop, in full view of the sterner inhabitants of the area. He shuddered to think of the newspaper headlines the next day. They'd be forced to marry, quickly and sneakily.

"Go. Back. Inside." His enunciated words sounded louder than Laura's hissed whisper. He waved his arms, in between snatching glances around the square to ensure nobody was watching. The stubborn woman either didn't understand or was ignoring his order, because she leaned even more of her body across the sill. He circled his arms like a lopsided windmill, while praying she'd retract her torso before his heart stopped. The image of her toppling to the ground and smashing her beautiful face sent a shudder down his spine.

"Winchester, stay there," she called in a cheerful and oblivious way. "I'm coming down."

Damn the woman. Damn her impetuous nature. She ought to be locked up. If his family emblem on the side of the coach hadn't highlighted his identity before her neighbors, calling out his name would have informed them who the peer was standing on her footpath and dancing around like a man possessed.

Whatever had possessed him to come anywhere near Jamison House at this time of night? He glanced around. Thankfully, no curtains twitched in the upper story windows of her closest neighbors. He ordered his coachman to drive slowly and quietly around the square and wait for him at the furthest corner.

He walked up the steps and stood in the darkest corner of her porch. By the time she pulled open the door a few minutes later, he'd recovered a little of his composure and was rehearsing his sermon. This time he was fully prepared to berate her, to have his sternly-delivered ultimatum stun her into obedience. This time, he'd make her swear she'd stop putting herself into precarious situations and stripping any more years from his life.

How dare she think so little of her reputation or her physical well-being that she'd dangle from her bedroom window and brazenly open her door at this time of night? Yes, he'd tell her this sort of recklessness was behavior overlooked in a child running tame in the country. But it was not acceptable for a debutante who attended balls and routs in London, ostensibly to catch a suitable husband.

Laura stood clad in a nightgown and an ankle-length lavender satin wrapper, past which barely-there matching slippers showed. For the second time, she robbed him of breath and his rehearsed lecture flew from his mind as quickly as a feather caught in a wind gust.

Dark luxuriant hair shone in the gaslight like the blue-black of a raven's wing. The tresses spilled over her shoulders and flowed down her arms, and swung at waist level as she moved. He swallowed. They stood in full view of eagle-eyed aristocrats returning after their night on the town. To merely stand on her doorstep and stare was blighting the rules of proper conduct.

He pulled in a deep breath, relaxed his clenched fists and nudged her inside. Standing on this vixen's doorstep and gawking at her far-too-tempting body, like a randy sailor on shore leave, was becoming a pattern. Risky behavior that he, as the more experienced of the two, must ensure never happened again. He tugged the door closed behind him, remembering at the last moment to not slam the door and wake her servants. Or worse, rouse her aunt or sister.

She stood in a shadowy recess and watched him, head tilted to the side in that assessing way she had, obviously unaware that the candle-light from the wall sconce behind her illuminated her form in the shiny robe. Each dip and curve of her barely-concealed figure was clearly visible to him and warmth radiated from her bed-time body, her night-time musky scent teasing his nostrils. He inhaled deeply. He'd watched many females arise from bed after a sweaty bout of sex and knew the variations in a woman's scent, from her first light stir of interest in a bed partner to the heavier aroma of dampness and satiation after their hot and energetic romp between the sheets.

Laura's fragrance hinted at an anxious woman, whose senses were heightened and passion stirred as she anticipated the return of her lover and imagined how their reunion would proceed. And despite them not being lovers, Richard could easily imagine Laura rising from his bed. When they collapsed in exhaustion after making love, over and over, she'd look at him like this, soft and dreamy, but her naked body would shimmer and the smell of satisfaction would emanate from her in waves. In his fantasy, though, he'd lay his lover on the newly-washed linen on the bed in his house and they'd hide in their love nest away from her family, and his, and their never-ending troubles with the Consortium.

It was even easier to visualize her inquisitive nature pushing her to try, enjoy and master every exotic position he suggested. The lucky man who married Laura would never tire of sleeping with her naked in his arms, nor of waking her by kissing each secret place on her body. She'd wiggle and squirm, awaken fully aroused and eager, and squeal with delight. And she'd probably demand more, and even more. Oh, yes, it was so easy to imagine thinking himself drained to the last drop and Laura, hair swinging, leaning over him and doing things with her mouth that would leave him begging. But what would happen after they were lovers?

His affairs never lasted long; they burned out and died a natural death within a month or two. Laura would be different. He couldn't picture ever becoming bored with Laura as his lover. But she was a termagant. A defiant and passionate lady, whose wild nature couldn't be subdued enough for her to fit comfortably into his well-ordered household. He shook his head. No, her nature would prevent her ever becoming a staid wife, and she'd be hopeless at chaperoning his sisters. She was still reckless enough to need her own chaperone or constant attendant, to stop her leaping feet first into difficult situations.

Richard cursed his ancestors. If he hadn't inherited these blasted chivalrous traits from a long line of Winchester forbearers, he'd be free of a conscience. He could make love to Laura without being wracked by guilt, and accept any flirtations she offered in the same way he accepted the advances of wanton widows. If Laura had the voracious appetites of those women, the only sort he dallied with as they understood any affair between them would be temporary, scratching their mutual physical itches, with neither party mentioning a long-lasting relationship.

Oh, yes, if Laura wasn't a debutante, he'd taste her lips over and over, delve into her wet mouth and titillate every sensitive niche on her body. The irony wasn't lost on him. If he adhered to the rules of a true gentleman, he'd ban Laura from his dreams and forbid his mind to dwell on any erotic images, most especially those of undressing her, button by button.

All his focus should be on the welfare of his sisters, and his thoughts for the future fixed on increasing their family wealth so he could provide for them in the present, and his countess and children in the future. Until now, he'd thought the best time to bring another woman, a wife, into his sisters' lives would be in two years, perhaps three. The way his emotions and yearnings were at the moment, he'd be stupid to postpone taking a bride to his bed for that long.

His physical needs were well met through casual affairs, yet this craving to have a woman in his bed, only one woman, had become like an itch he couldn't scratch. This unfamiliar yearning tossed all his carefully thought-out plans out the window and left chaos in their stead.

No, a rational man must choose a sane and safe path. And if he didn't pass his conflicted attitudes on to Laura, she'd continue to walk her own path to marriage. Eventually she'd choose one of those ungainly and socially-awkward scientists she favored and he'd be the devoted husband she deserved.

Again he opened his mouth, ready to deliver that scathing lecture, but instead his attention locked on her hand. With a careless movement, she ran her fingers through her long locks and tossed the curly ends back over shoulders, uncaring when they fell in a haphazard tangle. His mouth dried and he could feel the pound of his heart against the wall of his chest.

The last time he'd seen that glorious hair, flying as free as the raven she resembled, they'd been young enough to take summer swims together in the lake. Governesses and tutors had strictly supervised their adventures and Laura's body had been well-covered, her hair caught back with a ribbon at the start of their swims. Due to her tomboyish ways and her determination to copy their dare-devil leaps into the lake, she had invariably ended their swims with strands flying every which-way and her head of hair as unrestrained as her nature.

Now, her magnificent mane flowed over her shoulders and swung to the sides at each movement. His body had tightened and his willpower was evaporating faster than a mist melted by a summer sun. More than taking his next breath, he yearned to touch her hair and discover if the texture was as silky-soft as it appeared. The urge to run his fingers through her luxurious dark strands was so compelling, that he was barely conscious of his actions when he used his teeth to tug off his gloves and carelessly tossed them towards a table.

He lifted a curl and was mesmerized by the way it twirled around his bare fingers, trapping him as easily, as she had, unwittingly and unwillingly, secured a place in his heart. Curling strands trailed across his hand and drifted back into place, while he stood and watched and felt himself be carried away by the current and unable to regain his footing.

He shook his head, determined to clear the haze of lust from his mind. Determined to halt before he was lured further down this dangerous path. They were headed for the point of no return and she, the novice, would be both mortified and regretful in the light of day. Apart from the consequences if her aunt came down the stairs and discovered them together. A shot-gun wedding wasn't what either of them was looking forward to. He shuddered and dropped his hand.

"Are you completely insane? Do you never consider the consequences of your reckless actions?" His tone was sharper than he intended, but he felt like a yacht tossed off course by an unexpected change of weather, and wanted to rock her foundations as well. Her eyes widened and she took a step back, though his rudeness had one beneficial consequence: she'd put an arm's length between herself and his sudden and annoying surge of lust.

He didn't want to frighten her but she was well-read and a devotee of the natural sciences, so surely she knew how a man, any male, would react to the picture she made, illuminated by candlelight in figure-hugging nightclothes. Her body was more enticing than any flamboyant display of flesh from a Covent Garden courtesan. His hands reached out, desperate to hold her, to run his hands up and down her barely-covered curves and carry her upstairs and back to her still warm bed.

He'd undress her, step by slow step. Her robe would slide away from her pale-skinned shoulders, allowing him to kiss each exposed inch of bed-warmed-flesh. Her nightgown was already pulled across her abundant bosom so, aroused by his longing look, her nipples would contract and pebble. He licked his lips, imagining their shape and taste when he sucked through the fabric. They'd be as round as one of her perfume bottles and would smell and taste like her skin, of fine honey and the dew of arousal.

He sucked in a deep breath, a pathetic substitute for an aroused nipple drawn slowly across his teeth and into his hungry mouth. Good Lord, he needed to stop. One more minute and he'd be matching actions to his fantasies. With a great deal of reluctance, he forced himself to turn and study one of several paintings of old Roman sites that covered the walls.

With his back to her, he said, "Don't you know better than to open your door at this hour of night? Where's your damn butler?"

"The poor man is suffering terribly again with his rheumatism. We never allow him to wait up till this hour."

He heard her move, tiny rustles of linen from behind him, and his cock jumped in response. He cleared his throat, trying to sound strong and dignified. A footman, then? That rude one who thinks he rules the roost?"

"Ah, well, he has enough trouble remembering his manners after a decent night's sleep. If he's awake all night, goodness knows how he'd speak to visitors the next day."

He turned towards her, raising one eyebrow. "Have you ever thought of hiring a better type of servant?"

"And leave more thieves on London's streets? No. At least here they have an alternative to their previous occupations."

"Ha! You mean you hide criminals in Jamison House, removing

them from the long arm of the law? Knowing a constable won't come knocking on an earl's door?"

"Perhaps." She grinned and shrugged, her wrapper slipping down her shoulder and causing another jolt to all his male parts. "And though you criticize my impetuousness, I am not a lack-wit. I'd never answer the door unarmed at night."

He hated that Laura continually misconstrued his need to rein in her impetuous nature. She imagined he wanted to tame her wildness by caging her, and that was far from the truth. Even when they'd been children, he'd tried to damp down a little of her girlish brashness. Though not to gain control of her as she thought, but to stop the top-lofty owners of the manors around their home villages labeling her ill-bred or to prevent any gossip about her behavior.

In his eyes, Laura's refusal to conform to rules made her unique. And the potions she mixed, with so much care and love, to cure ailments, set her far above those women who called for smelling salts if any family or servants fell ill. Laura always put the well-being of others before her own safety, and he wished she would lose a little of her independent nature and, in turn, let him care for her safety.

Something prodded his hip and he looked down, only to curse his distraction, because he'd been so focused on Laura's face and hair he'd not looked down at her hand. A naïve mistake for someone who could walk any street in this unruly city without having his pockets emptied. A gent who was alert enough to avoid being coshed on the head.

Yet, he'd let a cascade of hair and a swaying bosom blind him to his situation. Laura's left hand rested on the curve of her very feminine hip and dangled a very unfeminine weapon. Her fingers were looped in a desultory fashion through the trigger of a much larger caliber gun than the smaller woman's pistol she sometimes carried in her reticule. The gun swung in small lazy arcs beside her thigh and he stiffened, realizing how close the weapon was to his own thigh. Despite knowing how skilled a shooter she was, Richard possessed every normal male's dislike of even the smallest threat to his manhood. Best, then, to postpone his prepared lecture, at least until he'd unarmed this vixen.

The situation was as Sherwyn had often said. Any hero's well-meaning attempt to extricate a Jamison woman from a hazard often turned face-about and threatened the life of the savior. Better, then, to err on the side of safety and shift his vitals from the vicinity of her weapon, and before he opened his mouth and put his foot in it.

"Perhaps we could continue this discussion somewhere quieter? Somewhere we won't disturb your aunt. And of course, your poor overburdened servants." At his sarcasm, she simply raised one shaped brow and continued to circle her gun. "And perhaps we should secure your weapon. I feel very nervous having it near any part of my anatomy."

She chuckled. "Now you sound like your cousin. Despite Sherwyn being the one who taught us to shoot, and extremely well, he's as jumpy as a new-born foal whenever Becca waves a loaded pistol."

He scowled at her. "Men, or at least those who fancy themselves as legendary lovers, or who need an heir in the future, are very protective of their lower torsos. Future generations depend on us keeping our bollocks intact. And that means staying well away from any Jamison female brandishing a weapon."

With another small gurgle of laughter, she placed the gun in a drawer of the hall cabinet beside them and spun away without another word. She walked to the far end of the hallway and waited for him to follow. He hadn't known the room, a tiny cubby-hole with its odd shaped walls and tucked away under the steps, existed. Intrigued, he dipped his head under the low lintel and stepped inside the dark space, standing still while Laura secured the door. From a stained-glass window high up on one octagonal wall, dim rays of moonlight streamed down and created enough glow to make out the shape of pieces of heavy furniture. He took a step towards what he assumed was her desk and banged his forehead on a low beam.

"Ow!" He lifted his hand to rub the area at the exact moment Laura reached a finger towards his mouth, motioning him to silence. But their hands collided and he held her bare fingers, stilled them, and then lifted them to his nose. "Honey," he murmured.

He nuzzled higher, along her bare wrist, and opened his lips over her skin. Skin so soft that he could have been kissing the rose petals she collected for her lotions. Dewy, velvety, and oh-so-intoxicating.

The sound of her rapid swallowing was music to his ears. He needed this stubborn woman to be as unraveled by their close position as him. Wanted her as undone by his aroma as he was after inhaling the scent of honey on her hands. He began his campaign of seduction by sucking each finger into his mouth, one after the other, wanting her so aroused that she squirmed in his arms and begged him to relieve the unbearable tension.

"I–I mix a little honey." Her words were spaced between breathy pants that corresponded to each deep pull he gave on a finger. "Wi-with my base lotion."

"I like it." He pushed the sleeves of her robe and nightgown up her arm so he could nuzzle further upwards.

"I could mix you some." Her words were said with a breathy gasp that did wondrous things to his libido.

"I don't think it would taste nearly as good on my skin."

He licked a small path up her forearm and she shivered. Her wide-eyed look and frozen silence told him more than words.

"Do you like that?"

She nodded and then licked her lips. His body hardened and he instinctively pressed closer. His last remnant of sanity urged him not to frighten her with the growing physical evidence of his lust. Laura's knowledge of a man's anatomy would be far more advanced than most unmarried ladies, because of her fascination with science and Darwin's theories about the attraction between genders.

No one could spend time with the Jamison family and not know of their unorthodox views and their love of a good argument. Meal times often resembled rounds of boxing, rather than polite dining table conversation. Every Jamison sibling read ferociously, held strong views on numerous scientific and political topics, and felt free to debate them, regardless of gender or topic. It stood to reason that Laura would notice his arousal, because it strained against the placket of his trousers like a hungry horse pushing its nose over its stable door towards the feed bucket.

The only unknown factor in this situation was Laura's response. Any lady raised in a household of peers would be entitled to, and encouraged to, slap his face. Good and hard. Considering this particular lady's prying nature, she was far more likely to react by asking him a hundred questions, ones he'd be hard pressed to answer rationally while he struggled to retain some semblance of sanity. If she explored his body too intimately, chances were his hunger for her would break its bounds and push both of them into actions beyond their unacknowledged, yet strictly-adhered-to limits.

Sanity be damned. If he didn't touch her, he'd be driven as mad by repressed desire as Lady Hetherington was by her incessant greed. He leaned in slowly, the way a horse breaker gentled an unbroken steed, and touched his lips to hers. The kiss was the gentlest he'd given in many a long year, and not the sort he engaged in with his normal bed partners. His willing widows or high class courtesans liked him to show more aggression, a nonsensical notion that he'd been told gave them a feeling of being 'taken by a lusty lord'.

His shared touching of lips with Laura was nothing like that, being more of a test of control—on both sides—yet the sweetness and innocence of this kiss sorely tested his control, stretched his famous self-discipline far more than he would normally allow with a woman, and proved that once again her mere presence had goaded him into another arrogantly stupid move. Still, when she slid her soft hands up and around his neck and directed his mouth back to hers, he followed her lead like the enamored and addicted fool he was.

Letting her set the pace, he stood as still as stone while she glided her lips back and forth across his, a slow and steady investigation destined to drive him over the brink if he didn't find the fortitude to stop her.

He opened his mouth to protest, but she touched his tongue with hers and all thought leeched from his mind. His hands shook and his knees threatened to sag. He'd never experienced a reaction like it, especially not to the kiss of an innocent. In the blink of an eye, their roles reversed and he was no longer the predator but the one who needed to beg to be released.

"No." He attempted to disengage himself, but his feet were glued to the floor boards and he couldn't force them to move, couldn't will himself to take the necessary step backwards, away from such dire temptation

"This-this is bad idea."

"I think it's an excellent idea." She cocked her head to the side and frowned. "Besides, I thought you wanted it too."

Even more than he needed to separate from her, he wanted to reassure her that there was nothing wrong with her physically or mentally. Part of his desire to be with Laura was his longing to inflate her self-esteem, to pump back the self-poise she lost each time her father chastised her for lack of talent. He touched his forehead to hers.

"Wanting has nothing to do with it. Five minutes with you, and I can think of nothing but exploring your sweet mouth and sucking in the exotic taste of you." He gripped her arms, undecided if he should push her away, or pull her so tightly against him that she couldn't help but feel how much he wanted her physically.

"But don't you see," he said with a growl. "That's the problem. If I gave in and laid my hands on you the way I want, the way you think you want me to touch you right now, your brothers will hunt me down and shoot me." He snorted. "Hell. Becca will return and join the hunt and she's a far better shot. In the light of day, when you come to your senses, you'll realize I was right. You're alive and vital and beautiful, and you deserve to have the best life possible." He shook his head. "We both know I'm not the right man for you. Dammit, Laura, even the smell of my sweat isn't right for your theories. How many times have you sniffed my cologne, my person, when you thought I wasn't aware? I've not said a word, despite being treated like an exotic specimen. You've analyzed me, written about me in your endless notebooks. But this." He waved his hand in the tight space between them. "This...thing that happens. It's...it's a curse. And a blasted nuisance. "

"See! You're supposedly far more experienced than I, yet you cannot name what happens when we're together. Before an audience, we circle each other like lions defending against attack. But alone, like now, I feel... I want... to experience things, with you."

With his face inches from hers, he scowled, tried to pretend it didn't matter and that he didn't want the same.

"What you feel," he snapped, so close to her ear that she jumped, "is simple passion. Desire. Arousal. Call it what you will." He took her hand and guided it downwards, holding it loosely over the hard ridge of his erection beneath his trousers. He ignored her sharp inhalation. "You can repeat, word for word, lectures you've attended at the Academy. You think you understand sexual urges." He pressed down on her hand, securing it firmly against him, before he slowly molded her fingers until fitted the curve of his cockstand like a glove. "Yet when it comes to men and what they really want from women, or the lengths unscrupulous rogues would go to get a beautiful woman beneath him, you've as little knowledge as a child in the nursery."

When she met his gaze, he expected to see her awareness. What shook him to the core was her look of wide-eyed wonder. And when her tongue darted out and swept across her luscious red lips, he forgot the purpose of his action. Forgot this was supposed to be about shaking her equilibrium. Forgot his own tongue wasn't forbidden from following the path of hers, and that he shouldn't be imagining the sweet taste of her again.

She swallowed, hard, and put her hands to her hips. Defiant Laura had returned. "I'm not a child and I'm well-informed on every aspect of anatomy and physiology." She smirked, with the look of a female who understands her power over the male species. "Besides, I've been surrounded by men all my life. My brothers, you, your cousins. Do you think I haven't learned things from all of you?"

"Nonsense. What you know is textbook anatomy, not an intimate knowledge of a man's body."

She scowled. "This," she said, giving his rapidly-increasing erection a squeeze, "is a man's innate response when in close contact with a female he's considering as a mate. For procreation."

"Ah. Another lecture straight from the mouth of the adolescent Mister Darwin. You've proved how little you know, my innocent, despite your endless discussions with other obsessed scientists. Men prefer to use this organ for recreation, rather than procreation."

Her mouth opened on a small ooh, and she looked down at their hands. His erection jumped in reaction to her scrutiny and, as so often happened with Laura, he saw far too late what his brain had valiantly tried to signal from the moment he'd accompanied this beautiful woman into her closet-like study. He swallowed.

Far from acting in any normal maidenly fashion and shoving him out the front door, this bluestocking, with her consuming interest in the science of procreation, had the wherewithal literally in her hand to indulge her rabid curiosity. Heaven help him, but by the look in her eye and her firm clasp on his precious manhood, she was delighting in each discovery. And seducing him so quickly and so unerringly, that he was about to be the one put to the blush.

Having years of town polish, he prided himself on his swift assessments of his sexual encounters and his ability to either speed them up, or slow them, according to his schedules and whims. He was dumbfounded by his own blind stupidity, because her eyes widened even further at the mention of recreation. He could follow each of her thoughts as she weighed up the possibility of testing the aforesaid recreation.

"Oh, no, no, no. Any man reacts this way if confronted by a half-naked woman. It means nothing." He turned towards the door, desperate to escape. "We kissed. Nothing more, nothing less. "

As he invariably did with her, he'd confused the situation, badly. If she'd been another sort of woman, well, yes, naturally he'd have taken full advantage of their intimate situation. Only if she was his bride, could he encourage Laura's thirst for knowledge and her desire for an exciting new adventure. If this was their wedding night, he'd push on, full steam ahead, to a mutually satisfying conclusion. And if she was a sophisticated woman, his rakish friends would be laying bets on how many days would pass before he bedded her.

But the woman standing within a breath's distance from him was Laura. Sister of his friends, sister-in-law to his cousin, family to a large group of males who'd be justifiably angry if he touched her virgin body and then thought to evade the parson's net. Every male he was associated with would urge him to run, to save himself, or at least his bachelorhood.

Her fingers began to move under his, a slow and steady exploration of his rock-hard cock. She investigated the breadth and the length of his member until he was groaning aloud and, by reflex, squeezed her fingers to increase the pressure.

"See. You're not the first man I've kissed. Nor will you be the only man. I intend learning as much as possible about men, their likes and dislikes, before I chose a husband. How else can a woman decide which man is right for her. Which man will bring her joy during her marriage?"

Despite learning, as did every boy at a new school, to never react to taunts, Richard couldn't conceal his fury. He felt every crease wrinkle across his brow and the uniform dig of each of his fingernails into his palms. Despite knowing this particular heckler would notice and, more than likely, rejoice in having disconcerted him. It was pure folly on his part to expect that in the arena of carnality, his particular field of expertise, this contrary woman would permit him to hold the reins or, in this case, his phallus. Utter stupidity to imagine himself slowing, or speeding up, their interactions.

How did one contrary woman unravel him, rapidly and completely, as none of his business partners or opponents ever managed? Laura made one of her fervent declarations and his plans to keep his distance, and not become emotionally involved, were overturned as easily as pieces of furniture in his sisters' nursery doll's house. Her endeavor to select her husband, using sensual experiments and exchanging kisses with numerous bachelors, had to be the biggest exercise in futility he'd ever encountered.

Why then couldn't he stop scowling? "Exactly how many men have you kissed? And who are they?"

She gave a deep sigh and slowly, ever so slowly, released his arm. "You've no right to ask me that, Richard, not when you've shown so little interest in kissing me yourself."

"Oh, I've plenty of interest alright. Never doubt that for a minute. Every time we're alone, I come within a hair's breadth of taking whatever you keep offering."

"I don't offer anything."

"Yes you do. Most likely, you're unaware of what you're doing to me. But trust me on this: your body is ready for intimacy, even if your head lags behind."

A few moments ago, she'd been eager and excited and looking to him for her tutoring in the bedroom arts. Now she stared at him in horror, making him feel like a puppy-kicking fiend.

"You've no need to fear though, my dear, as I've a hard-and-fast rule about never ever seducing innocents. No matter how they prod and provoke me into it."

"Why you arrogant…."

He grasped her hand as she swung it towards his face. "Oh, for heaven's sake. Be grateful I didn't take things further and ruin you." He shook his head. "Believe me, I wish…"

"Wish- wish what?"

"That we were…" He barely caught himself in time. If he revealed how many times he'd considered a union between them, even drawn up columns of For and Against, Laura would poke and prod and demand a full explanation. Apart from feeling disconcerted by her swift change of attitude, from horrified retreat at the wedding to flirtatious advances now, he'd seen how easily she could wring juicy bits of gossip out of the mouths of her generally close-lipped brothers.

So, if he revealed even the most minor of his reasons for crossing her off his list of suitable marriage partners, she'd be like a dog with a bone. Laura wouldn't let go until she'd argued him into a corner, and he'd be forced to admit his main reason: terror, pure abject terror, of being so head-over-heels in love with his wife that the rest of the world ceased to matter.

He'd decided at eighteen, when his parents had died, that duty was a much more powerful reason for marrying than love. Love caused havoc for those around you. Love destroyed families and ruined estates, and he would not be one of those peers whom the ton pitied because he'd sacrificed all but his titles in the name of love. Titles were cold companions in hard times. He and his sisters, plus his future wife and heirs, would all benefit more if he concentrated on long-lasting wealth and security, rather than some philosophical notion of love.

"Never mind." He shook his head. "I'm only here to tell you about your friend, Longman."

She fired off a succession of questions. "Did you find him? Where is he? Is he unharmed?"

Despite his will, Richard felt a sudden stab of jealousy over Laura's immediate and heartfelt concern for another man. Even if Longman was, by comparison to himself, hardly more than a youth.

"He's in a doctor's care right now. Expected to recover, though it may take some time. But he was kidnapped earlier tonight."

She gasped and wrapped her arms around her body, hugging herself. "I knew something was wrong."

He longed to haul back into his own arms, if only to offer comfort, but his yearning was too raw to risk any contact. "Yes, it appears your prediction proved correct. Again. How do you know these things? As soon as they happen."

She shrugged. "Perhaps it's my grandmother's Scottish blood."

"Your brothers seem to think you've inherited more than your grandmother's Scottish blood. They think you've the second sight, like her." She shrugged again, neither agreeing nor denying that she may have inherited pre-eminence. He prodded a little deeper, trying to prompt a response from her. "Perhaps you already knew. Because I'm certain that you still haven't shared everything you know about these new syndicates."

"Do you think Longman's public objections to the methods being used by the new consortium frightened them enough to abduct him?"

"Huh. Another change of subject, Laura?" She dipped her head and broke their connection, the stubborn fool. "If you don't confide in me, how can I help you? And you know I'll discover all you secrets eventually anyway." He growled his frustration when she remained silent. "So far, I know nothing about Longman's abductors. But the Yard have sent investigators. I'll visit my friends there in the morning and find out if they've discovered anything."

"It's going to end up like before. I can feel it." She threw up her hands and started to pace, though her recording room was so small she ended up walking around him in dizzying circles. "The elite members, the ones in the inner circle, will put pressure on their friends. Anyone who refuses to invest with them will be prodded into joining by other means. With Michael, they applied pressure by threatening to harm us, his siblings. When he refused to give them any information about our forthcoming share trading, the inner circle of the Syndicate harassed us by watching this house, day and night, and following us wherever we went."

Richard sighed, understanding Laura's frustration and worried about the dark circles under her eyes. Recent traumas had left them all restless and uncertain and robbed them of sound sleep, and Laura's crotchety disposition during the past week had only been another symptom of her anxiety. He certainly didn't blame her for being out of sorts. The wedding, his cousin's demands to ignore Laura's protests and stay close to the women, everything was making them wary and contrary. And not only Laura; for their normally serene sister, Lottie, had also seemed on edge at the wedding. The sisters looked in every direction each time they left the house, as if planning their escape routes in case they were accosted.

He reached out and took Laura's arm to stop her circling, and then led her to the old day-bed which was tucked under the ledge running along one of the angular wall. He seated himself beside her, but was careful to leave a two-foot space between them.

"You've been through a lot this past year. Neither you nor your brothers and sisters backed down from the Hetheringtons, even after they had Peggy killed."

"We had no choice. Scotland Yard needed our help. Becca wouldn't even have involved Sherwyn if we hadn't needed to search those houses for evidence. The Hetheringtons were becoming desperate for money."

"That's exactly why I want you well away from here." He shifted closer and took her hand in his. "Let me deal with Lady Hetherington. I'm seeing my friends at Scotland Yard in the morning."

"No. You don't know what that woman like I do. She will destroy you if she thinks you're involved with us."

"If she knows Sherwyn's gone, she'll already have me in her

sights. And if this new syndicate hasn't connected me with your family, they'll be contacting me anyway."

"Why?"

"Because they'll need to recruit every wealthy and highly-titled peer they can, so they have enough leverage to push others into investing with them. Without appearing immodest, I'll be one of the first they approach. And I can guess at the others they're most likely to ask. Time is short for them. People in a hurry make mistakes."

"If you're right, I hope their mistakes cost them, but not us."

"Indeed." He nodded. "And I promise you that if Lady Hetherington is in London, I'll find where she's hiding and have Scotland Yard send her back to the asylum."

"But will we find her in time? Before she brings more grief to our families."

The look in her eyes nearly brought him to his knees. Laura might not love him as a woman who had fallen in love with a man, but there was a depth of feeling reflected in her gaze that warmed his soul and pierced his heart. Who was he trying to fool?

No matter how many times he told her, or himself, that he wasn't the man she needed forever in her life, he wanted her to look at him, not as a brother related by marriage, but as the man she desired above all others.

She stared up him, eyes pleading. "Richard, we know how desperate the Hetheringtons were to eliminate us before. Please take care. I don't want you to be her next victim in her sights."

He smiled.

"What," she asked with a puzzled frown.

"I enjoy the times you forget yourself and call me Richard."

"And I enjoy the times when you forget yourself and kiss me."

"Touché." He touched his fingers to her cheek and she bent her head to his hand, nuzzling it like a newborn seeking solace. "If I hear more news of Longman, I'll send word."

"No, you'll come in person."

He nodded, accepting that he was destined to always do what he could to make her life easier. His news might bring her joy, and he wanted to bring a smile to her face. Or if Longman's condition had deteriorated, he wanted to be comfort her in her distress.

As she turned to open the door of their secluded hidey-hole he asked, "What is this room? I've never noticed it before."

She laughed. "Good. I prefer my dungeon to remain secret.

Solitude is impossible in this household, but I like to be alone when I'm planning a new mixture."

He chuckled at the picture of brave Laura hiding in here to avoid being dragged to Bond Street by her aunt. In contrast to most women of her age and status, she considered shopping a boorish chore to be attended to only when absolutely necessary.

"Rather prettily decorated for a dungeon," he said, as he fingered the silk shawls thrown across the back of the day-bed. Hues of every color of the rainbow in cushions and rugs lifted her hidey-hole from a cell to a tasteful and warm haven; so Laura must visit the importers' warehouses even she resisted the crowds on Bond Street. "A retreat fit for a princess."

She shrugged. "Sometimes I imagine I'm in the tower of a castle. Sometimes this is a laboratory and I am the first woman scientist to achieve world-fame. Here I concoct potions to wipe out all evil in the world. Depends on my mood." She dropped her gaze, as if embarrassed by her admission. "Besides which, this is the perfect place to avoid my father on his infrequent visits. The Earl and I disagree on which is more important, aromatic plants or large slabs of Roman rock. He considers growing lavender and herbs a waste of his land."

"I may have noticed his indifference on the last occasion I encountered him," he said dryly. "Why does he ridicule your friends and belittle your research?"

She dropped her head and he followed the movement down, noticing her tightly clenched fingers. "Father accepts that Becca and I are labeled bluestockings and prefers to think that is an endorsement of his intellect and teaching. He praises Becca because her share trading provides Papa with money, so he can leave and excavate Roman ruins all over Britain. And Lottie's physiognomy and phrenology?" She shrugged. "The Earl is unaware that his prettiest daughter refuses to use her feminine wiles to lure gentlemen into revealing their fiscal secrets. He would be horrified to discover she studies facial features and reads head shapes, a mystical science. He accepts brains or beauty in his daughters. I offer him neither."

"That is utter nonsense. You have a unique combination of both."

"Not according to the Earl. He only tolerates Mr. Lyell, because Charles's interests lie more with geology. A tangible science that an archaeologist can appreciate."

"Ah. So that is why the Earl encourages your visits to the Geological Society, despite sneering at its members."

She made a sound of derision. "Father has no interest in the formation of Pacific atolls, or the subsidence of coral reefs. He needs me to report on Charles's research into obsidian and other rocks. And he clings to the ludicrous ideas of Jonathon becoming the next Curate of the Society, and therefore being able to grant Papa money for more digs."

"I thought Charlesworth coveted the position of Curate."

She stared at him, her gaze shrewdly assessing. "For someone who claims to have no interest in these branches of science, Winchester, you are remarkably well-informed."

"I like to keep abreast of new discoveries in many fields."

Laura didn't need to know that his interest in these scientific societies was more about the nature of the men who frequented them, than any compulsion to classify rocks or which Pacific atoll was likely to sink first. Sherwyn did the same, as Richard had encountered his cousin at the Academy and the Geological Society and several of other scientific haunts. His cousin had laughed off Richard's declaration that Sherwyn embarrassed the family name with his love-sick following of his intended to all the most boring places in London. His large and looming presence at Becca's side, the Duke had explained, was a visible warning to the large groups of men his beloved exchanged ideas with: that the Duke of Sherwyn would personally deal with any man who looked twice at his lady-love or touched a strand of Becca's magnificent red hair.

Laura's opinions closely mirrored Becca's regarding men who ruled their women's lives with a whip hand. Both ladies would blacken the eye of any man who blocked their thirst for knowledge. For women were barred from university lectures, that left discussion groups at various houses or note-taking at in lecture halls across London. Richard justified his own presence by using his two sisters, younger versions of blue-stockings, as his excuse. He was nothing more than a devoted brother, who liked to keep a close eye on his sisters and their whereabouts.

Only a week ago, Sherwyn had raised his haughty brows and asked, "You're only here to watch over your sisters? No one else?"

He'd shrugged it off and replied, "Sherwyn, you and I know that, deep at heart, all men are rakes. When a desirable woman crosses their paths, good intentions often fly out the window."

"All well and good to mistrust other men's motives for befriending your sisters, Richard, but don't lose sight of your own good intentions when you're with any other desirable woman."

Considering how few women visited these meeting halls, Richard should have asked Sherwyn to clarify which woman he referred to, though at that moment he'd been distracted by the sight of one of Mr. Darwin's associates—was it his cousin?—who had leaned towards Laura and bent his head close enough to listen to her, so that his nose had practically bumped her chest. Richard hadn't been near enough to see exactly where the scoundrel was looking, but he had a pretty good idea that his gaze was directly down the front of Laura's bodice.

Only after Sherwyn had moved away, had Richard considered the incident. Had his cousin noticed how many times Richard and his sisters bumped into Laura at these places? Could Sherwyn suspect Richard's relationship with Laura—on the surface that of combatants—was not as it appeared? He'd caught the speculative look in Lottie's eye more than once, when she'd appraised the way he and Laura circled each other in public. Perhaps, despite his downplaying an amicable relationship between them, the entire family suspected his feelings were quite the reverse. That he cared far more for Laura than he showed in their prickly conversations.

"Apart from which," Laura was saying, "Father considers me the most boisterous of his children so, by assigning me this thick-walled room, my noise wouldn't rattle his ears or distract the servants."

Time someone advised the old Earl and his narrow-minded stupidity about the way he treated his middle daughter, and Richard had many powerful ways to make him listen. A letter might take weeks to reach the Earl, but Richard would feel much better after he'd written it.

"Out of sight, out of mind," he muttered, knowing her father considered Laura a nuisance and her studies insignificant and blight on the family name. He looked around. "You don't store your oils and herbs here."

"No. Another wise move on my father's part. After I burned down the gardener's shed–"

He chortled. "Another of your small mishaps?"

She scowled at him, looking as ferocious as the gargoyle that would have guarded her castle's fore keep in yesteryears. "My mishaps are few and far between, yet everyone is determined to recall them whenever something goes awry. The gardener wasn't pleased to have lost part of his shed, so my father decided to allocate me my own dispensary. This way, I can distil my oils and brew lotions to my heart's content, and if I inadvertently cause any small fires or explosions, twill be only me who is injured."

He disliked the indifferent way she announced the possibility of her own demise. "I'm certain your father didn't intend you any pain by his actions."

"Papa never intends pain. He simply cannot deal with real people in a living world. Which is why he escapes to his archaeological digs whenever possible and leaves us all to our own devices."

"Suddenly, I see things a lot more clearly."

She dropped her gaze to the carpet, and absently ran her hand along the spines of the leather bound volumes arrayed on the bookcase fronting the door.

"There is nothing for you to see, Winchester. I know you and your persistent ways. You never leave a thing alone until you unravel the entire mystery. Well, there is no mystery here." She flung her arms wide. "What you see is what you get."

"It's obvious that not only do you suffer from an insecurity about not living up to the high and exacting standards set by other members of your family–"

"I'm not jealous of my family."

She looked so defiant, so alone, that his heart broke for her. In a flash of intuition, her motives became apparent to him. Why she drove herself so unrelentingly and why she pushed herself to do more and more.

"Not jealous, no. Constantly comparing yourself to them and finding yourself coming up short. Yes. Your father's defection possibly started you on this path, but your own insecurities have taken hold. For no reason, either. Sweetheart, never think that if anything happened to you that people would not grieve."

"Would you?" As soon as she spoke the words, she looked shocked at herself. She shook her head. "No, no. Please. Do not say anything."

He took her hands, willing the trembling in his limbs to cease so she wouldn't notice the abject fear the idea shot through his being. "Sweetheart, if anything happened to you, my heart would forever be empty."

She nodded, and turned to walk him back to the door. The slump of her shoulders, usually held so high as an act of bravado against every detractor who stepped in her path, told the story. This fearless woman, still of an age when life should be treating her like a princess, and when compared to his years of experience barely an adult in age, deserved more. He wanted to make her promises for the future. To vow to take care of her, help her understand she was worthy of being fêted and protected and—

He stopped, shocked at where his thoughts were headed. Naturally, if someone asked, he'd say he loved Laura. He'd make the same declaration regarding her two sisters, even her madcap aunt. But what he'd almost admitted placed a different perspective on the idea of loving someone.

She looked at him quizzically.

His erratic behavior confused him. What must it do to her? She should hate him, revile his attitudes, yet tonight she'd offered herself to him with such sweet innocence, he'd been shaken to his core. Then and there, he vowed to hasten the process of locating Lady Hetherington. To uncover her financial center and take strong steps to shatter any plans she had, long before they came to fruition. Long before any of the dirt clinging to these evil people came within a whiff of Laura.

At the door, he turned, lifted her chin. "You're brave, strong and beautiful. Any man will be lucky to have you as a wife, Laura, remember that."

Unable to help himself, he dipped his head and touched his lips to her pursed mouth.

Once, twice, and again. He brushed back and forth, savoring her sweetness, and locking the memory away to be pulled out at future times, lonelier times without her.

"Goodnight, little temptress."

Chapter Eight

The next day, the Earl of Winchester leaned back in his desk chair at Martin House Minor in Berkley Square, so named in jest by the family to distinguish it from Martin House in Mayfair, the residence of his cousin, the Duke.

He linked his hands behind his head, faced his man of all work, Whittaker, and tried to concentrate on the present conversation, rather than dwell on what might, or might not have happened in the early hours in Laura's hidey-hole. For the past hour, he and Whittaker had been hammering out strategies for upcoming investments: coal mines in Wales, factories in Birmingham and new railway lines across England.

A few minutes ago, they'd moved on to a discussion of the new consortium, which was the main gossip around the Exchange and its surrounding cafes on Threadneedle Street. Financiers were abuzz with news of several new syndicates being formed, and everyone was guessing as to who the mastermind was this time. Had Lady Hetherington truly managed to escape the asylum? Was London going to be safe if she made some sort of triumphant return to the underworld?

Dammit, they still seemed to be behind the eight ball. Running to catch up to Lady Hetherington, or whoever was the new mastermind pulling the strings. The wedding had been disrupted by shots, people could have been killed, and Richard was frustrated they'd made so little progress in their hint for the shooter. Either his reactions were slowing down, or this group was incredibly well-organized. Not that he was about to admit that to Laura and her family.

"Whittaker, we're chasing our tails here. Getting nowhere. Round up as many likely lads as you can from the East End, who will welcome a bit of coin in their pockets in exchange for some decent information. Go to the kitchen and ask Saunders to help. Tell him he's relieved of duties here today. He has plenty of mates who are looters or lubbers, or some form of criminal. Between the two of you, throw a bit of money around and see if we can loosen some lips.

We need to know where Lady Hetherington is hiding. Which taverns her thugs drink in.

"If Lady Hetherington is resurrecting her organization," Whittaker said, "she'd have needed money to bribe her goalers to turn a blind eye when she escaped. And she'd need a bucketful of the ready to coax her previous gang to trust her again after the fiasco last time."

"You're right. I'm a blind fool. Chasing down a shooter in London is like looking for one worm in a tubful. Someone must have been backing the lady. How else would she have enough blunt to escape? And that someone has a vested interest in seeing our old enemy rise up from the almost dead and shake up the City."

Richard banged the desk and made the normally-unflappable Whittaker jump three inches out of his chair. "We need to look at those above ground now. Not the low-lives under it. Who do we know with pockets to let at the moment? Peers who are believed to be flush, but have managed to get into hot water financially?"

Whittaker shifted in his chair, sitting up straighter, and leaning forward with an eager look to his eyes. "My lord, you're brilliant. Without having a large lump of money to dangle before the noses of the greedy ton—" Whittaker's eyes went round with horror. "No offense meant to yourself, of course."

Richard laughed and waved a hand. "Get on with it, Whittaker. You know I won't take offense at anything you say. And we both know the majority of my peers are inbred lunatics, or are so busy praising their own greatness that they never have a thought in their heads. I only expect you to inform me, well ahead of time, if I'm also heading down the path to stupidity and ruin."

"You, my lord? Never," his man assured him with a grin. And, thankfully, Whittaker had more brains in his little finger than most peers had in their heads and was a man to be counted on to always tell the truth.

Richard tapped his mouth as he considered. "Knowing how many members of the ton are either tight-fisted or have empty pockets, Lady Hetherington is as likely to convince them to part with more money, as to persuade a flea to leave a dog's back. No, someone with a lot of influence is behind this and using the lady, her name and connections as a shield. If anything goes wrong, like last time, she'll be left to take the fall."

"I'll start checking into the stability of the usual top performers in the share trading market straight away." Whittaker was jotting down a series of notes down his foolscap page. "Put together a list of men who have over-stretched their finances and need a way to recoup their losses in a hurry. Try to work out who has most to gain from advancing the lady working capital to get another syndicate running." Whittaker stopped writing and looked across the desk, a serious expression on his otherwise complacent face. "And which of your enemies, my lord, would like to see you dead."

"Good Lord, Whittaker. You sound like Lady Jamison. Laura is convinced those bullets were aimed at what she calls my thick skull."

Whittaker chuckled, but covered his mouth when Richard scowled at him. "Wonderful. Now I have two of you imagining I was the target at the wedding."

"I think it would be a mistake to rule out any possibilities. Both you and Lady Jamison were nearly killed. Until we know more, my lord, I implore you to be careful. You've set guards outside Jamison House. You have someone following the ladies. You even have watchmen here, at Martin Minor, to safeguard your sisters. Yet you've taken no precautions for your own safety."

"Hmm. Point taken, Whittaker. Get Saunders to hire an extra man, one who can be very discreet. Because if I notice him following me about, he's fired."

"I shall inform Saunders of your requirements. And I shall concentrate my efforts on discovering the current financial status of anyone you have dealings with. This may not be a reincarnation of the Hetheringtons' empire at all. It might be someone trying to knock your own financial legs out from under you."

"You're suggesting a competitor with a grudge?"

Whittaker nodded. "Whoever it is, he or she must feel confident they are going to succeed. Perhaps you and your investments are all that is standing in their way."

"You're correct. Word around my clubs last night, was that rather forceful approaches have been made to several of my acquaintances. Therefore, one must assume she, or he if it isn't the lady herself, has been planning this for quite a while. Someone is providing the power, and possibly a large amount of money. If not, publicizing the scheme would be too risky."

"Interesting, my lord, but fortunes aren't so thick on the ground these days. Inheritances are much depleted. Therefore, the families who are still comfortably situated are not nearly so naïve about whom to entrust with their funds."

Richard laughed. "Are you including me? Because I trust you with the management of my family's funds. I also like to think I'm not naive."

"Yes. Now we simply need to narrow the list of possibilities by eliminating those of your acquaintance who are like you, my lord, in control of their own destinies. And then investigating the ones who are left. With roughly ten thousand possibilities, I should only take a day or two."

Richard came around his desk and slapped his man, his most trusted friend really, on the shoulder. He laughed again. "Whittaker, do I detect a note of sarcasm?"

***

Richard and Whittaker set out together for Threadneedle Street to attend one of the stock auctions, although Richard never bid for himself. He preferred to let a money man stand in his place, so he could blend into the background and watch the proceedings.

It amazed him how much could be learned by studying the facial expressions and the body movements of men when their fortunes were at stake. In the gambling dens, lives were dealt with on the throw of a dice or the turn of a card. But here, lives and futures depended on men trusting other men. Trusting that when they bought shares in their ventures, be they railways or mines or factories, that the men who owned and ran them were honest.

It proved to be a long morning and, after another three hours spent prowling the clubs over luncheon seeking information on Longman, or any snippets about the new consortium, Richard was exhausted. Therefore, it was late afternoon when he finally rode his horse into the mews behind his house and handed over his stallion to the stable boy. He yearned for the peace and quiet of his library where he could do some serious thinking, mulling over all the small pieces of information he'd gleaned during the tedious day.

As per his normal practice, he entered the house by the kitchen door. Cook always had something tempting on the table for the footmen's tea-time about now, and Richard often detoured here to pilfer two or three of her tiny lemon tarts. Perhaps a scone laden with jam and cream. He sniffed, then grinned.

Ah, yes. Today was tart-baking day. His favorite. Her back was turned to the trestle table running down the center of the room, as she instructed a very young maid on how to stir the enormous pot on the stove. A pot that seemed twice the child's size.

"Mrs. Baker, am I employing children to stir the soup nowadays?"

At the sound of his voice, both females jumped slightly and Cook twirled to face him, a hand to her heart.

"Oh, Master Richard! You scared me half to death. And Meg here's no child, as well you know."

She waved a negligent hand towards the girl who now faced him, and he realized his mistake. She might be small in stature, but the look in her eye proved that little of the child remained in her. She assessed him. Blatantly. Far more assuredly than any of his other maids did. He frowned; something tugged at his consciousness and told him things were not quite as they seemed.

"… And remember you said to employ her, my lord," he heard Cook saying, "as she's the daughter of the cousin of Jemmy, our own second footman, and from the family who comes from near your estate, so that's why you said she'd be fine as the extra maid we needed–"

"Yes," he interrupted quickly when Cook took a breath, knowing from experience that Mrs. Baker in full sail was impossible to halt. "Of course, I remember now. Meg, delighted to have you on our staff."

He dipped his head in her direction in a quick acknowledgement, as he reached for another lemon tart to add to the three he held in his left hand. Mrs. Baker tut-tutted at him, then handed him a warm apple puff to add to his feast.

"Oh, Master Richard, some things never change. You've had such a taste for my tarts since you were a boy. And I never can scold that you'll spoil your dinner, because you've the appetite of three men. Yet you've not an ounce of spare flesh on your form, and that's the truth."

He laughed. "Mrs. Baker, you'll bring me to the blush." He glanced at the new maid. "And embarrass our newest member of staff."

Again that nagging feeling of something… something he didn't know what. Strange though, the new maid from the quiet country village near his reasonably distant estate, whom one would assume would be fairly shy, demure, perhaps even unworldly, appeared not the remotest bit embarrassed.

Rather, he felt her gaze assessing him in the same way he assessed as prime piece of horse flesh he considered purchasing at Tattersall's. What was also strange was that it was normally he, as the predator, doing this sort of assessment of females he'd just met.

He had the distinct feeling the shoe was on the other foot. It left him uncomfortable, and not just in a sexual way. More a disturbing way. He shook his head. Ridiculous. She was simply a woman in a smallish body.

"Thank you, Mrs. Baker. Delicious as usual," he muttered, around a mouthful of lemony syrup. He turned to walk to the door, just as Jemmy came bursting through from the other side.

"My lord, a message," he gasped. "An urgent message has come from Jamison House."

Richard stiffened. Oh, God save him. Laura! His gut clenched. In three quick strides he stood before Jemmy, firing questions. "What's happened? Is Lady Laura harmed?"

Jemmy shook his head, although that wasn't enough to relax the tension in Richard's body. If anything happened to Laura and he'd failed to protect her, he'd never forgive himself.

"'Twas Lady Laura what sent the message asking Your Lordship to hasten around to Jamison House. It's the elderly Lady Jamison. And the younger one."

"What's wrong with them?"

"The message said ruffians set upon them outside the park this afternoon. Somethin' 'bout tryin' to abduct them. And they was hurt, tryin' to fight the men off."

"Bloody hell. I hope they're not too badly harmed!" He was already racing to the door as he called, "Pardon my language, Mrs. Baker."

"Tis of no matter, milord, when you're so upset." She clasped her hands to her bosom. "I'll pray for the ladies' health."

Chapter Nine

When the Earl arrived at Jamison House ten minutes later, it was a close contest who carried the bigger lather of sweat, he or his horse. Tossing his reins to a waiting footman, he took the stairs three at a time, barely waiting at the entrance to speak a word to the clustered servants.

He rushed past the butler and strode into the first room, loud voices announcing clearly where the ladies were gathered. Noise always foretold of a Jamison gathering, and this was certainly no exception.

"Winchester," their Aunt Agatha called, the moment she spotted him in the doorway. "Oh, thank the heavens we have a wonderful man with us now. I pray you've come to protect us, three women at the mercy of cut-throats."

He swung his glance across the three women, once, twice, three times, assuring himself they were, all three, conscious and alert, though not all upright. Only then could he manage to dip a quick nod towards where Aunt Aggie made an elegant picture of dishabille, sprawled across a sofa and with her feet propped high on a tasseled ottoman.

However, for the life of him, he couldn't force a single word from his throat without stepping first towards Laura, reaching out a shaking hand and touching her. Ridiculous, when she was the only one of the three Jamison women who was on her feet, as Charlotte was propped on the sofa opposite her aunt with her feet elevated as well, one wrapped in a sodden cloth that dripped water into a basin placed on the carpet below.

One moment to reassure himself that Laura lived and breathed, that blood still flowed warmly through her veins, and then he would be able to deal with all the other traumas in the room. First though, he needed that one soothing moment, as a baby needs rocking to sleep in its mother's arms. To feel the beat of a heart beneath your touch, and to know they are safe, is sometimes all one's mind can contemplate.

He swallowed past the lump in his throat as he saw the tentative smile she gave him, a smile freely given and warmly welcomed. A moment of truce in their ongoing war. At the same time, they reached for each other's hand. Fingers touched, clasped and held.

He swallowed again. "Laura, are you well?"

"Yes. I wasn't with them when it happened. Two ruffians attempted to kidnap my aunt and Lottie, though, thank the Lord, they fought them off long enough for help to arrive."

He squeezed her fingers, showing his relief to find her bodily intact. For once, he didn't care his affection was openly displayed, before her, before her family. Normally, he'd rather be hung and quartered than allow her even a hint of his inner emotions, fearful she'd use it against him. Not cruelly, for she hadn't a mean bone in her beautiful body. But he feared she'd read far more into his affection than he wanted declared publicly; far more fondness for their sister than he dared allow her brothers to witness.

Regaining power over his turbulent emotions, he turned to Lottie, to where she watched with her shrewd eyes. Eyes far too penetrating for his comfort, and far more knowing than a mere knowledge of phrenology would give her. Her reputed ability to see inside people's minds, to understand their thinking, appeared entirely too true for his comfort. Resisting the urge to drop his eyes, to shield his thoughts from her inquisitiveness, he stood his ground and attempted to appear unfazed.

He pulled up a light chair to the side of the divan. "Lottie, were you injured?"

"It's such a dreadful nuisance, and right at the vital time in our investigations, but it seems I've sprained my ankle. And so badly, the doctor will not allow any weight on it for at least a week. I'm furious with myself for letting this happen."

He reached over and grasped her hand, at the same moment their aunt declared, "Lottie, I have already assured you, it wasn't of your doing."

"But it was. Normally, I'd have seen those men hovering around the tree. Two men not dressed or carrying themselves as ones who belong in our square are usually very easy to pinpoint. For some unknown reason, today–" She broke off with a frown. "I cannot think why I was so distracted. Why I failed to see them until they were within smelling distance. And, even then, I'm positive that, had Laura been with us, their stench would have alerted her to their presence far earlier. Yet I remained oblivious. Something unheard of for me."

"Yes, we know, dear. It's why you and I are sent on errands to ferret out information from the park strollers each day. I distract them, while you extract the information."

Laura flashed him a small smile. "Michael equates Lottie's ability to one of those insects who entices their prey with their beauty. When she has sucked them dry of information, she supposedly devours them whole."

Aunt Aggie groaned. "And I've asked you to cease portraying such a revolting image. It never fails to ruin my appetite."

When Laura and Lottie shared an amused glance, he covered his mouth and feigned a cough, smothering his own laughter. It was a Jamison family joke that even if the sky was falling to earth, Aunt Aggie would still manage to ring the bell for tea and cakes.

He cleared his throat. "So, ladies, please tell me everything you can remember. Every detail about the men you can recall."

Aunt Aggie drew in an enormous breath and launched into the tale, expanding each detail with gusto. "Lottie and I were walking along the pebbled path that runs around the outskirts of the main strolling area of the grasslands... you know the path I mean?"

She stopped and raised a brow, and waited until he and Laura nodded.

"We were walking ever so carefully, so we didn't tread in a very large patch of wet grass right in the center of our favorite strolling spot. Most inconsiderate to put it there when Lottie was wearing her lovely new butter-yellow half-boots, and naturally, we didn't want to take our normal direct path, and chance walking through anything dubious, which might leave a stain on the leather–"

"Auntie," Lottie said, but soothed over her abrupt interruption with an apologetic smile, "Winchester doesn't have time to listen to a recital of our outer accoutrements. He simply needs the facts."

Aunt Aggie stared straight at him, fixed him with a beatific smile, and he pictured her charming hordes of men in her younger days. Having every rogue in the ton eating from her hand. Though, had anything really changed since those days? He could easily see her taking those daily strolls in the park with Lottie, under the guise of stretching her aging legs, but with the explicit intention of manipulating men of all ages directly into Lottie's path. Or snapping the more elderly ones up herself, and draining them of information.

The so-called enticing insect who lured her prey and then

sucked them dry. The two of them would prove a lethal combination in gambling halls.

"Well, two men, terribly unsavory sorts, one of whom has a French background–"

"How do you know that?" Richard asked.

"The poor man had dreadful oral hygiene, and reeked of garlic; the strong sort of odor which only comes from daily consumption of large quantities of garlic in his cooking. Oh, yes. Mark my words, his family is French, and every night he partakes of a large meal cooked in traditional French style. Also, for his luncheon, he'd eaten heavily spiced sausage, such as the butcher in our little village concocted in his smoking room. Or at least, until it became terribly disloyal to eat anything with even a…whiff of the French clinging to it." She smiled. "If you will pardon the pun."

"Good grief. You recorded all those facts, from only a moment's sniff of his breath?"

"Oh, I'm nowhere near as skilled with odors as our dearest Laura, but I do have a nose for food. When I was younger, well, of course it was between wars, so we were able to travel about more freely, and so as girls we sampled many, many Continental cuisines."

She clasped her hands over her ample bosom, gave a long mournful sigh. "Oh, how I miss the food the French served in those days. Things were still allowed to err on the side of extravagance, and therefore were a little more special. Our Queen, God bless her, though she has some wonderful ideas, doesn't have the soul of a gourmet. If left to her own devices, she'll soon have us eating only the most staid of foods, ones from the Continental countries with the most boring palates. Countries in which she has relatives." She shuddered. "German cabbage every day of our lives."

Laura burst out laughing, then turned to him. "I do apologize for my family's un-Victorian sentiments, in some cases at least. Food being one. We do love our country, and are all loyal subjects of Her Majesty, but...."

"But?" With a raised eyebrow, he prompted her to divulge the rest.

"But, in this case, I agree with Auntie. Some of the things we are being forced to give up…well it seems un- English."

She gave a little self-conscious laugh and ran her hands down the sides of her already straight skirt. "Still, we have no time for that.

Continue with the story."

"I'm afraid we were too distracted by other things to even notice when those two dreadful men appeared from behind that tree. They took hold of us, one each, and pushed cloth–"

Aunt Aggie shuddered and gave a loud groan of disgust. "Their cloths were of good quality, but they had wiped their hands on them while they waited for us and impregnated the fabric with their dockside odor, their grime and their warehouse dirt, and then when the one who held me expected me to calmly hold still while he inserted such a thing into my mouth…well, of course, no lady would stand still for that."

Aunt Aggie seemed oblivious to the stunned looks she received from the three onlookers, and continued ranting and raving about the inconsideration of the man who expected her to cope with a dirty rag, even if the quality of the fabric was high.

He looked at Lottie propped on pillows, holding her stomach because she'd laughed so hard. He glanced at Laura who had collapsed in a hiccoughing heap at Lottie's feet, having laughed so much tears were streaming down her cheeks. He opened his mouth but could think of no suitable comment, so he returned to his own contemplation of the scenario Aunt Aggie had described for them, and once again he too started to chortle. His low chuckle escalated into a laugh, until he joined the girls in insane and uncontrollable laughter.

After several minutes of this, they quietened and calmed.

"What is so amusing in that sordid tale? Auntie Aggie asked in a puzzled voice.

Laura stood and crossed to perch on the arm of her Aunt's chair. "Your recall of minute details amazes us and makes us feel inferior."

"It is true, Lady Jamison. We laugh at our own youthful ineptitudes, when thrown into comparison to someone of your years and abilities. To be blunt, you just made the three of us feel inadequate."

"There is no talent to what I notice, you know. Simply years of practice mixing amongst people of all classes and observing what occurs around you."

"No, no, my dear lady. You underestimate such talents. Most ladies pay no attention to the world around them. But to return to something you mentioned; the cloth smelled like their hands. And their hands carried the odor of the docks."

"That unmistakable odor of mud, fish and barrels of produce, and whatever else one may find at a dockside warehouse area. The sort of places where ships unload their cargoes."

Laura questioned their aunt. "How do you know so much about the smell of the docks?"

"Two of my relatives, distant cousins, were ships' captains, and as a young girl I was fascinated with the entire area. I begged them to take me there frequently. Over the years, I have revisited upon occasion." She smiled. "I enjoy the excitement one feels around ships and sailors. The constant coming and goings of the carriages and the traders."

She patted her niece's hand. "And do not fret, my loves, as I never go alone. There are always gentlemen who are eager to escort me on any little adventures I which to experience." Her smug smile had her two nieces groaning in unison and shaking their heads.

"Michael thinks you are chaperoning us, yet I often feel you are the one who needs more closely watching." Laura smiled as she said it and leaned forward to hug her aunt.

"Now, I am afraid all the excitement has wearied me. I shall retire to my bed, as you should be doing too, Lottie. Winchester, delighted that you are here to lend assistance. Please, please, take care of my precious girls."

She rose and walked to the door, as stately as ever, asking the footman to call her maid and to then send assistance to help Lady Charlotte to her chamber.

While they awaited, Lottie continued where her aunt had left off with their story from the park, filling in minor details Richard questioned her about. The more he knew about these men, the better chance he'd have of tracking them quickly. Hopefully, they could lead him to their employer. For he didn't doubt for a moment that someone with a larger intelligence than theirs was the puppeteer behind this attack.

"They attempted to thrust those foul cloths into our mouths, so we couldn't make a noise while they tied our hands behind their backs. They already held the ropes they intended using, so they only had one hand free each to subdue us. They assumed we'd be so overcome with an attack of the vapors, their work would be easy."

Laura shook and head and sighed. "I've no idea why men continue to underestimate the abilities of women in this day and age. One would think we still lived in feudal times, the way we are treated."

Richard held up a hand to the two women, as he said, "I swear when I catch these two reprobates, and catch them I will, I'll allow you to lecture them about the emancipation of women until their ears ring." He chortled. "Might even be a way to induce them to give up their information faster, if they are beset by lecturing females for hours at a time. Newgate may appear the better option."

As he said it, he backed two steps away from the girls, who both directed scowling looks at him. "Simply jesting, my dears," he managed to get out between bursts of laughter.

"Your wit remains a source of constant amusement to us, Winchester," Lottie conceded with a grin.

At least one Jamison sister saw no problem with his sense of humor, although some labeled it a little lop-sided. And many women of his acquaintance never laughed at his off-handed witticisms.

Recently, he threw out such quips to attract a smile to Lovely Laura's face. To remove the all-too frequent worried frown marring her features and contorting her brows. Ludicrous to admit, but he assumed a role of court jester, indulging in small nonsenses to bring her momentary joy.

"… Who held me," Lottie was saying, when he refocused on her, "had a problem with his hand. He seemed to not have maximum strength in his wrist so, thankfully, I twisted sideways in his grip and swung my reticule at him. I was annoyed that I caught him a glancing blow on side of head, nothing more, though it did loosen his hold."

Lottie, blue-eyed, blonde-haired, and with the look of an angelic cherub, was treating her attack as if grappling with unknown assailants was an everyday occurrence. Unfortunately, it probably was for these ladies. No wonder Michaels and Jonathon worried every time they had to return to their university studies and leave the ladies here. And no wonder they prefer to employ men who were more hooligans than servants.

"… Pulled out the gag. I did what any lady would do. Screamed. Loudly. Then I used my heeled walking boots to stomp as hard as possible on his foot, though I do hope I haven't done any permanent damage to my lovely new boots. And when Dirty-hair jerked forward, I hit him again with my reticule, though I am sorry I lost several beads from it. And I do so love that bag."

Richard waved a dismissive hand and answered, absentmindedly, while he considered the possible reason for the attack. "Please allow me replace your reticule, a gift to celebrate your courage."

"Goodness, Richard. I couldn't possibly accept such a personal gift from you," Lottie said, her glance flicking back and forth between him and her sister.

"I fail to see any impropriety. After all, we are now related."

Lottie frowned. Her gaze fixed on Laura, she said, "I still fear some may think it inappropriate to accept your gift. Though I thank you for the offer."

"If not a new reticule, I will find another way to make amends. I dread explaining to Sherwyn how you came to be attacked, when I was supposed to playing sentinel in his absence."

Lottie shrugged again in her dainty and feminine way. Her shawl slipped and his eyes were automatically drawn to the pale and elegant slope of her shoulders.

"Oh, for goodness sake," Laura said, moving to stand directly in front of her younger sister. "Not you too, Winchester."

"I beg your pardon?"

Laura rolled her eyes. From behind her back, he heard Lottie snort and chuckle, though she tried to smother the sounds.

Laura said, "We all accept that Lottie is beautiful. And we've all seen men turn into tongue-tied nincompoops around her. However, I refuse to watch you pant like a rabid dog in our own drawing room. Please refrain from embarrassing yourself, and Lottie, in my presence."

Her caustic set-down brought a rush of heat to his face, yet he would not allow Laura's misconstrued ideas to embarrass either him, or poor innocent Lottie, who was peeking around Laura's shoulder and watching him with keen interest. He sensed that Laura was testing him, and if he failed, would enjoy berating his male stupidity.

Lottie seemed fascinated with the interaction between him and Laura and was waiting, wide-eyed, for his reply. He had a dreadful feeling he would be dammed by one of them, no matter how he reacted, and though he didn't want Lottie to ever feel uncomfortable in his presence, he also didn't want to provide Laura with any more reason to mistrust him.

"Every man is bound to notice your loveliness, Lottie." He smiled. "I apologize for my gender if it discomforts you, but men are never going to stop admiring beautiful women. That said, and with no insult to your angelic looks, not every man prefers blue-eyed blondes. Or green-eyed red heads like Becca."

Laura stared, a small frown furrowing her brow, the workings of her mind almost visible to him as she struggled to understand his meaning.

"Personally, my preference leans towards dark-haired vixens whose eyes spit fire at a man."

Laura put her hands to her hips and continued to scowl at him. "Oh, really. Then explain about your countess. You know the one. Hair dyed using barrel after barrel of flowers in a futile attempt to make herself look younger and mousy hair appear golden blonde."

Richard battled the urge to burst out laughing at Laura's scathing, yet apt, summation of his former mistress. The countess had frequently declared, with dramatic flourish and usually while they were in bed, that her many assets were due to a benevolent God. He'd long suspected it was more a case of the lady fibbing in public and used beauty aids in private.

Perhaps he could ask Laura which flowers the Countess used to color her locks, because he hated not knowing facts. To accuse his previous lover of telling lies would have been undignified, but Laura, being a distiller, could at least give him the truth.

Or perhaps not. She was glaring at him as if mentally painting a target on his chest and priming her pistol to hit him dead center.

As a distraction, he threw his hands in the air and said, "Can you not forget the Countess?"

"Not until she has forgotten you, which seems unlikely judging by recent events."

Lottie's laughter bubbled up and Laura shifted her scowl to her sister. Lottie held up a hand and said, "I shall leave and allow you to finish this round of your battle without me."

Two burly footmen were summoned to assist Lottie up the steps without her putting weight on her injured foot.

When Richard was alone with Laura, he encouraged her to continue their story. Though he needed to hear more about the attack, he also wanted to prolong their time together. The arrival of the messenger at his house had scared him so much he'd lost ten years off his life span.

He listened, not so much to Laura's words, but to the inflections in her voice. Before he left, he needed to be sure Laura had recovered from the shock of seeing her beloved family members injured.

If she'd let him, he wanted to be the shoulder she cried on, and provide solidarity in the place of her brothers, or Sherwyn. If she didn't boot him out of her house, he'd happily watch her pace around and around this room, for as long as it took for her to walk off her agitation.

Even anger pleased him. If Laura was feeling herself enough to fight him, it meant she lived and breathed.

Chapter Ten

Richard understood Laura's distress, knew why she still paced the circumference of the drawing room.

She blamed herself for allowing her family to be harmed, although the incident in the park and their injuries were his fault. He'd let them down, all of them.

"Our aunt is a most intrepid lady," she said with a fond smile, "despite all her nonsense about needing a strong man to protect us.

"While Lottie was distracting her assailant, Auntie extracted her bonnet-pin and stabbed her captor in the face. From the way the thug screamed, she thinks she injured his eye. Two men on the other side of the gate noticed the uproar and ran to assist. Fish Fingers, as Auntie dubbed him, swung up one of his hands towards her face after his associate, Weak Wrist–"

He spluttered out his uncontainable mirth over their names, but at Laura's exasperated glance he encouraged her to continue with a hand wave.

"–called to him they must run. Not wanting Fish Finger to punch our aunt, Lottie fought. Kicked out at Weak Wrist. That's when he grabbed her ankle and twisted as hard as he could. He threw her to the ground and then they ran back to the trees. Auntie threw a rock and hit Weak Wrist a good blow on the back of his head. It knocked him off balance and he fell to his knees. But before their rescuers arrived, his mate doubled back and dragged him down an alley."

"An incredible tale. Grown men would take to their beds for days after being attacked that way. Where did you all learn such fighting?"

"You know Cayle taught us to shoot?" He nodded. "Michael frets about us while he and Jonathon are away studying. So they've taught us how to defend ourselves. Lessons my brothers learned from a Chinese instructor near the university."

"Thanks be to brothers with such foresight. Perhaps I should engage an instructor for my sisters, also."

"A good idea for any young lady about to be launched into a world of rogues and scoundrels. I've lost count of the number of times I've used some of the simplest maneuvers on supposed gentlemen of the ton who overstep the boundaries of propriety at social occasions."

"Tell me their names and I will ensure they never bother you again."

"Your interference is unnecessary. I repeatedly inform you that I am not your responsibility. I can defend my own virtue."

"You shouldn't have to. No young lady should be left in such an untenable position. I've been consigned to protect you."

"You make me sound like a ship's cargo. A barrel of rum, and you're my guard."

He ignored her. "I've let your brothers down and broken my vow to watch over all of you. Two of your family are injured, and the possibility hangs over our heads that a madwoman is on the loose, with a grudge to bear against all those who helped in her previous capture. Mainly you and I."

"You're overreacting. It is impossible for you to be in every place at once. Neither I, nor my family, blame you in any way for this mishap. Jamison women are well used to incidents of this sort. We are also well equipped to handle them."

He narrowed his gaze and fixed her with his fiercest Earl of Winchester look. The one that sent gossiping servants scurrying back to work, and trades people to amend their overinflated bills to truer prices.

"What exactly do you mean by that? What do you intend doing?"

"We have guns in this household, Richard. And we know how to fire them. Even Auntie. Her late husband, our Uncle George, used to say, and I quote… 'My adorable Aggie is a much sharper shooter than most of the idiots I'm forced to hunt with in duck season.' Our uncle was a darling man, who preferred the time he and Auntie spent on our estate hunting together, without outsiders interfering and getting in the way, than City seasons."

She paced across the room, fidgeting as she was wont to do when thinking. By now, he'd come to identify all her idiosyncrasies and label them correctly.

This procrastination, not normal for head-long, rash Laura, led to a problem she didn't want to share with him, he was certain of that. In all likelihood, because it involved danger to her person, something she knew he would expressly forbid her doing.

"The biggest problem we're now facing…" She touched at least a dozen items with her fingertips while she dawdled in telling him. "Is that Lottie is now unable to accompany me tonight to Lord Hetherington's old warehouse, where we intended searching his discarded paperwork together."

He watched her, stunned into speechlessness as she rolled her eyes and waved a negligent hand.

"Winchester, we've done it many times before. Picking a lock is my area of expertise, whereas Lottie's is to discover the pattern in the paperwork we often ….uh…discover…in desk drawers." She grinned. "Or in hidden compartments in wardrobes, and in secret areas on library book shelves." She noticed his horrified expression, and quickly tried to reassure him but made the situation even worse. "Stop worrying. We've become proficient in slipping into private places, and then disappearing again very quickly."

He swallowed down his fury, appalled that they'd planned this without telling him, but knowing his anger must be damped down in order to regain control over their actions.

"Tonight, your skills will not be necessary. I may not be as nimble as you at the fine art of lock-picking, but can assure you that either I, or one of my employees, will gain me entrance to the warehouse. Write down the address, then you may remain here and see to the comfort of your aunt and sister while I attend to it."

"Certainly not. I'll not remain quietly at home while you place yourself in danger in my stead. Besides which, I'm the only one who'll recognize the exact sort of incriminating paperwork Lord Hetherington may have left behind in his rush to vacate the warehouse office. My assistance will assuredly be needed if we are to hand over correct and incriminating evidence to Scotland Yard. Lottie and I were the ones, alongside Becca, who spent weeks going through every scrap of correspondence, every accounting ledger and every journal from Lord Hetherington's estate. It was because of our diligent efforts that we learned he'd paid rent on several offices and warehouses scattered throughout London."

"I realize what an enormous feat you ladies accomplished by doing all that, and I admire you for it. But my cousins and I, alongside your brothers and members of the Yard, have all visited several of the establishments listed and found nothing.

What makes you think this warehouse contains anything of interest?"

"Because we only heard of its existence today. We were sent a message by one of the women we assist–"

"Another prostitute?"

She visibly bristled. "Please do not to call them that. At least not in our presence. To us, they are women forced to make their way in life as best they can, and most of the ones who come to our Society for aid are from good homes, who have been left destitute by men's stupidity and greed and obsessions."

He dipped his head in acknowledgement. "Very well. You received a message from a...lady of the streets–"

'That name is hardly any an improvement. Can you not refer to them a...working women?"

"Ha! You must not be meeting the same ones I do, as for the most part, they consider what they do as entertainment, not work. Apart from some of the lower class gin drinkers, most courtesans enjoy–" Looking towards the ceiling, he threw his hand wide. "Why, of why, am I having this conversation with you. Tell me what the message read."

"This...uh..female friend of ours works in The Gilded Cage, an extremely hard establishment to access."

"I know the place."

Black brows dipped and midnight eyes turned inky, as her seemingly perpetual scowl at him this evening deepened into a ferocious look. "I am positive you do, my lord."

His lips twitched. "I shall amend that statement. I know of the establishment to which you refer. Know its location and reputation. The type of clients they cater for. However, it may relieve your mind to know that I am not a member there, and have never patronized the hostesses." When she started to speak, he held up a hand, palm out. "And may I add, I'd be appalled to discover your...friend...discusses with an innocent such as you, the rather extreme techniques practiced behind those walls."

"Repeatedly you refer to my innocence, a state I sought to resolve last evening, if you remember, and yet you have no knowledge of how much or how little my friends at the Society have explained to me. About what happens behind those closed doors of the houses in which they seek employment."

He smiled and stepped forward to touch her chin, lifting it so her eyes met his. "But I do, little one. Your kisses last night told me everything I needed to know. In every way that matters, no man has peeled back the many layers that make up the flower that is you, Laura, and dipped his tongue into the centre of your mouth, as I did last night."

"Damn you, Winchester, forever twisting my emotions into knots. One moment you treat me like an errant child, following me around an older brother. At others, you wax poetic about my looks and my abilities, until I have no idea what is the truth. Or what you want from me."

He groaned. "Unfortunately, that is the problem, my sweet. I also have no idea what I want from you. So shall we agree to leave personal feeling aside for now, and discuss the axe about to fall upon our heads in the form of Lady Hetherington? Does she have a connection with The Gilded Cage?"

"How do you do that? You leap from pillar to post with such lightning speed that I am continually lagging behind. You solve puzzles in the blink of an eye. You concoct spider webs of connections between people and times and places and occurrences that would take even logistically-minded people hours, weeks, plus reams of foolscap and bottles of ink, to work out."

"I've read that often people develop an over-activity in one area to compensate for something they lack in another."

"Ah! I see."

She spun away and said no more, leaving him puzzled, anxious and restless. Surely she could not mean that she understood his vague reference to mean his own defect. No, it was not possible that she had uncovered his secret. Still, time again to redirect the topic to the upcoming evening.

"I assume that to mean Lady Hetherington is involved in this broth—working house, which also means if we are getting messages about her, she may also be receiving news of us. Of how close we are to discovering her secrets, her location and how she is acquiring the funds to live and prosper."

"Which is precisely why we must go to the dockside warehouse tonight. If she discovers we are tracking her, she will likely take steps to dispose of anything we might remember that was connected to her previous life. Anything to do with her, or Lord Hetherington and their estate and the consortium they ran. She will be bent on destroying any establishment he owned."

"Assuming she knew all their locations."

"She announced the night of her capture that she was the

mastermind behind the entire affair, so I think it is safe to assume she knew each and every location in which her husband met with his cohorts and conducted his blackmailing efforts."

"And several of the offices we searched in the last few weeks proved that Hetherington, or his underlings, held secret meetings with larger groups of lower class men. Tradesmen, shopkeepers, bankers. Those with nest eggs to invest. By inciting them into frenzies over the enormous profits promising to be reaped in railway expansions, they threw their money at the upper tier members of the Consortium without a second thought."

"They say, a fool and his money are soon parted."

Fury sparked from her eyes. "I do not believe those people were fools. Merely gullible. And who would not be with the tempting propositions dangled before them. They saw men of high rank, your peers, gaining money through the Stock Market and thought they could too."

"And they could have, still can, if they invest wisely."

"I want to save any more innocent victims from the Consortium's deceitful tactics.

Stop them from using coercion, or force, all before it happens."

"It's a hell of a dilemma that you leave me in. If I go alone, I can slip in unnoticed, however, I'll not be able to skim through the quite possible mountain of paperwork as quickly as if I have your assistance. Neither will I be able to remove it all from the warehouse without being noticed."

She crossed her arms under her breasts, a too-distracting movement at this particular moment, as it lifted them closer to his view, and gave him a smug smile. Her foot tapped an irritating rhythm on the carpet.

"I am forced to agree. Not because I think it a good idea, because I don't. But due to the fact that your particular knowledge of Hetherington's other paperwork will help sort through it faster. And the quicker we can vacate that place, the faster I will relax."

"You will not regret this decision."

"I am positive I will rue the day we ever joined forces on anything, my dear. Therefore, I will have your promise that we spend a minimum of time there and when I say it is time to leave, you will depart whether we are finished or not."

She hesitated, then nodded. "Agreed."

"I will return this evening then. Dress appropriately and warmly.

It will be cold near the docks."

"I've old clothes belonging to Jonathon that I wear whenever we go –"

"Please! Don't tell me you've broken into warehouses at night before. Who'd be idiotic enough to allow you to do that?"

"Becca and I needed to enter offices when we were first collecting our evidence against the original consortium. But you needn't fret. We were well protected on those occasions. Michael and Jonathon accompanied us."

He ran his hands through his hair. "Your brothers are as crazy as you girls. Why? Why would they encourage you to do that?"

"We were desperate. Frightened. It was before Cayle agreed to help us collect the information we needed. Try to understand. Unnamed men threatened Michael. Our friend Peggy was murdered in her cottage, because the killer assumed our calculations and forecasts for the next stock releases were kept there, as she was our bookkeeper for the Society. Poor, poor Peggy."

Her breath hitched, a sob. "I miss her dreadfully."

Having three sisters should guarantee some sort of imperviousness to feminine tears. Over the years, he'd seen every type. Sisters who twisted him around their fingers from the time the toddled their first steps, by dropping their bottom lips and offering him their most woebegone expressions. Mistresses who'd used bouts of noisy weeping to extract more expensive jewelry, or a new carriage, from his pockets.

At the first wet droplet trickling over Laura's flushed cheek, his resolve broke, along with his heart. He moved, by instinct, towards her and drew her into his arms, stroking his hand over her hair as she sobbed into his coat. Her chest rose and fell, with deep wracking sobs, as she cried out all the stress she'd held bottled inside her for the past several weeks.

"Shush, sweetheart, shush. I know you miss Peggy."

When her sobs settled to shudders and then to trembles, he reached into the pocket of his trousers and withdrew a handkerchief to hand to her. "You're missing Becca, too."

She glanced up, eyes red-ringed and water-drenched, moisture clinging to her long dark lashes. Surprise showed in her glance.

"Do you really think me so insensitive I'd not comprehend the origins of your anguish?"

He snorted, shook his head. "I can see from your face you do.

No matter. For now, I suggest you also retire to bed. Try to rest. It's sure to be a long tedious night."

He kissed her brow, a fleeting touch, turned, and stepped away, before his arms reached for her of their own volition. Holding her felt so right, so perfect, the knowledge choked him.

Or rather, the knowledge that it must remain unspoken made it hard to swallow, hard to draw breath. Hard to move away.

No. Best to leave.

Now, right now, before his infallible will failed him.

Chapter Eleven

Later that evening, Laura tightened her grip on the hanging strap of the Earl's carriage, as it shuddered to a halt on a rutted road between rows of warehouses fronting the East End docks. The stench of stagnant water and rotting cargoes swamped her oversensitive nostrils, hitting with the force of a boxer's punch to her head.

Physically, she was an exhausted mess. Mentally, she stiffened her spine. Richard, prepared as always, produced two thick scarves from his coat pocket and moved behind her, wrapping one over her nose and securing it behind her head. With a couple of deft movements, he similarly prepared himself, before waving her towards the door and his waiting footman.

Gas lamps, few and far between, cast irregular streaks of yellowish light on the planked walkways crisscrossing the narrow and muddy laneways, increasing their precariousness. Unprepared to show any hesitation in front of her overly critical escort, she sucked her courage like a long drink of fortifying Madeira, and stepped onto the nearest boardwalk with one booted foot.

Silently, she blessed her younger brother for being of a similar size, and for lending her a suitable outfit, even if it was unknowingly. Boots outclassed slippers in ankle-deep mud, while trousers would outrun skirts and petticoats if they were discovered and she needed to flee. Testing planks with each step, she walked towards their pinpointed destination, a building diagonally across and set amongst a row of decrepit storage houses, yet far better preserved than its neighbors.

They'd discovered this address in the records of Lord Hetherington, after Scotland Yard had arrested and goaled him several months earlier. Many, many hours of sifting through dusty papers, account books and ledgers, had uncovered the addresses for all the properties Lord Hetherington owned.

Her brothers had systematically investigated each premise and removed boxes of papers that she and her sisters had been perusing, one mound at a time. This warehouse, however, was mentioned as being used significantly more often, and was better repaired than any of the properties Hetherington had used for his illegal activities.

She and Richard were certain he'd held the majority of his inner circle consortium meetings here. Secret gatherings of the highest ranking men in his pyramid scheme of investments, where attendees were gowned, masked, and re-enacted ancient rituals.

Theatrics had been added to Hetherington's sham investment schemes to lure the bored younger set, who were both gullible and coin-desperate. Also to entice the group of older men who still clung to fantastical beliefs of meager fortunes magically multiplying into untold riches if they could understand the Spirit of Life and penetrate its core.

After reading the Consortium's well-documented, Ten Steps to Greatness, about their investment pyramids, the Jamisons had uncovered Hetherington's tactics. Peers were enticed into tiers of his consortium with promises of a great leader—namely the conniving lord himself—who could interpret astrological charts in a way never seen since John Dee's proficiency in the occult arts had made him indispensable as magus to Queen Elizabeth the First.

These greedy but indolent men, angry that their inherited fortunes were dwindling while factory owners grew richer every day, welcomed someone of their own social standing who promised them never-fail investments. On three occasions at balls, elderly lords, devout worshippers of the art of alchemy, had asked Laura to dance for the singular purpose of interrogating her on the processes of distillation.

The most obsessed of the three gallingly informed her that if she experimented in her distillery and succeeded in turning lead into gold, he'd offer her his name and titles in marriage. Truly magnanimous of him! Did these idiotic men actually imagine if a woman was intelligent enough to master metallic transmutation, she'd then be so witless as to transfer control into their more far less competent hands?

Stopping before a smaller wooden door set into the wide road-frontage, Richard pressed close to her back and waved a gloved hand ."Shall we?" The scarf muffled his voice, yet his question seemed loud, too loud. The coachman had driven towards the corner, the fading echo of horse hoofs striking cobblestones the only other sound in the unnaturally quiet street.

She hesitated, determined to answer confidently, not like a quivering mouse. "Of course. I'm eager to begin."

The scarf made his expression hard to read, though his eyebrows rose in disbelief. "Unless you've had second thoughts," he muttered. "Or decided to show common sense."

She shook her head.

His hands went to his hips. "You could wait with the coachman while I go inside. Reconnoiter."

The dratted man peered into her eyes, perhaps even her soul, with one of those irritatingly all-seeing, all-knowing looks he used to scrutinize people. One point in Winchester's favor: his thirst for knowledge meant he chose his to-be-quizzed subjects democratically, being able to extract minute details and nuances from either the lowliest street-sweeper or the highest Parliamentarian.

His cousins described Winchester's tactics as burrowing beneath one's shallow façade, yanking on the ropes of one's mind, dipping into one's well of insecurities and hauling one's secrets into public view, by the bucketful. He left her raw, exposed and reeling. Precisely why avoiding the Earl remained higher on her list of priorities than avoiding the Black Plague.

Her family wrongly believed her frequent, loud and long-winded arguments with him upset her. Believed she preferred passing her time in her distillery, creating soothing lotions and potions. Believed she avoided him because she'd no time for gentlemen like him, who happily romped with outgoing and intelligent tonnish women, while at the same time declaring they'd only walk down the aisle with a simpering, dull-witted virgin.

So, though she detested some of his attitudes, she'd recently decided prudence was the better part of valor. Sooner or later, this man, one of London's most colorful peers, who by rights should have his mind fixed on who was the most voluptuous opera singer, or which gaming hell offered the best stakes for the night, would be bound to unravel her secrets.

To expose her fears.

To strip her bare.

Lady Laura Jamison could steam oils and essences, pick locks, forge signatures and decipher codes. Dealing with emotional upheavals, especially those caused by a man touted to be emotionless in his dealings with women, was beyond her capabilities and her comprehension. So when forced into his company, she used confrontation as her defense against capitulation.

She jerked the scarf away from her mouth, summoned her most scornful look, hoping, even in the gloomy light, he'd understand her silent warning. Naturally, undaunted, he spoke again. She held an imperious hand before his face.

"Bite your tongue, or I'll bite it for you."

His eyes widened, he pulled off his own face covering and chuckled aloud. Also to be expected: he'd pictured her command with the naughtiest connotation.

"I-I would never…" She, with a dark complexion she adored because it precluded all tell-tale maidenly blushes, knew her cheeks now radiated heat. They were hot enough to rival her aunt's bedroom fire.

His head tilted as he watched her, male to female, seemingly lost to their surroundings. Ummm. I think I'd enjoy you biting my tongue. I can picture your soft lips covering mine. Those sharp little teeth sliding down my tongue…."

"Stop." The lane remained quiet, empty save for the two of them, but she ordered, "Remember where we are."

She forced herself to look away from where his gaze still focused on her mouth. In an unconscious reaction, she ran her tongue over her suddenly dry lips. The always-in-control Earl's demeanor changed. There was a hissed breath, a stiffening of his posture, reminding her of an animal readying to leap. And, to her dismay, she appeared to be his prey.

No. No matter how much the notion of testing him intrigued her, enticed her to prod at his rigid rules and boundaries to see if they'd bend and break, the idea was fraught with danger. Still, she wondered how far she, someone far-distant from his usual type of woman, could disrupt his well-known control. Imagine him floundering out of his depth, this once, and proving his shell could also crack under pressure? Prove he could make mistakes, buckle under the force of human nature, as easily as she and the other females he scorned? Emotional ones. Demanding ones. Clinging ones. Loving ones.

"Remember?" One hand on the wood paneling above her head, he leaned forward, trapped her between his chest and the building. "Only our location is holding me back from the compulsion I feel right now."

She had to ask. "Wh-what compulsion?"

He glanced at her mouth, and flicked his tongue over his lips to thoroughly wet them. "Why, kissing you, of course."

A shiver ran up her spine. She laid her hands flat against the wall behind her, as he turned and walked the few steps towards the two larger entrance doors. Placing the lantern directly below the meeting point, he lifted a large padlock away from the securing metal bar and tugged hard.

Several attempts to loosen the lock failed, though he'd pulled it from side to side, stuck his boot on the planking and jerked the lock outwards. He shook his head, grunted, held it high towards the glow of the street light, and gave her an enquiring look.

"Hasn't been opened in a while. Can you do it?"

He turned up the lantern wick and moved aside. Visibility improved and gave her a better chance of picking the lock, though it also increased their chance of drawing unwanted attention.

Drunken sailors, thieves, and worse lurked in these alleys on the lookout for an easy chance. A wealthy toff wandering off the well-lit routes to home. A whore too gin-soaked to notice if her night's takings were gone from her pockets in the morning. A child who'd clean up nicely and be sold to a brothel.

Richard explained, lectured rather, if she insisted on accompanying him, they needed to be as quiet as church mice, slipping in and out without stirring too much interest. These were mainly storage sheds, but London's infamous housing shortage meant squatters claimed unused buildings and thieves grouped together, living in *flash kens* for safety. Mean and desperate, they'd fight to the death to retain right to their buildings.

Thankfully, most kept to themselves, scrounging out a living, unless confronted. Some lived in a perpetual drink-sodden world and would flee rather than fight. Others, the children and women mudlarks, ignored the world, apart from the mud, black and stinking, they dug for buried treasure at low tide. If lucky, they sold their finds for coin, a pie to fill their bellies, or perhaps ale to deaden the sour taste of their lives. Mudlarks didn't frighten her, because she'd heard stories of them from the women at the shelter.

However, she silently prayed other invisible watchers would heed their own privacy rather than poke their noses into this particular alley. Because she needed focus and force to keep pace with her co-thief, to prove her mettle, to disprove his theory of her being an unnecessary burden.

Though tonight, of all nights, her stiff-upper-lip dragged on the cobblestones, her spine sagged like a sodden wheat stalk, and their cat tiptoeing along a hot brick wall displayed far greater bravery than her standing in this alley. Perhaps breaking into one of London's notorious eastside warehouses on a ghastly fog-ridden night might see even a hardened thief high-wrought?

The lock dropped with a clunk out of suddenly nerveless fingers. Tears pricked and prodded behind her eyelids. When he touched her back, she jumped.

"Steady, Laura."

When he bent to squint at her face, her eyes, she ducked. Long elegant fingers, bare since discarding their gloves to better absorb the lock mechanisms, grasped her chin. She resisted, pulled away from his grasp.

No. Don't let him be kind to me. Not now.

With her nerves tightly strung for weeks, the smallest thing might snap them and bring forth those tears; something out of character, something he'd delight in mentioning at every opportunity.

"Be honest, Laura, just this once. Admit this place terrifies you. We'll return to the carriage, and within an hour you'll be safely ensconced before your bedroom fire, sipping cocoa."

She gave a slow shake of her head. "Then what? Will you promise never to taunt me, as my brothers did? Never to hold tonight's cowardice against me?"

"Laura," He took her hands, shook them lightly. "Many people fear the dark. It's nothing to be ashamed of."

"Who-who said I was afraid of the dark?"

His stance softened, and he leaned into her. She tried to tug out his grip, to hide her face, but he kept hold and dipped to look her in the eyes.

"The family all know. No one thinks worse of you because of it."

"Huh! Shows how little men understand women. The boys played tricks on me, horrid tricks. Left me alone in the dark. I screeched like a trapped animal. But now I'm an adult, nobody will ever again think me a coward."

"Puss, your brothers played childish tricks. But now they're older, they'd never ridicule you for being afraid. Everyone fears something."

"Except you. You challenged the old Stock Market regime. Became Winning Winchester and forced a more modern path. The Invincible Earl."

He snorted. "Those silly monikers acquired in the banking district, they mean nothing." He shrugged. "My feet are made of clay, like every other mortal."

"Utter rot." She lifted the lock, studied the keyhole. "Far easier to deal with a little ridicule from business associates than to be labeled an idiot, or a coward."

She heard him suck in a sharp breath and the lantern he held aloft jerked, dipped, before he straightened his arm again. "If you knew the true extent of my peculiarities, you'd shun me."

She twisted to peer at his face, trying to read his expression.

"Why would I shun you?"

But now he turned the tables on her by dipping his head, shielding his feelings. He pointed at the lock. "We're not here to discuss philosophical problems. We've got more pressing matters."

From her jacket pocket, she extracted a small roll of cloth containing her tiny tools, implements used by criminals, lock-picks, for practices taught to the Jamisons by a well-known safe breaker. Their family collected an unusual array of servants, mostly former criminals, who, once rescued from whatever predicament they found themselves embroiled in, invariably became family faithfuls. From these criminals, the five Jamison children had learned many survival skills, the sorts of thing necessary when one's father was absent more than present.

Absorbed in the intricate twists and turns of the keyhole, she fed a piece of steel through the hole and jiggled it. Her senses opened as each piece of the puzzle shifted, tumbled and fell into place. She became one with the mechanism, absorbing its thoughts and movements, until it rewarded her with a final click.

After unhooking the padlock from the metal bar, she slid it sideways, grateful for Richard's hands beside hers pulling strongly.

"Well done." His softly spoken words caused another shiver of awareness. She stilled, waited for the sensation to pass. Prayed one day her traitorous body would cease these bizarre reactions.

Be strong. Be calm.

While he opened the door, she pressed into the shadow of the overhang and surveyed the narrow alley. Wooden door slats scraped when he pushed open the door, the sound echoing loudly. Noise had diminished as nearby residents burrowed into their hovels, snatching a few hours' sleep before sunrise when their miserable routines would begin again.

"Anything?" His query, spoken into her ear, startled her.

"Don't do that." She scuttled around the door, grateful when he pulled it behind them and blocked them from street view.

"You're as nervous as a mouse avoiding a stalking cat."

"A stalking cat is a very apt description for you. Like a panther, prowling the jungle for its next meal."

"Best not to give me ideas." He held the light high and started weaving a path, between crates and traversing the storage area, with her close on his heels. "The only thing edible in this place would be you. As I promised your aunt to protect you from all menace, I'm including me. I'll behave as meekly as your fireside cat." He halted, gave her an exaggerated, leering look, and smacked his lips. "Just for tonight, this panther will sheath his claws."

She chuckled. "Thank you for making me laugh."

Unintentionally, she captured his gaze as she said it. Her breath also caught. He'd have gazed at hundreds of women that exact way, eyes full of seductive lures, promising untold pleasure. But despite her mind knowing, despite scolding herself with the truth, for a brief moment she wished he stared only at her with such intense focus.

That she, Laura Jamison, was more to him than any of the dozens he'd dallied with. The one for whom he'd renounce his rakish ways and live the life of a saint with her.

Impossible, foolish imaginings. Silly, girlish dreams.

She directed her attention to something more realistic, their immediate situation, as, side by side, they climbed a set of rickety stairs leading to an upper level of offices. Through glass inserts, they looked down onto a row of cubicles spread down one entire side of the warehouse. These viewing holes were originally designed so supervisors could stand above, like demi gods, and watch the working populace below. The glass, now covered in a thick layer of dust, allowed in very little light, but their lantern showed the equally filthy wooden flooring and highlighted any uneven boards.

Half an hour later, Laura stood before her fourth cabinet of drawers and heaved a loud sigh of resignation. Nothing in the last twenty drawers. Nothing in this lot. With the toe of one riding boot, she kicked wildly at the bottom drawer, which gained her nothing more than a sore foot and a scuff on her brother's boot.

"Nothing of interest?" Richard spoke from the other side of the room, having worked his way down, mirroring her actions, pulling open drawer after drawer, and thumbing through any papers he found.

"Nothing but old shipping records." Laura let him hear her frustration. "Some trading documents between one storage company and another. I was positive Hetherington must have stored his most secret records here. Who were the henchmen he used. Which peers he blackmailed, and who helped him compromise them. "

She shifted to the next cabinet and gave the top drawer a fierce tug. "Damn you." She pulled harder past whatever had wedged it in place, shifting sideways to give herself more leverage, but almost toppled over. "Bloody, bloody hell!"

Behind her, she could hear him laughing.

"Tut, tut! Dockside language from a lady. If we weren't near the Thames, I'd think it out of place. I suppose your criminal servants taught you to swear like a navvy, as well as pick locks."

"Actually, no. I learned those particular words from someone not from the lower classes. Many consider him a gentleman." She glanced at him over her shoulder, deliberately ran her eyes up and down his form. "Some women even consider him handsome."

"*Me*? I didn't teach you swear words."

"You've forgotten about the girl trailing around the estates behind you, whenever you and the other boys came home on school holidays."

"I remember an annoying hoyden, who displayed infinite adoration for my cousin. Not for me. Only Cayle. Mortifying for a young man bent on cutting a swathe through the entire female population of Upper Greensborough. It's a wonder I didn't run away in humiliation."

She laughed. "You're incorrigible. And you didn't notice my defection in the least. Every girl swooned if you set foot in the village. Bessie, the inn-keep's daughter, cried inconsolably for a week each time you departed for university."

His nose screwed up. "Which one was Bessie? The eldest?"

"No, Thomas's second daughter. And my compatriot in mischief."

"Ah, the cheeky one." He grinned, and motioned in front of his chest to indicate her breasts. "The one with the enormous –"

"Winchester!"

His lips twitched as he touched a finger to her nose. "I was about to say, her enormous... teeth."

"Luckily, they didn't interfere with you kissing her. Often."

He choked, spluttered a little. "You spied on us?"

"How else would an Upper Greensborough girl learn about the world? Certainly not from our governess. We decided if we didn't want a marriage similar to our parents, where Papa gallivanted about from one end of England to the other, and left Mama at home to raise us alone, we needed to learn all we could. About men, their mating habits–"

"Mating? You make us sound like rabbits."

"Rabbits were best for our studies. And we've you and your cousins to thank for introducing us to that fascinating arena. Apart from teaching us to swear."

She smiled. She'd stunned him into speechlessness, and she did adore gaining the upper hand with Winsome Winchester occasionally. Although, despite having dubbed him with that pet name long ago, she'd never utter it aloud. The Earl's conceit was already considerable, although not unwarranted in some areas. Though she frequently ranted to her family about his contrariness with her personally, for most people, in most circumstances, he was pleasant, engaging and charming.

"I'd never have discussed such things with you. You were girls. Children."

"They weren't exactly discussions."

"What then?"

At his confused expression, she experienced a pang of guilt, even pity.

"We followed you. Listened to you tell tall stories. Bet on who'd utter the rudest word each day."

"Why the hell didn't any of us notice you?"

"You were too busy with young men's posturing and posing to notice the girls trailing in your wake. Much of your time was spent watching those rabbits. Or the roosters, or other animals doing...."

She fluttered her fingers. It was embarrassing for someone who prided herself on her forthrightness and her scientific knowledge to be groping for a suitable word to describe a happening of nature.

"...things."

His lips twitched. She pointed towards his mouth.

"I saw that. You're hard pressed not to burst into gales of

laughter at my inability to express myself in a licentious manner."

Stifled amusement escaped in short bursts from between his clenched teeth until, finally, his mouth opened with full blown peals of laughter. He bent forwards, slapping his knee.

"I fail to see the humor."

"It's the image of a gaggle of girls...creeping around..." The words erupted between bursts of laughter. "...in the bushes, behind us lads. And despite all your scientific studies, you blush when speaking of lovemaking."

"Mating is not love—" She sucked in a breath. "It's ..."

"Intercourse? Sexual congress?" His eyes danced with mischief.

"Humph! Stop. You're distracting me." She waved a hand, turned back to her stubborn drawer. "Go. Search. Finish so we can leave."

"Ah, now you're eager to be rid of me. Earlier, you insisted on coming."

"My mistake. We always rub each other the wrong way."

His tone switched from teasing to sensuous. "Ah, but there are so many right ways we could rub together, my sweet." His huskily spoken words, with their deeper connotation, were his way of distracting her, and she thanked him for trying to make light of her fear of their dark surroundings.

Inadvertently, he also aroused her awareness of his blatantly male side, something she couldn't afford to acknowledge. She felt shaky, as if the floor itself rocked and not just her emotions. If his daringly spoken words affected her like this, he'd hold unimaginable sway over her if she allowed his flirting ways to fully seduce her senses.

Then the floor truly shifted, with a sharp rock and sway under her feet, while a loud blast assailed her ears. Planks groaned and screeched, loose items slid from cabinet tops and smashed around their feet. A glass pane fronting the office cracked, shattered and blew inwards, the force sending shards in every direction as, almost in slow motion, the window frame sailed out and down.

"Holy hell!"

She'd barely registered his gasp of pain before she was grabbed and thrown towards the corner. A blinding flash, beyond the gaping hole, lit the office. He landed across her, squashed her onto the planking in a protective gesture she associated peculiarly with him.

"Déjà vu," she muttered into his coat sleeve, as another lesser explosion from below sent a cloud of dust skywards.

Three more blasts followed at roughly three-minute intervals, until their upper floor swayed like a wind-blown child's swing. With her eyes squeezed shut, she huddled in the haven of his body and thanked God for the strong arms enclosing her in a tight hug.

Several minutes passed, while they waited with bodies tensed for another blast, one that would send them hurtling to their doom.

"For propriety's sake," she whispered, breaking the nerve-wracking silence, "we must cease meeting this way."

His face pressed into her hair and his chuckles vibrated through her. "Only you, pixie, could make jests. Most women would be screaming."

"As soon as I catch my breath, I'll try that." He shifted his weight, allowed her to breathe a little easier. "Will screaming help?"

"*Any* noise is likely to get us killed. Whoever set those detonations will be waiting to check they left no one alive. But they didn't think of the mezzanine, which was probably built later. A balcony, with reinforced supports, angled back to the wall."

She wriggled under him, turned to look upwards. "So there's possibly nothing left of this building except the boards we're lying on?" He gave a tiny nod of agreement. "So we're like Pacific islanders clinging to the only atoll the volcano didn't blow up?"

He gave her a strange look. "At least there'll be nowhere for the culprits to conceal themselves. They'll be outside. Or long gone."

"Someone will come. They'll find us."

"The problem is, friend or foe?" He'd moved so they lay side by side, wedged securely into the corner, and spoke more to himself than her. "Second problem? First blast here. Next closer to the door."

She frowned, waited for him to explain his train of thought.

"Main destruction at rear, next blast to bring down walls. Then the storage crates, and set to give the men retreat time after each one."

She gasped. "They knew! Knew we were here. Even if we survived the first explosion, they thought we'd perish in the rubble before anyone found us."

"If you weren't such a quick-witted female, I could feed you some Banbury tale about rescuers digging through to us."

"I trust you to tell me no lies."

The wood beneath them creaked, shuddered, and tilted to the left. She slid towards the steps, or at least where they'd been, and this time a scream escaped. She thrust out her hands and used her feet to stop her slide. "Ouch!"

"What? "His question came from a little above her, his hand latching onto her ankle and pulling her back towards him.

"Splinters. Hetherington didn't spend money on his office."

"I suspect this warehouse was a meeting place for gatherings to convince working men into handing over their savings."

"It seems awfully large for a meeting."

He shuffled them along the floor, rested his back on the cabinet and pulled her against him.

"Hetherington's other establishments revealed some information. Things your brothers wouldn't share with ladies." He cleared his throat. "Two or three larger localities, possibly in rotation, were used for gatherings of men. Plus twenty or thirty women to entertain them."

"They entertained them here? In a draughty tin shed."

"Hmmm. I imagine it warmed up quickly. The entertainers danced, flirted, flaunted, and curtained areas would have been for...as you call it... things."

"Oh!"

"Anyone who refused to join their syndicates—"

"The sham syndicates?"

"Mmm. They blackmailed them. Letters were to be sent to wives, families, or to a tradesman's clientele, disclosing their romps here with prostitutes. They forced every man to sign their ridiculous proposals, and ensured they asked no questions."

"No wonder Lady Hetherington claimed credit. It was far too ingenious for her pretentious husband to have concocted."

Deafening screeches had them covering their ears, pressing closer to each other. Their loft shuddered, broke apart, the far support bending and tipping them sideways, so they were no longer able to find purchase with hands or feet.

"Hang on."

He laced his fingers behind her back as she flung her arms around his neck with clasped hands and they entwined their legs, faint protection against the jerks and squeals of timber and iron. But his arms remained, firm and unyielding, shielding her body, as gravity tossed them through the cavity which minutes before had led to steps. During their downwards twists and tumbles, she screamed, a full-throated scream of dismay, horror and fear.

With a bone-jarring jolt, they landed, bounced, mercifully on something soft and rolled and ended in a sprawled heap on packed dirt. Above them, any remaining supporting beams were tearing away from the wall, creating an incredible ruckus and, with sick dread, she waited for life to be crushed out of them. Waited for death to find them.

Another scream, perhaps hers, she didn't know. Chaos erupted around them, a multitude of noises indicated crates splintering, chinaware smashing, as beams dropped on them.

Richard grabbed her harder, rolled them over and over, and brought them to a thumping stop against a disrupted pile of crates. Pieces of wood still fell on their heads and again he flung his body, like a protective blanket, over her.

They huddled for several more minutes, listening to debris falling, scattering and finally settling around them, until the only part not a pile of rubble must surely be the semi-circle of crates sheltering them. Through it all, she was clutched to his chest, the hard pound of his heart matching hers. Their lungs labored in unison, sucking air from within their cocoon, rather than attempting to breathe dust-laden air from the echoing cavern beyond.

Richard groped in his pocket and pushed a scarf over her chin, silently urging her to cover her mouth as she sensed, rather than sighted him do the same. His intent was clear. Try not to inhale more filth into their already aching lungs.

Again they waited, listened, tried to distinguish individual noises and the direction from which the last movements of settling timber came.

"We need—work—out—path—least—blocked—yes?"

Her question, hissed between pulls of air into her pained lungs, was more to reassure herself that the body wrapped tightly around her was alive, than from the need of a reply. Despite knowing his lungs worked, she needed a word.

A murmur. A reassurance *he* lived. That he was not simply her companion, the male defending her, but *him*. It was useless to deny it here, now. As she'd tumbled into black-nothingness, her immediate thought had been of *him*.

For his safety. Of his life. Of preventing his death. Her oft-times confident, her recent support, her present salvation, the man whose presence in her life had begun to mean everything.

He pressed a finger to her lips, whispered, "We can't move yet."

She nodded. Too soon to stand. To look. To breathe dust-smothered air.

"Listen."

At his command, she strained to hear what had alerted him. Gasped. Felt his hand smooth over her head, soothe her. Heard voices, near the entrance to the shed at a guess. Searchers moving through rubble between them and the doorway, checking in case they'd managed to avoid the first larger blast and had started to run to the door. Rough dockside voices echoed as they yelled to each other, giving instructions, complaining of the futility of their searching.

Richard edged them further into the corner, slowly lifted a timber slat and laid it across their opening, while she prayed the searchers couldn't see any better than they could through this haze. Moonlight streaked across some sections now, allowed in through openings blown in the high roof, though thankfully for them the major part of the roof has remained intact. A blessed relief that only wide lines of light split the haze and highlighted the twinkling of dancing dust-particles.

Buried in their hideaway, she prayed they'd not be discovered, and gave thanks that if this was to be her last moments on earth, she was spending them in Richard's sure and steady arms.

"Stay still," he whispered, his tone as always calm, reassuring, wonderful. "There's too much dust to see us. Even if they come this far." His grip tightened, as if expecting her reckless side to take over; expecting her to leap from cover and do something rash.

Many long, anxious minutes passed before the voices faded, minutes during which she clutched his hand as if she were drowning and he'd thrown her a rope. Hoping he'd excuse her lack of courage in this dark, and to her, terrifying place, as normal behavior from a gently-bred young lady. Her hand trembled and he squeezed them, passed on his strength, allowed her to recompose herself. To push back the roiling waves of nausea bringing bile to her throat. To concentrate on her companion and not on her abject terror of holes exactly like this one: small, dark, suffocating.

A scrape, a long screech, distracted her and indicated the warehouse door was being pushed closed. A clank, a slam, and hopefully the bar was being fastened across it. Please let it be so. Please let nobody have remained inside. He eased her into a sitting position beside him, leaning on a crate.

"Could you," she said, adopting a sure tone, yet leaving her hand resting in his, "understand their conversations?"

"Yes, unfortunately." He patted her hand. "They're returning at daylight to look for bodies. After the dust settles."

He made no move to stand, but, in contrast, her restless spirit saw her climbing to her knees after another few moments to look around.

"Don't you want to see?" She peered down at him, mystified as to why he remained seated."

"You can tell me."

She reached down, grabbed his hand and tugged to encourage him. Although he pushed to his feet, he kept a light grip on her fingers and didn't swivel his head, as he'd done when viewing the chaos. Fingers of fear crept up her spine. Gooseflesh broke out over her skin.

"What's wrong? Tell me."

"No need to worry. The first explosion blinded me. I'm sure it's only temporary."

She gasped. "The bright flash. That's when it happened."

"I imagine so. I smelled gunpowder. Glass shattered. Everything went black."

She shook his arm. "Why? Why didn't you say before?"

He shrugged. "You might have had a missish swoon over a minor wound. Might have cried out. Better to wait 'til they left. You might have done, what your aunt calls, an ear-splitting-Loud-Laura-screech."

She whacked his arm, her slap sounding much as a wet fish landing in a boat's bottom.

"Ouch!"

She scowled, realized he couldn't see her expression, longed to plant her palm across his cheek but in deference to his injury, attacked his arm again.

He tried to grasp her hand, missed, shuffled backwards. "Cease! I inform you I'm wounded, perhaps mortally, and you…" He rubbed at his arm. "Damn you, why are you hitting me?"

"I didn't hurt you. Though I am furious. You know perfectly well I wouldn't have taken any missish turn. Do you truly think me so dim-witted as to cry out and reveal our position to those roughs? Do you truly not trust me at all?"

"No, no. To the contrary. I thought, with your kind heart, you might have cried out in sympathy for my distress. Or thought to summon aid. In fact, I'm trusting in your indomitable spirit to locate our escape route."

She hesitated. "Do you believe we can escape? Truly."

"We *must* escape. Before daylight. Before no bodies are found. Before they question where they saw our lantern."

"Even if we find a way out tonight, they'll chase us."

"No, I don't think they realized who was trapped inside. More likely they were ordered to torch this building, then saw our lantern upstairs. Decided to kill three birds with five explosions, so to speak."

"Goodness. I do hope you're deductions are correct."

She groped around their immediate area and uncovered some necessities: a half-tub of water she presumed the entertainers would have used for washing. Plucking up her courage, she sniffed.

"What are you doing?" His voice showed his already-rising frustration with his role as bystander, while she portrayed the intrepid explorer.

"Smelling water." Silence, as she realized his agile mind would be working, that his others senses would be on high alert to compensate for being sightless.

"No rank smell?"

"Clean enough to bathe your eyes."

As she spoke, she collected her make-shift remedy and cleared a small area in which to perform her medical treatments. She slipped into a natural rhythm, this healing coming as easily to her as speaking. Something her family teasingly told her she was an expert in. And she'd applied home-remedies a hundred times, probably a thousand, for family, friends and servants.

But this time was more important than any of those others, and she wished sincerely her knowledge was greater. Wished her knowledge of gunpowder was as extensive as her youngest brother's, hoped her treatment would restore his eyesight, because she, of all people, understood how much Richard's life depended on being able to see pages.

To see writing. To absorb the written word through his sight. She knew his secret fear, just as he knew hers.

"I'm nearly ready. I need to cleanse your eyes of any gunpowder residue, the sooner the better."

Chapter Twelve

Richard slid down into position beside Laura, a small smile hovering around his mouth. If he had to be in this predicament, there was no one he'd prefer tending to him. Her skills as a home-healer were remarkable and he'd trust her with his life. Or in this case, his sight. He heard cloth ripping and turned his head.

"If my ears aren't playing me false, you ripped your linen."

"Just a frill from my petticoat. For a bandage."

He tensed, forced himself to remain still. "Damnation. Of all the times to not to be able to see. To ease an injured man's troubled mind, you might at least show mercy and describe your actions."

She chuckled, then began to dribble water over his eye.

"Describe how you tore your petticoat. Slowly. How high did you lift it? Were your ankles exposed?"

"Did I mention you're incorrigible?"

"Several times. Now, continue with your trim ankles… encased in red silk stockings… with matching garters…" Her tinkle of laughter soothed him as much as the cool water she applied to his burning eyes.

"Your imagination, sir, does you credit."

After her washing duties were complete, he felt a damp cloth placed over his closed eyelids, a gentle pacification to the increasing sting which had begun to worry him. Permanent damage was unthinkable, and he'd no time to even consider the dreadful possibility in their present circumstances.

He issued instructions, and listened as she investigated the circumference of their dusty prison. As she worked her way around, foot by dusty foot, searching for a door and testing windows, she called back to him. A constant stream of typical Laura dialogue that he welcomed with open ears and a thankful heart. With her own fear of the dark, she'd understand better than anyone how this grated on his nature. How much he loathed being blocked from the light, forced to sit still for fear of stumbling into fallen debris and worsening his injury.

"Keep talking, please, so I know you've come to no harm."

"The windows seem to be crisscrossed with bars. Barricaded from the outside. More than likely rusted."

"Don't try climbing too high and hurt yourself. Even we could shift one, it would be a long drop to the road outside."

"Whoever owns this warehouse," she called in an indignant voice, "should be ashamed. It's falling to rack and ruin."

His laughter rumbled up. "Should I point out the irony in that? Several blasts were set here not half an hour ago, my love. The most likely culprit being the owner. I don't think upkeep weighs heavily on his mind."

"Hers."

He considered in silence, before calling back, "I assume you're referring to Lady Hetherington."

"Richard, tell me you're not moving."

"Goodness, what acute hearing. And yes, I shifted a crate directly behind me because I heard water. Perhaps there's a pipe running into that barrel."

"A pipe?"

He listened to the clatter of rubbish as she clambered over rubble to return to him and held his breath, waiting for a cry of distress, ready to go to her if she fell. Christ, sometimes he wished his Laura wasn't quite so fearless. It literally robbed him of breath when she did things like that, things that put her life in danger.

Not until she touched his arm did he breathe easily, reassured when she knelt beside him on the floor. She took his fingers and directed them to the pipe she'd uncovered; a solid metal pipe.

"You're wonderful," she cried, and he felt her lips brush past his cheek in a quick salute of gratitude. "I didn't think to follow the water source. What sort of scientist am I?"

"A beautiful and courageous one," he replied automatically. No reply from Laura. He cursed at not being able to see her face. Not being able to read her expression after his slip of the tongue. Had he given too much away?

"Ah…the…ah…pipe," she announced, her voice fading as she moved away from him, "runs into a barrel and water fills the wash basin from a side tap."

He sighed. Had he ruined their friendship by saying too much? He'd long ago decided nothing could come of his never-ending infatuation with this woman, but he'd always hoped they could retain their camaraderie long into the future. Long after they were both wed to the type of spouses they'd pronounced many a time they desired.

"…and it disappears here, I think into the wall. Stay back while I climb in and look."

By instinct, he moved in her direction, drawn to her voice like a child following the pied piper. "I smell water."

"Yes, and close by, I think. In this wall, there's a door. Disused, but a door nevertheless. I'll clear a path in front of it. These crates look undamaged."

"Come, guide me to you. I'll shift the crates."

She led him, with great care, to the back wall and placed his hands on crates so that, between them, they tugged and pushed and exposed the door.

"I can unpick the lock, I think."

At her words, he put his ear flush against the wood and relayed any movement. "Yes. I can hear it starting to move. Keep turning the drop piece to the left. You're doing beautifully, my sweet. A little more to the right. Slowly. Yes, it's moving."

He placed his hand over hers on the knob. "Please be careful, sweetheart."

Another fleeting brush of her lips over his cheek before the door scraped. He reached for her hand, waited. But the only sound was the scratch of rodents' claws on hard ground.

"I can smell produce. Vegetables. Perhaps wine. I can't see much. Oh, barrels along each side of what looks like a tunnel. My nose tells me there's air, fresh air, somewhere at the end."

"If we're going to escape that way, we need light. Dawn."

"Yes. "He heard her deep sigh. "The tunnel's dank and dark. And I don't fancy rats nibbling on me."

"No. Better to make our way out at first light."

She tugged out his pocket watch and he imagined her squinting in the pale moonlight to read it. "Good. Still working."

"Do you have your spectacles?"

"Yes. We're fortunate. Your watch and my spectacles remained intact. "Another deep sigh from her. "If only your eyes hadn't been hit."

He reached for her hand, squeezed. I'm sure it's only temporary. Besides, it didn't prevent you from venting your spleen on me for not informing you."

"Nothing will prevent me from informing you when you make mistakes, my lord. Nothing."

He chuckled as she took his hand and led him into their nest, and fussed around to make him comfortable.

"I found a couple of coarse rugs we can sleep on."

"So, four or five hours until we can see to escape."

"Here." She pushed an apple into his hand. "Our gourmet meal is served, my lord. And I've a bottle of wine, if you've your knife to uncork it?

"Of course, dear lady," he replied formally, happy to join her game if it would ease her fear and pass the time. "Always happy to serve a gentlewoman her wine." He extracted his knife from his boot and opened the bottle. "After you, little one."

He listened to her long swallows, squirmed when she slurped on the mouth of the bottle, and imagined those same strong throat muscles performing the same motions on him. On his mouth. On his body. He squirmed even more and blessed the lack of light; blessed the dark hiding that body from her inquisitive eyes.

"Ah, yes." She touched his hand to push the bottle into his fingers and he jumped. "One of the best vintages I've ever tasted."

Like her, he drew long and strong on the bottle's neck, until she reached back again and tugged the wine from his grip. He listened to her take several more swallows over the next five or ten minutes.

She interspersed her drinking with short lectures on his stupidity in thinking she was the sort who would panic under this sort of pressure. For believing she wasn't as capable as him. She stopped only when she hiccoughed, loudly.

He chuckled. "I think, little love, that may be plenty for you for now."

A slight tug of war ensued, until, not wanting to hurt her fingers, he released it. More gulps, more rapid swallows, sounding very loud in the peace of their temporary haven. Once again, he covered her hand and used more force to retrieve the bottle.

"Oh, no. No, it's wonderful. I want more."

"Sweetheart, drinking more wine won't magically make your surroundings light. But I'm here, with you, and I swear I'll keep you safe from everything terrifying about the darkness."

"Even rats?" She hiccoughed again.

"No rodents will dare come near us, I promise."

He moved his courageous accomplice closer, tucked her under his shoulder and wrapped his hand around his arm. Her fears hung between them, unspoken, but hopefully his presence would be enough to damp down her anxieties until daylight. Her body rocked as hiccoughs popped up, several times in succession, and then her body slumped heavily into his side. Wine, fright, and exhaustion had taken their toll.

Her murmured words were almost too low, too slurred, for him to catch. "…wanted my own knight in shining armor… Cayle… to Becca." She sighed, a deep inhalation that lifted her shoulder under his arm.

"… never thought I'd have …strong …" Her words faded as she drifted deeper into slumber, though it'd surely be an uneasy one.

Hard ground and two prickly rugs laid between crates didn't make for a comfortable sleeping chamber. By using his jacket, he created a makeshift pillow for their heads and then, with her in his arms, he slid down to a full recline. They needed to snatch a couple of hours' sleep, so they'd have their wits about them if they encountered anyone on their escape route.

When he woke, he estimated an hour or two had passed, and her even breathing indicated she'd fallen into a deeper sleep than his. Her hair tickled his nostrils. Her curves molded, flush against his side, and despite the boy's clothes she wore, every rounded arch reminded him she was pure woman. A very desirable woman.

Beneath the blanket, she wiggled her bottom, shifting backwards in search of warmth, and pressing into his groin. His erection jumped into full awareness, long before his mind caught up.

He groaned. Bloody hell. Recite something; poetry, something long-winded. Anything to shift his mind from the unbridled lust he felt, the ache of unacknowledged and unacceptable want always lurking just below his senses when he was in her presence. Each and every time her delectable rear end, those soft pillows of flesh, pushed against him, he was forced to grit his teeth.

If not for the regular in-out motion of her chest beneath his taut arm, he'd swear the minx was wide awake and deliberately tormenting him. Punishing him, driving him insane.

Under his breath, he started to hum the first ditty springing to mind. *There once was a barmaid named...* No! Sailors' songs about prostitutes and whoring would make it far worse. Though now his mind had fixed on women with pendulous breasts, women with figures ripe to be used as models for ships' mastheads, plus all the things drunken sailors sang about. The pleasurable things they did with these women.

Not helping.

He eased back his thighs, retracted the muscles in his groin, desperate to ease the throbbing pressure. But Laura, following his most heated part, kept backing into him. She wriggled, circled and nearly sent him screaming. He clenched his jaw. Surely she would awaken soon. Surely he could allow her a little more warm repose.

Listing his stock portfolio distracted him briefly, long enough for his tense body to relax, for the cramps in his muscles to ease. She moaned, and in her sleepy state moved one hand arm. Without sight, he was helpless to see what troubled her, and he wasn't fast enough to soothe her back to sleep. If she awoke now, with him as randy as a paddock bull, her quick mind was likely to recognize his predicament. She had two brothers and two scientifically astute sisters. Not to mention a great-aunt whom, he was certain, neglected nothing in educating her extremely inquiringly-minded girls about marital relations.

"Sore shoulder," she muttered.

After an inward sigh of relief, he reached across and walked his fingers up her arm until he reached the spot to rub, the spot her hand lingering hand indicated.

"Ummm. Nice," she purred in a pampered-kitten voice.

Before he'd registered her intention, she rolled. A complete roll ending face to face, her front pressed tightly into his taut body. He hauled in a breath, stilled, tried to shift back, away from her, as much as possible in the confined space. Her uppermost leg lifted and hooked over his, anchoring him in place.

"Northern Railways. Two hundred and twenty-five shares. East Manchester Mining Company. One hundred and thirty shares. Middleshire Coal–"

"What are you muttering about?"

"Keeping my mind active. Reciting my shares."

Soft fingers touched his cheek and he flinched. "Is there something I can do to help you relax?"

Her innocent question, accompanied by drifting fingers down his face, to his neck, and coming to rest over his heart, sent a myriad of erotic images on a mad race through his head; a dozen different solutions to relieve his excruciating tension; ideas leapfrogging over one another in the hurtle to the finish line and gain the honor of being acted out by Luscious Laura.

Lord help him! No way could he survive another half-hour of

this torment, not without following the lead of this building and exploding from within.

A lazy hand drifted across his chest, toyed with his vest buttons, and then breached the defensive wall of heavy brocade to dip beneath. To delve further, to tiptoe under his linen shirt. Every muscle tightened. Despite the chill, beads of sweat broke out across his forehead.

"You...are...the devil incarnate." He gripped his shirt, held the tails to his trousers, and shoved her hand away from bare skin. He swallowed. "A temptress. Sent to dissolve my vows about not touching you. You, my love, are trying to shatter my promises to the men in your family. Those same chaps who vowed to rip the arms off any rake caught within breathing distance of their sisters."

With her nose buried in his chest, she giggled.

"Proving my point. Only a girl who is naive–" She nudged him in the ribs with her elbow. "Very well, through your readings of medical and anatomical articles, you consider yourself well-informed about matters of the bedroom. But if you continue trifling with me here, in our very intimate position, which I'll hasten to explain to your aunt wasn't of my doing, but something born of necessity–"

A hand covered his mouth. "Richard, you're babbling. You appear to be rather over-excited."

"Listen, little she-devil. My nerves aren't the only part of my anatomy overexcited. You've been rubbing up against me, touching me. I'm not made of stone, you know?"

Silence, and he didn't need light to know she would be frowning, pondering the matter. Head tipped slightly to the right, a tiny pucker between her brows her lips would be pursed in the delightful position which always reminded him of kissing.

"Ooh."

"Yes, ooh. Now, if you've any intention of arriving home with your virtue intact, you'll roll away from me. "

"Hmmm. What if I don't?"

He moaned. "Take pity upon me. I'm barely able to cling to gentlemanly behavior. To not fall upon you in a fit of lust. But I'll not last–"

Her lips touched his, robbed him of words, and his last remnant of manly resolve. Gently caressing, her mouth rubbed his, allowed him to feel the wet plumpness of her lips, absorb her sweet taste.

Without lifting his mouth, he moaned, quieter this time. The moan of a man whose will had been sucked out of him by a tempting mouth, whose surrender was inevitable when a willing woman was kissing any protests away.

More licks and sips, more brushes of petal-soft lips on his mouth, and his body shifted, changed, readied. Flight no longer seemed an option. Fighting impossible. Widening his mouth, he took back control of their kisses, lifted and spread himself until she lay beneath him, pliant, willing, and learning from the master.

Mine. Mine. Mine.

His head pounded, his blood rushed, the beat like jungle drums. A relentless rhythm, over and over. The kiss became hungry. He wanted to devour her, nibble, gobble and eat her every way possible. Taste her every taste, feast from her body as he already adored feeding on snippets of information she hand-fed him from her fast-whirling mind. With his lips, his hands, his senses, he opened himself to her and tried, at least in his humbly physical way, to demonstrate his need for her. A craving that ripped apart his carefully-built defenses, leaving him exposed and raw with wanting.

Their kisses were endless, on and on and on, as they tried to shift even closer, so close they ended wrapped together like clinging vines. Impossible to tell where one started and the other ended.

He ran his hands up and down her body, feverishly, memorizing her dips and valleys, wanting to fix her luxuriously rounded flesh into his senses to be brought out and remembered time and again. For no matter how good this was, they both knew it wouldn't stand the test of daylight, society, family stresses and their own hard-held notions of marriage. Better to savor the moment, remember it, and be able to recall it later.

His mouth moved to her neck, remembering the swathe of pure white skin he'd glimpsed earlier when he'd collected her in his carriage and she'd bent forward to descend. Her graceful neck, bountiful bosom…oh, hell…he wanted it all. Wanted to declare aloud that same refrain….

Mine. Mine. Mine.

Her warehouse-breaking-into outfit was an eclectic mix of her brother's out-grown clothing, yet it had looked anything but boyish on her. He tugged away the knotted kerchief she'd worn, pulled aside the two collar pieces. He could recall in exquisite detail the slash of white skin dipping into her ball gowns, and now he ran his tongue down, traced the path he could find unerringly, even blind, and felt the twitch in his groin, the extra hardening in response.

"Your skin is so white, here." His tongue flicked down the enthralling dip, then licked a path back up each side to nuzzle the underside of her neck. "And here."

His teeth nipped at one earlobe, and beneath him, she shivered, arched, and made a breathless little sound of arousal prettier than any bird's song. When he tongued the inner shell of her ear, she lifted from the floor and pressed upwards, pushed against his length, made tiny movements back and forth until he throbbed so hard he was certain she could feel it through their clothing.

Until he moaned aloud, though not attractive sounds, but raw, needful, agonized noises of a highly aroused male. While he busily expressed his adoration for each new part of her anatomy he exposed, she, not being a complacent sort of female, decided to return his attentions. And not in a passive way. Oh, no. His little minx didn't understand the meaning of passive. Her busy fingers tugged so many times his shirt came loose and, with her normal impatience, her fists gripped the hems and jerked, wrenching his shirt with utter disregard for the cost of fine linen up his chest. Not that he wanted to stop her. Breaking off his work around her neck and head, he lifted and hauled his shirt up and over his head. He tossed it behind him, not caring where it landed. Only caring her sweetly caressing hands returned to touch his bare skin, finished their exploration, put him out of his misery.

"Laura, Laura, Laura." As her palms slipped up and over his chest, and hesitated at his nipples, he chanted her name and, by flattening his palms over hers, showed her how to circle over his tiny, but tight-pulled, nipples.

"So much smaller than mine."

He gave a low raw chuckle. "And yours will be even more sensitive when I touch yours. Yet, the feel of your hands on me, there, is exquisite torture."

Another little hesitation, another pondering silence. "Really. You like it?

He groaned, dipped to kiss the back of her hand where it lay on his heaving chest. "More than like it, love. You can bring me undone with one finger."

"And will you touching my–mine, have the same effect?"

Using instinct for direction, he bent to her lips. Another long, languid kiss. More sweet little pants, more nails digging his neck, gripping tightly, holding him in place. He almost laughed. He'd lost all will to run. Lost the urge to back away, act in a gentlemanly fashion. Having gone this far, he'd die without at least a taste of her. Without the chance to keep her next to his body for a short time.

"If you enjoy kissing, sweetheart, when I touch your breasts," he reached between them to lay an open palm over her swollen breast, undone by the sharp pointed- nipple already protruding, already begging for his touch. "When my fingers rub *your* sensitive nipples, your body will come alive in ways you've never imagined. You'll know what it's like to want, you'll begin to crave things the same way I hunger for you."

She kissed him again, lightly, then leaned back to consider. "But I already do. Want more. Want whatever you can show me."

An inner battle raged, but fell defeated. Telling himself he'd stop soon, very soon, he vowed to give her a simple taste of passion. No more. Not because she didn't want it. He knew, had heard, felt, inhaled the signs. The scent of arousal filled the air around them, from him, from her. Inhaling deeply, he drew in her intoxicating odors. To know her acute response was to kisses, or his hands, thrilled him beyond belief.

The drum beats grew louder, stronger: *claim her, claim her. She's yours.*

Choice was ripped from his hands when she pushed onto an elbow and pulled her shirt from her trouser waist, using the same frantic action as when she'd stripped him. When she lifted her arms, he grasped the shirt and pulled it skyward, to fling it away in the same uncaring fashion that he'd discarded his clothing. All that mattered was baring their bodies for each other's enjoyment.

His fingers felt lace, the neck of her chemise, a feminine flimsy garment that would be glaringly at odds with the masculine coverings she'd worn. The disparity struck a boxer's upper-cut-knockout-blow to his already strained senses.

His fingers curled around the ties of chemise, gripped, argued, "Stop. A gentleman would stop. Because going any further…with you…"

A dozen scenarios raced through his head regarding him, with her.

... *Most likely an innocent*—despite her adopted air of worldliness.

... *One whom he...admired*—oh, so very, very much.

... *The sister of his friends*--who'd challenge him to a duel.

... *Related through his cousin*--who'd kill him, without the duel.

Therefore, a cowardly retreat seemed the sanest option. "Laura, I can't—"

She covered his shaking hands with her own, shifted his fingers, loosened the ties, laid open the placket, and placed his hands, flat, still trembling, on her warm, soft flesh.

"Richard, I've no idea the topic of your muttered inner debate, nor, at this particular moment, do I damn well care. Though if it's some idiotic notion of playing the gentleman, I'll not stand for..."

"Sweetheart, wait, please wait." He pulled his hands away from the temptation of skin and flesh and woman, and groaned.

Women, many, many women, if he were to be honest, had tantalized him with glimpses of clothing, various types, from ribald to silk lingerie from French designers. Dozens had discarded those layers of clothing, also in various positions, habitués, or during well-executed plans to impress or entrap him. Some for coin, some with hopes of becoming his countess. None had struck a chord in the same way as Laura's contrasting layers.

For something to do with his fists, wavering as if fighting the urge to delve into the snug crevice below her chemise, he grasped his head, forgot his injury and dislodged her bandage with his agitated actions.

"Hell! It's impossible to think. Not rationally. Not when you're lying there, half-naked," he waved one hand towards her and scowled when she giggled, "tempting me, taunting every smidgen of honor I possess."

"So, I tempt you, do I?" Her voice, husky, close, made him groan again and grip the hand she'd decided to trail up and down his cheek to further distract him.

He needed no further distraction, her hot scent drifting towards his nostrils each time she leaned upwards to stroke him, to mock him, was agony enough.

"You know you do. But if I were to continue...if a man shows someone like you...a young lady—"

Her limbs went rigid beside and beneath him. No, no, no, his own body cried. Stay with me. Don't leave me, don't reject me. Not yet at least, not until he explained.

Not until he delivered The Earl's Speech of Regret. The one he painstakingly addressed to each and every woman before he flirted with her at a ball, or dallied with her in a garden, considered bedding her or, whatever the case might be.

He caught her hands, imploring her understanding through body language and his carefully chosen words. Not for her would his well-practiced, sincerely-spoken sermon suffice. The one expressing profound regrets that his situation of raising four sisters tied his hands regarding marriage for some considerable years.

Not for her were his usual platitudes that in other circumstances she, whomsoever the female of the month happened to be, would be his preferred bride above all others. For she, his friend, his nemesis, would accept nothing less than authenticity and sincerity. Now, if only she'd listen.

"Richard, if you dare to deliver your infamous putdown to me, of all people, the one you use to warn off every female from sixteen to sixty, the Earl-Of-Winchester-Regrets-He-Cannot-Marry-You thing, you're so renowned for, I swear I'll not be responsible for my actions."

"Good Lord. You mean you've heard it?"

"Half the women in London, and ones younger than sixteen and older than sixty, can probably repeat it verbatim. You've been quoted, frequently, when un-entangling yourself from some convoluted situation. Women have actually fought over you, incredible as it seems to me, and men copy parts of it to break off their own relationships with women. Please don't say you weren't aware of this."

He chuckled, and she made a strange noise, almost a growl. He wished he could see her face. "Well, perhaps I've given advice to the occasional unfortunate man, who has been trapped by an overeager female and he wants to avoid the parson's noose. Though the bit about women fighting over me is rather flattering, don't you think? Ouch! You pinched me."

"Regarding your *disputable* attractions as a husband, I assure you I've no need to hear your regrets before we proceed. As long as you've no regrets afterwards, I'll be happy. You know I feel the same as you about marrying for propriety's sake. I'd rather live out my days in seclusion on a Scottish mountain, than be forced to marry someone over trivial details."

'That trivial detail could become the loss of your innocence, if we let things get out of hand, here, tonight, my love. My control can only be stretched so far, and you've always enjoyed pulling my chain, testing me to the limit."

"Tonight, I don't care what normally happens between us. Nor what happens after. Nor will I hold you to blame. Not when my body burns hotter than a furnace, my limbs won't keep still, and my senses are stretched, fit to burst. If I don't get something…something I can't even name…something you know about, can give me. Release from this torment. All I know, Richard, is that I need you. Now. Desperately. If necessary, I'll beg."

He'd always considered her character as layer upon layer of intriguing traits and quirks, but now, in broken and filthy surroundings, she'd stripped away the last covering with her own hands. Revealed the hidden gem at the center. Offered it to him, openly. A more delicate, more precious layer. Definitely a more enticing one.

"Oh, little one, you've no idea how glad I am to be the one you want to show you, to introduce you to new experiences. I'd give half my fortune to see you right now, spread like a feast for a man long starved for the sight before me. Though my eyes are blind, all my other senses are open to every part of you. Every precious inch of you I long to touch, to taste, to lick and to savor."

Her rising excitement, thankfully a match to his own wildly escalating passion, flooded those senses demonstrated by a sharp catch of breath, a violent vibration of her body, a shudder or shake through her limbs at every caress by his hands, which were now spread widely over her chemise. Over her breasts. Her tightening nipples. He felt them under his fingers.

"Your nipples are calling to me, begging me, wanting me to take them between my teeth and roll them and squeeze them and taste them until your flavor fills my mouth–"

Once more her hand covered his mouth.

"Richard, I never realized how much you talked before. No wonder we fight. But at this moment, I need actions. Not more words."

He nodded. "I can do that."

He slid his hands under the chemise and hooked his thumbs into the scalloped lace hem to drag it upwards with his hands. As his palms skimmed over the round globes of her breasts on their northward journey, he groaned again.

"Perfect. You're so perfect. Oh, God, I need light."

He felt rather than saw her head shake. "No, this is perfect. Being here with you. Here, in the dark, I can be someone else. Someone besides Lady Laura, the odd Jamison sister. Loud, often incoherent, and generally..." He leaned close to catch the softly-spoken word, "...misunderstood." The saddest word.

"I understand you perfectly," he said without thinking, busy removing her chemise without tangling her hair.

Her small hesitations, her small catches on words of emotion, were so much easier to read when he could see her eyes, when he could watch as she screwed up kerchief after kerchief into tight balls. Or ripped them to shreds, which is how many of his ended when they argued.

Perhaps he should simply stop offering his perfect squares of perfect linen, about which his valet lamented loudly after they were returned ripped, shredded, or sodden. Although, if he stopped offering when she'd used her supply of linen, she'd be too embarrassed to accept from any other gentleman their proffered personal item. So far as he knew, she'd never considered why, of all people, she didn't refuse his, her professed nemesis, whenever he pressed his urgently-needed linen into her hand.

Though unable to see the nuances of her emotions this time, he could interpret this one. "It's easy to notice the more–" A small jab to his ribs. "I was about to say... interesting qualities about you. Your eccentricities," another jab, "tiny ones to be sure, make you far more fascinating than most young ladies."

"If I'm so fascinating, why do you–"

"Now who's talking too much?" He chuckled. "Perhaps we could discuss other fascinating things about you, *after.* After exploring your, to me, far more intriguing physical side."

With a sigh, he settled to his task, his extremely pleasurable task. Flattened palms ran in unison over the two tightly squeezed buds pushing out in demand from swollen breasts, equally eager, equally determined to claim his attention.

Under his palms, his fingers, her muscles undulated, her chest rose and fell in a faster and faster rhythm, her skin rippled with sudden spasms, as he found and tormented particularly sensitive areas. And he reveled in every squirm, every wriggle and every moan. This is what he'd waited for all his life, this moment of pure enjoyment, yet an act of unselfish pleasure-giving.

Not that he ever left his bed partners unsatisfied. But right now he was content, more than content, to administer every type of sensation and experience to her willing form, and spend the entire night admiring his success, enjoying with her every miniscule of feeling and anticipation.

Sensing her climb, inch by writhing inch, higher and ever higher towards something wondrous, something she trusted him to provide for her, filled him with immense gratitude. Knowing he was the one she'd chosen filled him with pride, and possession. Mentally, he shook his head. It always came back to that with her: that feeling of possession, of wanting to reach out and claim her for his own, even though he'd spent many a night reminding himself why such an outcome would prove disastrous.

He pinched each nipple between two fingers, tugged, rolled, 'til his she-devil squirmed like a worm on his hook and begged with a mix of grunts, moans and demands for him to stop, yet never stop. When her tormented noises edged towards shrieks, part-pleasure part-tingling-pain, and he judged she'd reached the edge, he took a long slow draw on her elongated nipple, using the sharp edge of his teeth to drag it through a drawn-out release from his mouth.

He shuddered, the pleasure almost killing him. If he hadn't been reclining, he'd have been brought to his knees. This perfect peak was given all the attention it deserved, his hand cupping her begging breast and finally lifting it fully to his mouth, securing it with his teeth and fingers against her out-of-control wiggles and squirms.

Sliding across her chest with a long lick, he located the ignored breast, and at her urging, lavished it with the same concentrated treatment. Eventually, she grasped his head, pulled him away, her breathing jerky, her body twitching uncontrollably.

"Richard, oh, my goodness, Richard! Oh, you need to stop. Oh, my."

With one hand cupped around a breast and the other tangled in her disarrayed hair, pins holding it under her cap having long since disappeared, he looked up. Held his breath, waited. If she asked him to stop, he would, naturally, despite it being the most arduous task he'd ever faced.

"No, no, not the pleasure. Stop your infernal tormenting and teasing. Do something. I can't stand it." She grabbed hold of his wrist with both hands, shaking it, pleading, and begging. "You've years of experience. Fix this. Fix me. I'm about to explode. Shatter. Then nothing!" Her voice rose to a fevered chant as she shook his arm. "Do. Something. Now!" The last words screamed in his ear.

He chuckled and she stabbed his chest with a finger, punctuating her angrily-issued instructions. "Do. Not. Laugh. This is serious."

Try as he might, he couldn't smother his laughter, knowing the guffaws bubbling up every few seconds would raise her ire, rather than her excitement. He silently thanked the heavens their first adventure into sensuality was in a deserted area, not her bed chamber or an ante room off a crowded ballroom. At least Loud Laura could scream the roof off, or what remained of it, and nobody would hear.

"Shush, shush, sweetheart. I love knowing you're so eager to learn more about passion with me. But."

"Damn you! I sense one of your big brother lectures on behavior coming."

"The last thing I feel is brotherly. I want to be your teacher, your lover, not a family member struggling to do the honorable thing. This is neither the time nor the place to take your innocence, little one. I'll ease your pain though, relieve your rising pressure. But you must promise not to push me for anything else. The rest of the time we'll resist excitement. Discuss the weather."

He felt her nod. Whether she'd keep her word after he'd introduced her to her first taste of pleasure was debatable. He'd laid out variations of these restrictions, alongside reminders of the short duration of his liaisons, numerous times before. With numerous other women. And on many, many occasions he recalled, those women later paid absolutely no heed to his rules. Rules he'd set out before their very first contact, before their first assignation for mutual gratification. Women were not to be trusted in these affairs.

"No, listen to me. On the aspect of our time together, I'm making it clear. This is one occasion, one only. No repeat performances. No demands, no begging, no pleading for another night. No opportunity for your brothers, or Cayle, to discover what happened. No chance of them challenging me to pistols at dawn."

"Do not dare compare me to any one of your previous

mistresses. I've nothing in common with the preening empty-headed widows you generally escort about town. And I've no desire to monopolize your time. Nor your always-in-demand body. Plus, I've no more desire to be trapped into a relationship than you."

He heard her sigh, the softening of her tone. "Give me this one time, one chance to understand what more there may be to marriage. Knowledge to help me choose, at a later date, a husband who'll suit me in every way. If I've never experienced the delights as men are so free to do, how can I make judgments on whether a gentleman, or the next after him, will provide the right stimulation? Excite me to an extent such as you have tonight. If I don't find a husband, one who meets my requirements in every way, including the bedroom, I'll happily remain a spinster. Knowing I at least investigated every possibility, examined every avenue." She huffed. "Now, will you please shut up and move on to the next lesson."

He chuckled. "Absolutely, my delightfully demanding miss." He reached down and unbuttoned the flap of her trousers. "Lift up," he ordered, while tugging the trousers over her bottom and down her legs.

Leaving them tangled in her stockings and boots would thankfully provide another large road block, supposing passion carried him away and he missed the point at which he'd vowed his lesson in seduction must halt. His wandering hand touched warm and arousal-dampened flesh on its northward journey, and he sucked in a sharp breath at the feel of her hidden flesh moving under his.

"No—no drawers," he said between short gulps for air.

"Impossible to fit them under this clothing. Do you know how difficult it is too keep one of these wretched shirts tucked in? Keep the tails secured?"

"I do have some experience with that problem."

"And I imagined only women had problems with clothing when—"

His fingers eased through her nest of hair, the curls twining around his fingers, his imagination filling in their color. Raven's wing dark, with a blue sheen, even down there. A sharp jolt of arousal had his erection jerk, twitch against her thigh, and his fingers unconsciously tightened and pulled.

"Ouch!"

"Oh, damn, sorry," he muttered, hauling back on the reins of his self-control. Stopped his over-active imagination before it took any giant leaps forward and dived into the wetlands he sensed a fraction out of finger-reach.

Seducing Laura, or rather not seducing Laura, was proving infinitely harder than contemplated, and he'd assumed drawing a line, not crossing boundaries, would require every scrap of willpower. Wiggling one finger between the lowest part of her folds, he tested her response.

"Ooh, ah, ah, ah, ooh."

While she chanted a barely-comprehensible string of encouragements and audible displays of enjoyment, she arched, bucked and squirmed, although so far, he'd only inserted a forefinger, pushing it ever-so-slowly higher. When he brought her to orgasm, she was so responsive she'd quite possibly leap clear out of their little hidey-hole.

Groaning with a mix of agony yet delight at her response, he battled to ignore the throb and swell in his groin, the hardening and growing length of his arousal as it screamed for the same attention. But no. His vow was to make this night entirely about her, her voyage of discovery. Even if it killed him.

Her first experience would be joyous, exciting, leaving her panting for more. Resolutely, he pushed aside the image of another man having the privilege of teaching her the next lesson. For now at least, she was his.

A mere graze of her swollen nub, no longer hidden as the folds became engorged, saw her back arch, made her thrust herself forcefully into his waiting hand. He circled with his palm and with increasing pressure on the outside of her mound, continually dipping further, probing deeper at the same time. Two fingers could now slide inside with ease, twist, probe, retreat. Until she ran wet, the excess of juices dribbling between his fingers and down her thighs.

"Oh, God, you're so wet. So ready for me."

Her passage was soft, wide and brimming. Three fingers slipped inside, impaled her, and with the uttermost effort, he focused his other hand's efforts outside. A repetitive motion, round and round; rub and soothe, caress and pat and reward. Beneath him fully now, for she could stand no less, Laura panted, strained, reached, urged him to faster action.

'Reach for it, love. That's it. Now. Let it come. Yes. Come for me. Now, Laura. Show me. Show me how much you want it. How much you want *me*."

His thumb swirled in a merciless pace, while his plunging fingers relentlessly drove her, faster and faster, a frantic rhythm her body matched until, on an upwards buck, she screamed. A high-pitched wail of release, and eruption to out-do any one of her favorite island volcanoes.

Moving with lazy circles and caresses, he allowed her to ride out the violent climax, waited until her movements slowed, her breathing eased, and her clutch on his arm and shoulder relaxed.

It took several minutes before her breathing returned to normal and she flopped back. Her only noises then were tiny whimpers, reassuring him, because a non-talkative Laura terrified him, alerted him something was awry.

"That was...so...so much more...more than I ever dreamed being with a man could possibly be."

He snorted, leaned back, a spent man. "That, my innocent, was a teaser, a miniscule taste, of the pleasure to be enjoyed between a man and a woman."

She pushed up to sit beside him. Her hand touched his face, a gentle caress which undid him as much as any of her explosive screams of appreciation.

"Forgive me, for my selfishness."

Unable to see her face, and unable to comprehend the meaning behind her words, he frowned. "It's never selfish to find pleasure at another's hand, love."

"No, but you didn't...you didn't..."

Her hand touched his chest and trailed downwards, towards his waistband, where it lingered, drumming and touching, a tantalizing inch from his bulging and painful erection.

The witch would assuredly kill him tonight, one way or another.

"Ahem!" He flattened her hand with his, held it motionless while he fought to haul back on those continually slipping reins, and regain his composure. "I didn't find my own release, is that it?"

"Yes. And don't laugh at me, Richard. I may be a beginner pupil, but I do know men find it extremely painful. Um, if, ah, they don't do...you know, what I did."

"Ah, yes, you're a quick study, my sweet. Passion runs hot in your Jamison blood." He placed a tender and lingering kiss in the center of her palm. Cleared his throat. "Although my gratification may have been postponed, I nevertheless gained an enormous amount of satisfaction hearing, and helping, you reach your peak. To know you were so aroused, so eager to experience those things with me, here, for your first time. Well, it swells a man's head. Makes him feel ten feet tall. And with you, it was special."

"You mean because we called a truce? Our pretending to be friends instead of arch enemies."

"Not that, no. Deep down, you and I have always understood our bond, even if no one else has. We know it's too strong to ever be broken. Our families believe it to be a catastrophe our temperaments clash so often." Lifting her hand again, he trailed kisses from her wrist upwards along her arm. "For my part, I find our arguments are often the most exciting part of my day."

"After tonight, I agree." Her sigh puffed out against his palm. "Our times together can never be called boring."

Feeling around, he groped for their clothes. Leaning over to help him, one bare breast brushed his cheek. A mistake, a huge mistake, with his nerves so on edge, with his arousal still in full force. He stiffened and groaned. Planted his palms firmly on the blanket and willed himself not to lift them, not to touch the lemon-scented flesh so close to his nose.

One long sniff was all he allowed himself before he turned his head, pretended it hadn't happened, though the memory of a sweet-smelling breast pressed to his cheek would see him toss and turn during many a night to come.

Daylight seemed too far distant.

Too many long tense hours to pass before then. So the moment the sky lightened and the surrounding blackness started to recede, he shook Laura awake, perhaps more roughly than necessary. Better to distance himself now and indicate, in the clear and precise fashion he excelled at in business dealings, how they would proceed when facing the outside world. Reality awaited them and, loathe as he was to step into it, he knew they must, and quickly.

"Wake up. It's time to go."

He waited until she stirred and opened her eyes, looked up at him. Pushing herself into a sitting position, she reached up as if to touch his face.

"You can see me this morning."

He nodded. "A little. My vision is blurred, though I can now distinguish shapes, which is a blessing."

"Thank goodness. Hopefully, that indicates no lasting damage."

"Indeed. Though, if I was blind, my sisters would no longer be able to accuse me of burying myself in newspaper stock reports each morning."

She stared at him, blankly.

He sighed. "I meant it as a jest, Laura. Obviously, there'd be major inconveniences to my being blind. But come now." He offered his hand to help her stand. "We need to find our way out of this rubble before those men return. If the find no bodies, they may convince themselves, and their employers, that the lights in the office were nothing to be concerned about. A trick of the moonlight."

"I hope you're right."

He sighed, and hoped for that small piece of good fortune as well. Normally, he held an almost arrogant confidence in his own abilities to unravel the intricacies of puzzles. Generally, he could fire his mind in several directions at once, a handy trait when he needed to think like others. Such as the two criminals who'd too soon be unbarring the warehouse's door.

"Their coarse language," she was saying, "indicates they live in one of the areas around Cheapside. Perhaps nearer the docks."

He heard in her voice a frown, knowing she'd puzzle over their inflections until she decided in exactly which area they resided. Her ear for voices was as remarkable as her nose for scents. Many times he'd witnessed her astounding a group of acquaintances by detecting the precise area in which they'd passed their childhood. And after listening to a mere few minutes of their speech.

"Your skill amazes me."

He pictured her shrug, the one she gave whenever he, or her multitude of persistent admirers, paid her compliments. And again, her sense of inferiority stirred his irritation with her. "Why will you not accept compliments with good grace? Why don't you ever believe I mean the ones I offer?"

Her trill of laughter annoyed him further, with its obviously false note. "Richard, I've listened to you pay compliments of the same ilk to numerous other ladies. Naturally, I assume yours to me are offered in the same vein as all the others. Pretty words spoken to entrance. To lure with your charms. To draw the next conquest to your bed, for another meaningless encounter."

"Ha! I didn't speak pretty words last night, yet you succumbed to my charms, quite willingly, as I remember it." He let his anger deflate. "And, my love, our encounter was far from meaningless. At least, on my part."

He heard her loud swallow. Waited for a word of agreement, a crumb thrown to a waiting hungry bird.

"Let me bathe your eyes before we leave."

Ah, his wishes weren't to be. He tried to catch her hand, but grasped only air. Blast this woman. Another conversation he'd not wanted to start, yet when started, he became obsessed with seeing it through to the end. With hearing a truthful answer from her. And yet another time, when she'd avoided a direct answer with an adroitness born of extensive experience evading rakes and roués and every other sort of unsuitable men her brothers warned her away from.

Yes, yes, especially him. So why, then, did he continue to wait for her to speak a kind word to him, a word of encouragement, and a word of truth?

She bathed his eyes with blessedly cool water and led him by the hand through the maze of upended crates and spilled barrels.

Sight came and went in bursts of gray and white, shapes moved and sometimes formed into substance, but without her guidance he'd have turned black and blue from tripping over obstacles. Even so, they banged shins and stubbed toes often enough to cause them both considerable discomfort.

"Now, I'm putting my trust in you to lead us out. Trust in yourself, Laura. Use your remarkable gift and open your senses to the smells around us. I know you can distinguish the scents, separate the smells. Fruits, vegetables–"

"Wine. Barrels of wine along the walls."

He stayed quiet beside her several times while she did what he'd asked, opened her acute senses, and inhaled the odors swirling around them. Then, when she decided which way they should go, he followed as meekly as a lamb.

Greatly relieved to reach the tunnel's end, they halted in increasing morning light to haul in lungful after lungful of fresh clean air. They repeated the process several times before righting themselves, and their clothing, and retracing their step down the alley. Luck was on their side, as the narrow streets remained deserted, allowing them to walk, heads down, as if they belonged in a dirty alley in dockside, towards the adjoining street and his still waiting coachman.

Not until Laura was delivered, unharmed, at her kitchen door, and to all intents and purposes unobserved, did he take his first free breath. He'd deliberately kept his farewell brief, unbending and formal, while he'd repeated his familiar mantra.

Better to keep his distance. Better she thought him incapable of sustaining any real emotion. Better she recalled his fondling as a remedy to her fear of the dark. Better she clung to no dreams concerning the future.

He spent the entire carriage ride home, plus the hours remaining of night before he rose from his bed, plus a long breakfast at which his sisters required his presence, berating himself. Convincing himself he'd acted correctly. For both of them. The course he'd chosen, allowing her a sample and then retreating, had been the right one.

A gentleman's path. The noble road from the one more experienced in such situations. The only route he could travel, and still leave Laura free. Free to make future decisions about a future husband based on her initial taste of seduction. Free to pursue happiness with another man. A man who would be better suited...

Bloody hell!

If he couldn't even deceive himself into accepting the utter rot he'd been advocating, he'd little, or no, hope of fooling Laura. A woman who saw through all his outer trappings faster than her elder sister calculated a complicated column of mathematical figures. Easier than Lottie attracted men. Quicker than Aunt Aggie's grab for the plate of cream cakes.

Unfortunately for his peace of mind, Lady Laura Jamison was the singular female capable of peeling away his outer layers and exposing his secret. She was the one woman who attacked every obstacle in her path, including him, with the doggedness of the train engines her brother designed to chug up hills.

He retreated from her, often, through fear. Cold, raw terror of her seeing his entire naked self and not liking what she saw. Rejecting him as no other woman had ever done.

To himself he admitted it. He wanted her, needed her. But he'd resolved never to have her, not in that way, not trapped in marriage with him. Not tied forever to a man who could barely read the words on a page by the time he was twenty. To someone as courageous and intelligent as her, he'd never admit his failings.

Her scorn would kill his soul.

Chapter Thirteen

Laura lay back in her bed, reveling in the comfort and softness after so many hours spent in a cramped position on a cold hard floor. However, something seemed different, and left her lonely, unsettled. She knew what that sensation of loss meant, yet remained afraid to name the sentiment, even to herself. Richard made her feel whole, safe, and yet wanted, all at the same time.

Ooh! She thumped another hollow into the middle of her pillow, unable to doze, and wished Becca slept in her old room and could be roused for some middle-of-the-night sibling confidences. When she'd surrendered to Cayle, her elder sister had given into passion, experienced great pleasure, even while she'd remained stubbornly determined not to marry the Duke.

Now it seemed to Laura she was destined to follow her older sister's example. She longed to give in to passion, too. Each time Richard touched her, the yearning grew stronger. Yet, because of some asinine male twisted logic, he pulled back at the last moment. If only she could do what Becca did, and force Richard's hand.

She needed help. Leaping from the bed, she grabbed her robe, slid her feet into slippers and ran down the corridor, flinging open Lottie's door.

"Wake up, little sister. Time for another Jamison plot."

Lottie's head rose from beneath the coverings: tussled, blonde, and unbelievably beautiful.

Laura pointed at her. "Yes, that's what I need. You must tell me how to achieve that look you carry about always. The one for a glimpse of men grovel at your feet."

Her sister flicked back a swathe of curls and frowned. "What look?" She glanced at the window. "The sun is barely up. Must we have this discussion now?"

"Yes, it's vital that I start on my campaign straight way. Before anyone else digs their claws in to deeply."

At that, Lottie shot straight upwards in bed, reaching for a shawl to wrap around her shoulders.

"Well, it's about time you decided to take stronger action regarding Wonderful Winchester. Before that conniving countess…"

she gave an exaggerated shudder, "...sucks the soul right out of his body."

"You've been writing another gruesome chapter in your gothic novel, haven't you? No, don't bother answering, Guilt is written all over you face. You know Michael is terrified his baby sister will turn into one of those garish women who haunt the library circles around the City, begging to be allowed to read their latest masterpiece aloud. The type that stays awake all night hunched over a writing tablet, and creates lurid tales of murder and mayhem that scare little children."

Lottie clasped her stomach and rolled from side to side on the bed, laughing uncontrollably. "Thank you so much for that oh-so-charming and deflating description of me. And Papa worried that my looks may give me an inflated opinion of myself. No chance of that with four siblings."

Laura waved a hand in the air as she grinned at her stunning sister. "I shall allow you to wallow in the compliments gentlemen pay to your looks, but only a concerned sister would prevent you from becoming too full of your own self-importance."

They stared at each other, then collapsed into uncontrollable gales of laughter.

After they had finally recovered, Laura said, "Now back to planning my strategy. And by the by, that uncanny thing you do," she circled her finger next to her temple, "with reading minds. It can also be very sinister. You knew, even before I spoke, that my plot concerned Winchester and that...that feline pants chaser."

Her sister merely nodded, not explaining as usual. Lottie expected the family, if no others, to accept her gift without question. The family were also privy to the number of hours Lottie spent attending lectures and pouring over scientific and philosophical treatises on every aspect of phrenology and many other emerging sciences.

Instinct might lead Lottie into conclusions about people's actions and wishes very quickly, but it was intense hours of study and hard work that enabled her to predict accurately the outcomes of these actions.

"I've been considering the idea that I could do the same thing as Becca did. It worked wonderfully well for her."

Lottie chuckled. "That thing which would include driving Winchester to the edge of insanity and then, when his mind is in complete turmoil, seducing him into your bed, and then waving him goodbye? That thing?"

Laura jumped up and down on the bed and grinned. "Yes, exactly that. Richard will be so stunned by my seizing the initiative and seducing him, that he simply will not have time to do his normal move."

Lottie titled her head to the side and considered. "And what is his normal? Oh, I see. You mean the way he constantly advances and retreats in your presence.

"Precisely! One moment the man is like another over-protective brother, sermonizing on everything I do, arguing over every inconsequential subject–"

"And the next he rides to your rescue like a gallant knight on a white charger."

Lottie clasped her hand to her breast and sighed in theatrical fashion.

"So distressing to have a gentleman who is so besotted with one, that he regularly makes a complete cake of himself in front of his family and peers by rushing in where angels fear to tread to ensure your safety. So distraught is he at the mere thought that some harm or distress may come to the woman he loves, that he follows her like an avenging angel and draws his sword to face all combatants."

Laura glared at her sister and ignored her playacting. "Rubbish. You are confusing me with Becca, when Cayle charges in to play her white knight. Richard is more like a … a confused military regiment. Not knowing when to advance and when to retreat, and messing up the whole situation because he's forever tripping over me in his comings and goings."

"Oh, dear, poor Richard. A military regiment. How amusing. The one thing he does have in common with one of those is that he has more intelligence in his little finger than many regiments of men have between them."

"I will give you that. His grasp on situations is unbelievably quick. His decisions are made like lightning."

"Except when it comes to courting our Lively Laura, it seems." Aunt Aggie's voice startled them as she walked slowly into the chamber.

"Auntie," Lottie said. "We didn't mean to disturb you."

She settled her considerable derriere into Lottie's bedside chair before she spoke again. "We shall all endeavor to help you...ensnare the man you want, Laura, especially if it is Winsome Winchester."

Laura groaned. "Perhaps it is a bad idea. Much as I want to experience a little…" She broke off and glanced at her aunt, her liberal-minded aunt, but still her supposed chaperone.

"Yes, yes, Laura. We do understand what it is you want to experience and naturally, I feel obliged to warn you of the consequences of letting things go too far with any gentleman. But in this instance we are discussing Winchester, who has always been a particular favorite of mine–"

"Auntie," Laura interrupted. "We do recall that it was you who named him Winsome, and we do understand how much you admire him, but–"

"That is the point I am trying to make, if you do not rush me."

Both girls covered their faces and groaned. Luncheon would be served before Auntie reached her point.

Lottie faced her aunt with a sweet smile. "We need to formulate our plan for Laura, Auntie, as we would not want you to miss your breakfast."

"Oh, no, no. That would never do," the older lady fussed. She turned to Laura. "You have spent many, many hours trying to put into practice your theory and sniff out a suitable husband, by using the pheromones in his odor. Or should one call it his scent?"

She fluttered her hand. "No matter. And I understand why you girls hold such strong desires to test the waters with men before you will even considering marrying any one of them. The women we meet at the Society share so many horrid stories about their marriages and other…uh… relationships, and they all agree on the one fact that, when a woman marries she becomes the possession of her husband." She reached out a hand to each of the girls and patted their hands. "And, my dears, your own parent's marriage was a disastrous example for impressionable young people. Your father continually disappears, leaving his women behind to fend for themselves. Not that you haven't all coped admirably, but some, if not all, of that duty generally falls to the eldest male of the household."

Laura rolled her eyes at Lottie and shuffled up the bed to rest her back against the bedhead next to her sister. They settled in for a lengthy discourse, knowing from experience that rushing their aunt's rambling stories usually led to even more convoluted explanations, and even more time spent awaiting the conclusion.

For, inevitably, their aunt's summations of a situation held wise counsel. The time it took to be given this counsel drove even a saint, and their local clergymen, to impatience.

"Therefore, I do understand why you show such extreme caution when choosing a gentleman with whom you may be spending the better of part of your life, and I do comprehend how testing a man's prowess in the sensual areas, before being tied to that one person, appeals to you."

She drew in an enormous breath and continued, "However, in this instance, I feel it is past time that you took matters into your own capable hands, and arranged a date and a place to compromise Winchester and settle the matter once and for all, instead of all this pretense of seeking out other men and testing their aromas also."

Disregarding the open-mouthed expressions of shock on her nieces' faces, Aunt Aggie charged on like a runaway horse. "Everyone accepts that the two of you are soul mates–"

"But we argue constantly."

"Adds to the spice of marriage. Plus, everyone understands you'll marry one day–"

"But neither of us wants to marry."

"Everyone also knows, deep down, you're both far too conventional to disregard society's rules completely."

"But he wants to marry someone who is the complete opposite from me. Someone sweet, docile, dim-witted and–"

"Everyone knows men make those absurd statements because intelligent ladies scare them witless. Yet, if they trip up and marry a clueless chit, they're bored to tears within weeks." She pushed herself to her feet. "I'm away to break my fast, while you discuss details of how, and when, and where, we shall surprise Winchester." She rubbed her chubby hands together with glee. "Oh, such delightful fun. So reminds me of when I set out to compromise my own darling husband. Force him into marrying me. He proclaimed it the cleverest thing I ever achieved."

After their aunt left, the girls sat in silence for several minutes.

"Did our chaperone truly give me permission to pursue whatever I want? And to use whatever means to secure it?"

"Well, no one has ever called our chaperone *conventional*," Lottie remarked dryly.

The girls talked, throwing out one idea after another, until the maid came to helped them dress their hair.

When she walked into the breakfast room later, Laura was no closer to a solution. She and Lottie had run through a list of several different ways, and venues, for a seduction. She'd discarded them all. Not being completely shed of all propriety just yet, she didn't want her reputation to be tarnished permanently. Whatever she decided, she must handle it in as discreet a manner as possible.

Her stomach fluttered, and she placed a hand over the butterflies dancing there. Perhaps she could have what she had, deep down, always wanted, yet denied: a chance to sample the seductive powers of one of London's most renowned lovers.

She knew his reputation. Had read every tit-bit the gossip papers reported in the last few years. Secretly followed his life since he'd grown into adulthood, moved away and not visited so regularly. Despite the danger involved, Richard drew her as obsessively as a dull moth drawn against its will to a bright flame. So much so, he'd become the ideal candidate on whom to test her latest theory about an ideal man, or hopefully, husband. Neither of them was rushing into a permanent association, no matter the dreams and aspirations her auntie had voiced.

Laura's scientific studies had long convinced her that smelling a man's pheromones, testing his aroma, and comparing it to hers or other females, could assist in her search for an ideal mate. A husband who wouldn't cause problems like the spouses of other women she'd spoken with at the shelter.

Becca's old suitor had revealed his true colors by joining forces with the Syndicate, and then attempting to force the Jamisons to cooperate. Using coercion, or any other means. She sighed.

So many men became tyrants when handed even a small amount of control, women were always placed in a precarious situation in a marriage. However, by conducting an initial test on her chosen partner's sweat, she'd be able to estimate beforehand how likely he was to violent tendencies. Added to her tests, she'd ask Lottie to use her skills as a phrenologist to run her hands over the bumps and lumps in a man's head.

Lottie could predict very accurately which way a man leaned. Towards a quiet sensitive nature, or anger and violence. Between them, she hoped to determine how far a man could be pushed before his temper rose, before he resorted to verbals or physical abuse.

If he was likely to press his advantage if he could push a woman into a compromising situation. And, with the Jamisons' newfound wealth after Becca's magical touch with the share market, it was vital to discover how long a man would retain his honorable qualities if he was squeezed into a financial corner; was within a hand's breadth of gaining something he wanted.

Now her palms sweated. She played a dangerous game. Torn between the logic of waiting longer for the correct-smelling man or grabbing, with both hands what her body urged her to take now.

Him. Richard.

He was the only one to have ever had butterflies do flips in her stomach, or made her palms go clammy at the thought of him. Her previous hints, subtle as they were, that they could become lovers— only as a test—had horrified him.

Time to bring forth her Jamison side and conquer. She scowled at her rapidly cooling eggs. If the conniving Countess managed to attract Richard to her bed, several times if rumor had it correctly, surely she could easily manage to lure him there once?

Unfortunately, getting there didn't present the problem. Keeping him there was. An image of him tied to the posts of her bed while she ravaged his body filled her mind. She sighed. Small problem: she had no idea what ravaging entailed.

"I think I shall pay a visit to Madame Faberge's establishment this morning," she announced to her sister and aunt. "Before her house becomes…uh…too busy later in the day."

"I thought Michael had forbidden you girls from visiting that woman's premises ever again, after Becca rescued Cayle from that dreadful fire," Aunt Aggie said, her ferocious frown for once resembling a forbidding duenna's. "My dear girl could have been burned alive."

"Michael forbade Becca from returning there, Aunt, not me."

"I fear your brother will consider little difference in that argument. He will be angry at any of his sisters visiting Madame openly."

"Madame has pressing accounting issues that I am obliged to attend to in Becca's stead."

"Fustian, Laura. Everyone knows how much you detest accounting issues."

Lottie grinned. "I think Laura's meaning is that the visit is to assist her plans to bring Winchester to an accounting."

Aunt Aggie beamed. "Ah, well that is a different matter entirely. You wish Madame's advice on how to persuade a reluctant suitor. I understand why you would wish to do this, because it would be shameful to allow that hussy, the Countess, to best a Jamison. But do go quickly. Go early before there are many people on the streets. And have the coachman wait around the corner from Madame's establishment. And take our special footman as protection. And wear a veil. It would not do for anyone to see you visiting a notorious brothel. And if your father ever hears of this adventure and asks for details, do please tell him that I knew nothing of any plans to corrupt any gentleman. For some ridiculous reason, he thinks me an unsuitable guide for you girls."

Laura bade them goodbye with a smile upon her face. Today promised to be a day of new adventures.

She only hoped Richard thought so too.

Chapter Fourteen

Richard departed his house early, intending to begin his full day by scrutinizing the latest Stock Market reports at Threadneedle Street. Abnormally for him, neither the battle of wits needed for negotiations at the Exchange, nor the fiery discussion at the nearby coffee houses roused his enthusiasm. Heavy thoughts weighed on his mind, so much so that when he rendezvoused with his cousins, Brain and Tony, they regarded him with strange looks.

"Is something bothering you, Winchester?"

He scowled at Tony. "Nothing. Shall we box?"

For the next hour, he worked off some of his frustration with round after round in the ring at Gentleman Jackson's Boxing Salon, even sparring with his cousins in a more aggressive manner than normal. Time after time, he challenged them alternately.

Finally, when the three of them dripped sweat and could barely stay upright, Brian held up a hand to him. "Winchester, we surrender. Whatever worm is eating at your brain today, we can only hope half beating us to a pulp has helped ease some of those demons."

They walked to the benches at the wall and collapsed in a row, panting for air.

"However," his brother said, wiping his brow on a length of linen and hauling in several deep breaths, "we'd at least like to know why we are being used as punching bags."

He shook his head, his own chest heaving from the intensive bouts of exercise. More than his usual definitely. More than necessary. "I apologize. No need to drag you into my gloom."

"We volunteered to become your means of escape from whatever bothered you when you arrived. The ferocious look on your face warned us our session would be hard. We accepted that. Now explain why."

He raised his hands in a gesture of confusion, of indecision, of vulnerability. "A decision I've made is proving harder to follow that I imagined it would be. Difficult to keep telling myself my reasons are sound when–" Breaking off, he dropped his head to his hands and rested his elbows on his knees.

"Would this decision concern a woman?" Tony, always the most intuitive, could be depended upon to jump straight to the heart of the problem. "Or rather, a lady?"

He twisted his head towards Tony who sat on one side of him, peering down at his face. "You know?"

"Not hard to guess. All the signs have been there for several weeks."

"What signs? What lady? Are we discussing the Countess?"

Brian, though a likeable man and a good friend, lacked his brother's insight. It remained a family joke that Brian needed all aspects of relationships, and the nuances and emotions associated with them, pointed out to him in a direct manner. He continually failed to notice by himself.

Richard turned his head towards Brian. "This has nothing to do with the Countess. Our affair finished long ago and I have no intention of reigniting it."

"The countess seems to hold a differing view on that," Brian remarked dryly. "Unfortunately, she's regaled her bosom friends— the closest hundred that she's reconnoitered with accidentally, yet on purpose—with her view that it is only a matter of time until you come to your senses. No one refuses her, you see, so she assumes you shall be begging her to resume your relationship."

"Damn all greedy, grasping women to hell."

"Moreover…" Brian continued, giving him a wary eye.

He clenched his fists clenched, gritted his teeth, hoped the heat rising in face remained unnoticeable.

"…The entire London upper ten thousand now believes our infamous bachelor, the Earl of Winchester, angles after her favors, perhaps even the hand in marriage of the Countess. They assume that, as a renowned enticer of women, you'd be loath to acknowledge that you'd lowered yourself to crawling after any woman. Your lofty status, as one of the few eligible men in the City with the audacity and nerve to bed any woman he desires, would crumble in a week."

"Not every woman I desire," he muttered darkly, hiding his mounting wrath by fixedly staring at his feet.

"As we have departed the ring, I beg you to not start swinging punches again," Tony said, "for obligation forces me to divulge this. Your devious past paramour set it about that your current distraction with another lady, a young chit, will prove to be a passing fancy.

Your more experienced mistress–"

After a growled exclamation of annoyance, Richard emphasized, "Past mistress."

"She declares the lady's naïve attempts to hold your interest past the time of your temporary guardianship will never bear fruit. You'll be sniffing around her more experienced skirts within days. No innocent can match her own skilled charms. In bed or out of it."

When Richard glared and uttered another low growling noise, Tony held up his palm. "Or so your past lover has the City believing."

"May the bragging bitch be struck down by lightning for spreading such lies amongst the ton's gossips? How dare she smear any young lady's name, or character, for no good reason and without a shred of proof?"

"Indeed. These fabrications—if they're lies about you resuming your liaison--"

Richard made his opinion of the stories clear, by a series of low angry noises and a fast nod of his head.

"These untruths, these rumors," Tony said with a sigh, "may devastate the standing of the poor young woman involved."

Brian scowled at one, then the other. "For goodness sake, tell me which lady."

Richard and Tony ignored his question.

Tony asked another of his own. "So, dear cousin, why are you so afraid to commit yourself to a woman you so obviously care about? I can guess at what stops you, but still, if you wish to unburden yourself, we are your friends, Richard."

"And your family," Brian added, still looking confused by the conversation.

"Families. Ha! Therein lies the crux of my problem."

He looked between his cousins. "You two know more than anyone how families can set a terrible example for anyone considering marrying. For years I've avoided marriage, as I saw my own father—your uncle—impregnate my mother on such a regular basis that she died from the number of miscarriages she suffered. One too many pregnancies. Why she never refused him her bed, I'll never understand."

Tony gave one of his philosophical shrugs. "Love conquers all."

Of all the cousins, Tony thought and dwelled the most deeply over matters such as interactions between the families and the support each member should show for the others. Recently, Richard's appreciation of this cousinly support and counsel had increased enormously.

With Sherwyn away, Brian and Tony took on the role of his close confidants. Perhaps unburdening himself to them would clarify his own mind, untangle his feelings, as their insights into marriages came from similar situations to his own. Peerage couples and their related families tended to carry on unusual relationships.

Most contracted initially for the sake of blending titles and wealth, some became cold, some distant, some degenerating into complete family feuds. Unions based on love appeared rarely and even when that happenstance occurred in the beginning, the false and formal lifestyle the genders were forced into often drove a wedge between couples.

"Surely my mother could not have wanted to risk pregnancy over and over in order to please my father."

Brian leaned across to lay a consoling hand on his back. "I'm afraid, Richard, as we were all too young when your mother passed to understand the circumstances, we may never know the answers to those questions." Brian's thick brown brows arrowed together and his forehead gathered deep creases as he frowned, his habitual expression when concentrating hard. "Though, 'pon my word, I never heard a cross word between your pater and mater when we played together as children. As far as I recall, your parents acted as though they were besotted with each other all the time."

"The majority of couples in our extended family's history," Tony said, "tended to love each other so much, and wished for such a large tribe of children, it endangered the women's lives."

"By the stories, the pairs that loathed each other were the minority," Brian said, "Pairs such as our father and our now banished step-mother. I still shudder thinking about how much harm Julia tried to cause our brother, and all the Jamisons. Incredible that she teamed up with Lord Hetherington. We'll never live down that embarrassment to our dying days."

His brother nodded agreement. "Yes. Thank goodness society forgave us, the St. Martin men, for her misdemeanors. By trapping Lord Hetherington, we prevented hundreds of minor investors from losing their savings to that unscrupulous and manipulative consortium."

"Trouble is," Richard told them, "we're now tackling the same problem all over again with Lord Hetherington's insane wife. Until we can apprehend her, for the second time, and ensure she is institutionalized permanently, none of us is safe. She could have us all in her sights as targets to be killed. Murder didn't disturb her before. I doubt that disposing of a few members of our family, or the Jamison family, would do much more than give her a few moments' pleasure."

"If we redouble our efforts, we may still have this mystery solved before our brother and his bride return. Sherwyn's dealt with enough. Time we settled this once and for all."

The three of them discussed the latest information they'd uncovered, shared snippets of gossip that might prove relevant, and agreed on their next plan of attack over the upcoming week. Brian, by recruiting more friends to the cause, could cover more ground around the lower class districts, the brothels and the gaming halls. Lady Hetherington's money source was too full, too frequent, for it not to be supplemented primarily from one of the City's vice areas.

"London accommodates roughly one hundred and fifty thousand brothels," Richard said, groaning at the enormity of the task ahead of them. "And we've checked into …how many? Not a fraction of that number. We'll never locate Lady H. Not before the next share allotment is due for release, anyway, and if we miss that opportunity, she'll likely buy up more than we can afford. Therefore, we may face a future with that crazy woman owning more of the new railway line than we do. I shudder to think what would happen them. What inane decisions she may make, or which government officials she may apply pressure to."

"It seems likely that she is already applying pressure in high-up government circles. Possibly by blackmailing men holding mid-level posts in government offices."

Richard moaned and shook his head again. "I fear in this instance, we may be defeated." His two cousins stared at him, then displayed their confusion by glancing at each other and shrugging. "What silent communication just passed between you two?"

"We wondered why your normal cheery confidence–"

"Plus your everlasting and often exhausting zeal–"

"Not to mention your doggedness over completing every endeavor you commence. Well, we do wonder why those ingrained traits forsook you at this crucial point in our investigation.

Especially," Tony said with emphasis, "when a satisfactory completion of this situation means removing a certain young lady from danger. Ensuring her future safety allows your own consciousness to rest easier. It also, and by your displays in front of the family this is something for which you yearn, allows you to distance yourself from the aforesaid person for whom you hold responsibility–"

"Enough!" Brian scowled between his brother and his cousin. "I appreciate that I may be a little slow to evaluate the same nuances that my brother does when it concerns the female gender–"

"A little slow? Why just last evening Tessa Prendergast invited you to stroll in the conservatory with her, Brian, and you replied that it would be too risky as the damp atmosphere might make her curls go even more awry."

"Simply trying to be helpful."

Richard and Tony burst out laughing. Richard nudged his cousin in the arm.

"Tessa's a known bed-hopper, Brian. That's the customary lure she throws out to invite a new man to indulge in a fast and furious romp with her, while her husband remains occupied in the card room." He burst into more gales of laughter. "By speaking of her unruly curls and not accepting her blatant offer, Tessa's self-image may be so badly dented she'll never recover her composure. I'd wager no man has ever refused her in quite such a way before."

Brian looked at him and gestured in a vague way. "You mean…You've accompanied her to a conservatory."

"Yes, although, in my case, it was the butler's pantry during a dinner her husband hosted for his Parliamentary cronies."

"Good Lord! During dinner? And you weren't exposed by the serving staff?"

"I did say romps with Tessa tended to be hasty, didn't I?"

"Mine with her took less than the time it takes to ask a lady to dance."

Brian's glance spun to his brother. "You too? My brother? And my younger one at that. Blather it! You two show me up as a complete slow-top when it comes to the fairer sex." His brows met in the middle again, no doubt churning over his missed opportunity.

"Take heart, Brian. Nothing's fair when it comes to Tessa. Positive man-eater. Don't fret, she'll not approach you again. Fish that got away, that sort of analogy. She'll want to prove no man's immune to her charms."

'Yes, well, cousin, if I have a man-eater after me, so do you. The Countess abhors your rejection of her, especially publicly. She's determined to show her *bon amiss* she can reel you in anytime she wishes. Hook, line, and sinker."

"May we dispense with the fishing metaphors and return to our more pressing problems, as luncheon calls. I've been invited to join Porch ester at White's for a succulent slab of beef and a burgundy or two. His Lordship is one of the dozen gentleman who refused the advances, the most persistent advances, of a business man who approached them all at their weekly meeting of the Anthropological Society. This unidentified man-of-affairs claimed he represented an anonymous party, who held the rights to land a new railway would need to cross in order to extend the line approximately seven miles from Ravenglass to Dalegarth, near Boot. Several of the men, including Porchester, had already committed their next allotment of money to be speculated to you, Richard."

Richard dipped his head in acknowledgement. "So those men said no straight away. Other declined for various other reasons. Apparently, the man then became agitated, swearing and claiming he'd be killed if he hadn't filled his quota. They were clueless as to what this signified but, thankfully, Porchester thought to send me a message as he'd heard we were seeking just this sort of information."

"Well done, Tony. This could be the link we've been missing. Some clue as to what sort of people Lady H is using and where and how they are being recruited." Richard grinned. "I may recover my optimism today after all." He slapped his younger cousin on the back.

Tony glanced at his pocket watch and grimaced. "Drat it. I've only ten minutes before I must depart to dress for White's, and Porchester is a stickler for time." He fixed his intense and all-too-knowing stare on Richard. "So, care to share what bothers you so deeply about your latest dalliance?"

"There's no dalliance!" As soon as he'd snapped out the answer, Richard regretted it.

His tone, if not the sour-sounding words, conveyed his anxiety. "I've never done anything so despicable as dally with an unmarried and gently-bred lady." He rolled his eyes. "Most especially when I've made promises to her male relations to lay down my life and protect her from rogues such as myself." He stared at his cousins with a jaundiced eye. "And you two."

"Not fair to include me in that description. I can hardly be classified as a scoundrel, if I failed to notice the bait Tessa dangled under my nose last evening. A rogue would have obliged her and taken advantage of her advances."

"By that description of a rogue, I am indeed one," Richard said with a mournful sigh.

"Ah, I see," Tony said with a huge grin.

"Luscious Laura has also thrown herself into your arms, unable to resist your well-noted charms, and by necessity you've refused her no doubt tempting offers. Dreadful dilemma."

He ignored the scowl directed his way and grinned, before continuing in a teasing tone, "Stay strong, adhere to your morals, but wallow in so much misery that you're compelled to box for hours at a time to relieve your rapidly increasing frustration. Your other alternative is to seduce the woman you're obsessed with. Make her your mistress."

"Tony, cousin or not, I'll still plant my fist in your smug face."

Tony laughed. "Idiot! Of course you can't make her your mistress, even if you have already seduced her–" He broke off and looked at him questioningly. Richard shook his head, aware that his expression betrayed him nonetheless.

"So, you haven't gone so far as to seduce her. Yet. Though, knowing how you feel about her, it's only a matter of time."

"Is this Lady Laura we're discussing?"

Now it was Brian who stared at him with an accusatory look. Again he nodded.

"Am I to understand that you hold feelings for Luscious Laura?"

"I may do, and please cease from using that derogatory name to describe her."

Both Brian and Tony laughed at him. "Might we remind you that it was you who coined that particular term to describe her ample assets?"

"At the time I didn't realize we may be attributing it to my future wife."

"Ah, the crux of your dilemma at last. To wed, or not to wed. That is the question."

"Now see here," Brian said, his face reddening. "Tis not gentlemanly of any of us to discuss such a lovely lady this way."

"Brian, I realize you've always been slightly smitten with Lady Laura, but lately I've also come to the understanding that my own feeling for her are somewhat more than that."

"Never say the Escaping Earl, the one who's adroitly avoided any talk of love and romance with all his previous lovers, has now succumbed to what we call the more feminine emotions. Never say you're in love."

He frowned, the word jarring somehow. "No, no, no. I'll freely admit to being in lust. Who wouldn't when Laura truly is magnificent? Love? Never!"

"Then the only obstacle to your future happiness that I can foresee," Tony said, leaning back and crossing his legs an adopting an unconcerned pose, "is if the lady in question has more good sense than to want to marry you. Perhaps it is one of us she prefers, after all."

Tony's smug grin made Richard's fingers itch and his fist curl into a ball. His cousin judiciously slid a few inches further away along the wooden bench, although his grin didn't decrease. It widened.

A sharp chortle of laughter was forced from between his clenched lips as he watched his cousins' reactions to his news. "I suppose I may as well reveal all, as you'll both badger me about it for days otherwise."

"Wise decision."

"My dreams have been haunted by Laura for weeks now. But just when I'd decided to offer her marriage, stubborn and contrary Laura—"

"I find those her more endearing traits," Brian said, smiling at his brother. "Do you recall that evening, a year or so ago, when she slipped out of her home against her father's wishes to attend a meeting of the Council on Education?"

He looked at Richard. "Think you were still on the Continent. Villages, including the ones bordering the Jamison's estate, argued that schoolmasters needed to be paid more than a carpenter or blacksmith."

Tony laughed. "Yes, Laura was magnificent that evening. Like Joan of Arc. She demanded that the council increase teacher's pay, so a better class of person could be enticed into the situation. The Council members, all male of course, took offense at what they termed a slip of a girl issuing them orders, and the meeting deteriorated into a riot."

"Good Lord! I hadn't heard that particular story of her exploits. Though several others are enough to turn my hair gray. If we marry-- after we marry, I shall have to curtail her exploits."

Tony rose and grinning widely, slapped his cousin on the back. "I wish you good luck with that, but I fear you'll have as much chance as Sherwyn has of taming her elder sister."

Sitting in silence for a few moments, he reflected on the excitement he felt when becoming embroiled in arguments with Laura. Quick to concede defeat if proved wrong, she also stubbornly stuck to her principles in disputes about women's rights, the working conditions of children, or any other Chartist ideas she adopted.

He looked up at his cousin.

"In this case, she is being so contrary that she has declared herself willing, no, not just willing but eager to become my lover."

Brian's brows raised. Tony whistled.

Richard stood up and fixed them both with his sternest earl of several estate's intimidating glare. "I trust no word of this will ever pass your lips."

Brian appeared horrified. "Certainly not. I would never break a man's confidence that way."

Tony looked affronted yet his eyes twinkled with mischief. "Especially when it concerns a woman that our relative thinks he may someday be able to convince to marry him."

"Your faith in my ability to win fair maiden's hand is truly touching," he said, clasping his hands to his heart and allowing them to see his sarcasm.

"More to the point, we're all privy to Laura's mind-set about marriage. Her brothers have shared all the details about these experiments she carries out. Sniffing everyone. Done it to me several times."

"Really?" Richard raised a brow in query. "And what conclusion has she drawn after sniffing your person and, I assume, making those copious irritating observations in her ever-ready little notebooks?"

Brian smiled. "Oh, she's told me often enough what good friends we are–"

He took a menacing step towards Brian. "How good a friend?"

When Brian shrank back onto the bench and raised his hand to protect his face, he groaned and stepped back again. "Damnation.

Sorry, didn't mean to take another bite out of your hide."

"Understand, old man. When bitten by jealousy–"

"I'm not jealous!"

Both Brian and Tony nodded affably, though it was glaringly obvious they didn't believe a word of his denial. Not for an instant. Hell. Perhaps his feelings were written across his face, printed for all to read like a Fleet Street newspaper. He prayed only his close acquaintances had noticed the recent disturbance to his stability.

"Nevertheless, the problem remains that Laura will not cease with her observations, until she has found the perfect match for her criteria. A mate. Ridiculous idea. Like recording an animal's behavior, and matching it with an animal of similar temperament. I've tried to explain to her that it will never work."

"You mean she tackles it the way you do when putting that stallion of yours to mares. The way you fuss for weeks beforehand. You write letters to prospective owners of mares across the country. You study the horse parentages, and cross examine every groom over the characteristics and stamina of their sires and dames. You draw intricate charts of their pedigree and trace their ancestors back for generations to ensure a perfect coupling."

He threw up his hands and put his hand to his hips, glaring at Tony. "Fine. I concede there is some merit in her theory. And, yes, Laura uses similar classifications as those I use to breed my horses. But I tell you right here and now, I will not agree to Laura's demands and take the confusing minx to bed merely to satisfy her curiosity. Nor so she can cross another tested name off her ridiculously long list."

Brian laughed. "Yes, she's mentioned on several occasions that your scent is not quite right." He did that beetled-brow thing again and tilted his head to one side to peer at Richard. "Which seems terribly contradictory, when one considers it. Why would Laura insist on testing your bedroom prowess if she's already decided you're not going to be a marriage match?"

"That is what I cannot decipher. As a gentleman, I dare not trifle with her affections, nor her virtue."

"Michael and Jonathon will draw straws to see who challenges you to a duel."

"Oh, it won't come to that," Tony said, grinning. "Our brother will have already gutted him with his knife long before it comes to that."

"So reassuring! Thank you both for your assistance."

Tony placed a hand on his shoulder.

"If I was you, I'd take the delectable Laura to bed. Teach her all you know. Make her so eager for more, that she will forget all her notions of experimenting with other men–"

"Ooh! Thank you of also reminding me of that part of her plan. Rest assured, no other man will come within six feet of laying a hand on her."

"I should hurry then and secure her hand for yourself, because each time she is out in society, the crowd of worshipful admirers falling at her flirtatious feet thickens. Very soon, she'll decide an odor, a tang, attracts her correctly, according to her research and legends, even close to acceptability, and she'll sail forth with her plan to test that as yet unknown gentleman in her bed."

"Over my dead body."

"Oh, I'm sure Sherwyn could arrange that."

With those parting words, Tony and Brian walked towards the door. Richard gathered his coat and hat and followed them, but as he reached the door behind them, a messenger rushed towards him.

"My Lord. An urgent message from the lady waiting in the carriage outside. She wishes you to join her. Immediately."

Brian and Tony also halted as he asked the messenger, "Which lady?"

He bobbed his head. "Not rightly sure. 'er husband's an Earl. Big crest on side of 'er blue carriage."

"Ah, ha! It seems your determined previous mistress has tracked you to Gentleman Jackson's. This should prove interesting."

He scowled at Tony's grin. "Didn't you have a pressing appointment at White's?"

"Damnation, yes. Must be off. Sorry to miss the fun, though. Brian, be sure to regale me with the entire sordid tale later."

Winchester strode out of the boxing establishment, with Brian following, mentally comparing himself to an overworked steam engine. His anger rose, hot and humid, like a blast of compressed air tunneled through a pipe. How dared the woman? If it was that conniving Countess, her ears were about to receive a blistering blasting from him such as she'd never heard before.

Reaching the carriage, definitely hers, he grasped the door handle and threw open the door, intimidating the attending footman with the ferocity of his expression. He sprung inside and threw himself onto the seat opposite her.

"What is the meaning of this? And how did you know where I would be anyway?"

Seated with her the skirts of her fashionable gown spread wide, she gave him a look designed to portray innocence.

"I needed to see you, urgently, and I knew you always boxed here three morning a week. This is one of those mornings."

"Your intimate knowledge of my daily routine is enough to make me squirm in my seat, but any guesses I may make at why you might need to see me, in an urgent way, brings a sweat to my brow."

She trilled a laugh, a false, forced sound that twanged his taut nerves like the string of an over-tightened harp. "Oh, no! Please, you silly man."

She reached across, placing a gloved hand on his coat sleeve. He flinched, despite his best efforts to show her the implacable calm of a marble statue.

"Let me set your mind at rest."

Cold fingers, a sign of impending doom, sent shivers running up his spine. Her fingers tapping on his arm, though light, reminded him of a cat stalking a mouse and toying with it.

"Dispel any pressing concerns. The Earl hasn't connected us in any romantic way. You're not about to become a father."

She gave her version of a girlish giggle, a high-pitched whine that also grated.

"That thought never crossed my mind. The extreme precautions I take ensure it will never eventuate."

"Besides which, I'd never ruin my figure that way." She waggled a finger near his nose. "No, no, no, my love. We've much more important issues to discuss."

Here it came. The cat readying to pounce. Moving in for the kill.

"You and I, Richard, are alike. Two of a kind." She purred.

"We're nothing alike. Nothing. You're a greedy manipulative bitch. I'm not."

Her sucked-in breaths hissed and sizzled between them. "I suggest you play nicely with me, my lord, as I have something you'll definitely want." She smiled, a-mouser-anticipating-its-next-meal sort-of smug smile. "It concerns your newest lady-love, the overly-talkative one who sniffs at your skin like a bitch on heat."

"As I already explained, the only bitch I've spoken to recently is you. And I'm about to end this conversation, and any lamentable association we may have had in the past, right now."

He opened the carriage door and bent to leap out, anxious to be on the footpath where he could draw his first breath of clean air. Away from her suffocatingly sweet French perfume. Away from her clawing clutches. Away from her.

What he'd enjoyed about her—apart from the glaringly obvious thing of a willing female body thrust into his hands—he couldn't now fathom. Even on the occasions when she'd enticed him between her silken sheets and between her satiny thighs, he'd known. Deep down, he'd recognized the obsessive way she'd kept him there, clutched him, tethered him with guilt and tears and embroidered stories of her unhappy marriage. So why?

Because he'd understood that a woman so shallow, so false, could never affect him emotionally, never touch his heart, so giving in to her erotic demands was an easy option. Far easy than giving in to the deeper, more sensuous entanglement he faced with Laura.

If he surrendered. If he gave in to her. Or rather, to himself, and his own ever-growing desire for her. If he committed himself to Laura–

If. If. If.

If he did, it would be a body-and-soul, unswerving, faithful-to-the-day-he-died type of devotion. The idea scared the living hell out of him.

Trying to calm himself, he drew in another lungful of air. Ironic that the City's heavy, coal-dust ridden air seemed to him far more pure than the choking atmosphere in the carriage he'd left. He opened his eyes and directly in front of him stood Brian, an anxious expression on his face as he peered over Richard's shoulder at the carriage.

Damnation! He realized the cause of Brian's distress. The carriage lingered, an enlarged version of the dangerous feline seated inside. A jungle panther, sleek, slate black and stationary on the steel rutted roadway behind him. He eased in an edifying breath, before turning to face the still-open door of her elaborate equipage. The satisfied smile on the Countess's countenance, as she leaned out the window, warned him in advance. She beckoned to him with a crooked finger.

Without shifting, he said to Brian, "I fear the Countess failed to comprehend my last message."

"What did she want?" Brian murmured the question close to his ear.

"Me!"

"Bloody hell!"

"Exactly."

Steeling himself to not cause a disturbance in this busy area where many of his peers came and went on a constant basis from their own bouts of exercise, he took one step closer to the window. Dodging the rolled fabric blind, he pushed his head into her space and forced her to shift backwards on her seat, sliding a little more into the interior of the carriage.

Better! Much safer. No need for onlookers to glimpse her appearance, perhaps recognize her, nor, he hoped, for them to attach any importance to a conversation the Earl of Winchester held in the street with an anonymous figure in a coach.

"Was there something delaying your departure?"

"Oh, yes, my elusive love. You may think you can best me in this, but I hold the upper hand. A full house in this case."

She giggled again.

Out of the blue, he recalled why the noise ground on his nerves. It reminded him of the young girl who'd drowned on his estate two years previously, while running away from a group of lads who'd inadvertently frightened her. Poor demented child. After a dreadful birthing, her mother had died and the babe barely survived, and then, as the years passed, it became obvious that the child would never lead a normal life.

Still, her father and brothers doted on her for seven years and ignored her high-pitched giggles, screeches and other inappropriate noises, as did the entire village. Nobody held a forever-child responsible for her frequent outbursts or sometimes outrageous behavior. She was incapable of controlling her emotions in situations that overexcited her. Incapable of knowing right from wrong and good from bad.

How peculiar that the giggle from the Countess sounded much the same, an uncontainable outburst of inappropriate sentiment. Those blasted cold finger tickled his spine again. Blessed enhanced intuition, something that ran in his family, was fast becoming a nuisance.

"I love gamblers' vocabulary, don't you? But of course you do. As a constant speculator on the Stock Exchange, you gamble every day. So you understand that holding a full house puts me in the position of power."

"Is there a point to this diatribe?"

"As you've been so reticent to discuss this civilly here, this morning, I've changed my mind. If you wish to acquire the information I hold about your precious little flirt, you now need to visit me at my home."

"Out of the question!"

"Your choice, though possibly a dangerous one for the lady involved."

"How do I know you're not bluffing, to use another of your gambling terms?"

"To call my bluff and see my hands spread out, in all their naked glory–"

He frowned at her. "Are we still discussing information, or something else?"

Another of those irritating sniggers. She snapped her fan hard on his arm and he jerked backwards. "Naughty, naughty man. You'll need to call at my house at three sharp to unravel that little mystery."

She reached across and rapped hard on the open doorway of the coach, and the liveried footman standing at attention on the footpath sprang forward to fasten the door. The nasty-looking footman called to the coachman, who readied his horses with coarse shouts and slaps of leather reins. Left with no alternative, Richard and Brian moved quickly away, before the large coach lumbered into a swaying motion as he maneuvered into the stream of traffic on the crowded street. The surly sounding coachman continued to hurl abusive comments at anyone brave enough to cross his path.

"The immoral employer seems to keep equally nasty servants around her," Brian remarked, that pondering frown telling Richard that his cousin dwelt on something of importance. "One wonders why she carries so much force on her town coach."

Brian pointed to the back of the departing coach where another brute of a footman balanced on the back board, his scowling gaze riveted on them.

"Hum, now you mention it, an interesting situation. I'm certain she never carried such a show of brute strength with her before."

"So what did she want this second time?"

"Me."

"Bloody hell!"

Richard snorted. "You're repeating yourself. But once again, I agree with your summation of the situation."

"You'd not be idiotic enough to take her up on her proposition a second time." He looked him in the eye. "My brothers would never forgive me if I let you consider something so mindless without issuing you a severe warning."

"Don't fret, my friend. Mixing with the Countess may possibly have been the most foolish thing I've ever done in my life. I'd never dive into that cesspool again. Though I do wonder about those protectors of hers. Was it to impress me? To call me to heel?"

"More likely she is frightened of something. Or someone. Perhaps one of her other past lovers is threatening to reveal all to her husband. Though hard to imagine what he'd gain."

"In my opinion, nothing. The Earl is only too happy to have his wife taken off his hands. Leaves him in the clear to pursue his own rather peculiar little foibles."

"Oh, not another high-titled peer with strange bedroom habits."

"From what I understand, yes. The Earl frequents those bawdy houses that cater to a specific type of patron. Probably the reason he's never sired children with the Countess."

Brian sighed. "Seriously, I start to believe they should extend the number of padded rooms in Bedlam. Lock away the entire upper ten thousand."

Richard laughed. "It's all the inbreeding from previous centuries. Never works well with horse-breeding for many generations either. Can't see why it would prove any better with humans."

"Perhaps we should all refrain from siring any children."

A sudden picture of a brood of red-cheeked and dark-haired children playing around his feet flashed before his eyes. Another babe sucking from the breast of their mother. The woman looked up at him, her dark eyes glowing and giving a loving smile to him.

Laura's eyes, Laura's smile.

Of course it would be. He couldn't escape it, no matter how far he ran. He heaved in a deep breath. No other woman could fill the role of mother to his heir and his other children. Why not accept it and start making it a reality, instead of producing one feeble reason after another to avoid it?

"…Nevertheless," Brain was saying, "you must avoid the Countess entirely."

"I wish that were possible. The conniving woman dangled Laura's safety as bait in front of my nose, knowing I'd do anything to secure it."

"What are you talking about? What did she say about Lady Laura?"

"If I'm to discover something she knows, something concerning Laura, I must visit the Countess one last time. Today. At her home."

Brian shook his head. "Oh, no, no, no. Not a good idea. You have no idea what her plan is for you once she has you there."

"I must go. She knows that. Anything that involves Laura, involves me."

"Oh, hell. You're in deep, aren't you? You're in love with Laura."

Richard glared at him. "We've had this discussion. At present, I'm her friend. But I want to be her lover, her only lover. And I've decided to become her husband. And soon. As for love, I'll leave sentiments of that sort to those of a more poetic bent."

"Utter rot!" Brian grinned. "Deny it all you want. But you're already up to your ears in love with our Lovely Laura." His smile was replaced by a serious frown. He shook his head, his detested cowlick flopping across his forehead. "This visit this afternoon, it truly doesn't bode well. I should accompany you."

Richard laid his hand on his cousin's shoulder. "I appreciate your concern, but it's better I confront the Countess alone. If you're with me, she may not speak freely. Although, I do have a way you can assist me without actually entering the house."

He grinned at his cousin. "Are you and Tony any good at sweeping streets?"

As they walked away from Gentleman Jackson's, Richard outlined his new plan to Brian.

Chapter Fifteen

Laura rose from her chair beside Lottie's bed and collected three plates and teacups, the remains of their shared and rather early luncheon, a light repast they'd taken in the bed chamber to save Lottie and Aunt Aggie from another painful trip to the dining room.

After placing the crockery on a tray for the maid, she turned to look at her recuperating family members.

"I'm worried about both of you."

She looked towards her aunt, whose bruises on her arms had turned from black and blue to yellow and purple. Lottie's foot, wrapped in the doctor's tight bandage, was propped high on a mound of pillows. "Perhaps I should dispatch a messenger to Winchester and send my regrets. We can visit the Society another time."

"No need for that, my dear," her aunt reassured her. "We're both recovering perfectly well."

"One more day off my feet and the doctor says my ankle should be strong enough to start some light walking." Her sister grinned at her. "One might start to wonder if these delaying tactics are because you cannot face the Winchester at the moment. Did you two have another spat? If so, I'm sorry I missed it. I do adore seeing the sparks fly between you two."

"That is because they're both too stubborn-minded for their own good," Aunt Aggie said, nodding her head in an all knowing fashion. "Neither of them is willing to concede defeat in any of their squabbles."

"Ah, ha! Another reason for me not to go. If I stay here, I cannot fight with the supercilious man."

Lottie looked at her, her brows raised. "He may appear arrogant on occasion, but the man is invariably correct in all his statements."

"I know. That's what makes him so hard to work alongside. When I go with him to the Society this afternoon, he'll be all willing, available, affable, smiling, harmonious and–"

The other two had burst into gales of laughter. She flashed them an irritated look, willing them to understand her predicament.

"Not towards me. Oh, no. The man is never that pleasant to me. He's that way towards all the women who beg his assistance with their accounts. As so many of them do. Frequently."

"Laura, I think it is time you readied yourself. The Earl be there ahead of you otherwise, and who knows what mischief all those doting women may get into without your strong hand to guide them."

Laura rolled her eyes. "I do know when you are funning me. Fine. I'm leaving now. After the Society, I have several other calls to make. And if I finish early enough, I wish to call at Mr. Roberts, the bookseller. So do not expect me before four or five. And I shall leave instructions about opening the door to callers. We need to take precautions while there are so many criminals–"

"Laura," Lottie said.

"Yes?"

"You're rambling again." She made a shooing motion with her hands. "Go, go. And when you get home, we'll have more time to discuss the advice Madame Faberge gave to you this morning. I can't wait to learn more ways to tempt a suitor."

"Or in your case, to dissuade an over-eager one," Auntie said, with a fond smile at her youngest niece.

With a little laugh and a wave, Laura ran down stairs to issue strict instructions to their butler and footmen as to whom would be admitted to the house while she was out.

"On second thoughts, perhaps tell everyone that we're not receiving at all. That way no one will be allowed enter, and we'll not have to worry who they are, or what they may want, or who may have sent them to spy on us."

It took her several minutes, but at last she felt she'd covered all eventualities. At least, as best she could. So why, oh why, did she feel this irrational fear? One that prevented her from taking that step outside their front door. Winchester and all the women awaited her. They needed her help. She must go. Yet, she lingered, certain something was wrong.

For the third time, she instructed their butler, until accompanied by their footman, Warren, the one Winchester considered a criminal and not a house servant, she placed a firm step on the stairs. In a quick rush, she descended to the carriage, and settled back to spend the journey to the house where the Women's Society met in deep contemplation.

Though she loved her family desperately, on occasion she wished for a few moments' peace and quiet. A chance to catch her breath and consider her future. She sighed.

As always when alone, her thoughts leapt to one person. She took her notebook from her reticule and turned to the well-thumbed page near the back: the one man she longed to be able to write about in her research, to describe his smell as a perfect counterpart to her own; one that drew her immediately and set her senses reeling.

Botheration! Why could it not be him?

Winchester's titles and names were generations old. His family's veins ran with blood at least as blue as her own. He possessed the high level of intelligence that intrigued her in a man.

His body...oh, yes, the manly physique that she regularly admired in secret, made every unmarried woman in a room turn her head when he entered. To her annoyance, several married women also turned their eyes to make a survey of his attributes. Even more frustrating were the blatant advances that followed their visual appreciations.

For Laura, Richard's wealth attracted her the least. He drew her to him with his wit, his uncompromising support and his vulnerabilities. And, though she hated to admit it, she craved security.

Her greatest fear remained that she'd remain a spinster after never finding a man through her research; left with no husband and therefore no precious children of her own. Michael and Jonathon would eventually marry and she'd have the unenviable choice of residing with one of them and becoming a fond aunt to their children, or wandering archaeological digging sites with her father.

Her carriage pulled up before the Society's premises and the door opened to show her Winchester's smiling face.

"I'm pleased you've arrived."

She looked towards the walkway to the neat terraced house, and at the windows where anxious faces pressed against the glass. "You could have gone inside without me. You're the one they're waiting to speak with."

He turned to the row of chattering women who had moved outside to rim the doorway and, in a graceful gesture, tipped his hat to them and smiled.

"Oh, no. Far too terrifying to face a room of these women by myself."

He raised his elegantly gloved hand and treated the women to a little wave. The chattering rose to a crescendo, like a flock of excited birds. His nonsense forced a laugh out of her.

"Twaddle. You've faced hundreds of women in hundreds of ballrooms for years and never worried. In fact, you exalt in their attention."

"With that class of ladies, I know where I stand. Know when to flirt, when to retreat. Know that the majority of them don't expect anything more from me than some inane comment regarding the day's weather." He indicated the women watching them.

"These women are far more intelligent. Far shrewder. I'm terrified of making a mistake, because they will most certainly know. And condemn me for it."

She didn't laugh this time. Under his words, tossed about like a jest, she sensed the hint of true anxiety. Knew he truly feared failing these women who were depending on him so much. Linking her arm through his, she started to walk slowly towards the door of the Society. Though her stomach clenched, she turned towards him and lifted her mouth in a small semblance of a smile.

"Shall I tell you a secret, my lord?"

He patted her hand where it rested on his coat sleeve. "If it is something that will give me more confidence in facing these women, please, by all means."

"I, too, am terrified each time I come here."

He stared at her with lowered brows and his even white teeth worrying his bottom lip.

She nodded. "You see, like you, I fear not measuring up to the high standards set by others."

He cocked an eye at her. "Becca?"

"Yes, Becca, with her mathematical acumen, helps these women so much. A hard person to imitate when my own skills with accounting are decidedly hopeless."

He grinned. "So the sole reason I'm allowed escort you on days such as this, is so you may bring me here as a substitute for your sister. Should I have donned a gown?"

"Oh, no, I assure you, these particular women would rather see your more manly attributes displayed."

His mouth twitched.

"My problem is wondering if any of these women may have seen any parts of me displayed at the...ah... places where they work."

She swallowed. Her hands covered her mouth. She spoke between her fingers. "I–I'd never considered that you may know any of the women we assist."

He shook his head and pulled her hand away.

"Sorry, sweetheart. That was a jest. A stupid one. It's because my nerves are a little frayed today."

"Why? Has something happened?"

"No, no, nothing to concern yourself with. A small problem that my cousins and I shall deal with, and hopefully terminate once and for all, later this afternoon."

He placed her hand back on his sleeve with his usual finesse, yet he appeared ill-at-ease. Tense somehow. And she knew it was not any silly fear of meeting a room full of past or present street walkers. With his reputation, he'd no doubt encountered hundreds of them.

That image did not sit well with her and now she felt uneasy. Perhaps the small problem he and his male cousins had later on concerned females. That image caused her stomach to roil and her fingers clutched at his sleeve.

He gave her a little frown and eased the grip she held on his sleeve. "And Lottie? Do you feel the need to compete with her?"

"A little, yes." She shrugged. "My younger sister is also brilliant in her own way. Apart from her study of several of the new sciences–"

She giggled.

"When you giggle like a school-room girl, it's like music to my ears. When others give silly laughs, it's like fingernails scraped down a plaster wall."

"That comical image of Lottie worshipping the hills and dales on your head with her fingertips caused my mirth. Apart from her love of lumps and bumps, Lottie interprets people's movements and facial expressions. From studying them, she attributes emotions and intentions and motivations. She also understands several languages, so she can interpret the nuances of people's spoken words as well. There are few secrets that are withheld from her when she wants to learn them."

"Good heavens. I think I'll remove my head and my expressions from her vicinity. Can't think of anything worse than someone knowing my every thought."

"I share little of Lottie's skills, and only a small amount of her knowledge of the new sciences. I've been with her to some demonstrations of the theories of Franz Gall, where they try to show that our characteristics and criminality are determined by the shape of our head."

"So, when we catch Lady Hetherington, Lottie will read her cranial bumps and see if her criminal traits have always been with her, or if living with a corrupt husband led to adopt the same procedures."

"Oh, very good, Richard. You've been studying it."

He gave one of his careless shrugs that didn't fool her for a moment. The man devoured knowledge faster than the printing presses could produce it.

"I purchased George Combe's boring book and read all of forty pages before throwing it at the wall."

She snorted. "Good grief. Not…um…*The Constitution of Man and Elements of Phrenology*?" When he nodded she burst into laughter. "Nobody else of my acquaintance has managed the first ten pages. What a hero you are. Why did you attempt it?"

He gave another of those shrugs that gave away nothing, then grinned. "Perhaps I did it to impress you."

She squinted at him to see if he was again testing her patience. Though he looked at least half way serious. She sighed. She never knew where she stood with this frustrating man.

"Hum. Well, perhaps I'll frighten you with the knowledge that I can sense a lot of your thoughts."

His eyebrows shot upwards. "That would terrify me. But I know you're lying."

"How?"

"Because if you'd read my thoughts when you bent to descend from the carriage, you'd now be blushing from head to toe. You see, from my position, I could peer straight down the front of that deliciously low neckline and see—"

She gasped, looked down, and attempted to hitch up the neckline of her gown with one hand. It stayed tightly adhered to her bosom. 'You couldn't see anything of the sort, you liar."

He flashed her a wicked grin. 'No, but I do have a truly vivid imagination."

She gave him a small slap to his wrist and marched to the door, shooing the inquisitive ladies inside as she went. As had always happened before when he'd accompanied her, the women were grateful to have Richard's help with their accounts, and he mingled easily with them, standing on no ceremony, no matter who they were or in which street they resided.

He demonstrated a simple way to keep a tally of the money they earned in a notebook and then subtract their expenses each month to show what they might be left with, and how much they might afford to use for their investments.

Then he wrote down an up-to-date list of the share opportunities coming up and gave his personal forecast for each. Because he regularly visited Threadneedle Street, he spoke to the eager listeners about recent discussions in the coffee houses amongst the traders.

These women knew—as did Laura—that for them to go to these places would cause a stir. There remained the old guard, who disapproved of women being involved in anything to do with the banking or market precincts and often forcibly removed them.

Having the Earl, a direct participant each day, relay the latest news was far, far better than paying for news sheets and pouring over them by dim candles at night.

He set them to work on their accounting, and strolled around the perimeter of the room to watch and be on hand if anyone needed assistance.

"You're very good with them," Laura said. "Most gentlemen would never set foot in this house, and would never agree to teach women in trades how to budget their own money."

"I enjoy doing it. I struggled with schooling when I was a child and I know how demoralizing it can be to not be able to undertake simple tasks like these for yourself. And while we spend two hours here, I have my men out working on our other problems."

She groaned. "Something warns me that we are falling behind in this race. That the Syndicate is winning. I also worry about Lottie and my aunt at home while I am here. But they assured me they would be perfectly fine without me while I attended to several errands."

"You didn't send me a list of the addresses you intend visiting this afternoon, as I requested."

"And you haven't told me where you're going. So we are even."

"I need to know so I can accompany you. Protect you."

"And who protects you?"

"I can take care of myself."

"Your hypocritical attitude becomes annoying. You insist on knowing where I'm going. You want to accompany me everywhere. Yet now, when I have finally accustomed myself to your irritating presence, you acts in a secretive way and have a mysterious rendezvous. If I was a suspicious sort of female, or your wife–"

"Heaven forbid," he said with a cheeky grin.

"I'd assume you were visiting a new mistress." She leaned closer and her eyes widened.

"You're wearing your nighttime cologne. The special one I mixed with musk and sandalwood. The one you said puts you in mind of a seductive evening."

Her mouth opened but she couldn't speak the words. The size of her blunder mortified her. She felt her face redden.

"Oh!"

He shook his head and tapped her mouth closed with a finger.

"No, my curious little cat. I do not have a new mistress, and no, I'll not discuss this subject any further with you."

She remained mute, disconcerted, considering the situation as he prowled the room and performed his duties with effortlessness and honesty, unperturbed by their conversation.

In return for his able assistance, the women were eager to share the news they had collected around the back streets and alleyways of the city. No one mentioned the reasons they were out working on these streets, or in the houses fronting them, late at night.

Laura and Richard accepted every tiny piece of shared information as though it was a gold bar. Each piece of the jigsaw would help them piece together the bigger picture. Hopefully very soon.

"Ruth, you must take care when you search the receipts of your abbess," Richard told the doe-eyed beauty almost sitting in his lap.

"We know Lady Hetherington's organization has control of as twenty broth... ah...visiting houses, and perhaps even more. Her blackmail schemes seem to have netted her many, many unfortunates who are now obliged to do her bidding." He patted the girl's hand. "I'd be devastated if any harm came to you, pet."

"Oh, my lord, I does it all for love of you."

When the other women all tittered, she flushed. "And for us. If 'un the Yard catches these crooks fast, we'll be safer goin' 'bout our business at night. More trade means more coppers to save in my little tin box." She smiled up at Richard, with a worshipful smile. "And the more you'll 'av to 'elp me with me sums."

Laura cleared her throat, but no one took any notice. She did it again, louder.

"I think it is time the Earl and I departed. I know he has another pressing appointment this afternoon."

Did she imagine it, or did he squirm slightly at her words? He didn't meet her gaze as he disengaged Ruth's clinging hand and stood to his feet. He bowed deeply.

A collective sigh rose from the women, some old enough to be his mother. One who had long retired from rough trade could even be his grandmother.

This was too much. These women, who should be immune to every man's charms, looked about to swoon at his feet.

"Ladies, it has been a pleasure as always. And remember, if you hear word of any men going about the local tradesmen, the shopkeepers, or the owners of your establishments, and trying to set up rings of investors, send word to my townhouse. You all have my card with the address."

In unison, they nodded. "We need to stop these men before they convince any more innocent people with a little cash to spare to invest in their fraudulent schemes."

As they walked to the door, the women's chatter came to Laura's ears.

"He's ever so handsome."

"I do envy Lady Laura having that one dangling on her line."

"Hope she knows how to reel him in."

"Hope she remembers some of those tricks we've taught her and her sisters."

Beside her, she could hear Richard's snorts and chuckles as he struggled, unsuccessfully, to keep his mirth under control until they reached her waiting carriage. He lasted until he'd handed her inside and waited until she settled her skirts. He leaned in the open door.

"I'm simply breathless with anticipation to know the tricks you've learned. Especially if Ruth taught you."

He ducked his head back from the opening in time to dodge the object she'd flung at his head: her notebook. He bent to the ground and retrieved it, flicking through a few pages as he held it up in the air. "Always wondered what you wrote about me in here."

"You wouldn't dare!"

He grinned and stepped back, signaling to her coachman to drive on. "I'd dare anything where you're concerned, my dear."

As the carriage pulled away, he waved the notebook jauntily in the air, his mouth wide open with a smug, self-satisfied grin. She leaned as far out the window as she could and reached for it, but only grasped thin air.

She let out a string of curses, the sailors' ones she seemed to only use in his presence. His laughter rang in her ears. She banged her bonnet back against the upholstered head rest, not caring that she crushed its pretty brim. Ooh! She hated more than anything the times when he got the better of her.

Especially when she lost her temper over it. Like now.

She trusted him to not read her private scribbling, yet, if the situations were reversed, she doubted she'd be so keen to guarantee his privacy. The temptation to take a peek into his private thoughts might prove too much for her.

Would it for him though? Double blast the man. She tried to calculate the weeks until the bride and groom returned, and she could be relieved of some of her duties involving the Earl. She still wasn't sure whether that was a good thing, or a disaster.

Laura's bad humor evaporated some time later, not from any excitement over paying two boring and regulated duty calls, but due to her excitement over the four paper-wrapped books that rested beside her on the carriage seat. She loved books, adored them. And now that the Jamison's finances were once again sound, she could afford this little occasional extravagance.

A visit to Mr. Robert's shop meant a long journey home, but she smiled, appreciating the silence inside the carriage in contrast to the busying traffic outside, as working day people began to wend their way home. Some were on foot, some in omnibuses, and some via the train companies that the majority of their investments were with. She leaned her arm on the window ledge and watched the hustle and bustle in each new street they turned down.

So often in the City they were travelling at night, on their way to attend dinners, balls and musicals, and she saw little. Today, however, the yellowing afternoon light softened the normal glaring grime of gutters and streets and made them appear lighter, more habitable. She smiled, enjoying the moment.

As the carriage wound around streets she rarely travelled, Laura checked her little watch. If the rest of their trip continued on this way, her aunt would be fretting because she would be late.

Perhaps she could take home a small gift to appease her anxiety. She pulled opened the roof flap and spoke to her coachman, ordering him to stop a few streets further on at the tiny sweet shop that sold the boiled sweets her aunt adored.

John coachman pulled the carriage to a halt in front of a long stretch of parkland and turned to lean down and speak to her.

"Sorry, my lady, but this 'ere's close as I could manage to yon shop. Street's too full of cart sellers. Small market goin' on."

He waved towards the side of the road, where carts piled high with fruits and vegetables stood side by side. "You keep Warren close behind you, mind, 'cause 'is lordship gave orders that we keep you safe."

Laura hid her annoyance. Richard's issuing orders to her servants irritated her, yet she understood his reasoning well enough. She also knew why John coachman and Warren would be eager to not upset the Earl.

Richard's cold stare could freeze the blood in an enemy's veins, and she'd seen grown men quake in their boots at a few sharp words from him. She managed a small smile for Warren.

"Stay close then. We wouldn't want to upset the Earl, would we?" Not expecting a reply to her dry comment, even from outspoken Warren, she turned and walked down the footpath, twisting and weaving between wagons and pedestrians.

Once or twice she checked over her shoulder to reassure herself that her escort followed close on her heels. Reaching the shop, she indicated to Warren to wait outside, opened the door and stepped inside, smiling as she inhaled the familiar sweet smell.

The plump rosy-cheeked wife of the proprietor boiled and rolled children's peppermint sticks in her back room, on the same stove where she cooked Aunt Aggie's favorite toffees. The mix of strong smells, caramel, vanilla and lemon, flooded her nostrils, the power of it almost too much for her oversensitivity to cope with. She withdrew her kerchief from her pocket, used to this occurrence after so many years dealing with oils and aromas and blends of fragrances.

"Oh, my dear Lady Laura, so lovely to see you again," the beaming little lady gushed, "although I notice the kerchief is already to your nose, you poor dear, and yes, I do understand, because I too suffer with same affliction, on many, many occasions, and especially on those occasions when I'm mixing a particularly large batch of sweets that need a strong, stringent base oil to give the flavor or aroma and–"

Laura pulled the kerchief away from her nose long enough to interrupt the flow of words. "I'd love to stay and compare ingredients and blends, as I know you're like me and have so few people with which to discuss things such as distilling oils. But I must purchase my aunt's gift and depart, or I shall be very late for dinner and she'll fret."

The darling woman apologized several times for keeping a valued customer waiting, as her husband wrapped a large quantity of toffee in a paper roll and secured it with a pretty ribbon. The pair, as round and happy as a pair of summer robins, escorted her to the door, still chattering, still smiling. Being with this couple never failed to lift her spirits.

She stepped outside and Warren fell into formation behind her, speaking loudly enough to gain her attention.

"That sweet-maker would talk the ear off a cow. Talks even more than you, Lady Laura."

She gritted her teeth and pretended not to hear him, as she concentrated on keeping her edible package held safely in front of her, and away from anyone who bumped into her.

Honestly, they might have rescued Warren from goal, and he might have been destined for the hangman's noose, and he might be a common thief with no schooling, and he might have reached adulthood in the roughest part of the slums, and she conceded that he had been orphaned at a very early age—

But surely, even those things shouldn't excuse him from displaying a modicum of manners, now he was in their employ. Someone needed to tutor the insolent servant. Someone needed to curb his tongue. Only not her, and not now.

She quickened her pace, retracing her path back towards the carriage through the thickening crowd, praying the raindrops hitting the brim of her bonnet did not forewarn of an imminent downpour.

For the hundredth time, she cursed her own impetuosity. Her family reminded her countless times that her actions invariably landed her in predicaments from which she required rescuing.

She turned around. "Warren, we should make haste. Perhaps walking along the outside edge of these carts will prove faster."

She slipped between the two nearest wagons, lifted her hems, and stepped across the gutter. Her gaze fixed ahead, not on any refuge that might swill beneath her feet, she reached the paved road and felt slightly comforted by the sound of Warren's heavy breathing immediately behind her.

As a footman Warren was far from ideal. As a keeper, his towering size and uncouth attitude made him perfect. Her carriage came into sight, standing at the corner of the next crossroads.

When she saw John standing upright on his box, turning this way and that, evidently on the lookout for them in the crowds, she expelled a sigh of relief. Not normally fussed by encroaching crowds or loud storms, something in the atmosphere today disturbed her.

Either the approaching bad weather or her unshakeable feeling of impending doom set her nerves on edge. Increasing her pace, she strode along, looking neither right nor left through the increasing rain until she reached the corner.

John coachman recognized her, smiled, indicated that he'd descend to the side of the coach and open the door in readiness for her quick entrance. Lifting her hand, she waved her acknowledgement and started to call out a greeting.

The sight that entered her line of vision on the steps of the house on the opposite corner stopped her in her tracks. She stood like a marble statue, her limbs so heavy they could have been carved from stone. Warren, driven by his own forward motion, banged into her back and knocked her off balance.

She cried out, startled, but more shocked by the image still burning holes in the backs of her eyes. Warren's large hands shot forward to grip her forearms and prevent her from toppling to the ground and being trampled underfoot.

At the same moment, John's shocked voice rang out, "Lady Laura, oh my goodness! Lady Laura, take a care, I'm coming."

Around them, the other walkers separated and then surged past and left her tottering in a small cleared area, Warren supporting her. Her legs refused to hold her upright and she breathed in panting gasps, as if she'd run a race.

Out of the corner of her eye, she saw Warren's gaze swivel towards whatever had caught her attention. Warren, and most likely John coachman, would see, as she did, the Earl of Winchester being farewelled in the open doorway of a large cornerwise townhouse.

The owner of the house wasn't known to Laura, though whoever resided there possessed immense wealth, as the windows, standing to soldier-like attention in two neat rows, fanned out for a great distance down the sides of the two bisecting roads. It was a very large residence indeed. Heavy gold brocade curtains draped the windows, and all the exterior window sills were of a reddish colored wood, polished to such a brilliant gloss that the streaks of afternoon sunlight bounced off them and hit passersby in the eye.

Winchester's back was too them, yet Laura knew it was he, in the same way she sensed his presence every time he entered a ballroom or galloped across the end of a park.

Without conscious thought, she started across the street to greet her friend, thinking to offer him the comfort of her carriage as a dry haven from the increasing rain. Her feet touched the pathway below the townhouse's step, she settled her hems back over her ankles and looked up in time to see a lady.

For she now accepted the fact that it wasn't one of Richard's many male acquaintances, as she glimpsed of swirling skirts around his legs and the blonde hair near his darker head.

When she'd first seen him from across the street, instinct had told her he was visiting a woman but she'd pushed the idea away, rejecting it as untrue, as he'd told her he wasn't visiting any new mistress today. She might have called Richard many unkind names in their continual conflicts but never, ever a liar. No, this lady was not a new mistress. Most likely the wife of a business associate.

Feeling somewhat reassured, she took a few more confident steps across the walkway towards the bottom step, her intention being to wait until he'd completed his call and offer to convey him to his home. It would be only neighborly as they lived in such close proximity.

She stopped at the bottom of the wide steps and clutched her parcel and reticule to her chest, hoping to keep them slightly drier in the shelter of her body, and waited. Rather than Richard retiring from the lady's side, the petite, blond-haired woman stretched upwards and pressed a lingering kiss on Richard's cheek.

Laura watched in stunned disbelief as he shifted the woman's hand from his shoulders and lowered them to her side, yet not letting go of them. He kept them clasped in his gloved hands, swinging them a little at thigh level to emphasize whatever point he made to her as he bent his head and spoke near her ear.

"Oh, my goodness!" Laura's hands squeezed hard against her chest.

Beside them, a gray-haired and exquisitely liveried butler waited with solemn patience to secure the doors. The butler's gaze fixed on some invisible spot away from the couple, as if a renowned Earl and an elegantly gowned lady bid farewell on the doorstep every day.

Perhaps they did in this household, but certainly not in the majority. A most bizarre happening.

Laura lost track of time. Things happened in slow motion after that. Half- awareness informed her that Richard turned...walked down the steps...towards her.

But her unwavering gaze stayed locked with the motionless figure in the doorway. The now visible title-holder stared down at where Laura, her almost-visitor, waited on the street.

Even from where she stood, Laura clearly saw her brows lift in surprise and her mouth open. The lady raised her nose in a gesture of disdain. A smug, fox-cunning smile spread across her adversary's face.

The Countess of Newbery.

Chapter Sixteen

"Lady Laura!"

Cries came from two directions at once.

"Milady. Lady Jamison."

Richard startled, lifted his head. Oh, Lord, no! His gut clenched and he gripped the railing as his knees shook.

Laura had barely flinched when shot at—twice—yet now, her expression of horror told him someone had inflicted much worse damage to her person. Him! He'd wounded her this way. She'd seen him leaving Gloria's house. She'd witnessed Gloria kiss and cling to him. God knew what she thought, what she imagined.

Those calls of Laura's name. One from in front of him. Warren arrived in a panting mound of distress to surround Laura's heaving body with his own bulk and shield her from foot traffic or eager viewers in coaches. One from behind him.

Richard swung around in time to glimpse Gloria's profile, as she turned to her butler and the open door behind her. In time to glimpse an emotion that sent gooseflesh racing over his skin. Despite their prolonged conversation, despite her begging entreaty for assistance, despite her desperate avowals of innocence, Gloria's face radiated triumph and glee and an unholy excitement.

Hell! What had he let loose? Surely he couldn't have been so deluded by feminine tears and pleas?

In front of him, Warren had taken Laura's arm and was leading her across the street. She appeared dazed and disoriented, as the footmen needed both hands to steer her in a straight path to her waiting coachman. The sight of the open carriage door and the thought that she'd walked away without a word, a question, or a scold, finally freed him from his frozen state.

"Wait, please, wait," he called, raising his hand and running after them. He dashed onto the street without checking and nearly went under the hooves of a fast-turning curricle as it rounded the corner. The young buck driving it called a few words of abuse, but he made no effort to respond or to apologize.

Go to Laura

Explain to Laura.

The refrain pounding through his head blocked out everything else as he weaved between the jostling wagons and carts, and raced to reach her carriage before the door closed. From somewhere offside of him, Brian and Tony ran to catch him up, calling as they ran, but he didn't dare stop.

Tell Laura. Tell Laura. Tell Laura. It beat faster and faster in his brain, until his mind fogged and his vision turned red. From a few yards away, he heard Warren call to the coachman to start off, and realized that Laura was seated, the door was fastened and she was leaving him.

"No, no, wait. Please, Laura, wait," he called, and waved in desperation as her face went past his view and the coachman maneuvered her equipage into the stream of traffic. "No, no, no," he moaned, over and over, as he dropped his hand to his knees, gasping for breath. He shook his head as his breath hitched on an almost-sob.

Brian and Tony joined him, both in the same out-of-breath state, both having raced from their positions as observers. Their disguises as street sweepers had been good at three this afternoon but now, disheveled as they were, they could easily have taken up their brooms permanently with no one being the wiser.

Brian touched his back in a tentative but comforting manner. "So sorry."

"Terrible timing," Tony added. "When I saw the Earl's country conveyance coming around the corner and stop, before driving towards the mews, I imagined it would be he discovering you with his wife. Especially when she stepped outside, in full view of the street."

"Newbery arrived home? While we stood on the steps?"

"Can't say for certain if Newbery himself saw you, but it was definitely his coach that arrived. Great lumbering thing, loaded up with enough goods and chattels for a battalion, the way he always travels."

"Hell!"

"Yes, didn't think you'd be pleased. Had visions of the Earl shooting you in the bollocks."

"Brian, you know I had no intention of becoming involved in any sort of relationship with Gloria again. We spent the entire time conversing. Nothing more."

Brian held his hand up, palms out. "Whoa, my friend. It's not me you need to convince of that, it's Lady Laura. When she ran past me, she looked like someone had shot an arrow through her heart."

"Her face resembled a bleached sheet."

Richard bent down to pick up the white paper at his feet, the bright-colored ribbon having caught his attention. As soon as he lifted it higher, he recognized its contents, as he was a frequent customer at the same sweet shop along the road. He unfurled the crushed paper and examined the contents. What he revealed made him feel like the worst rogue who'd ever walked the earth. Toffee. The type that Aunt Aggie favored.

He knew now why Laura had been on this particular corner. Yet he had no reasonable explanation for the appearance of Newbery, considering Gloria had told him, several times, that her husband was safely out of the City. His views on life made him too skeptical to believe in coincidence.

"Dammit! I have to go to her. Explain. And you two will come with me. Describe your part in this afternoon's surveillance. Why you were there. What you saw. Instinct tells me Gloria played me for a fool today, the question is why."

"You think she expected Newbery to return around three, when you were with her?"

"Not just expected, arranged for him to return and discover us together. Although we did not leave the drawing room the entire time."

"It makes little difference which room you were in. It only matters that you are starting up again with your former mistress."

"Someone went to a lot of trouble to make it seem that way. And Gloria, well, she possesses beauty and delights in a wide variety of sexual activities, but she is incapable of developing a long term plan of any kind, and even less capable of applying normal methods of organization. She's laughed often about Newbery despairing of her reckless spending, and of her incomprehension of even the simplest of household accounts." He shook his head.

"No, if this was a trap set for me, Gloria needed someone else to lay it for me. She was only the bait."

With Brian and Tony accompanying him, Richard hurried around to the stables in the mews behind Newbery's house to fetch his horse. As he waited for his cousins to change clothes, he questioned a groom, one of Newberry's men, on the recent comings and goings of the Earl and the Countess. For a few gold coins, he was rewarded with excellent information. Pieces to fit into their puzzle. Pieces that might very well be the key to solving it.

At Grosvenor House, Winchester addressed Thompkins, the Jamison's butler, in his most formal tone and asked to be announced. He hoped the formality might jolt the servant into doing what he wished, though he held no real hope for it, as the servants here followed their own strange code of behavior.

Loyalty to the Jamisons stood as number one, and possibly numbers two, three, and four, on their list of duties. Other than that, they tended to do what pleased them.

Obviously it didn't please Thompkins to allow him to see Lady Laura so, in a gesture of pure bluff, he announced that he and his cousins would sit in the drawing room and wait until the lady was free. They waited in silence for fifteen minutes, each second minute of which he checked either the mantle clock or his fob watch.

"She intends avoiding you," Tony remarked.

"Don't imagine she'll speak to you today, or next week, or next month," his brother added. "And it seems the other members of the family are also sending you to Coventry."

They both rose. "It may be better if you do the initial explanations alone. If the Lady ever agrees to listen to you."

His cousins departed, leaving him to pace the room alone. Anxious, guilty, and above all, aggravated. He strode to the door, inactivity driving him insane. Warren hovered in the hallway.

"You there," Winchester adopted his Earnest Earl expression, "where is Lady Laura?"

The man regarded him with a hostile look, and Richard could well see why he'd been a valuable part of a criminal group before the Jamisons had removed him from the temptation of stealing on the streets.

"I'll never allow you near our wonderful ladyship, no after wot you done to 'er."

"Now see here–"

The footman shook his head. "No point in going all hoity-toity with me. Used to respect you, we did, the servants here at Jamison House. Knew you was family to the Duke. Knew you helped those street-workers with their accounts, same as our good ladies do. Thought you had more sense."

Hell! Now a footman was making him feel even worse, heaping mound upon mound of guilt upon his head. As he deserved every word, every curse hurled at him, he stood there and took it.

"If you're going to carry on with that piece of strumpet again, and believe me when I say that makes no matter if a woman takes money for what she does or not, some are harlots no matter what class they was born into." He sniffed and ran his footman's uniform sleeve under his grubby nose. "Least you could've done was go about it quiet like, behind closed doors, and not on the steps of that Countess's house for every man and his bloody dog to see. Humiliatin', that's what 'tis for my lady."

Christ! His shoulders slumped and his fists clenched.

"After you gone and told her you weren't bedding that man-chaser no more, and my lady, well she don't say nothin', but a man's got eyes in his head, and he knows when a woman thinks something special about a man.

"Don't like to see her upset like this. Crying like her heart is broke in two."

Richard rubbed at his chest, trying to ease the pain over his heart.

"Won't speak to her sister, nor her aunt."

He pushed past Warren and strode towards the staircase to the upper floors. Glaring at the footman he said, "Don't even consider trying to stop me."

Warren grinned, his missing teeth turning it into an evil lopsided leer. "'Bout time you did the right thing." He slapped Richard's back and turned away towards the kitchen.

Richard was momentarily stunned, but eager to grasp the opportunity to make things right between him and Laura. Leaping up the stairs, he strode straight to the bedroom he knew to be hers and knocked on the door. No answer. Nothing but the sound of sobs, non-stop wretched sobbing.

He opened the door and hesitated. This was wrong. As a gentleman he should not enter a lady's boudoir. Yet he wouldn't leave without speaking with her.

"Laura." Nothing but sobs from the heaving mound of shoulders exposed from the top of the bedclothes. "Laura, it is I. Winchester." Silence. "Please, sweetheart, it's Richard. Speak to me." Each time he spoke, the sobs hitched, then recommenced.

He closed his eyes and prayed for guidance. A soft sigh sounded beside him and a wrinkled hand came to rest on his sleeve. Aunt Aggie. He started to from his apology, but she stopped him with a finger to his lips.

"She refuses to speak to us of what happened. Go. Comfort her. I shall sit on this chair next to the open door, as chaperone. Trust me. In a household where Laura is revered by every servant, no one will gossip about untoward behavior."

"Thank you."

As he walked toward the bed, what he assumed to be her head turned towards him. She'd recognized his footsteps. He sat in the bedside chair and touched her spine through the bedding, rubbing softly.

"I'd like to explain about my visit to Countess Newbery's townhouse this afternoon." Silence. "I am so, so sorry if seeing me there, with that particular lady, caused you this distress."

Her tousled head appeared about the blankets. Red rimmed eyes stared at him in accusation. "You, Winchester, are a bare faced liar. A distorter of truths."

"No, no, I've never lied to you."

Her finger came out to point at him and he noticed she still wore her afternoon gown. Probably best. A miserable Laura distressed him. A wretched and dressed-for-bed Laura would tempt him to climb under the blankets beside her to offer careful, yet caring, words of consolation. Rubbish. He'd offer a damn sight more than that if he could get beneath those covers with her, and once he had her in his arms he'd find a way to convince her to stay there. For the rest of their lives.

"You said your appointment this afternoon wasn't with a new mistress."

"It wasn't."

"You neglected to add it was with your past mistress. A lie by omission."

He grasped her finger and held it still. "No. The Countess came to me, implored me to meet with her, as she'd learned something important." His eyes roved her drawn features, looking for encouragement that he'd caused no permanent damage to her fragile feelings. "A threat to someone very important in my life."

She frowned.

He stared into the deep swirling pools of her eyes, willing her to understand. "I'm a dullard, a foot-dragger, and any of the other names you delight in calling me at times like this, but it doesn't need a lightning strike for me to realize that, without this person, my life would be insipid, mind-numbing and not worth contemplating. That most important person is you, my love."

Her eyes widened with genuine surprise. "Oh."

He truly was an idiot. During their habitual sparring, their game of advance and retreat, he'd forgotten something of importance.

Laura's level of participation in these games was of a novice. The bond that grew and strengthened every day between them became mind-bogglingly clear to a rogue with his level of sensual and sexual experience, yet, she possibly assumed it to be commonplace.

Another misinterpretation for him to deal with. Later.

"Gloria—"

"Do. Not. Speak. That woman's name to me." Laura's brows furrowed into one of her infamous scowls.

His spirits rose. An angry goaded opponent he could deal with. A sad one confounded him.

"The Countess informed me she knew who was behind these latest threats on your life. The rifle shots. The injuries your family suffered at the park. I couldn't take the chance of not going. Couldn't risk missing hearing about a vital segment of our conundrum, especially if it concerned your safety."

She pushed up onto her elbows. Her curls tumbled around her shoulders and the tips settled like tiny dark halos close to her nipples. He sat on his hands. Better that discomfort than a slap to his face from her aunt, if he reached across and traced one of those swirls with his finger.

"… swear you didn't go to the Countess to resume your affair?"

With great reluctance, he shifted his gaze back to her mouth. "I do."

Unable to help himself, he reached over and brushed a thick lock of dark back from her cheek and tucked it gently behind her ear. Her body may still be street clothed, but her hair flowed ready for his bedding.

"My association with her could never have been deemed an affair in any case." He shrugged. "I admit we were lovers on a few occasions—"

She gave several small gulps for breath that ended on another of those heart wrenching sobs. When she turned her head away from him, he put his palm under her chin and turned it back.

"But nothing more. I know you cannot possibly understand, but there is an enormous difference between a man and woman enjoying each other's bodies and–"

"And what?"

"Becoming the lover of someone you care for deeply."

Her eyes widened and her fingers clutched at the blankets at her sides. He'd said too much. Revealed too much of his deepest yearnings. He cleared his throat.

"I just remembered. She said... *'I've won.'* What did she mean?"

Now he needed to clear his head. "Pardon?"

"Your countess–"

"She's not my anything," he said, trying not to grind his teeth.

"My mistake. That lady stood on her steps and she said those words, 'I've won'. She looked more awake, excited. "And now, Richard, I understand her meaning. She heaped scorn upon my head because her scheme, whatever or whomsoever it involves, with you, had succeeded." She shook his arm, her eyes widening, color flooding back into her pale face. "And that made her feel...exalted."

He tried to follow her train of thought, her quick mind and rapid speech hard to follow when she was in full flow. "How do you know what she said? You were nowhere near her."

He saw her cheeks pinken before she dipped her head. "Oh, my goodness, how stupid of me." He slapped a palm to his forehead. "How could I not have guessed? I've always known there were hidden facets to you, more skills you took pains to hide. Some were obvious, some I guessed, but this one...this one I didn't know. Doesn't anyone else?"

She shrugged a shoulder. "Only my auntie, my brothers, my sisters."

"Not your father?"

"He's the reason I learned how to do it." He cocked a brow. "Even as a child, my father always thought my skill as an aromatherapist less important than other proficiencies a normal young girl learns at her mother's knee, or from her governess. I believed, wrongly as it happened, if I could make myself into what Papa wanted, he'd stay. He'd want to be our father. Most of all, he'd love us. Especially...especially me."

He winced. The compulsion to defend this brave woman grew stronger. Despite her resistance to his shielding of her in situations of danger, he'd glimpsed her moments of vulnerability.

Searching ballrooms each night looking for something she wasn't going to find, the perfect man, seemed pitiful and a cause for ridicule to many of their peers. Yet he admired the courage it took to follow her research through to the end.

To cling to the hope of finding that one superior male specimen. A pot of gold at the end of the rainbow.

She shrugged. "It was easy. I took to following Papa when he went about the estate, watching him when he talked to himself over his archaeological treatises, when he ordered an ale at the inn. I tried to learn his every thought by reading his lips. After a while, I began reading others' as well. For similar reasons. I thought if I understood what people said about me, why some of them distrusted my skills in mixing my herbs, oils and blends, I might convince them that I'm not some medieval witch–"

Oh, hell. The burn in his belly became a gnawing pain.

"I might convince them to see me as a normal sort of lady. The sort that capably presides over a large manor house. The sort that never get herself into inextricable dilemmas. The sort that a proud papa would introduce as his beautiful and clever daughter."

Do something, anything, his conscience screamed. Spill his guts. Tell his secrets. Reveal his sins. Rip out his heart. Soothe this wondrous woman's wounds.

Stop her blaming herself for a father who was too self-absorbed to see past the end of his nose. Too detached to show her any love. He wanted to haul the absent Earl back from whatever God-forsaken kingdom he'd lost himself in this time.

Stop her making excuses for superstitious bigots who labelled her a witch. Ingrates who should thank the Lord for the cures and potions she dispensed to save their lives. He wanted to push their noses to the earth and make them kiss the ground she walked on.

Loving Laura grew up expecting nothing in return for her favors, for her goodness. She expected little and assumed she deserved even less. Yet, from somewhere, she'd found the courage to march through the flotsam and jetsam of male society for that rare specimen: a husband who admired her merits, who worshipped her uniqueness and treated her like a princess. Treated her far better than her father.

Before he could stop himself, he started to speak. Started to reveal his secret. If he shared his insecurities, his failings, it might offer her some comfort, lessen her own fears.

That, and his heart, were all he had to offer.

He took her cold hand in his, rubbing it between his palms to warm it. It took several deep swallows, plus a clearing of his throat, before he found his voice. "You've naught to be ashamed of, my sweet. You're far, far, more intelligent than I."

She chortled. "As if I'd believe that make-believe story."

He shook his head. "It's true. In fact, only this afternoon on our visit to the Society, I experienced several bad moments with the women. Do you remember when Ruth asked me to read through those multitudes of pages from the solicitor? The one who is in charge of making the investments for all those women under their pseudonyms."

She frowned, nodded. "Yes, but–"

He placed a finger over her lips. "No. Let me finish. I may never summon the nerve, nor have the opportunity, again. I made an excuse to Ruth that I was tired, and then asked Josie to read it out instead. I know Josie is rather withdrawn, but I also noted how well educated she is."

Laura glanced at him with eyes as shrewd as Lottie's, making him wonder if his secret was not so secret after all. But this afternoon he hadn't imagined she'd seen anything amiss. Other than that he was too lazy to read aloud sixteen pages of script.

"Funny how life changes in the space of a few hours. This afternoon I remained determined to not let you get too close to me. Not close enough to uncover my closely guarded secret. And yet now, I am eager to unburden myself to you. In the hope it will show you that none of us is perfect. Apparently, my mother not only suffered several miscarriages, but the births she had were all long and difficult. Especially mine."

"Ah, and you decided to continue being difficult through the rest of your life." Her mischievous grin was balm to his soul. He laughed with her.

"Like you, I've studied many research treatises. Only mine were concerning the damage done to a baby's brain after a traumatic entrance into this world. Evidence points to the fact that a long, hard birthing can cause damage to a baby's head and brain."

She pushed up again on one forearm and looked at his head. "But Lottie says your phrenology bumps indicate a high level of intellect and a steady character. No mental disturbances and no criminal tendencies."

"Yes, and I'm eternally grateful for that, as it's allowed me to compensate for my deficiency. You see–"

He wiped his sweaty palms down the sides of his trousers. "I cannot read." He shook his head, trying to clear his thoughts and explain in words she'd comprehend. "No, no, actually, I can read now, but I couldn't read, not for a long time when I was a child, nor at Eton. I hid it, you see, from everyone, and because of it I took many a beating at Eton so that taught me to overcome–"

'Richard!" She laid a hand on his sleeve and tugged. "Goodness me, Richard, you're rambling again. Is that what this is about? Your big confession. Your huge sin." She flopped back onto her pillows and waved a hand between them. "I knew that long ago. About your reading."

"You–you already knew? Bu–but how? Wh–why didn't you say something? Accuse me."

"Accuse you of what? It's not a crime to be unable to read. Beside which, I know that you now devour books with an unquenchable hunger for knowledge. I also recognize the degree of bloody-minded determination it took to teach yourself how to fathom those damn, blasted pesky letters on a page."

He chuckled. "I do so enjoy your demure language."

"In truth, Richard, the knowledge that you managed to not only learn how to read, but kept the fact hidden from most people for all these years, intimidated me dreadfully. Made me feel even less sharp that you."

"So share your secret. How do you know about my difficulty, when even those who have been close to me for years didn't realize?"

"Years ago, an Irish priest visited our village. He'd suffered an injury to his head when a child. Said it made it impossible for the words to stay still on a page when he read them. They leapt around more than the leprechauns in the bottom of his garden."

"I referred to mine as dancing fairies when I was younger."

"Still, like you, he found a way of fixing the look of letters in his mind, so that when he saw a word he recognized it. Didn't need to spell out each individual letter the way most people do. I've watched the way you worked your way down a page of writing, using your index finger as a guide to each word. Not the letters, but the word in its entirety."

"I cannot believe that you saw all that, yet said nothing."

"The only puzzling thing is why you never told me yourself."

"The idea that you might think badly of me held me back. I've experienced the shame of being thought obtuse. It happened when I struggled in some classes at school. And even later at university. Although, by then, I'd become proficient at covering up my deficiencies. Using every method at my disposal, I avoided any actual public readings. In my own mind, I balanced my backwardness with books by out-stripping my peers in other fields."

"Let me guess. Mathematics. Sciences. Engineering."

He quirked a brow. "Those subjects weren't hard to determine. Your investments tend to run to inventions, machines, anything where you can view the mechanisms in person and make visual evaluations."

"You're not a witch. You're a mind reader."

"Huh! Many people imagine it to be the same thing. Another reason I hide my gifts, in the same way you damp down the things in which you excel and secrete the ones in which you struggled. Extremes of any sort invite condemnation and ridicule. None of us enjoy being dissimilar, or risk being ostracized for our differences."

"Ah, my wise one. We all make do in this life with whatever gifts we are given. And your gifts are unique. You should treasure them."

At the door, their chaperone cleared her throat to indicate that he'd lingered too long. He began to stand but Laura gripped his arm.

"Come back to me. Tonight," she whispered.

Sweat broke out across his brow. His palms went damp. He shook his head, a last bid to deny what they both wanted. To do the correct thing for her family's sake. "You—you don't know what you're asking."

She nodded. "I do know." She gripped his hand. "This is the perfect solution for both of us. You cannot deny you desire me."

He swallowed. "No more. I've tried." He snorted. "It does no good. You can read everything I think."

"... and it will be ideal for me, because I can conduct my research with you. Experiment with someone I trust implicitly. I trust you to take care of me."

He groaned, thinking of her aunt standing guard at the door.

"....and neither of us wants to marry the other."

He flinched. How could he admit those white lies he'd told himself, told his family, told her, told countless husband-hunting women, no longer showed his feelings?

"....sooo... there's no risk one of us will be hurt. Not when we've done tests. The scent ones. And remember, your aroma didn't call to me, not in as strong a way as I wished. And of course, I will never, ever, try to trap you into a marriage because of anything we may do. So, please, promise you'll come back tonight."

He rushed his farewells, desperate to distance himself from the sight of Laura, in a bed, a large soft bed, begging him to return to her. Any true blue-blooded and well-bred gentleman would have responded in the negative, in an instant. No hesitations, no second thoughts involved.

His own taut silence verified that trying to abide by every convoluted rule of gentlemanly behavior was beyond the capabilities of any red-blooded male. Especially him.

Chapter Seventeen

Standing in the garden of Jamison House many hours later, Richard hoped his raging inner debate may have resolved itself. At long last, his head might even clear enough to focus on other pressing problems. Such as, was it Lady Hetherington, an escaped madwoman who'd set men after them? Was she trying to kill them?

Or merely frighten them sufficiently that they would withdraw from the race to buy shares in the new railway line about to expand into northern England? Or the proposed one in regional France that the French engineers had requested their assistance, both physical and financial, with.

Or how long before a lunatic and her greed-driven followers succeeded? Those were the sort of nitty-gritty problems a logistical brain like his relished solving.

No wonder he'd scrupulously avoided emotional entanglements. No wonder every male his age did.

Men, by design, weren't equipped with the convoluted reasoning necessary to untangle excesses of sentiment. Though he was wise enough to never share his peculiarly male reasoning with his sisters. All four of them were avid supporters of the new thinking women's movements, even going so far as to carry placards down Oxford Street if a cause fired their imagination.

On those days, he'd learned to hide or invent urgent business appointments or country races. Any excuse that took him outside the Town precincts.

In recent weeks, the clamor in his veins, the depth of his desire, the instinctive and primitive need of a male to claim his mate, had risen, grown, heightened on an almost daily basis. Reminded him every minute, every hour, what had commenced as light-hearted banter and mild family disagreements had progressed into friendship, then crystallized into desire, and now burned hotter than a fever.

Standing beneath Laura's window, he wanted to act the fool and yell at the top of his lungs. Beg Laura to play his Juliet, throw wide her window, and listen to his heart-felt words. Ha! A theatrical reenactment of Shakespeare's love story here, below her window, would scandalize the entire square.

He threw back his head, laughed in silence. He didn't give a damn. The tension left his body and his shoulders sagged in relief. For the first time in days, weeks, his heart felt light. He craved Lady Laura. All of her, all the time. What's more, he'd reached a momentous decision.

Nothing less would do than she agree to marry him. Become his countess. Bear his children. He groaned. Convincing his argumentative adversary might prove the most taxing negotiations he'd ever undertaken. He'd need all his persuasive skills, all his knowledge of stage-managing and dealing with a difficult opponent.

Laura openly admitted she yearned for more demonstrations of his skills as a lover, but getting her to agree to be his wife wouldn't be as easy as asking her to join him in a bed. No. It would need considerable rakish powers of persuasion to convince doubting Laura that the aroma surrounding his clothing and skin could be altered. Changed to smell exactly the way she perceived her future husband's aroma should smell, should waft up to her sensitive nostrils. And no, he refused to accept being merely her part time bed fellow.

He shook the trellis, decided it seemed sound. The rose bushes fanned out higher up. The snarled roots nearer the ground merely needed to be passed without any destruction of his clothing. Since his latest midnight escapades with his partner in crime, Lady-of-the-night Laura, his valet expressed grave concerns over the state of his master's magnificent wardrobe. Bemoaned the fact he'd appear on the streets equipped like a common beggar.

Ah, yes! Perhaps this was his solution. Begin his nights with his scandalous cohort dressed as the low class criminals they invariably ended up mimicking, as they crawled through broken warehouse windows and searched through dusty archives. The things he did for love.

He tugged on the bottom wooden slats, once, twice. Nothing pulled away from the wall, so that part seemed soundly fixed. Reaching up, he repeated the process on the next three levels. All held still. He'd forgotten the items he carried, the reasons for this clandestine visit. Dim-wit.

With difficulty, he looped their strings through his coat opening and, as an extra precaution, tucked them into his vest. He looked up.

The window appeared a long, long way above his head. He groaned.

Generally, the women he liaised with were so eager for his nocturnal visits to their bed chambers, they provided a discreet escort through the front doors, every effort being taken to ensure his comfort along the corridors. By contrast, he didn't make a practice of visiting the chambers, nor even the front greeting rooms, of unmarried innocents. Not without at least two of his sisters as a safeguard to his bachelorhood.

Still, if Romeo had managed it, Richard could. Juliet, or rather, Laura, was worthy of any slight risk to his manhood. Hand over hand, he started to climb, managed his own height off the ground before the first tremble rattled the wooden structure.

Hell's teeth.

The trellis wobbled. Shook. Collapsed.

Whoosh! He fell backwards and landed flat on his back, rose thorns scratching his face in his backwards tumble. Air was knocked out of his lungs and he lay gulping for his next breath. He grabbed his stomach, only to remember the parcels secured there. Gingerly, he opened his vest and felt the wrappings. They appeared intact. The joke would be on him if he'd managed to destroy the same gift twice in one day.

When he could breathe again, without feeling like a horse had kicked him, he rolled to his knees to stand. Directly in his line of vision stood a pair of legs, ones resembling tree trunks and attached to sturdy men's working boots. Warren! Well, he'd plenty of experience bluffing his way to a win in high stakes card games, so surely he was equal to the task of fooling a belligerent thief turned footman.

"Warren, just the man I hoped to find."

Between the full moon and ample street lighting in the Square, he had no problem seeing the skepticism on the man's face. He stood upright, adopting what his sisters referred to as his fiercest about-to-scold expression and what his servants called his, 'Look out, the Earl's after something' stance.

"I brought these packages for the ladies–"

"Ladies, my lord, or one particular lady?"

"Very well. I brought these items to deliver to Lady Laura and didn't want to wake the household, so I thought to drop them over the sill of her window." The man stared at him with an evil eye. "Onto the floor of her room. Without waking her. Or anyone else."

"Terrible thoughtful of ye. Sure 'er aunt will want to thank ye. When she 'ears of this little 'appening in the mornin'."

'Really, is there any need for her aunt to learn of my visit? She might fret more over her niece's safety."

"Sure she would, sir, sure she would. Which is why I'm out 'ere at night, prowlin' , watchin' for rum coves tryin' to climb a rose trellis."

Warren bent to pick up the broken pieces of wood and moved them to the edge of the garden bed.

Richard sighed. "All right. How much will it take to silence you?"

"A bribe, sir? You think my lady's safe nights can be bought away with coin?"

He resisted the urge to grind his teeth. Barely. "I realize you don't trust me after today's activities, but is there anything I can do to assure you I mean no harm to the lady?"

Warren smiled, a terrifying sight. The gap-toothed crooked grin was only slightly less horrendous than his normal scowl. "Ye can show me what you intend leavin' for our gracious lady, and ifin' I say it's orright, I'll take you up there meself."

Richard shock must have been evident, as he couldn't stop his jaw dropping and his body relaxing into a slump. "You'd do that for me? After you saw me at the Countess's house this very afternoon. I assumed you'd want to punch me in the nose."

"On 'pon my word, me and the other footmen drew straws to see who had the luck to flatten your face for you, but Lady Laura wouldn't hear of it. Said you must've 'ad a good reason. And that was before you came a callin' and gave 'er your sorries. If you're good 'nough for our lovely lady, you're good 'nough for us."

He refrained for laughing at this dubious honor. Somehow, he did feel fortunate to have passed inspection by a house full of Laura's devoted servants. "May I ask you, Warren, why you are all so loyal to Lady Laura?"

"Oh, we're grateful to all the family, and that's God's truth. I'd've been in me shroud. Planted deep in the dirt if Lord Michael hadn't rescued me from those bloody nabs. Same for most of the servants "ere. Nothin' we wouldn't do for any one of this family. But 'tis Lady Laura I owe mostly. When me little one took sick–"

"You've children?"

"Yes, sir, two little ones and another on the way."

A hair-raising vision of the streets of Cheapside swarming with red-headed insolent thieves, miniature versions of Warren embedded itself in his brain. He shuddered. Thank heaven Warren remained on the right side of the law these days. Then he thanked the good Lord again that Warren guarded Jamison House at night. The man deserved a bonus. He must remember to arrange for Whittaker to send a large basket of food and toys to Warren's domicile. Assuming Warren intended letting him live to see morning.

"When me little Petie took da croup bad, 'twas milady who mixed one of 'er brews and carried it 'round to me missus. Sat up all the night with Petie feedin' him her curative from a spoon. 'til Petie stopped the coughin'. Saved me boy's life. Saved many another life too wit' them potions and lotions milady mixes in the shed out back of the garden. Terrible sad, though."

He raised his brows and showed his curiosity, encouraging Warren to continue with his insights. Modesty would prevent Laura ever revealing such details about how she spent her hours, instead of frittering them away at one social event after another. She'd never blow her own trumpet.

"The old Earl - though he's supposed ta be master, he's never done a good thing for these lovely ladies. Most 'specially not for Lady Laura. Made Thompkins build milady's distillery over far side of the garden. Far away and outta his sight as possible."

"Hear no evil, see no evil."

"Beggin' pardon."

"Ah, no, nothing. Merely an old nursery mind came to mind. Laura's father liked her out of his sight, so he could put her out of his mind. As if his daughter never existed."

"And milady with her wondrous nose what smells the sweat on a person's skin and knows straight off what ails them. And them hands what mixes things to make ye sickness go away. 'Tis a marvelous gift. And 'tis a crying shame more can't see that it is."

Richard blinked several times to dispel the moisture gathering in his eyes at Warren's tribute to his employer.

"You're quite correct, Warren. 'Tis a terrible shame Lady Laura is forced to hide her skills." He nodded, slapped the other man on the back. "I think it's well past time someone did something about that, don't you?"

Warren nodded, his own eyes streaming with tears. The footman used his enormous paw to swipe away the trail of tears on his cheeks and then beckoned to Richard to follow him.

Together they made their way to an unobtrusive side door, a servant's entrance, where Warren slipped through and waited for Richard to enter.

The footman pointed at the tight steps leading up to the bedrooms. "De-li-ver ye parcels. Nothin' more. I'll be waitin' right 'ere to let ye out ag'in."

Ah, well, that settled the question of whether or not he'd join his beautiful temptress in her bed when he reached her room. He'd spent the last hour convincing himself he possessed enough fortitude to do what he'd come for, and then leave. Yet, he'd also been honest with himself. If Laura awakened and looked at him with seduction in the inky depths of her eyes, his weak will might have been tempted to surrender to her charms. Give in to her coaxing and continue their lessons in love. No question of that now.

He reached her room and padded inside. Beside her bed, he stopped and peered down at her. Slate black curls wound like the fingers of streams through the marsh at night across her pillow. Her arms were thrown up above her head and her fists were clenched as she groaned and murmured in her sleep. As he watched, she twisted and turned, caught in some wild dream.

"No, no, no," she called out.

"Shush, love, shush, it's just a dream."

If he didn't quieten her, one of the other women would rush to investigate her noises and discover him here, standing like a forlorn lovesick idiot staring at her linen-covered form in her bed, waiting for her to throw him a few crumbs of pleasure.

She rolled from side to side, groaned again, louder this time and thrashed her head against the pillows. He dropped his wrapped parcels on the bedside table and sat on the edge of the bed, drawing her fists down into his hands. With his fingers, he unfurled their clench and soothed their soft interiors until she relaxed her tense grip.

"That's it, love, just a dream." He reached up and stroked the damp strands of hair away from her face, marveling at the softness of her skin. Honey again. Something like the lotion she used on her hands.

On impulse, he bent closer to her face and licked a light trail up one side. She tasted like pure heaven. One more and he'd stop. Only one more taste of her skin on the side of her face meant another on her neck and, finally, a light lick across her slightly-opened mouth.

He'd go to hell for this, but he couldn't resist. He opened his own mouth against her and stilled, closing his eyes against the jolt of pleasure rushing through his body. The joy signing through his limbs and the blood heating in his veins. Just once more. He sighed softly against her lips, feeling his breath brush over her warm flesh and come back to invade his mouth and his senses.

Very slowly he pulled away and opened his eyes. Damnation. A deep, dark, dazzled gaze met his. Using extreme care, he stood and started to back away, hoping she slept and hadn't really opened her eyes and stared at him. Hoping she'd imagine herself to be caught in the throes of a dream.

"Stop." Her hand shot out to grasp his wrist, pushing the bedclothes down past her waist. Though her expression looked sluggish, half asleep, the grip on his arm was firm. "Richard?"

He sat again, and resumed a soft stoke of her hair, willing her eyes to close. After several long heart-stopping seconds, her lids drifted shut and her hand dropped back to the bedclothes.

"Don't go. I need you." Her words came as a sleepy closed-eyed murmur. "Dreams. Bad."

"I know, love. Shush. I'm here. Go back to sleep."

"Help me. Love me."

No man could resist her sad begging voice and remain sane. No man could walk away and leave an angel in pain. And especially not a man who cared more for her well-being than for his own life.

He moved to the edge of the bed and stretched out beside her, keeping his boots away from the pretty coverlet. Large, dirty, man-sized footprints on her spread would tell everything if noticed in the morning. By tucking one arm under her neck, he could raise her slightly to meet the downward quest of his mouth.

"How can I help but love you, my darling?" He murmured soft words over and over as he brushed his mouth back and forth across hers in time to his soothing nonsenses.

Her free arm lifted on the other side and came across his neck, anchoring him in place, pulling him closer. Her limb draped him limply, yet gave implicit orders as to what she required from him. Nothing differed from when she was awake.

Still demanding. Still greedy. Still his.

He kissed her now as he wanted, letting her feel his own greed and raw need. Not of a depth to frighten her, merely to demonstrate the depth of his desire and the care he was prepared to take with her tutoring. Not tonight though, Not with Wicked Warren watching for him below stairs.

He dragged back an inch and slid his mouth further south on her body. Gooseflesh pebbled along bare skin and her nipples rose to instant attention and pushed through the thin lawn of her nightgown. He swallowed.

"You're so responsive, so passionate," he murmured, his face snug against her warm breast.

She'd better agree to marry him, quickly, or he'd need to be locked in Bedlam with lunatic Lady Hetherington and her henchmen. He wanted her so much that his body shook with it. His fingers trembled as they hovered a hair's breadth above her breast. He cupped it, the full round shape of pulsing female flesh swelled against his palm and wrung an unbidden groan from his lips.

Sliding down a little more, he twisted so he half covered her body with his and lowered his mouth over her areola, sucking the entire area into his starving mouth. Adopting the age old rhythms of a beloved, he sucked, tugged, squeezed and pulled on her breast, and marveled at the newness of the sensations he experienced only with this particular woman.

At the same time, he felt he'd been her lover forever, knowing the intricacies of her body, the ways she twisted and shifted when she wanted him to move to the other neglected breast; the sweet sucking sound she made with her mouth in unison with his noisier ones, as if urging him on, stronger, faster, longer, and always more, more, more.

Her unspoken chant resounded through his head. Give me more, she cried. Give me everything. He slid one hand beneath the covers and felt for the hem of the gown, sliding it upwards with his fingers in a soft slow sensuous glide over petal-soft skin. He pictured her thighs. They'd be milky white, smelling of honey from her lotions and dripping with cream from her womanly center.

His middle finger touched liquid: smooth, flowing, wet. Oh, so very, very wet. So ready for him. As he was ready for her.

No, not yet.

He touched her folds, the gentle kiss of a butterfly landing on a beautiful flower, and she arched from the bed. Her hips lifted towards his hand, seared back and forth, seeking. Her eyelids lifted a fraction, her dark lashes fluttering several times as she struggled to focus on his face.

"Richard, I need you."

"Oh, sweetheart, I need you, too. You have no idea how much I want you right now. But I can't. I promised Michael. I promised Cayle and Becca and–" He broke off and gave a quiet chuckle. "And even Warren standing guard downstairs. Believe me, I will soon claim you in every way possible. But not here, Not tonight. Not when your sister or aunt may come into the room at any moment. When I have you, little love, it will be at a time when we can enjoy each other's bodies. When the desperation to join with each other is so overwhelming that nothing can stop us. Do you understand?"

She nodded and relaxed back against the sheet. She squirmed. "It hurts."

He chuckled again. "I know, my sweet. It hurts me, too."

He shifted slightly on the bed, trying to ease his own rising discomfort. His hard erection pushed against his trouser seams, begging for release. He reached down to ease it into a more comfortable position, but encountered another hand already there, reaching, searching.

Laura's touch on his aroused flesh, even through the layers of cloth, was so exquisite he could die happy right now, simply from knowing the pleasure of her hand moving over this throbbing part of his body. He swelled into her palm and groaned again. Unable to stand the suspense, he reached down and tugged opened the first two button, freeing his erection to jut into the air. Her hand sought it blindly again. Placing his own palm over her hand, he guided her to where he bounced and bobbed beside her hip, his engorged flesh expressing its delight at escaping its tight confines.

Her fingers wrapped around him, sweetly, softly, femininely, and his eye rolled back in his head. He swore.

She jerked back. "Did that hurt?"

He shook his head and then realized she couldn't see those sort of movements in the darkened room. They were both working on their other senses; those of touch and sound and smell.

Yes. That might be the way to convince her they were right for each other, after all. Not his outer distillery concocted fragrance, but his essence. He retracted his finger from where it had still rested inside her tight secret passageway and, taking her hand in his, swiped both their fingers across the head of his penis, taking up his pre-come.

He lifted his fingers between them. "Open your senses, love, the ones you are so good at. Use your acute sense of smell and tell me what you notice.

"Yes. Musky. Salty."

"That's you and me. Our mutual desire. Swirling together. Mixed. The blends in that aroma, do you smell them? High note. Low notes. Isn't that what you look for when you try to mix the perfect perfume? Two oils that blend seamlessly together without ever separating in the future."

"Yes."

"Then I want you to remember that tomorrow, and the next day, and every day thereafter. Whenever you try to tell me that you've run your extensive series of tests on me, on the odors my skin emits, and we're not an ideal match."

Ruthless now, desperate to make her understand his hidden message, he lowered both their hand to her own sex once again. "Yours," he circled her swollen nub, delighting in the hard push of it against his finger. "Yours is so musky with your desire that it brings me to my knees. The thought of how much you want me.

"This lotion, as sticky as the cream you use on your hands," he thrust her fingers deep inside herself, "it drips onto our fingers, as finely the best quality new honey from the abbey monks."

"Richard," she moaned again, and started those little upward pushes with her hips.

Each push thrust their joined fingers a litter further into her entrance, and he used his own digit to circle the sensitive nerves he knew rested around the rim. Short panting little gasp told him he'd found the right spots to arouse her even more, even faster. Not that his passionate little love needed any encouragement from him to enjoy herself. She was already in that self-absorbed space in her own mind where she could only concentrate on reaching that elusive goal. Freeing her body from this torment.

She grunted her impatience at him, as if his deliberate delaying tactics must cease immediately, or she would reprimand him in her normal daylight fashion. Bedding this woman every day for the rest of their lives would be a delight, as she'd never let him rest on his rakish laurels, would always demand more and more adventurous sexual behaviors to attempt with him. He couldn't wait.

"Easy, love, easy. Let me stop your hurting."

It took so little time that he was actually disappointed, wanting to prolong the bliss for himself, if not for her. But she was so ready, so ripe for her release that a few quick short thrust with his imbedded finger and a few swirls of his thumb around the exposed nub, and she shot to her peak like a shooting star in the night sky in the Pacific Ocean.

Her orgasm was prolonged and profound and he guided her through it with his fingers, until every twitch and shudder had subsided and she flopped back into the mattress with a loud whoosh of exhaled breath.

"That was so–so–"

"Soothing?"

"Exciting. Stimulating."

She pushed up onto her elbows and beamed at him. Wide awake. By rights, he should wait until their wedding night to initiate her fully into the world of sex, knowing her passionate nature would see her adapt to it like a duck to water. He also knew he was in deep, deep trouble when she directed a knowing feminine smile at his bobbing erection.

She licked her lips. Bared her teeth. Her expression was that of a hungry dog about to gnaw on a meaty bone. His bone.

He held out his palm. "Oh, no, no, no. Whatever you are considering, it is not going to happen. Not tonight at any rate."

She stared at him, her gaze intent; her intent clear.

"No, no, no," he tried again.

Too late. She took his throbbing member in her hand and bent her head. He'd had mistresses who'd never get this close to a man's most private parts, who believed a penis the province of only street whores. His breath caught. His mind reeled as tried to fathom her intention.

Her hair feel forward as she peered closer. One hand came out to the bedside table and she groped about, searching for something. He glanced down to see what it was she sought.

From his position he had the better view, for what little light was thrown from the candle standing at the back of the nightstand slashed across in his direction. His body blocked her view.

"Glasses," she muttered, still groping.

He passed the gold framed spectacles to her, placing them into her outstretched hand, and she pushed them onto her noise, securing the wire ear pieces and then bet once more to her intense study of his erection. She pushed him to one side so the light illuminated his manly parts better, caught its skyward lift.

"Aw, hell, Laura. You refuse to wear them when you go dancing and bump into all the other couples on a dance floor. You refuse to wear them for a walk in the park as would-be suitors might regard you as a blue-stocking. Yet now you'll don spectacles to study my anatomy as if I'm one of your scientific specimens. I feel like Michelangelo's statue of David in Rome, the naked one that all the schoolgirls giggle over in their father's illustrated art books."

"Oh, you're far more interesting than any cold marble statue."

He chuckled. "Thank you, I think."

'For one thing, you're a lot warmer, and the tip of you glows blue like the color of those pretty worms that burrow into berry leaves–"

"Oh, for goodness sake. A worm?

You're comparing my most precious bodily possession to a common worm?"

She giggled. "Not a common one, my darling, but one of those special ones the Chinese use to spin silk cocoons."

He heard her words through a fog, for his mind had stopped at the name she called him. Did she realize what she'd said? Confessed. No, he was certain she didn't. Although, he had a clear recollection that it was her exact expression.

She'd not called him irritating, or arrogant. Or impossible. No. She'd called him, *my darling*.

Something that had been wound tight as a spring inside him for weeks, eased. The first around his heart loosened. It was going to be all right.

"What did you say? What will be all right?"

He looked at her and smiled, his inquisitive little nemesis. "I told you I'd enjoy you doing to me anything I did to you. Better than enjoying, your touch on any part of my body is a miracle to me."

She gave him a suspicious glance but returned to her task. The one involving sliding the skin of his penis in a jerky, yet incredibly erotic, journey, up and down. She dallied over the tip, bending to study the underside and then stared, wide-eyed, when it jerked in response.

"I feel like an ant being watched by a small child who is lying on the ground beside it."

She smiled briefly, but went back to her explorations, her

examinations, giving little sounds of joy at each new discovery.

"Enough," he finally cried, grasping her hand and setting it back into a strong and steady rhythm. When he'd climbed those stairs, this hadn't been his intention. But now, two choices lay before him. He could walk past Warren wide-legged, in agony from his blue balls, and suffer Warren's knowing grin. Or he could spend a minute, for that would be the meagre amount of time required under her present ministrations, and relieve his weeks of celibacy.

He pushed aside his third choice.

His non-interest in several blatant female advances in recent weeks had become a topic of high amusement amongst his friends, only his closest, like his two cousins, guessing the reason. Bedding another woman held no appeal when his mind was filled from daylight to dark with this woman, the one gripping his shaft as if was the staff of knowledge.

His rational self emerged long enough to pull a handkerchief from his coat pocket and thrust it under the end of his cock, without a moment to spare. His entire body jerked, several times, his shaft thrusting over and over through Laura's fingers to spill and spurt into his waiting linen. With a deeply satisfied groan, he wrapped the evidence of the most incredible orgasm in his sexual life and thrust it into his pocket.

And without even being inside her tight passage. Without even the joy of spilling his seed high in her womb and praying they created a miracle together. Praying for their first babe. When he finally gathered strength, he opened his eyes to find her watching him closely again. He snorted.

"Don't tell me. I shall be recorded in your notebook under, *Species Studied in the Aftermath of Sexual Bliss.*"

Her eyes widened. "Was it bliss?"

He bent to plant a light kiss on her questioning mouth. "More than bliss. A gift such as I've never given or received before."

She worried her bottom lip.

"What's worrying you now? More study needed? More tests to run on me? Feel free, use my body any way you wish. My anatomy is at the services of Madam Scientist."

"What worries me is my intimate tests with you contradict every other study I've made. I've tried to predict if our chemical smells attract each other and they don't. Never. Not once. Even in dog and cat populations, males and females find each other by smell. Those silk worms I mentioned: they have the same sort of sensory drive and release an odor to attract their mates. The fan bee waves her wings and wafts out an odor to attract the swarm to the hive."

He sat up and rubbed his hand through his disheveled hair, trying to make himself presentable before he faced Warren's stare.

"You are unbelievable. No wonder we always argue. I've just introduced you to pure pleasure. We both collapsed in each other's hands. And you—you now want to debate whether or not animals and insects know more than our bodies do. Well, I can assure you, my little disbeliever, that I know more about your mind and your body than any research will tell. More than years of taking notes in notebooks and calculating the results will mean to you. We belong together. And if that little experiment," he gestured to where her nightgown still lay high on her wide apart thighs, "didn't prove it to you, I don't know what else to do to convince you."

Without saying another word, he checked that his gifts rested safely on the table and stood and left the room, and the floor, before he gave into the temptation to turn around and go back. Warren half-dosed in a chair in the tiny entranceway, but came to his feet at Richard's footsteps.

Richard drew in a sharp breath and prepared for a fight. He held a hand up to the footman. "If you want to retain the shape of that nose of yours, you'll keep your mouth shut."

"Well, I'll be a sow's ear. I gave you extra time, trusting you to do right, but thinkin' all the same that you'd come down 'ere lookin' a damn sight 'appier than went you went up. You gentry know how to make a mess of lovin'. It aint that 'ard to make a woman 'appy, you know."

"And I don't need you giving me lessons on managing a woman."

"Huh! If you be thinkin' to hustle milady, I'll tell you now, you ain't got a pig's chance in hell. Need to talk to her smart side. With all them fat books on plants and insects and how they catch their wives and with writin' rolls of men's names like when we make a legal vote, milady'll only fall under the spell of a man who outsmarts her on her own list making."

Richard's mouth dropped open in awe. The bloody footman was right. That was exactly how he needed to manage - oops, wrong word. How he needed to coerce that stubborn woman above them into his way of thinking. Ah, yes, now he felt better. He liked knowing he had control of the situation again.

"Warren, your advice is excellent. Fight fire with fire."

The footman scratched his head. "That 'nother one of those nursery songs?"

"A proverb. Meaning I need to counter-attack. Assemble my own arsenal of scientific treatises to prove my side of the argument. Everyone who undertakes research knows things aren't always what they seem, so we need to dig deeper, look at the wider picture. In this case, we need to sail other oceans to acquire new knowledge."

"'Fraid you've confused me there, sir. What good will it do sailin' off now, You need to be 'ere to fight off all those other la-de-da gents what comes deliverin' flowers every day of the week for milady."

His eyes narrowed on the man. "Flowers? What flowers, and what men?" If a giant of a man with more scars than cheeks could blush, then Warren turned as red as tomato. Richard took a step closer to the footman, clenched his fists. "Tell me all of it. Now."

"Well, twas a kindness really, from 'er ladyship to ye. She said ye didn't suit her for a marriage, so she still needed to find other men to add to those lists of names of 'ers, ye know?"

"I know." Richard nodded his encouragement at the man. "Lists, like on ballot papers."

Warren nodded his huge head. "So, she said 'twere kinder if ye didn't guess there were a lot of other gents, plenty of em when I adds 'em up, who fitted the chem– chemmie something or other–"

"Chemicals?"

"That'sit. Stuck with her chem-min-icales."

His jaw clenched. "I am going… to throttle… the little twit." He swung around to storm back up the staircase but Warren, despite his bulk, was light on his feet. The footman beat him to the first tread, and planted himself firmly in his pathway. Crossed arms completed Warren's picture of impenetrable force.

"How dare Laura decide what might anger me, and what mightn't."

"Think milady got the right of it though, didn't she? Ye've blue steam spoutin' outta ye ears."

When Warren put a beefy arm around his shoulders, he winced, but stiffened, determined not to display any weakness in front of the outspoken servant. He hadn't yet decided if the man was friend or foe, but felt it better to err on the side of safety.

"Now, milord, why don't ye go along 'ome? Spend the rest of the night ponderin' that little thing about other oceans. See if ye can think of some way to make milady 'ave ye that don't involve no sail boats heavin" off to the seven seas."

Richard blinked at the analogy, but then recognizing the wisdom in the man's words, nodded. Furious as he was with Laura—nothing unusual there—he needed to hasten along the formal process to their marriage. Only by creating his own force of nature would he sweep Lively Laura into a fast decision, without giving her enough time to ponder on all the ramifications of marrying him.

If she debated the wisdom of surrendering her prized freedom to a man she felt unsuitable, he'd he facing the same up-hill battle his cousin, Sherwyn, had had to face in getting Becca to agree to a date to meet him in church.

The Jamison women might be noted for their stubbornness, but the St. Martin men were noted for being able to outwit and out-maneuver the most formidable opponent. He'd not taken Laura's virginity, but it was only a matter of time. Quite probably only hours until his unruly libido raised its head again, and refused to be pushed back into his trousers and ignored.

A single thought of Laura and her passionate nature stirred him to craziness, so in another week or two he'd be begging her on bended knee in the middle of Bond Street to become her love slave. Then he'd know true humiliation amongst his peers. Right now though, he had calls to make. His friend also kept strange hours, so he'd be up working on problems. Fine. He could help work on Richard's instead.

He needed a solution, and he needed it quickly. He needed someone smarter than himself when it came to science.

He cursed all the times his eyes had glazed over when Laura had set forth on her favorite topics. What were those terms he racked his brain to recall? Olfactory? Perspiring?

Damnation. There was nothing wrong with plain old sweat and plain old smelling.

Chapter Eighteen

"Where are you taking me?"

They were seated in his carriage, and she'd asked the question three times already.

"To meet a friend of mine. You'll like him."

"Why have I never met this particular friend before?"

"Because Gerard tends to shun society." He grinned. "Partly for the same reason all bachelors avoid it like the plague. Too many matchmaking mamas and far too many scheming chits with money and titles in their sights."

"You seem to have avoided both quite nimbly for several years. At your ripe old age one would assume you're too slow to outrun them any longer."

He grasped his chest. "Oh. A direct hit. How you wound me speaking of my addled years catching up with me."

She shook her head in mock reproof. "Sometimes, I don't know what to do with you."

He gave her a lecherous leer. "I can think of many things you could start with, my love."

She burst out laughing, then stopped abruptly when the carriage pulled to a halt outside an opulent townhouse in a street she'd never been in before.

"Do I need to know the other reason he remains reclusive?"

"Umm. Better to let you perceive that for yourself. I can hardly wait to see your reaction."

"By the way, I wanted to thank you for your gifts last night."

He gave her a long leering look.

She reddened. "Not that one. The toffee you replaced for my aunt. You must have needed to waken the shop keeper in the middle of the night to buy a new packet."

He shrugged.

"And thank you for the notebooks. My old one. And the new ones. They are beautiful. So many vibrant colors."

"They reminded me of you. I thought you might like to write about me in one sometime."

"You mean you didn't read the old one of mine? Not curious to see what I wrote?"

"Oh, I was eaten up with curiosity. But I'd never invade your privacy. Not without being invited. I hope you invite me to do so again. Soon."

She swallowed. Loudly. Visibly.

Ten minutes later, a severe-looking butler guided them through an incredible number of hallways and corridors to the back of the house. Large double glass door opened into an enormous conservatory and, although he'd been there many times before, the sight never failed to impress.

Beside him, Laura gasped, loud and long, and when he turned towards her, those incredible eyes widened with awe and pleasure, and her mouth open with speechless wonder. In fact, her eyes had held the same unfocused glazed look as when she'd climaxed in his arms. An image that tightened his muscles and sped his pulse.

He wanted to taste that pleasure on her skin and place his mouth over her wide-opened one.

She placed her hand on his coat sleeve, pressing down in her excitement. "It's… it's…"

"I hope you are about to say it's incredible and a credit to its architect," a deep honeyed voice said from directly in front of them. "Not that it's a frivolous waste of money."

The owner of the voice that brought women everywhere to their knees, stepped up to meet Laura's eyes and held out his hand to her. By habit, she extended her own and he lifted it to his lips to place a lingering kiss upon her gloved hand.

"Ahem." He deliberately dispelled the tension filled moment. "Gerard, must I remind you that a true gentlemen never actually lays his lips upon a lady's glove. The idea is to hover above it."

His friend grinned, but didn't move his direct gaze from Laura's eyes and kept his hold on her fingers. "Like a circling hawk, readying itself to pounce on its prey."

He reached across and removed Gerard's fingers from Laura's. "Did I not request that you behave yourself if I brought her to meet you? I also asked you to be suitably attired." All three of them looked down at Gerard's chest, a deep slash of it exposed in the opening of his lawn shirt.

"I donned this shirt in courtesy to a young lady's sensibilities." He dipped his head to Laura, who still hadn't spoken.

Winchester rolled his eyes. "Suitably attired includes a vest, coat and cravat." He glanced down. "And stockings and shoes."

"I prefer these Dutch clogs. Much more comfortable for pottering around my laboratory."

Laura's eyes flared with interest. "Laboratory?"

Gerard smiled at her. "Richard told me that would capture your interest. You are a distiller and a perfumer, he tells me. Fascinating."

Richard took Laura's arm and drew her away from Gerard. He indicated the conservatory, where towering palms grew towards the glass panels in the rooftop and row upon row of exotic plants vied for space in the humidified atmosphere. "Shall we explore?"

Gerard laughed, but turned to show them the way down an aisle filled with flowering orchids. "Lady Laura, what did our friend here tell you about me."

"Only that you shun society. And yes, Richard, I can now understand why."

"Ludicrous isn't it? Though apparently your younger sister suffers the same inconvenience."

"She does, although we have learned to utilize her stunning attractions for the good of our cause. We dangle her as bait to attract the fishermen with the most catch to display."

"Ah, a euphemism for coercing men of the ton into spilling their secrets."

"I'm certain, with your strikingly handsome looks, you've found a way to use your to gain you something."

"Gerard dangles himself as bait, and the women jump like eager fish into his catch basket and beg to be eaten."

Laura chuckled. "What a skill to possess. I imagine Richard is green with envy."

"Ah, but now he has you, Lovely Laura, it is I who is envious."

"I don't *have* anyone," Richard muttered.

Gerard flashed him a grin, before draping a lazy arm around her shoulders and walking beside her towards the back of the conservatory, heads together, new friends already. He tried not to allow it to niggle him, although it did, as he'd instigated this rendezvous for a purpose. They reached Gerard's workroom and, with a flourish, he threw open the door and allowed Laura to proceed him.

Again she gasped. "This is even more incredible than your greenhouse. Did you design this as well?"

"I did."

"Quite staggering how much you remind me of my younger sister. She also tunnels her intelligence into creative projects as a way of compensating for all the hours she must spend on display, pretending to be nothing more than a beautiful woman. You've also found outlets for your talents to counterbalance your…ah…"

As he caught up to them, Richard said, "Please, don't let my presence stop you describing my friend's attributes. He adores it so much. Women call him an Adonis. An angel. Compare his perfect features to a cherub's."

"Very droll, Richard. I loathe it. Nature endowed me blond hair and blue eyes and a dark complexion so, for some inscrutable reason, a rumor began in society that I am some sort of God. A lucky charm. And that by being bedded by me they absorb some of my cherubic qualities. Stuff and nonsense, I know. As any intelligent person does. But nobody ever claimed that those who inherit titles also inherit intelligence."

Gerard guided Laura to a lengthy workbench, stretching along one entire wall. Set up at regular intervals were a myriad of thin glass flasks set in wire stands over small burners. Hundreds of small vials and bottles lined up like soldiers on narrow, especially-built shelves.

"This is where I conduct my experiments. I've been collecting pollens and seeds from plants and flowers and using a number of different methods, trying to create new variations on several old receipts for medications. My parents were noted scientists. They inspired my interest in curatives, preventatives and the mixing of them."

Laura became excited. "Many of your experiments must overlap mine. I distil plants, leaves and barks and mix the oils I extract into treatments for many common ailments to treat my family and friends."

"I know you also have an acute sense of smell," Gerard said. "I, too, have done research into something of that sort. In some cultures where men are allowed more than one woman, a husband chooses his woman for the night by how they smell. It is said that he can pick the woman who is most ready to conceive his child by her general scent."

"That is the theory I have been testing but it hasn't worked. I thought by sniffing men and detecting their pheromones, I could find a husband." She flicked a quick glance Richard's way, but her excited words were directed at Gerard. "Can you tell me why my theory isn't working?"

"Have you considered that it is working but in reverse?"

Richard watched Laura frown, rub her forehead, try to puzzle that out in her quick brain. "I am afraid I do not understand."

Gerard gestured at Richard. "The man can also chose by scent. You should allow Richard the chance. The results may surprise you. I now believe that when two people belong together, either one of them may detect the other first. Or notice first." He beckoned. "Richard, explain to Laura what you told me. About her scent."

When Laura looked at him with raised brows, he stepped closer to her and took her hands. "I started thinking about your ideas. The frustration you're feeling that you're wasting your evenings searching ballrooms looking for an invisible man. I wanted to help you. In any way I could. So, I asked Gerard how it linked to his own research and how it would affect yours and he explained that although your theories were sound and had been proven by scientists who had researched primitive tribes in several countries and–"

"Richard, slow down," Laura said, as Gerard chuckled quietly beside them. "You sound nervous. Like Aunt Aggie, when she is excited about something and can't stop talking."

"Allow me, my long-winded friend. If we wait for you to complete your explanation, our luncheon will be cold. Not only can the women in other cultures scent their mates. Men are also capable of doing that."

"Perhaps, Richard, you could demonstrate to Laura what you mean."

"I know your scent and can recognize you in a crowd of people. Your aroma calls to me."

"Ha! That theory is contradicted before you begin, because I do not wear any scent." She stabbed a finger in the direction of his chest. "It interferes with my ability to detect the natural odors in others."

Turning to Gerard, he threw his arms wide. "Do you now see what I suffer here? She argues over every minor detail. This stubborn termagant is so opinionated over this particular matter that she refuses to listen to anyone else's ideas. She makes everything in our lives far more complicated than they need to be."

She stomped one booted foot on his own. Hard. He jerked his leg back away from her reach, so she could not repeat the insult as he pointed a finger towards her nose. However, his mouth twitched. He could never remain angry at her for long.

"Will you please stop doing that," he pleaded, circling his finger near her nose. "My valet is becoming upset that the shine he takes hours to perfect is being scrubbed away from every pair of boots I possess. Do you truly imagine that I spend countless evenings in your company, yet I cannot recognize that the only aroma that clings to your skin is your natural scent? The ones you absorb as you go about your day."

She frowned and him, planting her hands on her hips in her normal belligerent stance. "You are full of fustian."

"When I prove my idea correct, you'll be required to pay me a forfeit." He held up a hand before she spoke. "One I will devise at a later time. We wouldn't wish to embarrass our host."

Gerard grinned. "Please, don't mind me. I'm enjoying myself. Perhaps I should take a notebook, and write my findings and conclusion from this interesting experiment." Richard glared at his friend but he paid no attention, staring at Laura in an irritatingly intense manner.

"Very well," Richard said. "On Mondays, you carry the odor of lemons about your person, after you've helped with the linen and bedding at the fallen women's shelter. I assume you are involved in preparing beds for women and children who are escaping untenable situations, and need a place to rest and regain themselves."

Ignoring Laura's stunned look he continued, "Two Wednesdays each month, you return to your house smelling of the forest. Like the pine trees and cones you've spent the day helping the children from orphanage collect and load on wagons. You enjoy ensuring those visits to the country give them enough wood to burn in their fires."

"I–I had no idea. Your nose must be very sensitive."

He shook his head. "The only person about which I've acquired this intense sense, what soap they've used, what petals they've used in their hair rinse, or what lotion they use to soften their hands....is you. Only you, my love."

Gerard broke the growing tension between them. "You shouldn't be discouraged, Laura, as I'm certain your skills would allow you to discern the same sort of everyday scents about our friend."

"But all I ever detect on him is the cologne I mix for him. Bergamot and lemon. The soap I blend especially for his use."

Gerard said, "Don't you detect other things about him? Things giving you a sense of the activities Richard's followed during that particular day?"

"Well, yes, of course. Because he doesn't always apply cologne."

She turned to him, standing so close he could smell today's visiting scent.

"Roses today, in the lotion on your hands. You intend paying visits to some older ladies, ones who appreciate very subtle floral fragrances drifting around them as they drink tea and reminisce."

He grinned at her. And she smiled back, a genuine smile of understanding.

Perhaps it would be all right after all.

Perhaps she would give them a chance. It was all he asked.

"On Mondays, you smell…male."

"Male doesn't sound terribly pleasing. Amongst well-bred gents who frequent the toffiest clubs to pose, one daren't mention people perspire."

"A little perspiration is good," Gerard added.

"It could be classed as one of those essentially strong male caveman smells which attract the, supposedly, weaker gender. The need of a woman for a protector."

"You attend boxing bouts and, knowing you as I do, you put every ounce of effort into winning each round. Therefore, your clothes will absorb the perspiration from those efforts. Not a repulsive smell. Simply a strong one that indicates the activity it took to achieve it. On Thursdays, after you've been to Tattersall's, you'll naturally carry the smell of horses, leather and men smoking. It clings to your coat and to you skin. I've been ridiculously narrow-minded over this issue, haven't I?"

"No, no," Gerard assured her, grasping her hand and earning himself a sharp grunt in disapproval.

"Yes, yes. I realize now that Richard's smell is one of everyday comfort and familiarity, and I completely ignored it as I refused to name the subtle layers of his scent. I believed the ones I mixed for him so suited his characteristics that I arrogantly looked no deeper. Good gracious! What sort of a scientist am I? I skewed the results in whichever favor suited my purpose."

She turned to him. "Please, please accept my sincerest apology, Richard. I truly believed the only scents you liked were mine, the ones I created."

"Tell her the entire story, Richard."

"Well, in truth, I don't particularly like the strength of the bergamot you mix for me. It makes me sneeze."

Her hand went to her mouth as she tried, unsuccessfully, to smother her loud gasp. She shook her head back and forth. Backed away from them. "All those times you sneeze. I caused them. You have an allergy to the orange base in the oil."

She groaned and dropped her head. "Oh, no. I've remembered now. In your youth, eating too many oranges gave you a rash. Why, oh why, did you not tell me? Why did you wear it?"

He looked at her and shrugged. "You created it. Of course I'd wear it."

"I'm mortified over my own stupidity. You suffered such discomfort simply to not upset me."

"We're friends. I didn't want to upset you. Besides which, my reaction to oranges is a minor discomfort. Not worth mentioning."

"Of course it's worth mentioning, you conciliatory idiot." She hit his arm again. "We may disagree, argue, and irritate each other." She tried to stomp on his foot, but he jerked it back in the nick of time. "But I would never, ever, wish you harm."

Chapter Nineteen

Around midnight, Laura pulled her over-large man's coat tighter around her shoulders to stave off the chill from the damp corridor, as she tramped along behind the laughing men. Their plan—hers, to be truthful—to walk in the front door as patrons of a brothel, had gone awry. Desperately, stupidly, awry.

Behind her, the stomp of Richard's footsteps should have offered some comfort, but she knew his prolonged silence indicated the level of his anger. When they'd concluded, over luncheon at Grosvenor Square, that a visit to this particular establishment had become a priority, he'd insisted that he, Brian and Tony would take care of the matter. Then his cousins had rushed off to assist in the arrest of six identified members of the Syndicate involved in the abduction of their friend, Longman.

Richard insisted on waiting. She persisted with the argument that, by the next night, the evidence they'd been told existed in this brothel would've been moved, as the ownership had changed hands. This little adventure had been to collect enough written evidence to prove that Lady Hetherington owned this pleasure house as one of several she'd acquired by illegal means. It was one of the girls working there who had sent an urgent message to Jamison House.

The brothels might have been acquired by coercion and blackmail, but the cunning lady intended selling them now, one by one, and using her ill-gotten gains to purchase every share she could in the new railway extensions. Thus turning dirty money into clean money. The woman might be mad, but underneath that craziness was a shrewdness that had led them a merry chase for weeks. Now, tonight, they were moving in on her. Or so they had thought.

Laura had made one teeny weeny little mistake in her calculations. A mistake he obviously intended holding against her forever.

Judging by the unnecessarily heavy stamp of booted feet behind her, and the angry mutterings interspersed with swear words she'd never heard before, Richard's head of steam was building to an explosion. An explosion aimed at her.

"I'm sorry," she whispered over her shoulder. "Are you ever going to speak to me again?"

"No."

"How could I have predicted those men would want me that…that disgusting way?"

"What did you expect?" His words were as cold as the walls they passed. "You came to a brothel, and you dressed like a prostitute. Men come here with the express intention of doing …*that*! They come to do many sordid and disgusting things with the women who work here."

"I– I–" She sniffed.

"You're not crying, are you?"

"Of course not," she lied. "The cold is making my nose run. But truly, Richard, call me naïve if you wish, but nothing Madame Faberge explained to us involved six men purchasing one woman. Plus, I always assumed that even a brothel worker would be given a moment to formulate their reply when the offer involved an uneven number of participants. To decide if they were rested enough to participate in a–a–"

"An orgy?" The word was offered with acute sarcasm. "And whatever possessed you to call yourself Madame Fabergé? Every one of those gentlemen will visit her establishment on a regular basis. They'll know she has red hair, not black.

They'd know that the idea of six men and one woman wouldn't send Madame Fabergé into a blue fit. Nor would a true bordello Madame slap the faces of the wealthy men suggesting it."

"I didn't think–"

"That's the problem with you, Laura. You don't think. You rush in. You place yourself in danger. It's far, far too frightening for me to keep enduring. When we're married, when you're my wife, I'll not allow you to take such risks."

"Married? Wife? Allow?"

"Stop repeating my words like a sailor's parrot."

"Nobody said I was marrying you."

"I did."

"I didn't."

"I don't care what you say. You are marrying me. As soon as we get out of here."

Laura came to an abrupt halt, slamming in to the mountainous back of the brute she followed. "Ow!"

Richard rushed up beside her, trying to put his arms around her, but his hands were tied at the wrists. "Untie me, you idiot. Let me see if you hurt her."

"Listen up, you two squabbling children." The man turned to face them both, holding his lantern higher so they could see the fierce look on his face. "My ears is ringin' with your fightin'. And makes no matter if you say you goin' to marry the gent or not, lady, cause come mornin', our boss lady upstairs is goin' to have you both killed, anyways."

He scratched his fat belly, then threw back his dirty-haired head and laughed. His mate up ahead stopped and called out, "What are you doin'? Come on. Bring 'em up 'ere. Time for our supper."

Between the two guards, they were pushed and pulled towards a dark and dank basement room. Garlic breath, their old friend, threw them into a cellar, without ceremony, then turned a key in the outside lock as he left.

He pushed his nose back through the grated section of the door. "My lady upstairs is too busy to see you tonight. But she knows you're here. Said to tell you she's been expecting you here for days. She'll deal with you two interfering bastards in the morning. After the sale of this ere place is finished. After all the patrons has left. Big celebrations upstairs tonight. The lady is going to very wealthy, come mornin'."

The other man, Weak Wrist, laughed. "That lady is right clever, for she knew you'd be comin' and searchin' for us. Ever since you broke into the warehouse. Said she hadda feelin'--some sorta sensation in her bones—that it would be those bloody interfering Jamisons again."

"That's why we've been keepin' such a good eye on all of you. But have to tell you, you've got her right angered, and she doesn't like being angered."

Richard stepped in front of Laura, pushing her behind him. "Our friends will be here with Scotland Yard to arrest all of you, long before morning. You'd better let us go now and get away while you can."

"No I don't think so. Think I'm goin' to enjoy dealing with the little lady here, all by myself. When we get you out of the city in the morning, and find a nice quiet spot, we gunner have a little sport with you. Pay you back for upsetting our plans so many times."

"And for being so bloody 'ard to kill."

"Madame, or the good Lady Hetherington to those that know her, only wants us to kill you quick like, but Nifty is right. You've been a thorn in our hides for too long. Time for some pay back."

"The lady says you deserve to be punished for all the grief you've caused, and all the delays you three sisters have caused for her. She want to control that whole Stock Exchange. Kick out all the men. Take it over for herself. Then we'll all be rollin' in the coin."

"That's utter lunacy." Richard stepped up to the man's face. "If you believe that will ever be allowed to happen by the stuffed shirts members of the ton who have all their wealth invested there, you're as crazy as your controlling mistress. No, your best chance is to let us go. Now. Quickly. Before anyone realizes."

The man shrugged. "We all know Madame's lost a bit of her wits somewhere along the way. But we don't care. None of our concern. She's making us rich."

"That's all we care about. What happens later is anyone's guess. But the two of us, we they don't intend hanging around long enough to become involved in the end. We'll have our money and be long gone."

"Though Madame doesn't realize that. Yet."

The two man laughed heartily at their shared joke.

Richard leaned up to the bars. "I'll tell her everything. Including where you and your families live."

"You're bluffing. 'Ow could you know that?"

He looked at garlic breath. "I know your family has a food stall at the markets at Cheapside. I know your wife helps your mother and father sell French food there six days a week."

Garlic Breath sucked in a gasp of air and then exhaled, blowing out his stinking fumes over them.

"If you untie me, I'll tell you how I know."

Garlic Breath considered it for a moment. "Makes no difference. You'll be dead in the morning anyway." He reached through the bars and undid the knots on both their wrists, Laura groaned. Rubbed the circulation back into her hands. "Madame isn't going to either hear you, or believe you, come mornin', so no matter what happens, you're dead meat."

"Hey, Nifty. Might be better for us to move them at first light. 'Fore Madame is awake. So she can't have no chance to speak to them. Won't have no proof of nothin' against us."

"Yeah. Good idea." He looked at Laura and Richard through the bars. "You two settle in for the night. We'll be back at dawn to have a nice little talk and a game with the two of you."

As soon as the men left, Laura and Richard searched every wall and corner and hidden nook of the room. To no avail: there was no exit except through the locked door. Instead, they made plans for whenever anyone entered with food or water. Their pathetic plan was to knock them on the head and escape. Sounded easy.

Now they needed someone silly enough to put their head underneath the heavy end of the wine bottles they each held as weapons. They waited in tense silence. Finally, the door opened again. However, the head that poked around the door was one that Laura recognized. Ruth's elder sister. Another one of the street girls they'd helped.

"Margie, you need to let us out of here."

'I will, but not until it's quieter upstairs. There are too many people coming and going at the moment. Too many guards on the doors. Madame is having a big celebration. She is telling everyone how clever she is. How she has won the race."

"Oh, no. This doesn't sound good."

"Me and the other girls, we got no idea what she means. Only that she is selling here tonight. Intends fleecing every gent in town for as much money as she can. For her last night. Has big, big plans for all the money she's been making."

A noise sounded from up above and Margie flinched.

"I have to go to work. I'll be missed. But I've brought a piece of bread and some cheese from the kitchen. Early in the morning, when everyone has finished for the night, I'll sneak down and open the door."

Richard gave Margie instructions as to where to send a message to Brian and Tony, if by chance any of the gentlemen she knew came tonight. Margie, eager to help, wanted to repay the kindnesses Laura and her sisters had shown her.

"Madame is a cruel mistress, and us girls are watched. Every minute. The guards beat us if they catch us do anythin' outta place."

"You're exhausted," Richard said later in the night, laying Laura's head on his shoulder. "And no wonder. You've been playing nurse maid to Lottie and your aunt, as well as trying to meet your obligations within the Women's Society. You do know how much I admire what you do for everyone, don't you?"

He felt her shake her head. "I think you're amazing. I think you'll make me a wonderful countess."

Her head popped up. "Yes. About that. The statement you made earlier. You cannot simply announce we're to be wed."

"Why not?"

"Why not?"

He laughed. "There's the sailor's parrot again."

She gave him a little punch to the arm.

"And when you're my wife, you'll not be allowed to man handle me any longer. It's undignified for a man of my station to be picked on by a woman of such miniature size."

She growled and he laughed.

"That's more like my lively Laura. I was afraid for a short time there that you truly were going to burst into tears and have fit of womanly vapors. You're much nicer when you're being loud, difficult and argumentative."

In the dim lantern light, she peered at him. "Are you deliberately angering me to ruse my fighting spirits? To not let me sink into the doldrums?"

He shrugged. "Possibly. Is it working?"

"Strangely enough, yes. So thank you. "

From upstairs, came the sound of loud shouts and cries and running feet. It sounded like a stampede of elephants on the floor boards above their heads.

"I hope Margie hurries. Something is wrong up there. There's too much noise."

"Yes, I'm afraid you're right, little one. Even for a brothel celebration there are too many people yelling. Too much running about. I wish we knew what was happening."

"You know they intend raping me, don't you?"

"Sweetheart, it will not come to that. I won't let it. I'll defend you with my dying breath."

"I know. That's what concerns me most. You'll get yourself killed trying to save me. No. We must get out now. We can't wait for Margie."

"You're right. We're not going to die down here without at least trying to let our families know what has happened to us."

"Or without being able to free our families from the danger hanging over them all still. We need to let them know about Lady Hetherington and her mad cronies."

"Laura, I need to tell you something. In case–"

"No, no, no. Don't say that."

"Listen, love. In case something happens to me, I want you to know. I love my sisters and I've always wanted my own family. Like the Jamisons, with your closeness. I want children, but I've been held back by a dreadful fear that my wife may die like my mother. I thought if I married a chit who

didn't really affect me emotionally, it wouldn't hurt so much. If anything happened."

She stomped on his boot again.

"Ouch! I wish you'd stop that."

"No. That's a dreadful attitude to carry into a marriage."

"I know. That's why it never happened. Couldn't bring myself to do it. Not when I could see how different it could be with someone else. Someone special. And now, now I'm terrified I've missed the chance. That I'll never get the chance to have children, or marry the wife I love. I didn't know until now, when it may be too late, how much I craved it."

"No, don't speak that way. Neither of us is going to die until we've done all that. Made love with the person we love. Known what true love is and have had the joy of holding a baby."

She strode to the door and pulled a pin from her hair.

'Do you really think you can manage this lock," he asked, wondering even as he said it why he would doubt her skill in anything. His Laura could do anything she set her mind to.

The next hour was a blur of activity. Laura picked the lock and they crept upstairs, expecting to have to fight their way past Lady Hetherington's henchmen. But upstairs in the main rooms, an unexpected sight met them. They stood in the open doorway and laughed.

Instead of brothel patrons, the room swarmed with Scotland Yard policemen, in the process of taking away at least twenty men in handcuffs. Lady Hetherington sat in regal splendor, on a brocade couch near the door. Her hands were also in chains, as were her ankles. The constables were taking no chances this time.

Brian and Tony greeted them with huge grins on their faces. "When we got the message Margie sent, we were already on our way here to meet with the police. So to smoke the ruffians out, we set a fire in the front rooms as a distraction, hoping it would give us time to get inside and down to the dungeon to rescue you."

"But I see our services weren't needed." Tony looked down at the pin Laura still clenched in her fingers. "Let me guess. Lock picker Laura to the rescue again."

Richard turned to Laura, as Lady Hetherington was led away, hopefully to stand trial this time. "It's over, sweetheart. You can go home and rest."

But upon their arrival at Grosvenor Square, they discovered that Becca and Cayle had returned.

They had been concerned about Lottie and her inability to walk, and Auntie and her bruises, and about leaving Laura and Richard together to solve all the problems. So they'd cut short their honeymoon trip.

That evening, they gathered for a family dinner at Jamison House to discuss the outcomes, but much to Richard's frustration, he couldn't manage a moment alone with Laura. She seemed determined to avoid him and he knew why. His blundering declaration that she would marry him wasn't exactly a romantic proposal of marriage. Not the sort of thing she deserved at all.

When he finally managed to corner her for a conversation, the entire family assumed they were about to commence another one of their regular fights.

He dragged her into the library, cave-man style, and slammed shut the door. "What's wrong? And don't lie to me. I can tell when you lie because your nose twitches."

She glared at him. "Rubbish. You're trying to frighten me into divulging secrets again." She sighed. "The problem is, Richard, you're an honorable man."

"I've never considered being honorable a problem."

"You made several promises to me, last evening, in the dungeon. But I know you said those things to comfort me, to reassure a frightened woman who was about to be raped and killed. And I certainly won't hold you to anything said under such extreme duress."

"I knew it. Knew you'd find some paltry excuse to cry off marrying me."

"Paltry?"

"But I never thought you'd be so cruel as to leave me to the ridicule of the entire ton. And if, after everything we've been through together, you still cannot trust me, and my declarations, then there's nothing more I can do, or say." He stiffened his spine, lifted his chin, turned to the door and walked away.

When the door closed behind Richard, Laura threw herself down on her back on the settee, sobs shaking her body. The entire family stared at her with identical stunned looks on their faces.

"Oh, no," she said, covering her face with her hands. "What have I done? I've ruined everything."

"No, no, Laura," Becca said, tugging Laura's hand's down from her face. Becca laughed. "Sweetheart, all the St. Martin men are made of much sterner stuff than that. I think Winchester's dramatic exit was partly his wounded pride, and partly to make a point. Possibly to shake your composure a little. After all, the Earl values family loyalty above all else, and you did reject him in front of the entire family."

Lottie plopped down on a footstool in front of Laura and took her hand. "There's always time to mend fences. Don't forget, Winchester is a warrior. The type who fights to the death for something he wants, so I cannot see him giving up on you so easily. You're an intuitive person, Laura. You'll think of the perfect way to convince him he's the man for you, if that's what you want. Is it?"

She sat up, clutched her sisters' hands and said, "Yes, I'm sure of it now. Winchester's the right man for me. I've been stupid all these weeks to deny the attraction I felt for him. I denied us a life together simply because I wouldn't let go of my belief that my scientific calculations were perfect."

"Ah, Laura. I don't think love remembers to follow any of the rules of science. Love often veers off the straight and narrow pathways simply to trick those of us with analytic minds. The strategy then is to recognize when we've been wrong, admit our mistakes, and move on."

"Like you and Cayle?" Lottie asked.

Becca laughed. "Yes, if I'd continued to cling to my belief that I was better off without a managing man in my life, I'd not be married to Sherwyn, and not be this happy every day of my life." She patted Laura's hand. "The other trick is to let a gentleman of honor think he is in total charge of our lives and our finances, while in actuality we still maintain a high percentage of control of our own affairs."

Cheered up, Laura climbed the stairs to her bed, determined that first thing in the morning she would go to his house and tell him how she felt. They couldn't lose what they had together.

Chapter Twenty

As he climbed the steps to Laura's bedroom two hours later, the Earl of Winchester patted his pocket for the tenth time. A reassurance that the ring, a family heirloom, rested safely there.

No more mistakes. This time he'd propose in a dignified and proper way. This time he'd explain all the honorable and logical reasons why they should marry, and as soon as possible. In his mind, he rehearsed a lengthy speech worthy of presentation before the House of Lords.

He sucked in a deep breath, opened the door and moved on silent feet towards the bed. Laura sat upright against a mound of pillows, the white coverlet lying in rumpled folds around her thighs. Her arms were widespread in a lazy pose that raised her breasts to push against the thin bodice of her lawn nightgown. When he managed to drag his eyes upward from the region of her bosom, he realized she was awake and aware.

Her eyes glowed in the lamplight as she met his gaze head on. "You're late," she said, as calmly as if he'd been a minute delayed to take their regular drive in the park. "I expected you an hour ago."

He planted his hands on his hips, threw back his head and laughed, not caring if the entire household roused and came running to investigate the noise. "You minx. You knew I'd come."

"Of course."

"Why."

"Because I knew you loved me. I realized it when I saw what you'd written in my new notebook. I recognized you were the only man I ever wanted to write my observations about."

'Thank God you've finally realized, because you're mine, all mine. And I'm never giving you up." He stalked to the bed and tugged his cravat free of its knot, slipped it from around its neck and flung it to the floor. "Now, get your notebook ready," he said as he continued to undress.

"Open it to the page I notated. The one that says, *The Countess of Winchester's Scientific Observations on the Sexual Techniques of the Earl of Winchester.* I'm going to teach you so many things, you'll fill that book. And many, many more."

"Winchester."

"Yes, my one and only love."

"Stop talking and start teaching."

Trust her to have the last word. Again. But he was only too happy to make love to the woman he loved.

Over, and over, and over.

Note from author: Reviews are like gold to authors! If you've enjoyed this book, please consider leaving a review and/or rating the book.

About Suzi Love

Tag Line- Making history fun, one year at a time

Hi, I'm Suzi Love, an Australian author of historical romances from the late Regency to early Victorian years, with a little bit of the Australian outback thrown in.

I've had a lifetime fascination with all things old, weird, and exotic. I love to travel, visit historic places, and talk to crazy characters. I also adore history, especially the grittier and seamier side, so I write about heroes and heroines who challenge traditional manners, morals, and occupations, either through necessity or desire. I hope you'll travel with me again.

If you'd like to be one of the first to know when I release a new book, plus enjoy some special 'Mailing List Only' benefits, sign up for my mailing list at the top right of my WEBSITE.

If you liked this book, I'd appreciate it if you'd write a short review or rate the book.

Or, keep up to date with what I get up to each day via my Rebel Mouse Magazine or Suzi Love Daily Gossip newspaper.

I love hearing from my readers, so feel free to write to me and tell me what you think.
Suzi Love
Cannon Hill Post Shop,
PO Box 191, Cannon Hill,
Queensland, 4170,
Australia

Where to find Suzi Love:-
Please visit my WEBSITE
Follow my books on Goodreads
Enjoy my historical images PINTEREST
Like me on Face Book - Follow me on Twitter
Email me here:- suzi@suzilove.com

Excerpt: The Viscount's Pleasure House

Please enjoy this excerpt from my historical erotic romance, The Viscount's Pleasure House.

Early in the reign of Queen Victoria;
Hawkesbury House in Belgravia, London

With a wave of his hand, Justin said, "If you're new to the profession, love, there's no need for modesty. We've seen it all before." He indicated the high flyers that filled his room with cheap perfume, cheap clothing and hopeful looks. "As these girls know, you'll earn better coin performing for me for a short time, than from a year's worth of peddling yourself on the streets." He flicked a glance at the ornate clock, another thing he'd inherited that he didn't particularly like, but that he had, either from apathy or defiance, left in that same position since his mother had been banished by his father years ago. "But, please, if you're staying, get rid of your clothing. If you're going, leave now."

A buxom redhead sat straddling the arm of his wing chair and waited for his return. Naked to the waist, she'd spread her legs wide in a blatant bribe to hire her as one of his dancers. Justin grinned at her, though he spoke to the black-clad woman. "I've several pressing matters to attend to."

"Pressing matters, indeed," she said, rolling her eyes and not trying to hide her scorn. "I promise to not take up more than ten minutes of your...*valuable time.*"

He gave a small snort of laughter. In response, the strumpet in his chair giggled, an out-of-place girlish sound, cupped both her large breasts, and lifted them higher, to better display her claret nipples. Like lush cherries, they were waiting for a man to open his mouth around them and suck.

"Justin, old boy," Bart said, his face split with a grin.

"You'd better hustle. Those titties are so ripe, they're about to drop off their stalks. If you don't come, it'll be my tongue under there and catching them as they fall."

Justin chuckled. The three men trusted each other implicitly, whether it was with their fortunes or their women. They'd combined their talents, their earnings, and had taken enormous risks in the money market until now--and though they didn't advertise this fact, they owned sizable slices of London property and English factories.

Without his friends' unflagging support over the past three years, Justin would never have had enough coin to employ dozens of investigators to search across England and Scotland for his mother and sisters.

The woman cleared her throat, loudly, clearly determined to pull Justin's attention back to her. "My lord, please listen to me. I have a proposal to discuss with you."

"Look around, pet." He waved at the posturing demireps. "Every girl here is offering me something tonight."

Desperate for well-paid employment, the girls took their cue and swarmed around Justin, draping themselves suggestively all over him. There was a chorus of cries and entreaties. "Oooh, yes, yes, my lord", or "Pick me, my lord." Added to these, were many highly exaggerated tributes to his manly physique and his awe-inspiring sexual prowess.

Hearing the outrageous compliments the girls were flinging at him, Bart and Thomas roared with laughter. Above the women's loud and flattering cries, Justin heard several loud sniggers.

Ah ha! His mysterious lady paid attention, even if she declined to reveal herself, or her intentions, quite yet. He smiled inwardly and, as her height was only a couple of inches less than his, looked at her over the tops of several bent female heads. The girls were occupying themselves by licking or kissing every inch of his bare skin they could find. He squirmed, but more from being tickled than from arousal.

"What makes your offer any different?"

"In contrast to these...eh...women," she said, her eyebrows rising to show what she thought of their antics. "My proposal doesn't involve anyone undressing. Or at least, not tonight. Perhaps later, though I'm not certain about the specifics."

It was damned hard to concentrate on the woman's stumbling explanation, but her insecurities intrigued him. Such a refreshing change from the brazen claims made by many of the titled bitches he'd been forced to deal with. He clasped the hands of the girl intent on unbuttoning the flap of his trousers so he could listen. "I'm offering you an exchange of information and services. One of benefit to us both."

He was distracted again by a saucy raven-haired temptress creating a ruckus in the middle of the room, a determined effort to claim his attention. She dragged back a large corner of Persian carpet and stood posed, center stage, until she could catch his gaze with her mesmerizing eyes, the color of which was obsidian, often found in the peoples of nomadic gypsy tribes.

After raising her bare arms, she began to clap and dance and sing in the wild and passionate rhythm of the Rom, the one the gypsies used for arousal. He shrugged an indifferent shoulder and was amused when the fiery girl hissed at him.

The teasing vixen reached down to drag her gaily ribboned skirts to her waist, lifted her leg, and proffered her toes for him to suck. She struck an eloquent pose and waited for him to acknowledge the sensual heat of her performance, her compelling eyes issuing a blatant invitation to him for her to join him for more intimate acts later. Justin happily obliged her first demand by drawing her toes, one by one, into his mouth and making loud sucking sounds. Her other unspoken demand he ignored.

Muttered but angry-sounding words beside him reminded him it was past time to deal with the black widow, and his throbbing head told him to ignore her proposal, whatever it was, and call a finish to the evening. By now, he should have chosen his line-up of Cyprians and sent them away, so he could crawl into bed--alone.

He addressed his assembly. "I apologize for being out of sorts tonight, but this shall be my pièce de résistance. You'll form the most exotic group of harem slaves ever seen in England, created to entertain the crème de la crème of our society. I shall then be retiring from the Pleasure House."

"Dammit, Justin, I wish you would reconsider selling the club." Bart lifted his blond head and fixed him with piercing blue eyes. "I do so enjoy our evenings at the house."

Justin turned to the woman and gave a half-bow.

"So you see, madam, I really don't care who you are, or what you have to offer. My time in this noble profession is about to come to an end. It appears that you like to watch, though. Stay until we are finished, if it entertains you. Otherwise, my butler will show you out."

At that moment, Justin pitied his intruder. There was something in her eyes, a weariness that matched his own and, for a split second, she'd looked as weighed down with worry as he felt. As if, despite her head making a decision to leave, her body hadn't agreed and kept her feet nailed to his floor. Like a lion cub hovering near the shelter of its den while it summoned up the courage to venture into the unknown. Nevertheless, her standoffish attitude had far out- lasted his small store of patience.

He stepped closer and in reaction she moved back. As if remembering her reasons for coming, she shook her head and moved that same pace forward. Not as close as before, yet near enough to appear fearless.

He sighed, and rubbed a fist across his aching eyes. "I'm fatigued, out of sorts, and my friends and I have business to conduct. Either join in, or leave."

He waved toward the door, hoping she'd walk out and leave him in peace, but also hoping, ridiculously, that she'd unveil, undress, and stay. Because something about this particular woman was different. Something about her stirred his first true sexual interest in many months.

He smiled a little. "I'd still like to see a little more of you. I can't even see the color of your hair." He pointed toward her groin. "Top or bottom. Here, let me unbutton you," he said, his fingers set to work on her top button, brushing the soft skin of her nape as he did so.

She flinched and held tight to the gaping neck of her dress with clenched fists. "Please. Listen to me. I'm not seeking employment."

"Ah, then you're simply a bitch in heat like all the others. Wanting a lusty tale to recount to your upper-class friends over tea and cake. Perhaps compare notes on Viscount Hawkesbury's infamous prowess."

If you enjoyed this excerpt, you can read more of The Viscount's Pleasure House here:- Print Book
Amazon USA   Amazon UK   Amazon Australia   Amazon Canada
Amazon Brazil   Amazon France   Amazon India

If you'd like to see some visuals of The Viscount's Pleasure House, take a look here: Web Page   Face Book   Pinterest